Mekong Meridian

MEKONG MERIDIAN

A NOVEL OF THE VIETNAM WAR

Steve Maguire

ISBN: 1541363116
ISBN 13: 9781541363113
Library of Congress Control Number: 2016921594
CreateSpace Independent Publishing Platform
North Charleston, South Carolina

ACKNOWLEDGMENTS

Original cover design and illustration by
Britt Taylor Collins, 2017
(BrittTaylorCollins.com)

DEDICATION

To Suzy
For everything,
and never ever failing to have my back.

INTRODUCTION

MEKONG MERIDIAN IS A WORK of semi-fiction. Although most novelists insist that none of their characters bear any resemblance to persons living or dead, I cannot. 1969's men depicted here are an amalgam of the many still-vivid recollections of my once-upon-a-time world: Vietnam's Mekong Delta, an infantry battalion in the 9th Infantry Division, my leading a reconnaissance platoon in combat and the considerable blood I shed there. This stone-hard, unchangeable reality comprises my memories of our war and the men I fought with and knew.

Many fellow grunts became life-long friends in Nam's aftermath with my several circles sharing one ardent belief; we saw the United States as the world's last hope against the metastasizing spread of communism. We knew that, to defeat this spreading totalitarianism, we would inevitably have, as our fathers' generation had, to take the fight beyond our nation's shores. Coming from towns and cities across America, those soldiers found a confluence with my life. For my generation, the location of that confluence just happened to be the Republic of Vietnam. This country was very beautiful, very foreign and, for 58,267 Americans... very deadly.

By the late 1960s the forces of communism had seized nearly half of the globe. On the march for fifty years, literally and metaphorically, their armies of "liberation" had installed brutal regimes in one country after another. Any fragile economy or mismanaged government was ripe for the picking, almost always by proxies of the Soviet Union or China. Vulnerable countries didn't always topple like predictable rows of dominoes, but they fell just the same.

In 1954, Ho Chi Minh's communists in North Vietnam signed the "Geneva Accords," a faux truce, which gained them UN recognition for the half of Vietnam they'd already won in battle. Before the ink was dry, the communists reorganized to seize the rest. They didn't go unchallenged. Anti-communist forces in South Vietnam tried to stop them. Ill-prepared and ill-equipped, they fought on through the following nine years. During the Kennedy presidency, the U.S. sent thousands of military advisors to assist the South, but the communists trumped that effort by shoring up their guerrilla forces with divisions of regular army troops from North Vietnam. Fully supplied with Chinese and Soviet weaponry, they began to conquer the South. Acting to block a communist takeover, President Johnson responded with divisions of American soldiers and Marines. For those of us who went, our motives for going and degree of dedication spanned the widest spectrum imaginable, but among us the likes of Carney were not rare.

This is First Lieutenant Gavin "Mondo" Carney's story, his thoughts, words and actions unfolding during five days. Fiction is the invisible cement between him and the all-too-real attitudes, sights, and sounds that comprised this side of the Vietnam War. Carney, Paul Keneally, and John Braccia may never have existed, but men just like them did. The reality of their exchanges, the tactical operations, the geography and the circumstances in which they are depicted, all lent a hand. They are lifted, undisturbed, from scar tissue formed around a memory branded by a white-hot gun barrel, one so hot it would burn forever as an unending reminder of the totalitarianism we fought and the beautiful land and its people we tried to save. It was a grievous crime that it ended the way it did.

PROLOGUE

"I SPENT THIRTY YEARS IN the Army, Paul, thirty years as an infantry officer. From leaving West Point for Benning in nineteen-fifty, to my last assignment at the Pentagon, I came to know a lot of soldiers. But now, retired longer than all those years spent in uniform? Too many unforgettable men don't seem to have names anymore. As for names I can remember, who they belong to is the problem. Plenty of guys remained real in every way though – more from my combat tours. The Infantry's like that. Working together in harsh conditions, in life-and-death situations forges lifelong bonds."

"Where does Carney fit," I asked.

"From my sixteen months in Korea and three years in Vietnam, Gavin Carney'd be one of a small number I couldn't forget if I tried."

I was sitting in the Texas home of a now elderly Colonel J.J. Braccia, reminiscing about our days in Vietnam. He'd been our boss when he'd commanded 3rd Battalion, 41st Infantry. Carney was the reason I was there. We met while I commanded E Company, both of us first lieutenants at the time. Our friendship was instantaneous.

"When he reported in, Paul, this sharp, confident, twice-wounded Airborne-Ranger, I took an immediate liking to him.

My Recon Platoon Leader had just gotten hit, so replacing him with Carney was an obvious choice. From then on, I called him by his call sign, *Tiger Claw Six*."

"You did, John, but you probably heard other officers in the battalion calling him 'Mondo.' It was a nickname he picked up in college –from an Italian movie, '*Mondo Cane*'."

"Never been much for Italian movies," Braccia offered, "Italian as I am. It translates to 'A dog's world' – college life?"

"No, it was a play on words. New Englanders pronounce Carney and Cane the same, CA-nee."

"I definitely remember Tiger Claw's Rhode Island accent. I know he went to the University of Massachusetts though – distinguished ROTC grad."

"Mondo almost didn't get into the army at all," I told him, "The same week he finished his final exams and took his Regular Commission, he got into a serious car accident. Two badly broken legs and he saw his Army dream fly out of his hospital window. So he crutched and limped his way through a masters in Russian history, then spent a summer in France. Two-hour workouts, seven days a week for a year and he presented his iron-hard self to an Army medical board. But fixated on his old X-rays, they refused to see the new Mondo. In his inimitable way though, that son-of-a-gun convinced someone to sign off."

"Knowing Tiger Claw, he probably hoisted some doctor's examining table onto his shoulders and ran around the room just to prove he was alright."

"No doubt he was," I agree. "A month later he breezed through Airborne and Ranger schools. Hell, remember that time he took a bullet in the leg? It hobbled him about as much as a muscle strain. Tenacity personified. Being a combat soldier meant everything to him."

"Yes it did, Paul. Everything. You and he were quite a pair: You the quiet sort, a lieutenant older than most of my captains, and of all things a former Peace Corps volunteer, and Carney, a whip-smart officer with a wise ass observation about everything. Give either of you a spare minute though and you'd pull a paperback out of your thigh pocket and be reading. As for you Paul, there wasn't an administrative or logistical problem you couldn't solve in five minutes."

"But," I added, "if you'd needed someone to go all the way to Hell and set fire to the Devil's ass, you wouldn't have to look any further than Carney."

"How true. You know, Paul," Braccia's voice sounding wistful, "when I first got to Vietnam, as an Arvin advisor, JFK was still in the White House. So I was there in the beginning, the middle and the end. Could we have won? Sure, but only if we'd crippled North Vietnam's ability to continue prosecuting the war. With the half-a-million man force we had, we could've. But, our strategy never called for winning. Is it any wonder it ended like it did?

"Carney epitomized an attitude and will to win that our muddled leadership lacked. Sure, they were committed enough for us to fight, but that's all. If they'd been half as committed as those fifty-eight-thousand warriors whose names are on The Vietnam Memorial, we'd have neutralized the communists' ability to keep fighting. Democracy would've grown in South Vietnam like it has in South Korea. And, there'd be a lot fewer black marble panels at The Wall."

"Mondo's view for sure," I said, "and his blunt way of expressing it, had his platoon sergeant thinking he wanted to win the war himself."

"Brash is a better word, Paul. Reminds me of this one evening in our firebase. I was having a few beers with some officers in the mess. The talk turned to where the war was headed and Carney, unabashed as usual, spoke up: 'Since we're trading off the lives of tens of thousands of soldiers, we need to have *something* to show for it. But all we've got is the ground we're standing on. Have we chewed up the communists to the point where they can't continue fighting? No. *And* they're going to do what with their huge, well-disciplined, limitlessly equipped army after we pull out? If our generals think this place is soon to be coming up roses, why is it that the only thing we see sprouting is punjis?'"

"Well, I thought my XO, Hal Tinderberry, was going to have a heart attack. He took it Carney was insulting the entire chain of command, and worse that he'd thrown in with the anti-war crowd. Later, I clued Hal in on how mistaken he was, but he disliked Carney so much, he probably didn't hear a word I said. Hal valued respect and tact above everything. Trigger-level, whites-of-their-eyes combat was outside the wire, far away. With others keeping it there, qualities like guts and bravery would always be alien to him. He was a great staff officer, the kind you want when an IG inspection's coming. Look at death from point-blank range? No, not his idea of a career-enhancing activity. But wha'do I know? I retired as a colonel, and Hal wound up a major general."

"There's still one thing I'm curious about, Paul. Seems right after Carney got hit, there was talk going around about this Vietnamese girl, a real looker. How in the world'd that happen, like where did she come from? And was she really implicated in his getting wounded?"

"That talk came from me, John, but outside of wanting to see you again after so many years, it's why I've come down here." I opened my bag and hefted up a three-inch thick packet of paper. "I got this manuscript from Mondo and need your input before I get it published. You'll be pleased to know that all your questions are answered right here."

Paul Kencally

I
The Unit

CHAPTER 1

THROUGH THE CHOPPER'S WIDE OPEN doors, a cool wind buffeted the six infantrymen sprawled inside. Downturned heads and low-brimmed bush hats obscured expressionless faces. Whatever the thoughts idling in their minds, the wind-whipped rippling of camouflaged uniforms was the only thing moving. Listless with exhaustion, from unrelenting discomforts, they seemed impassive to the relief, not that it wasn't felt. Grunts knew how to compress these cherished moments of rest, how to force a shutdown of all physical movement, to buy ten minutes from an available five. I understood. I, 'Mondo' Carney, was one of them.

Our five choppers' impending descent back into an infernal heat, and my platoon's resumed slog through more muck and obdurate vegetation, had an indiscernible effect on us. Resigned to it, we grunts grasped that if there were any pleasures left in this work, they'd be short lived.

While mud slathered trousers dried and sweat-soaked blotches became outlined with encrusted salt, they stolidly watched the variegated land draw beneath them. Rice paddies silvery-skimmed with water and meandering brown rivers outlined with green jungle stretched to the horizon. Rising up, a great fleet of motionless clouds loomed, their contours billowing like the spinnakers of tethered ships.

The choppers carried Reconnaissance Platoon, 1st Battalion, 43rd Infantry. I, First Lieutenant Gavin Carney was its Leader. We were en route to another helicopter insertion into an unknown jungle, another assault into the maw of enemy held territory.

"This is Tiger Claw-Six over." I spoke into the handset, a reflex to my RTO's having nudged my shoulder with it. Spec4 Nunziato and I had been together long enough that what we needed to say had become non-verbal. Repositioning the handset firmly against my ear, I faintly made out the voice of my battalion commander, LTC Braccia.

"This is Pain Maker Six. You might've been right about this area, Tiger Claw. I've been flying around for the last half hour, and haven't seen anything that turns me on, over."

"Roger that Six, over."

"Let's forget about targets Bravo, Charlie, and Delta. They all came from the same intel source. Screw 'em. Instead, I'm putting you into a place some ways from here. Prepare to copy: it's X-ray Sierra, eight, two, eight, four, niner, five. Do you copy, over?"

"Roger Pain Maker-Six, I've got eight-two-eight, four-niner-five, over."

"That's affirmative Tiger Claw. Arvin artillery's fired two hundred rounds in there. From where we put you in, move south – all the way to the river. Follow it west for a few hundred meters, turn north then make your way back. Let's see what you can turn up, over." Mentally, I was already traversing the U-shaped trek that lay before us.

"Roger Six, over."

"Pain Maker-Six, out."

I gave the handset back to Nunziato and broke out my map case, knowing by instinct that our new objective was about thirty klicks south-southeast from our present position, grid square XS8249 lay near to Rach Gò Công. I refolded my map to center it. That meandering river would guide me.

Indicated by a splotch of dark green, the objective was about two kilometers long and just north of Tinh Gò Công. 'Why's Braccia dropping us into such a pacified province? It's the outer periphery – maybe things are about to go bad. Whatever the intel, the VC know what they're doing and have intimate knowledge of all this Delta terrain. So, every familiar square foot of ground I can know, is one less boot on dirt the bastards'll be able to use against us.'

This place, named Xa Khoi, looked like a very out-of-the-way area. There were no nearby roads and no canals or rivers running through it. My map showed no habitation, with no reason for trails to exist. Across this vast river delta, habitation was universal, until it wasn't. This was just the kind of place transient NVA would like.

Through our chopper's windshield, I recognized my reference point, a looping bend of the Rach Gò Công coming up on our left front. From our altitude, it lay featureless, more a motionless beige stripe than a fat hundred meter-wide river. The confluence of the smaller rivers, Song Go Gua and Rach Cai confirmed the location of 'known points.' Our LZ lay exactly two klicks south of there. My eyes glanced from map to the green ahead then back.

"Hey, Lieutenant Carney," came a voice from behind. Sergeant Starcup, of Second Squad, pointed out the chopper's other door at the first evidence of the artillery barrage. The unmistakable 105 craters appeared as scattered flecks of out-of-place color, but in seconds a more overhead view revealed them as scores of fresh- divoted cavities that hadn't filled with water, hadn't yet been turned into shiny round discs of reflected sky.

The terrain swelled with dense stands of nipa palm, taller and more robust than usual. Their thick pinnate fronds rose thirty feet and obscured the slues of deep primordial mud from which they grew. On my map, solid dark green represented dense vegetation. An unbroken blotch of it covered nearly all of a grid square. I scoured for a speck of sere brown against the greenscape below. What I saw confirmed my map. No hoochs, the place was totally uninhabited.

At two o'clock from our heading, I spotted Braccia's Command and Control bird marking our LZ. On the ground beneath them, a gout of crimson smoke billowed rapidly, then ran into a long stream, as though the earth itself had been spiked with a bloody wound. I rechecked our incoming azimuth.

Smoke in sight, the choppers pitched downward. Dropping at a thirty degree angle, they bore in on a small splotch of pale green. Facing outward, I kept glancing through the windshield to maintain a sense of our direction. The choppers leveled out just above the nipa and banked to the left. I lost track of the red smoke. Then with the uppermost fronds of the last stand of nipa brushing the chopper's skids, we plunged headlong into a clearing.

In sudden unison, the outside door gunners opened fire at our flanks. The M-60 next to me pounded a wincing pain into my right ear. I clasped my hand over it. Squinting from its intensity, the leafy vegetation swirled as it rose up around us, the gun still jack-hammering lead into it. Its belt of shiny brass jerked steadily upward from an ammo can, a mouth of bolt and chamber chewing rounds in a ravenous incessant blur. Spent cartridges and links spewed out, tumbling away in the wind. I pressed my hand tighter. Each round's banging felt like an ice pick being jabbed straight into my eardrum.

Our tracers angled right and left, scoring the green backdrop with a furious crisscross of red. The quiescent jungle sucked the bright dancing lines into itself. Hundreds of deadly bullets tore into its insides with an incomprehensible futility. We neared the ground. No matter, *suppression* would keep enemy heads down long enough for us to debark and get to cover.

My guys were ready. The skids slid into the soft ground, everyone's gaze fixed on the nearest line of jungle. In a single motion, men scrambled, jumped, and spread out. Without a word from anyone, they moved swiftly ahead, as if pushed by the blade-driven wind at their backs. As the last boot hit the mud, the choppers were already lifting back into the air.

A thirty meter run and the platoon hunkered in a loose skirmish line along the edge of the woodline. The gunfire ceased. The sound of jet turbines faded in the distance. A quiet fell over us. Suddenly, everything seemed muffled. An invisible, thick quilted blanket of silence had dropped on us. I scanned the bush. It looked as mute and imperturbable as a photograph. Was it just me? I could hear my men moving on my left, but their scant sounds to my right were overlaid with a dull ringing. I stuck my index finger into it and massaged its ebbing pain, not for the first time. 'It's getting worse – should've plugged it with something. The last thing I need is to become half deaf in a place where the crack of a twig at fifty paces means the difference between life and death.'

I checked both flanks. Sergeant Olivera and some of his third squad adjusted their initial position. The first of them crouched in front of a berm, the vestiges of an old dike. The rest of the platoon was strung out along the edge of where we'd landed, in a large overgrown rice paddy.

Settled and hard from lack of cultivation, the ground seemed like it hadn't been tilled this century. More gray than brown, the soil was unworkable. Closer to the berm, the short stemmed reed growing at our feet, became dense. On top, its sepaled flowers, a thick carpet of them, had been pulled over it. Their features obscured, the dikes looked like moles the size of Volkswagens had mounded them up from underneath. Rain and time had reduced parts of them to little more than lonesome oblate humps. I could barely make out the geometric symmetry that had once formed the original paddies, but the reeds' clear preference to propagate where it had, helped.

"Olivera!" I shouted, "Take the lead. Move down that line of nipa. Stay alongside the dikes – *not on top*."

In a ragged line, he and his men approached the old dike. Their point man, a guy we called Spot, inspected for trip wires. Satisfied with its relative safety, he crossed over. The others followed. First squad slipped into a file behind them, five meters between each man.

When I reached the rise, I stopped to look around. My vantage improved slightly. It was all I had. I scanned the area for another avenue of approach. Fifty meters ahead, a stockade of giant nipa rose into a formidable wall. Iron-rooted in slues of mud slimier than fifty-weight oil, it wouldn't be impregnable, but we'd go through them only as a *last* option. 'This nipa'll be my very last.'

Craters from the artillery rounds scarred the middle distance. One salvo had landed innocuously in the reeds. Anyone caught here in an early morning rain of steel would've been torn to pieces. But no bodies lay anywhere in sight. 'Yeah, our old friend Charlie has a solid knack for avoiding heavy weather.'

My Platoon Sergeant, Cedrick Mounds, came over and pulled out his map case. I opened my own, holding it so he could copy the key points.

"The Colonel wants us to go all the way down here." I indicated the coordinates and traced my finger along the route. "Then we move inland and come back." He grease-penciled a mark for our farthest point, X-ed our LZ, folded the plastic case, shoved it back into a thigh pocket, and took a deep breath. He pushed his bush hat back and looked at me. Barrel-chested, he huffed every time he exhaled and spoke.

"I want to move in two parallel groups, Mounds," I informed him. "We'll maintain no more than a fifty meter interval between us. If anything's in here, I don't want my maneuver element to have to come from way back and get hung up in the shit while trying. Sergeant Olivera and his guys can keep going like they are. Crowder's squad can follow. Stick with them. Get Olivera to make his way through that gap over there." I pointed to a just-wide-enough defile of vegetation other than nipa.

"How we goin' to keep from driftin' apart, Sir? All them slooze-a goddamn nipa'll make us be zigzaggin' all over the place. We'll lose sight of each other for sure."

"True, but patches of low shrubby stuff intersperse this area." I pointed to where Olivera was heading. "And there's a few old paddies like this one. We'll use those spots to connect visually. Don't forget, we're moving due southeast, like one-three-zero. Bear too much to your right, and we'll converge. If you see the Go Cong River, you've gone too far to the left. Keep your eye on your compass. When we get to the bend, it'll become one-seven zero." He pursed his lips and looked down at his map.

"It's goin' to be pretty hard for one group to keep from falling behind the other." 'He's right, I'm breaking the important rule of never dividing your forces. But fifty meters doesn't constitute much of a split.'

"Look, if it winds up being too difficult, I'll pull us back together."

"Wouldn't it be easier to just do it now?" Mounds asked.

"Everything's easier, until something bad happens. Then you'd always wish you did something else." I tried to make it sound like a well-known maxim, one that he didn't pick up on. He looked at me blank-faced. "One last thing – stay between Crowder and Olivera's guys. You've been spending too much time bringing up the rear."

"Sir, you think there's somethin' wrong with Olivera handlin' his squad?" It was more an accusation than a question. He'd cut it close enough that I chose to ignore it.

'Mounds is getting harder to figure by the day. He's competent enough, but we've been together three months and my confidence in him is what? It's not growing – not that he's ever done anything wrong. But out here, guts are everything – and my gut says I've got me an undercurrent of dissension. Problem is, he and one of my squad leaders are right in the middle of it.'

"No," I spoke, looking him straight in the eye. "Olivera's fine. I just prefer to have you up there." He nodded and headed back to pick up the end of third squad. "Hey Tra," I called to my number one Tiger Scout. He moved up and stayed with me as I went over to join Sergeant Starcup and second squad. "Tra, what do you think of this place?" I asked.

"Here me think no VC."

"Uh huh," I said, musing over what had brought him to that. "Why'd they dump a shitload of arty in here then?" Tra looked to Tho, 2nd Squad's scout. They swapped comments in Vietnamese.

"American make this?" he asked.

"No, Arvin did," I told him. He exchanged a few more words with Tho and turned back to me. I caught a twitch in one of his shoulders, an involuntary shrug.

"Sometime Arvin shoot – sometime ah, me no know why."

"Yeah, sometimes they shoot just 'cause they get fresh ammo. Shooting it up makes them look like they're actually fighting the war. Shooting it into a place like this, guarantees that nobody gets hurt – which is weird. If the Cong had it, the first thing they'd do is stick it up the Arvin's ass."

Tra adjusted the brim of his hat and stared fixedly at the uncompromising terrain. His upper lip curled. The exposure of his gold eye tooth indicated deliberation. He was constitutionally taciturn, but between my volubility and his intense desire to help, he could loosen up just enough for what I needed to know. I always kept him close, sharing whatever thoughts came to mind. Tra helped me fashion random impressions into linear thinking. With a few heavily accented words, fresh realities formed like photographs in a developing pan. In this strange and hostile land, his native mind was as valuable to me as my CAR-15, a ready weapon to answer any of my *'what'* questions.

"I'll bet you, Sir," said Starcup, "that a chopper was just flying by and spotted some old man hunting crabs in here then reported it as a VC base camp. That'd be worth at least a couple hundred rounds of arty wouldn't you say? Hell, they're probably drinking a toast to their *estimated* body count right now."

"That sounds way too American for me," I said, following him toward the front of his squad. "Tra, how come nobody lives around here?"

"People no can stay in this place."

"Yeah, but why?"

"Here can no do rice. Numbah ten this." He tapped the ground with his boot. I nodded, eyeing the unyielding clay soil. There'd been ample time to utterly exhaust every nutrient in the past few millennia, but that could be said of this otherwise fertile Delta. 'Something's different here. What? The stalwart flora? The nastier ones look rapacious enough to eat small animals. The lack of them proves it… except for that rat I saw scurrying from the chopper wash. But then, rats always out-nasty death.'

"You can't grow rice," I went on, "but why can't VC hide out here?"

"Water come," he said, tapping the ground again. 'It's not the least bit mushy. He must mean it has a high water table. Bunkers would immediately fill up with water. But we're in the middle of the monsoon. Every bunker in IV Corps is already full of water.'

"Water from where?" I asked. His index finger gave me an ambiguous wave across the nipa to our left and the Gò Công two hundred meters beyond. "Yup, plenty of water there." 'it must be some alluvial quirk of nature he doesn't have the English to explain. We'll get to it in time. When he says there aren't any VC, there are no VC. I trust his word. Okay, and when was it they last sent us to a VC-free zone?'

I studied Tran Van Tra's thirty-five-year-old face. The only way he'd gotten to be the oldest man in our platoon was from having street-smarts in a place with no streets. It was from an intuition keen enough to glean information from sources unavailable to the rest of us. 'Merlin-esque is what he is. Sensing dink presence from the way the wind ripples paddy water or from the patterns of flying birds can't be anything else. The thing is, he's been prescient on our imminent future enough times that I can't discount him.'

Tra had been at this war for a long time, but like few others, had fought it from both sides. He'd explained to me that a decade earlier he'd found himself hotly agitated over the Diem regime's operations in his local district and become an easy recruit for the Viet Cong. Energetic and diligent, he'd risen in the ranks to a leadership position. Then, after seven years of combat and communist indoctrination, a swift disillusionment severed him from the cause. There'd been a death, a summary killing of someone close. Whoever it'd been had galvanized his hatred of the Cong with a burning passion. Intense and focused, it was ever-present enough that my men treated him with the wary respect you'd show if you were trying to make a pet of a poisonous snake.

I'd searched all over the brigade for guys like Tra, ex-VC with a personal animus for the communists, the deeper the better. Tra had a major deposit of the stuff. Any encounter with the VC and an igneous-eyed anger would roil up in him. It'd seethe and bubble deep down inside him like some pool of hot magma quaking in the bowels of the earth. A reservoir of malice, it powered the lethality of his actions. These eruptions subsided only after his weapon had done its work, his smoking gun-barrel a surrogate fumarole to the venting of the vengeance within. It was the kind of hatred that would never let me down.

Tra's underlying enmity for the Cong was actually icing. My unalterable trust in him was born of a few compressed seconds when he'd risked his life to save mine. The two of us, plus the two walking point, had walked unnoticed into the middle of a small VC encampment. The air exploded with automatic gunfire. Everyone scrambled for cover, us and them. Having expended my own magazine in the direction of the ones I'd seen, I wriggled off the trail to reload.

A dink popped up from the bush like a Jack-in-the-box. Too far away to leap on him, and too close to roll away, my eyes locked on the yawning black hole of his muzzle. In that sliver of a second, Tra flashed in a blur, hurdling into view, materializing from the air itself. The dink jerked his AK toward him. I expected bullets to tear him apart, but Tra knocked the gun barrel aside. With a continuous motion, his other hand came up in a steel-bladed uppercut. Burying the knife to the hilt, it penetrated all the way into the back of the guy's brain. That dink's expression and those hard eye blinks seemed like he'd been trying to comprehend what had just happened, while making the acceptance of it the last thing he'd ever realize. For Tra's total disregard for his own life in saving mine, I'd worked hard to ensure he received the Silver Star, the highest medal the US would award a scout.

We passed through an area where the artillery fire had been more concentrated. Our file weaved between the upturned earth around us. These craters were deep penetrations, the work of delayed fuses. From the minimal shredding they'd done to the adjacent foliage, they'd blasted narrowly back at the sky from where they'd come. 'Okay, delayed fuses are useful in destroying bunker complexes – if you know exactly where they are. So, where are they?'

Our file wound its way cautiously through the low bush. I continued to muse over the intent of the delay fuses, and the barrage itself. 'This place is isolated enough to be a VC or NVA basecamp, but assumed possibilities don't make for great targets. U.S. artillery fires thousands of rounds at bad intelligence all the time. Arvin don't. It's their back yard, they know the score a lot more than we do, and they're always short on ammo. What the hell's going on?'

I studied the upturned terrain and expanded my speculations. 'Natural bowers of nipa and jungle vegetation make for one-after-another places where whole squads of VC can set up camp. Odd though that the shell craters still don't have any water in them.'

We rounded one of the holes. I kicked a large clod of dirt from its rim. It broke in half and I crushed one of the pieces with my boot. Picking up a small chunk, I smushed it between my fingers and felt the smooth gumminess of clay.

"Tra," I prodded. "Now I can see why they can't grow rice here, but how were they able to do it a long time ago?" He squinted and looked at the scattered reed at our feet.

"Long time?" He asked, meaning how long ago had I meant.

"Ah, never mind. There's not any water in this ground." I pointed into the middle of the crater. "What the hell kind of water were you talking about before?"

"Water come all way here from rivah."

"You mean when the tide comes in? It comes all the way to *here?*" He nodded. I scrutinized the area for clues again. 'It doesn't have the look of being inundated twice a day. *That* kind of place would be a vast mud flat of nipa or mangrove with no solid ground. Nothing else would survive.' "I ain't buying it Tra. No way is that water coming in here all the time."

"Sometime water come. Sometime no come."

"Okay, how about today?" I asked.

"I think maybe. Maybe no. I no know this place. Never before I come here. Now I look, see ground, then I think, then I talk you maybe." I nodded and motioned for Davidson, one of our platoon RTO's, to come up so I could call Mounds.

"Hey Five," I said, "Tra thinks there aren't any dinks in here… on account of some kind of irregular tide thing. It's supposed to wash all the way up in here – sometime."

"When's that Six?" Mounds asked.

"Good question. It might only be seasonal."

"Yeah, and we right in the middle of rainy season."

"Well, maybe every so often then. Doesn't look like it's been in here real recently. Whatever's the deal, my chart says the next high tide's at nineteen twenty eight hours. With the progress we're making, we'll be out of here before then so it doesn't matter."

"Roger that Six," Mounds added. "I can confirm on them gooks, cuz I ain't seen a lick of nothin' nowhere."

"Yeah, just the way they like it."

"I ain't getting' how this water business keepin' gooks out of this place," he added, "but from what I'm seein', ten bucks says Tra's right."

"It isn't a guarantee, just a best guess. I don't care if they're here or not. We are. That's all that matters. Let's just keep pressing on. Out."

"You really think there might be some dinks in here?" asked Nunziato.

"No," I replied, "it's just not out of the question. Only a dumbass would rule them out altogether. Like this ain't your mom's kitchen."

"Yeah," he said with a laugh, "You can go ahead and rule out any being in there. Besides this here being a lot bigger, it's got a lot more places to hide."

"Inhospitable as it is – even for them. But it's also just enough out of the way..."

"You got that right, Sir."

"Chances of anything popping up in this crap still looks slim, but seven months in this steaming mud bath has taught me to stay ready for dink surprises."

"Damn straight we've seen a few, Sir."

Over the next three hours, we continued along a mazy, uneventful course. It kind of paralleled the Gò Công, because some of the nipa swamps cut almost a hundred meters inland, forcing us to make wide lateral deviations from our main direction. My two elements became too far separated. I had to call Mounds so we could link back up. Not wishing that he feel vindicated, I told him I needed to make better time. Only two clicks covered and neither element had found so much as a footprint. Then the rain came.

A late afternoon monsoon drove in from the south with a nipa-bending blow of wind running ahead of it. The first fat drops slapped our faces as hard as slung pebbles. Relief from the torrid heat was quickly exceeded by the storm's sheer intensity. We crouched and turned our backs to its horizontal fury, to wait it out by watching each other get pounded. Slashing torrents of wind-pelted drops smacked into us and dibbled the ground like bullets. It whirled the foliage in a mad, rending whipsaw. We squinted through the rivers of water that ran from the brims of our bush hats and into air white with water. It poured from our chins and noses like spouting gargoyles.

The rain didn't last long, particularly the maelstrom gnash of its sallying front end. Like a colossal dragon of swirling water which had suddenly become distracted by another quadrant of dry land, it moved on. As quickly as it had occupied the air and sky, the monsoon deflated into the mizzled calm of countless dripping leaves. And just as easily, we moved on too.

I ended our southward progress at the small river where the colonel wanted me to turn. Swinging to the west, we looped around and followed it for a while, then began heading north. A skim of water covered this entire area, first one or two inches, and then three to four. We were used to slogging our way through water and muck. I paid it little notice. Amid a landscape of rice paddies veined with slues, canals and rivers, the omni-presence of water was as inescapable as the infernal heat, the clouds of mosquitoes and the boot-hungry mud. During the next half hour, the water became incrementally deeper, past the tops of our trudging boots. We sloshed more noisily. Our pace slowed. Still, a foot of casual water sitting on firm ground was a stroll in the park compared to a lot of other places we'd been.

My point team of Corchado and van Wyck saw it first. They stopped, both of them raising hand signals. Corchado waved me to join them. With Tra as my shadow, I pulled up between the two. Nobody said anything. Corchado pointed at a body. It lay ten meters ahead. I couldn't tell from the grimy shirt, but the barely visible blue shorts gave it away as NVA. We spread out again and moved slowly forward, our eyes more alert to booby traps. Second squad automatically fanned out behind us for security.

Lying fetal and almost completely awash, he had the macerated look of someone who'd been taking a warm bath for three days straight. His color was that special pallor that set in fast when you were dead.

"He's shot up," Corchado said, a flat declaration of the obvious. We'd all taken note of the half dozen bloodless bullet holes. The body had no weapon, no pack, no shoes, nothing but a thin khaki shirt and those blue shorts.

"Yeah, he's good 'n' dead too," van Wyck said, as if to clarify Corchado's ambiguity.

"Not to put *too* fine a point on it," I said. "Tra, check him out will you." I motioned the others to move back, as Tra stuck the muzzle of his M-16 into the man's torso. Pushing slowly with a cautious eye for a booby trap, he nudged the body over onto its back. Nothing. "Not much of a chance they'd rig one under water here, but you never fucking know."

This random, dead-dink presence seemed about as meaningful as the expression on the face that looked up at us. The loose open mouth and amaurotic eyes gave him the stultifying look of befuddlement, frozen in that final moment, not in horrified surprise, but in the total inexplicability of what was happening to him. 'You never thought it would be like this, did you? Not that day... not that way. In your last block of training up in that Cambodian camp, did your instructors put out the details of what it'd be like when an American gunship caught you in the open? But however you got here, a dead dink's still a dink. There's meaning in that, but what's it mean for what we've got to do next? Keep a sharper eye for living-breathing ones for starters.'

I elevated one of the dead guy's arms with the toe of my boot. It flopped over in the water with a splash. From his elbow I caught a coppery glint, the protruding tip of a bullet. I knelt down in the water, hefted the lifeless arm, and lay it across my thigh. Then with my knife, I sliced open the soft gooey flesh, and exposed a section of clean white bone. I incised the blade point into a crack and dug at the round. It popped out and fell into the palm of my hand.

"M-Sixty," observed van Wyck. "Who-ya think got him with that? When?"

"My guess is he got fired up by some gunship. Tra, how long – couple of days?"

"Maybe two," he answered, kneeling down beside me. Placing a finger on one of the eyelids, he pushed it open. The cloudy orb was still intact. "Maybe tree, maybe four day." 'It's not really bloated, but is that due to time or its being preserved by immersion in water? This warm amoebic soup – seems like that might accelerate decomposition. But covered with water, it's been protected from maggot-laying flies.'

Tra's pondering expression suggested he was drawing from a deeper well of on-the-job coroner's experience. I'd seen enough bodies to keep me going for a while, but it'd be piddling compared to what he'd witnessed. All the ones I'd ever come across had just been killed. Even in the remotest parts of the Delta, a dead dink didn't lie around long before someone buried it. 'So why hasn't someone buried him? Nobody around to do him the favor? Okay, no civilians.... Where are his comrades, his weapon, and gear? Maybe the water had been higher and he'd drifted away from them.'

"Okay you guys," I barked, "all the fun shit's over. Let's get a move on."

Consulting first with Starcup and Tra, then Mounds by radio, I decided to check out the immediate area more thoroughly then press on to an open space three hundred meters this side of our original LZ.

After making just a hundred meters, water splashed above our knees. Our pace slowed accordingly. It rose to mid-thigh within another half hour. I called together Mounds and the squad leaders for a powwow.

"I don't know what the fuck's going on here, either we're imperceptibly going downhill into a totally inundated area or this water's coming up fast."

"You said way back there Sir," Mounds grumped, "that water's *supposed* to be comin' up in here." He tipped his bush hat back slightly, his gaze resting on something behind me, some invisible entity from which he might gain affirmation.

"There maybe," I said jerking my thumb back in the direction of the Gò Công, "but not here. We're at least five hundred meters from the fucking river."

"Well, Sir, I don't remember us comin' *up* no hill, for us to be now going' down."

"It'd only be a change of a few feet, Mounds. Spread over a whole klick, we wouldn't have noticed anything."

During my time in Vietnam, I'd humped on foot across a hundred Delta grid squares and flown over a thousand more. It was all the same, totally flat. With the exception of Ha Tien Province far to the south, there wasn't a single contour line on forty map sheets. This is where the not-so-far-away ocean and its tides came into play. Our persistent need to cross small rivers and canals made carrying a table of its twice-daily fluctuations mandatory. Many weren't crossable at high water and treacherous when running out hard, but at ebb they could shrink in half. And although the amplitude of Delta coastal tides was significant, they only rose to the top of river banks, *not* over them. If they did, the entire Delta would be uninhabitable. No one lived here, but we were still *above* the river bank.

"It looks to me Sir," said Crowder, "like the more we keep heading this-a-ways, the deeper it gets."

"If it's flat and the tide's coming in here," Starcup joined in, "wouldn't it just get deeper no matter what direction we're going? I think – like this daggum Delta's flat as a pool table."

"If it was that flat," I said, "the whole province'd be just like us, standing in two feet of water. Trust me, they ain't. We're obviously in some kind of slight depression with an in-coming tide. Tra says it only does this every so often. If it did all the time, the whole area would be one big continuous nipa slue. He couldn't say why it does when it does."

"The *when* don't matter much, Sir," quipped Mounds, "when it's the *now* you got to deal with."

Standing still as we talked, I could feel the cool water encroaching on my testicles. It confirmed what I guessed was true. Starcup realized it at exactly the same time.

"Gives me the feeling," he said, "like the whole fuckin' world's sinking right under me."

"Look," I said, "let's move on an azimuth directly away from the Gò Công. Sure as shit, if this area happens to be into some weird inundation thing, the further we get away from it, the less its effect will be."

We cut left and pushed on. Yet in spite of our moving directly away from the Gò Công, we trudged through steadily deepening water. It was as if we'd been heading straight *toward* the river, not away from it. Our progress dragged in proportion to its mounting depth. I became more than concerned. 'Why isn't it at least leveling out?' Baffled, I got hold of the TOC to let them know of my situation.

"This is Tiger Claw Six. I will not be able to make Lima Zulu at planned time. We need an early pick up, over."

"This is Three Bravo. What've you got going on, over?"

"Tiger Claw Six, I am in the middle of beau coup dense nipa. We've got to get clear of it. Right now, bringing in birds is a negative. I need some time, over"

"How much you need Tiger?" I was speaking to Lieutenant Pete Dahl who was on duty in the TOC. I gauged that as a plus. His ability to make things happen was a known quantity and his switch to informal radio procedure meant he was fully engaged.

"Don't know, Three. Progress is slow and the sun is going down. Wait, out."

Moving with as much speed as we could muster, we fatigued rapidly. Additional efforts gained us little distance. We ran into larger, tighter packed stands of nipa. Extensive, they cut off further movement to the west. Busting our way through nipa wasn't impossible, but we were already exhausted. Traversing deep mud under a yard of water rendered the idea hopeless.

We skirted the labyrinthine nipa in a tortured route for the next half hour. The trek kept us out of the slues of mud, but cost valuable time and didn't get us any further from the river. It didn't get us into a clearing either. The water rose past our waists and kept rising.

"Sir," Starcup called out from behind me, "I think it'd be better if we went back to where we were. It *was* anyway."

"Yeah, '*was*' is it. Who's to say that by now, back there isn't deeper than here. Besides, all I've been trying to do for the past hour is find a place that's good enough to bring in the choppers!" I looked behind us, to a panorama of darkling nipa palm against a purple sky. Their dark greens had already begun to striate with black. Standing in the motionless unbounded body of water, its sinister vastness gave me the feeling that there might not be a square foot of dry ground left within miles. Clouds of blood-starved mosquitoes swarmed to our scent in the close humidity. Hard and fast, I studied what lay before us.

"Corchado!" I yelled, pointing to what was looking like a cul-de-sac. "Can we get through there – or what?"

"Maybe, Sir, but it's where we'll be in the morning if it don't go nowhere. Thickest shit I ever seen."

"Shit is *it*!" I hissed in absolute frustration. "We're fucking boxed." From a distance, it had looked like just another defile but in the fading light, their mute forms seemed taller and as imposing as a looming phalanx of black-clad VC gargantuans. I stared at the point where the two walls of nipa came together. Rising from the dark water all around us, their stiff fronds bristled like primitive weapons, raised at the ready. They'd moved in shoulder to shoulder and closed us off.

"I think we damned sure gotta go back now," said Starcup.

"Back fucking where?!" I fumed, realizing for the first time that the entire platoon was in jeopardy, something more serious than a temporary navigational problem. Only this far from the coast, tidal drops could be as much as twelve feet. 'It was almost low tide when we got here. How much higher might it get? Suppose it comes up just another three feet?'

"Nunzie!" I barked. He was a few meters away. It distressed me to watch him fight his way through the water to get to me. On his passing it to me, I keyed the handset and brought up the TOC in a single motion. I spoke each word like it was a separate sentence, trying to communicate urgency over the radio, while displaying an air of cool for the benefit of my men.

"Three, I need an immediate pickup. I say again, *Immediate*! Over."

"No problem Tiger Claw, we've had the birds standing by waiting for your call."

"Look, Three, I've only got forty minutes until high tide. We're almost name-tag deep in this shit already. At the rate it's coming on, we're going to be using our gun barrels as snorkels before it crests."

"Roger, Tiger Claw. I've got your location – can't you just move west to what has to be higher ground?"

"Negative. I've been trying to do that for the last hour. We're blocked off by a big-ass nipa swamp – thick as shit – taller than anything I've ever seen."

"How 'bout if you went a little further north then?"

"Negative Three. *I say again negative*! You've got to trust me. I can't go anywhere. I want you to get us out of here – like *Now*! Do you read?!"

"Wilco Tiger Claw, you going to be okay for say twenty minutes? It'll take the birds all of that to get out there."

"It doesn't matter," I barked, giving up on cool. "I'm out of options. Just get those fuckers out here!"

"Roger. Hold tight, we're getting them up right now, over."

"Roge' – and oh yeah, one more thing. They're going to have to come in here one at a time. We're stuck in a spot barely big enough for that. I've got lights and will give their leader instructions when he comes up on our net."

The exchange reminded me of an infantry axiom that went back to the time of Alexander: '*The further away you are from your friends, the less able they are to help you when you need them most.*' That observer should've added something about the capacity of darkness to increase distance.

Sergeant Mounds shoved through the blackening water toward me.

"Damn, Sir! What the hell's going on? We ain't moved an inch in the past ten minutes. Alls the while, this here water's gettin' deeper." Not yet apprised of the situation, he appeared to be as upset with me as I was with our being there. No matter how I chose to define it, no matter who I chose to blame for putting us in here, the situation was all mine. Every life that was inside every face that looked to me was my responsibility.

"I thought we could get through over there, but it's completely blocked off by that line of nipa. Sink in that mud, and the water'll be over our heads. If we try and press on, we'll be fucked good."

"Sir, if we don't do somethin' pronto, we're goin' to be fucked no good."

"Just the kind of sage advice I was looking for Mounds. The birds are on the way. Take everybody and start preparing to get them out one chopper at a time. I'll bring them in from that direction." I pointed to a wide split between two tall stands of nipa. It would allow a single Huey to drop in, hover just above the water, then pull out over some slightly lower nipa at the other end, if that nipa wasn't too tall to get over. I checked the azimuth.

Word came from Crowder's squad that they'd just chanced across the vestiges of an old dike. We could stand on it. Trouble was the underwater lump of high ground could only elevate half a dozen men by a foot. That was meaningful to my short Tiger Scouts. I sent them over to it.

More minutes passed. With each of them, the water crept higher. Steadily it rose on our fatigue shirts and submerged our equipment. The RTOs unslung their radios and hiked them up onto their shoulders. My nervousness jolted with every lost fraction of an inch. It crept to the middle of my chest. It licked the collars of the scouts, underwater rise or no.

Tra and Tho were nearest to me. Although hard to see in the fading moments of dusk, I made out their serene heads. Their composure really got to me. There they were, calm and confident in my ability to somehow get them out of here, while sliding slowly into the gullet of this unchallengeable monster. 'What will we do if everything goes from bad to worse? What if our choppers *can't* get us out? My course of action…?'

"Okay you guys," I said, speaking in a voice meant for the entire platoon. "Here's the deal. If those choppers aren't here in fifteen minutes, anyone who's short will have to get up on some taller guy's shoulders. If our birds can't come in – or can't get us out, this is what we'll do. We ditch all our equipment – everything but M-Sixteens, one bandoleer, boots and pants. Anyone who's not a good swimmer had better drop everything but their dog tags."

"Drink all the water you have left. Then we move from here to the nipa and just hang on, riding up with the water. Those stands over there must be thirty feet tall. Up to half way, they're as rigid as steel poles. In a couple of hours, the tide'll be going back out and we can get our stuff – and wait for morning. They'll definitely get us out then." 'Yeah, all that, if I'm reading this water right and Motha-earth hasn't jolted herself into a new Precambrian Period with the whole planet now covered in water.'

"Tiger Claw Six, this is Greyhound over."

"This is Tiger Claw over," I said with undisguised relief.

"Roger, inbound your location, E-T-A, one- zero."

"Roger Greyhound. Okay, here's what we've got. The LZ is only big enough for one bird at a time. We're standing in water up to our necks. You'll have to hover. Your gunners will have to help pull us up. Come in on azimuth Three-One-Zero and look for the white strobe. The green light is your near end and the red is your far end. Stay right on that line. If you don't, you're going to be in here with us – commanding a submarine."

'There might not be enough time to make five one- by- one extractions. We've got to lift out from that submerged hummock – take the scouts and part of first squad first. If I don't, the last of us'll be left in too-deep water. Damn, that spot's so close to the nipa, every one of these pilots better be a friggin' flying acrobat.'

Pushing air against the ground or water, the UH1-E could do a stationary hover. But it couldn't simply go straight up into the sky. It required forward movement. We had some room for that, but the nipa was so tall, I was close to asking them to imitate a Polaris missile. And loading a Huey with six combat equipped grunts was the equivalent of a big pile of rocks. I'd seen choppers go down. Part of the pilot's decision on whether to come in or not, would depend on what I told them. And at this point, most of me wanted to tell them *anything.* I knew what kind of horror that could be. If they couldn't get out loaded, but tried anyway, we'd all go down. The vision of *that* nightmare would keep me honest. Such sobering possibilities weighed on my hopes like redundant layers of sodden sandbags.

The first Huey dropped in with little effort and hovered over the underwater rise. I shouted into my handset for him to switch his lights on. In the sudden globe of white glare, I instinctively flinched at the chopper becoming an instant tracer magnet. I looked away to preserve my night vision. The chopper moved forward, its lights illuminating only the area to its front. It cast the nipa as more monstrously eerie than ever. With their tips disappearing into the blackness above, they looked a hundred feet tall. In the shuttering shadows, the pale, ignis-fatuus green of Sergeant MacAlier's flashlight gave his face the look of an illuminated ghoul. Bundt's red one compressed our god of darkness into a single bloody eye.

The scouts and a couple of guys from first squad wrenched free of the water and onto the skids. Door gunners grabbed at their gear and hauled them aboard like huge fish. Trying to grab something secure, they flopped and wriggled on the floor, gaffed. The light moved forward and by the changing pitch of the blades and whine of the engines, I knew they'd begun their attempt to lift out.

I heard the dismaying crack of nipa being weed-whacked by the lift blades and held my breath. 'Are all five of those engines at a hundred percent? Is each one, right here and now, pulling every single horsepower it's supposed to?' Clearing the nipa, the whupping sound moved away in a robust and steady rhythm. I felt relief in one having made it, but the four scouts in it, meant it was two hundred pounds lighter than the others would be.

The second and third choppers each took down additional amounts of nipa. The blades were strong, whipping around at high speed scything off the tops of fronds. Strong too was nipa, and the further down that fibrous central stem, the more indestructible they got. If they hit any of them low enough, the ends of the blades would lose. They'd shatter and such an aircraft would assume the glide path of a footlocker full of bricks.

The fourth chopper dropped into our watery clearing. We were down to a dozen men. Ten of us had squeezed ourselves onto the little knoll, and the two tallest remained in place to mark the LZ. Water lapped at our necks. Coming in, the pilot misjudged his position or maybe tried to over-compensate the nipa on his left. The chopper's skids plowed right into us. Heads bobbed and ducked. Curses cried out in the swirling noise. Those designated for this load reached eagerly for the gunner's hands. Those of us remaining behind pushed at their legs and shoved them up over our heads. The chopper began to stray. Its skids slid across us. We ducked underwater and found ourselves directly beneath the aircraft.

Steadying its sideways drift, it began to swing diagonally. Its rear came around and the delicate tail rotor began sawing right into a thick stand of nipa. The steely fronds buzzed and splintered. 'Any deeper and that nippa's going to win and shatter those blades. Then the whole chopper'll lurch out of control and come down on top of us!'

I leaned into the water to get away from the aircraft's body. That only returned me to the fury of the whirling blades overhead. I feared them slamming into us as it tipped over, a giant eggbeater, destroying itself in a maelstrom of water and soldiers.

The Huey pulled back as if in a stagger. It shuttered, trying to lift a weight that was beyond its capacity. Then lunging ahead, it rammed itself into the wall of nipa. Incredibly, it kept going. The lift blades appeared not to have hit anything, so they just dragged the bird through. Teeth clenched. It could still crash. I listened. It pulled away and faded away into the night sky.

My last problem was to bring the final chopper in to the signal lights, then get the last of us into it. The doing would be even tougher than the one before. With fewer of us below to push, it would be a lot harder for the guys to climb up and get pulled aboard. Our chopper tried to maintain a stationary hover, inside the closing-in walls of nipa. It tried and tried, but slowly began to fail. It drifted to the left. Heads inside turned, to watch the inevitable.

The last two, Nunziato and I, arm-locked the skids… half in an effort to climb aboard and half in a reflex to hold the chopper in place. We both lost our footing and fell down too low for the others on board to get hold of us.

The crew chief got the pilot to descend a couple of feet. I felt the mound under my boots. Nunziato had the weight of the radio, so I boosted him up toward the grappling hands of two others. To get to the skid, he used my shoulder as a step, forcing me back and down. Beneath his full weight, I lost my grip. The inky surface closed above my head. I came back up, but the weight of my equipment altered my balance. I went under again. Pulling at the water with a one-arm breaststroke, I started to straighten up. 'That fucking pilot can't pull out now! I'll drop off into nose-deep water – and he won't be able to come back!'

I gasped for air, my hand swept across something. It stopped my heart. 'Somebody's submerged head?' Stunned, I reflexively grabbed for it. Swiping across it again, I closed my hand into a fistful of longish smooth hair. This clue blasted me with the horrifying image of a Tiger Scout who'd been left behind. Weighted by his equipment, unseen in the dark and unheard in the chopper's noise, he'd lost his footing and slid below the surface. To silently drown! I frantically hauled at him with a forearm across his neck, as the chopper vibrated and pitched over the wind whipped water, too long overtaxed, and too urgent to wait any longer. I pulled the body into my arms.

"Ahhh!" I screamed, "*The fucking dead gook!*" With a vile revulsion, I shoved flailingly at the NVA corpse, that same dead dink that I'd so carefully inspected only hours before, but he hardly moved. Somewhere, he was hooked onto me. Grasping the skid tightly, I kicked at his slimy body. The chopper drifted back. He bobbed against me *again.* He was clinging. *"I'll kill your ass, you…!"* I drove both of my boots into him. Then grasping someone's arm, I got one leg over the skid. In the wake of my attempt

to kick free, he drew in yet again. Caressing my other leg, he nudged at my thigh, as if in his spirit-wandering existence, he was either trying to hitch a ride or take me down with him.

Multiple hands wrenched fistfuls of my fatigues and I burst from the water like a cormorant taking flight. Arms hauled me upward and through the door. Heavy with water and exhaustion, I fell face down in a heap on the metal floor. A comforting tremble of engine vibration swept across my whole body. I brought my head up and the wind of accelerating lift lashed at my face. It rattled me to anticipate a need to dive clear of the chopper, and to hope that it wouldn't gain too much speed before catching the insidious nipa that would bring it crashing down. And oh yes, I imagined my host, still there, with his open and welcoming arms, undulating gently like sea grass in an ebbing tide.

CHAPTER 2

NUNZIATO AND I WERE THE last of the platoon to leave the LZ, a road-wide dike separating a pair of abandoned rice paddies that lay just outside the wire. As we trudged toward the perimeter, still dripping, I called the TOC and let them know we'd returned from our mission to 'Atlantis.' We followed the others in the irksome process of finessing our way through a section of the barbed wire entanglements that encircled most of our fire support base. Its pyramids of looping coils, interlaced with the warp and weft of many ad hoc additions, had become disorganized snarls of razored steel. It might impede an enemy attack, but our own going in and out was another story. A zigzagging lane had been created for troops to get through, but in order to pass, men still had to take turns holding strands down for each other with their boots. This tedious course from the LZ was used so often that most of the springy mesh had been bent flat.

Daytime called for just the occasional duck or leg over. Darkness though, turned our mutual exchange of holding and stepping into an exercise in not catching nuttage on a barb. A wire-free walk around to the front gate was further, and took ten minutes longer. Grunt algebra's equation said that the walk around equaled two additional sweat-drops of energy. So dark or not, through the barbed wire we went.

I unlocked and pushed open the door of my bunker. Swiping for the naked bulb hanging from the center beam, I snagged it and gave it a twist. The room filled with a dreary light. The only bulbs we had were dim little twenty-five watters. It'd be dreary with stadium lighting. My hooch, consisting solely of rough dirt caked timbers and sandbags had previously been a perimeter fighting position. To grab a modicum of privacy, I'd taken the bunker over and turned it into my living quarters. A mosquito ridden hovel was all it would ever be, but on the positive side, it could withstand a direct hit from an 82 mm mortar round and the worst of its overhead leaks missed my bunk by at least a foot.

As I shed the heaviest of my gear, the light began to flicker and brown-out. A voice called out from the First Sergeant's hooch. In the further distance, I could hear our little generator struggling to within the strength of a mosquito's bicep of conking out. I played the good soldier and unscrewed my bulb. The engine instantly began to gain in RPMs. 'Why the hell is my measly wattage always the culprit?' In the dark, I stripped myself of sodden jungle fatigues and lit a candle. While sliding into a pair of clean, dry, cut-off trousers and an OD T-shirt, a boot thumped my door open.

"Expect you could use a couple of cold ones about now."

"Paul," I said, "they should make you a four star general, immediately – on your powers of intuition alone."

"A mere administrative oversight on Congress's part I'm sure. So tell me what happened out there. I thought you Rangers never got far from your rubber boats."

"You're confusing us with SEALs. Rangers specialize in dry land operations and only dabble in rubber boats. It's vice versa with Seals. I tell you though I wouldn't have minded dabbling a little tonight." I reached up and turned the light bulb. The distant engine changed its tone only slightly so I left it alone. "Hey, what is it with that generator anyway? It's supposed to be a 1.5 kw. If you add up the six or seven bulbs coming off of it, we aren't even getting a quarter of that. All I want is one little bulb."

"It's an old ratty-ass generator. What can I say? The older and rattier, the less they gen. But I'll have you know, tomorrow, I'm picking up a pretty serviceable three-point-five. Added to this one, people'll mistake this place for the *Great White Way*."

"Yeah, we've already had *The Bob Hope Show*," I said. "Why not *'Vietnam! The Musical?'* Man, I can see him now, Luke the Gook, in his biggest role yet, center stage, singing and dancing his way through my platoon and right into our hearts."

"He'll bomb in New Haven before that ever happens."

Paul Keneally sat down at my table and watched me hoist my first can of cold beer and slug half of it. He and I had become close friends when he'd been the Four-Deuce platoon leader. Two months ago, he'd been given command of the Company, but nothing had changed between us. He put his uncommon dedication and considerable talents at Recon's disposal. This was a huge plus for me, because I no longer had to fight for what we needed. No grunt deserved to go without.

Keneally was more than four years older than me and at almost thirty was the oldest lieutenant in the battalion. I thought of him as being miles ahead in worldly accomplishments. If you needed a guy who looked smart, Keneally would be your man, a view he enhanced by the way he carried himself. The older-than-his-years creases in his face communicated a deep knowing concern and the bright-eyed intensity of his focus made me feel that it was reserved for me alone.

Inherently taciturn, he had a lot to say, if sufficiently engaged. My volubility proved the right catalyst. I'd toss him whatever came to mind, from non sequiturs on life, to splenetic rants on operations in the field. A perfect backstop for wildly ricocheting ideas, Paul kept me sane.

"I could only hear the TOC's half," he said, bringing my attention back. "I got the distinct impression you were in a trick out there."

"Trick 'n a half. Man, I was only this far from being slammed in a friggin' hurt locker." I squeezed my thumb and forefinger as though holding a mosquito by one leg. "Yeah, one with big fat Billy Buddha sitting on the lid. When I tell everybody at the TOC tomorrow, nobody's going to believe it. And what did we get out of it? Not a single dink – not any live ones anyway. We did come across this dead fucker though. He was just out there floating around – floating in, floating out. Who knows what he was up to. The dude could do a perfect dead-man's float. Perfect."

"He wasn't your KIA?"

"Nope. Some cruisin'-around gunship probably kacked him a few days ago." I slipped on a pair of foam-rubber flip-flops, but anticipating a mucky walk to the mess hall, kicked them back off then went outside to fetch my other pair of boots. Having baked in the sun all day on a pile of sandbags, they were as stiff as wooden shoes. "You know," I called in to him, "I dry them out, but to soften them up, I need to get-'em wet again. That's known as a *Catch-Twenty-three*." I clubbed them together to break out the hardened mud from between the cleats. "Anyway, since that dink got greased, it looked to me like he'd just been paddling hither and yon – maybe looking for that 'Right Way Path' to Buddha-ville."

"I thought you said he was dead?"

"Yeah deader 'an dog shit. But that didn't stop him from trying to take me down right when I was pulling myself out of the water and into that chopper."

"Mondo, I don't remember putting any LSD in that beer, but hell, maybe I did."

"Didn't need to. Trust me, you go out there and it'll be a *trip* you won't forget – a new hallucination every minute. Betcha by now it's under five hundred fucking feet of water. No, I take that back! It's probably sitting right back the way it was when we got there – like nothing ever happened – just waiting for another shot at gulping down some unwitting platoon. Fucking Arvins tried to kill it with arty before we arrived, but they lacked the atomic warheads they'd have needed."

"I'll steer clear of that place," he laughed, "easy, with my entire life confined here to God's little, brown-muddy acre."

All infantry lieutenants were usually assured of spending at least six months in the field leading a Rifle Platoon. But Keneally had only been out there a few weeks when battalion suddenly needed a school-trained four-deuce guy, with him being the only one they had. Seven months later, Braccia made him E Company commander.

'Keneally's right. He'll spend his entire tour in the relative safety of the firebase. But if I had a wife and little boy, how eager would I be to play hunt and seek with the North Vietnamese Army? Braccia offered me that transportation platoon in HHC when I came up from 1st Brigade; and what'd I do? Even with two Purple Hearts already, I chose Recon. What's that say about the value I put on my engagement and fiancée back home? If she asks I'll just tell her the truth; *because there's some shit needin' to be done!*'

"Check this out, Paul," I went on, "right in the middle of me doing this one-armed dangle from a skid, I thought the slick pilot was going to take off – like plunk my ass back in the drink. Fuck-it, I was already ahead of him. I can deal with it – yeah, all mentally prepared to spend the night floating in the nipa, me and my little buddy. You think a dead dink hanging around your neck could kinda act as some strange-ass lucky charm?"

"Sure, Mondo, it'd be the first thing I'd look for."

"Hey, a dead dink hanging around your neck has *definitely* got to be good luck."

"Dead-dink lucky charms..." Keneally pondered my inanity with a perspicacious nod. "A little outsized though, huh?"

"How 'bout those Amazonian dudes who tie shrunken heads to their belts. They seem to've gotten *that* whole issue under control."

To me Keneally's life seemed both conventional and not. A native of Philadelphia, he'd graduated from Penn, stayed on to take an MBA at the Wharton School, and gone off to newly independent Tanzania for a two-year stint in the Peace Corps. I'd asked him early-on why he'd taken up war as his 'logical next step to peace, given the number of guys who'd found volunteering there to be a respectable dodge to military service. He'd told me grisly stories about his experiences with Marxist revolutionaries in Africa. Alone and unarmed, his exploits there seemed harrier than mine here in Nam. He'd reacted by taking an infantry commission. His attitude was, different continent, different communists, same conflict.

"By the way, they're not sending us out in the morning are they?"

"I don't think so," He replied. "I was on the horn with Major Grizwell when you were flying back here. You're slated to rest, then around sixteen hundred tomorrow afternoon you're going out for a night ambush – northwest of here, operating there all the next day. He said not to worry about getting tomorrow's targets until first thing in the morning."

"I won't start worrying about anything 'til then," I said.

A growing swarm of flitting bugs had collected around the naked bulb and my annoyance grew with their numbers. Outer orbiters landed on our ears and collided with our faces. I picked up a can of Army insect killer and shot a misty cloud around the light. For a few seconds they flew unfazed, in and out of the hanging drizzle. Half of them suddenly fell to the floor, motionless. The others began flying erratically to safety, lighting on the far walls, only to drop and die. Tiny winged carcasses littered the floor.

"They can't fool me. NVA bugs – sent here with the specific mission of lowering my morale. Nope, they ain't gonna fuck with me."

"Doesn't look that way, Mondo. I'd say you've exacted a heavy toll on them – for just trying."

"Fuckin-ay. You better not dick around with a genuine superpower. Because, *'I'* have *the Bomb.*" I patted the side of the dull green can. "Please note that my itchy finger is sitting, *right on the button.*" Hearing the sound of my men passing by as they headed for the mess hall, I drained the last of my beer. "You need to excuse me Paul. I must dine, while the grease is still hot."

"You got it – that often maligned elixir of life in the infantry."

"Yeah, you never know what delights'll be found floating in it."

The last one to the mess hall, I picked among scant leavings and assembled half a meal. Recon had gotten the leftovers from three companies. I sandwiched paper plates around my scraps and took them back to my hooch. This practice was prohibited because it drew rats, but I decided that rank had to have at least one privilege. That was only a one-legged reason though. Eating shoulder-to-shoulder in the field was as common as the C-rations we ate, but things changed when we came in. 'Sitting with my men in the mess hall's enlisted section looks like fraternization, but sitting all alone in the officers' section looks stupid. Eating by myself in the quiet of my hooch solves everything.'

I turned on my transistor radio and the tinny sound of *"Marrakesh Express"* filled my hooch, the song's high harmonies exaggerated by a trebly 2-inch speaker. By moving my light bulb's wires to a different bent nail, I got it to hang right over my table. Now, I could eat *and* read, today's intellectual interlude from *Ramparts,* compliments of my girlfriend, a senior at Smith College. From a cellophane-covered, eight-by-ten color photo thumbtacked to the wall, my fiancée, Maureen Donegan, overlooked my doings.

Any random thought of Maureen drew me to look at her. My eyes always ended up riveted. That pose warmed me, her smile, the long blond hair, the curvaceous figure and choke-a-horse breasts that made me weak in the knees. What made it my favorite was her come-hither expression. The hint of *take me* hadn't escaped the eyes of any dude who'd seen it. She'd seen it too, and pleaded with me to trade it for one that would show her in a different light. Never. It was why I'd taken the negative and had it enlarged to the threshold of graining. I'd brought it with me to Vietnam to remind me of what I'd left behind and had waiting for me. 'Maureen, that come-hither look has gotten me through eight long months of combat and depravation. I love you for that alone!'

It'd been a year since the picture had been taken. I saw it as I always did, a single frame cut from a huge reel of motion picture footage. Mute and frozen in a thin membrane of time, I still saw her in that very moment, what we were doing when it was taken. 'All photos are like that. But this one's the perfect timeless reflection of her. Its immunity from evanescence will keep her just that way.'

The illogic of such a notion reminded me of what she'd written me only a week before. She'd described having to cut her hair and was letting it grow out brown. '*Having to?* What does that mean? She knows I'll hate it. That's why she didn't send any pictures of *the new me.* Okay, it'll take more than a chop-job to mar her looks. But why's she needing to change a part of her she knows I love? Look at those soft dun-colored ropes of it, the breeze tossing them into the air. How can it be gone? *Gone!*'

Continuing to study her enticing attributes, I noticed a hint of something new. Maureen was a beautiful flower, at the peak of bloom. Her Damp velvety petals never stopped beguiling me. But this blossom was giving me the strange sense that its roots were developing some kind of incipient blight. I couldn't quite understand the changes, they were like an invasive catabolism just beneath the surface. From ten thousand miles away, through a year-old picture, she was drawing my attention to something unnerving.

It'd begun with, 'stop the war and bring my boyfriend home.' But that'd led to a political drift, measured by the ominous tones of anti-war articles she enclosed with her letters. I'd become alarmed over their '*The enemy is us*' theme. Her being a dove was okay, war being hell and all, but my denial that she'd thrown in with the anti-Vietnam War movement was breaking down.

As swept up as she seemed to be, my rejoinders were having no effect. I was impervious to leftism and thought she would be too. 'Based on what, my faith in our relationship? That's all? I haven't heard the sound of her voice in eight months. If I could just talk with her, things'd be different. Or would they? She's been marinating in anti-Vietnam hostility for two years. That long, and leftism will've seeped all the way to her marrow. And here I am half a world away, the pure embodiment of all that's *"wrong."* No wonder I'm a cry in the wilderness. Every day, she's listening to voices sympathetic to commie goals – their enemy's always going to be America – and *me.* Where's *that* put our relationship? For starters, it classifies the genus of that mold, those furry spots breaking out on once-healthy leaves.'

I jotted down my impressions while reading her torn-out *Ramparts article.* By the end, I'd filled several pages. Covered with cross-outs and insertions, I copied them into a readable letter.

Dear Maureen,

I read that Ramparts piece and my first question is: Why are all these "anti-war" doves so infatuated with communist fortitude? They seem to believe that virtue flows directly from it. An eagerness to die for a cause has no relationship with moral rectitude. The Jap Army had an abundance of fortitude, but what good did they spread? Plenty of terrible causes have been perpetrated by tenacious fighters.

So, the solution for corruption in South Vietnam is communist totalitarian tyranny? Medicine strong enough to kill a patient is okay if you can tell yourself it was for his own good?? Rule One: There's no price in lives that's too high for communist leaders. Obtaining and maintaining the supremacy of state power is their only goal. Marx's "dictatorship of the proletariat" is justified by whatever means. Historically that's come to mean the deaths of tens of millions of people - human lives to them being nothing more than the expendable fuel for their engine of state power. The history is unarguable. You know this has been the center of all my studies, but right now, I'm facing Mao's "barrel of a gun." Between the classroom and this lab work, I've got this shit cold!

On a patrol today, we came across the body of a dead NVA soldier who'd been lying out there for a couple of days. It affected me in an unusual way. As an individual, he seemed symbolic. Discarded and left behind like a piece of debris, his very body spoke his epitaph: "HERE LIES A MAN WHO FOUGHT ONLY THAT HIS LEADERS MIGHT MAINTAIN TOTAL POWER OVER HIS LIFE, FROM HIS ACTIONS TO HIS THOUGHTS. HE HAD NO OTHER PURPOSE." He gave his life for this!

Sometime back, Ho bragged that twenty of his men could die, for every one of ours and he'd still win. Knowing that we value our one as highly as we do, and that his twenty are as unimportant to him as they are plentiful, he figures he can lose every battle and still be victorious. Think about that - lose every battle and still win! That epitomizes it. He sees our placing such a high value on the lives of our men as a military, political and societal weakness. He's betting that tying us down long enough will frustrate us enough to quit. You know we passed that point back in your sophomore year, when you joined Sam Brown's gang and went campaigning up in New Hampshire for "Clean Gene."

The communists have lost a million men, but to what consequence? None. To extend their power into the South, Ho will pour as much of his own countrymen's blood down the sewer as it takes - hundreds of thousands of innocent civilians too - the very people of whom he claims to be the savior. Then the guy who wrote that article (motivated only by his deep love of peace) wants us believing that communist willingness to shed blood, evinces some kind of wonderfully transcendent nationalism? It only proves to me that these professional doves are communist appeasers. He'd ridicule that, but just as quickly dismiss Red mass murder with their old "moral equivalency" concoction - to project communist crimes against humanity right onto us.

The government in Hanoi is just like every other red regime. It doesn't just possess total power, it exercises it. It's inherent to communism and been plain to see since the Bolshevik revolution. It absolutely blows my mind how their utopian rhetoric remains so intoxicating for so many, right square in the face of a sinister reality - ruthless cruelty and bloodshed on a colossal scale. As for war, it's their essential tool in their final phase of conquest. Because they are tyrannical totalitarians, communists deserve only to be stopped. That's why I'm here.

So then what does the willful ignoring of all their horrors mean? Doesn't it make you an accessory? And how on earth can a "Peace Movement" that's openly sympathetic to red conquest, even helping facilitate it, have any claim to advancing peace? <u>You</u> need to face this stuff.

Way past weary of the subject, I was too dog-tired to spend another minute on it. 'Will a six-page lecture be that much better than five? No-o-o, I'll just send it like it is. But not quite.' Fetching my K-Bar from its sheath, I laid the last page on the table and aligned the blade perpendicular to the bottom quarter, in order to slice off the last three questions. '...Don't need to be raising the ante on our long-distance fight. But shit! They're fair questions – and like any one of her enclosures aren't worse provocations?' *"Oh sure Gavin, stopping the killing with more killing..."* 'Exactly Maureen, how the fuck else do you stop a Commie with a gun? Yup, they're totalitarian butchers, only because we've provoked them. Otherwise, they'd be just a real fine bunch of guys.'

I mulled over our intercontinental letter writing and its descent into this game of wits. It was a match where she and a coterie of confederates assisted her in scoring points on me. I guessed when she got enough of them, the argument would be over. 'And where the hell would that leave *us?* Me here and her there – with one of her *special* collaborators?

I put down my knife, folded the pages and crammed them into a fat envelope which already contained an unfinished, pure, boyfriend-girlfriend letter. My affections for her having taken a fresh dive, I decided to revisit both of them in the morning. My sentiments were always more circumspect with a morning cup of coffee, than with late-night cans of beer. I pushed back my chair and checked my watch. The numbers read *23:13*.

I glared at the envelope laying there, the dissembling article from Maureen, and her unsettling letter. I shook my head at their contradictions and my sour feelings. *'Goddamnit Maureen!* It's so exasperating. Your letters speak so longingly of *us* and our eventual reunion. But your pledges of love sound like they're becoming perfunctory. You set me up with your embrace, then pound me with all your campus politics. It's like your warm loving kiss followed by a hot pain of a knife stuck in my side.'

Back when I'd started going with Maureen, she'd held opinions that were uniquely her own, an elemental measure of her personality and how she saw the world. Insights sprang from her by the minute. With a brash exuberance for everything, she had me falling in love with her from our first date. 'And now? She's jaded, with her thoughts on loan. Fucking ironic – Me here, maybe a day away from being turned into another notch on Victor Charles's AK... while she's somewheres in the Berkshires, entwining the sounds of Kumbaya with pot smoke into a more-perfect *truth*.'

I redirected my emotional reflections by straightening up the things on my desk. Tossed on a pile were the lyrics of a song she'd sent, *"Story of Isaac,"* by Leonard Cohen. According to her, its ulterior meaning symbolized the inhumanity of this war. She found the lines about sacrificing the children with blunt bloody hatchets and how we shouldn't do it, to be profound. I read the last stanza again, still deadlocked on what it meant.

When it all comes down to dust
I will help you if I must,
I will kill you if I can.
And mercy on our uniform,
Man of peace or man of war,
The peacock spreads his fan.[1.]

Maybe Cohen's monotone death croak added something to its comprehension, because it sure didn't jump off the page at me. I knew the real reason; I was the last of the Cro-Magnons. My antediluvian thinking always made her profundities opaque.

I grabbed a book my dad had found at a yard sale, an old copy of Robert Graves's *Count Belisarius.* Its vivid picture of 6th Century Byzantium was interspersed with longueurs so deadening it could put an amped-up speed freak to sleep. But I didn't feel like going to sleep.

"*Fuck it!*" I hissed, flopping the book down in trade for my bush hat.

I left my hooch and moseyed into the platoon's quarters. The lights were out. I walked between the wooden bunks, toward a dim glow at the far end. Silhouetted by it, the mosquito-netted hulks of my sleeping men seemed like rows of giant pupae cocooned on stout wooden shelves. I passed through the bay and turned down into our equipment area. At the far end, we'd constructed a makeshift bar from old scraps of plywood and artillery shell crates. Several guys were sitting at it, hunkered over beer cans, their dark forms flickering in the wan light of a single candle. A stratus of hazy gray cigarette smoke hung head-high around them.

"This isn't NCOs only is it?" I asked.

"Oh, ah no Sir," Mounds answered, with the kind of startle he might have emitted on realizing that I'd just overheard some indiscretion. "We just shootin' the shit. There's a beer or two left." He, Crowder, Starcup and Olivera, my three squad leaders, were the only ones present.

It wasn't an unnatural group, but without a new operation to get ready for, they had no business to discuss. Besides, Starcup and Olivera weren't ever absent their sidekicks, Dean and Corchado. Those two wouldn't be absent without being excluded on purpose. This bull session had the air of something conspiratorial.

Leaning over the big metal cooler, I fished around through cans of soda and pulled out a cold beer. I punched a pair of holes in the can and sat down. 'If they're engaged in a soldierly critique of anything, it'd have to be this evening's adventure in Xa Khoi.'

"So what's the three best things about Xa Khoi?" They all looked at me as if I'd just told them we were heading back out there in five minutes. I took a slug from the can and pulled out a pack of Luckies.

"To my way of seein' it," Mounds said at last, "there ain't three best things about downtown Saigon. "But Xa Khoi? I reckon that place damned near swallowed up our whole platoon."

"Well," I said, "it might have been fucked up, but without any AK-packin' dinks running around in there, it wasn't about to claim anybody." I lit up and blew out, the small truncated cloud of an interrupted first drag. "The way I see it – not one swinging dick."

"If that water'd come up any higher, and them choppers hadn't made it in, there wouldn't have been a need for the gooks to do nothin'."

"What about my contingency, Mounds? I put the word out, right when the water got up to our chests. Didn't you get it? I know you did – you were only twenty feet from me."

"Yes Sir, but the question is, would it've worked?"

"Of course it would have." I blew out another inhalation of smoke, this time aiming it down between my shirt and the bar. "If it wouldn't have worked, I wouldn't have put it out."

"Well, Sir," Mounds grumbled, "there ain't no tellin' how high floodin' like that might get or how long it might stay high."

"Flood from what? I countered. "It was only some weird-ass tidal situation. There *are* physical limits to how high it could've gotten – and for how long."

"I ain't never been in a flood, but it sure looked like one to me, and they ain't ever good."

"Sure Mounds, any time you got water as far as you can see, it'll look like a flood. Did your family move to Chicago because of the Great Flood – the Mississippi in 1927? Stories of that'd spook anybody."

"I doubt it. They come up from Alabama durin' World War Two. Anyways Sir, alls I'm sayin' is that some of the platoon might not do so well in eight foot of water."

"I understand that. That's why people've got to follow my instructions, scared of water or not. Like I've said many times; fear wants to keep us from doing what we need to do, even saving our own asses. That's why we always need to *act in spite of our fears.*" 'What really would've happened if things had gone like he feared, our pickup failing and water coming up over our heads? Short as Thanh is, anything past his chin would've been last-resort time.'

I conducted a mental formation of the platoon and began reassessing their swimming abilities squad by squad, soldier by soldier. I'd observed them around water plenty, but outside of a handful who were strong swimmers, I didn't know what the rest could do. 'How comfortable would everyone be in water over their heads? Non swimmers don't handle that very well. Some panic even when hanging on to something. We've crossed rivers that were over our heads, hand-over-handing it on a rope. It wasn't so wide or deep, but everybody'd done it, swimmer or not. Mounds is probably a not, and worried about sinking like a dropped grenade if he ever lost his grip. I need to find out who my questionable swimmers are and carabiner them to the rope anytime we use one.'

"I didn't come to Vietnam to drown," I said at last.

"I reckon not too many have," Mounds retorted, "but sometimes I gets the feeling' that you wouldn't mind at all, going out some other way – 'specially if it had gooks involved in it. I don't want to be alls that close when it happens."

"Huh?" 'What the hell's he talking about? Does he think I'm reckless or that I don't care if I live or die? That's what he's saying. Do the rest of them think this too?' "I promise you Mounds, no matter how it looks to you, that's not the way it is. You guys have been with me for a while. You know how I operate. People would be asking to go back to one of the rifle companies if things were so iffy, but nobody is. You know you can – any time."

"I don't know about after tonight, Sir."

I looked straight at Mounds then shifted my gaze to the others, one by one. 'Are their expressions backing him up?'

"Who are you talking about?" I asked.

"Well, nobody in particular," he answered. "It's just that some of the guys are pretty fucked up about what went down."

"Okay, so tomorrow you make it your NCO business to find out exactly who *is* fucked up. Then, you go and *un*-fuck them. Failing that, you let me know their names, and *I'll* go and un-fuck them. However, I'll remind you that it isn't a PL's job. It *is* one of the most important parts of being a good NCO though."

"You know we ain't got no problem with that, Sir," Mounds insisted, "It's just that we all knew there weren't any gooks in there, but we went busting our asses through that shit anyways. You even told us that the water was goin' to come in."

"One, *I don't pick our targets.* Battalion does – the Colonel. He tells me where to go and that's what I do. I just bring you guys along for my protection." I smiled at their drawn faces. And two, I told you that sometimes it came in. When that was, even fucking Tra didn't know. It definitely wasn't a regular thing. In any case, now we know why they weren't base-camped in there.

Before the water though, it didn't look all that out of the question and remember, there *was* that one dead dude."

"He could've come from five miles up-river the day before," Crowder interjected.

"True enough. Okay, looks like I need to go over the big picture with you a little more. First, we got *sent* in there. Second, our number one priority is killing dinks. Right? The more of them we get, the fewer of them there will be to get us. If we sandbag our operations, others might too. No dinks get killed; we lose."

"If you ask me Sir," Crowder began. The drawl of his words gave me the feeling of him trying a window after finding the doors to be locked. "Some of this battalion's already sandbagging. Look at that platoon in Bravo."

"I know, but they're an exception. We're Recon. Aren't we the standard for what to do and how to do it? We can't control them. That lieutenant over there is a fucking..." I wanted to say coward, but discretion won out. "...a fucking dipshit. He tries to cover it up by big-mouthing over how he's looking out for everybody – how he's keeping everyone alive."

"Can't beat staying alive!" Starcup cracked. "I just love the feeling."

"Staying alive isn't exactly our mission, but listen to what I'm saying. I don't expect that the mission should take precedence over absolutely everything – all of the time. We'*ve got to stay alive* – to do our job. But our essential welfare can't become some kind of predominating priority. If I let it, I'd be operating like Lieutenant Ass-wipe over in Bravo. To make sure nobody ever gets hurt, we'd just hide in a defensive perimeter every night and wait till morning. No mission. You all know by now, that I'm never going to do that. I don't think any of you really want me to either. If you do, you don't have any business being in Recon. To the best of my ability, I want to win this war." I let that sink in. No one said anything. I motioned the end of my cigarette toward the three squad leaders. "You all okay with this or what?"

"You know I am Sir, answered Starcup. I looked at Olivera and he nodded. Crowder turned to Mounds, who offered no expression.

"I'm with you... up to a point," he said at last. "I guess."

"You *guess,* Mounds? Don't we both need to *know*?"

"I'm not sure how it is you're goin' to win the war," Mounds cut in. "I can see us gettin' in some major shit tryin' *that.*"

"Gee-zuhs Mounds, I don't mean all by ourselves, but we sure as hell aren't going to be the fucking horseshoe nail that loses it either."

"Sir, I..." Crowder started, "I think he means just tryin' *too* hard." Mounds got up and went over to the ice chest.

"How many guys have been lost since I've been here?" I demanded.

"Well, I guess only one."

"Right, one. Do we want to talk about whose squad Prine was in, and whose element he was with on that operation? Or, about some of the circumstances leading up to it... I don't think we do."

"No Sir we don't," Mounds said in a quick defense of Crowder. "This here's ain't about Prine. We was just talkin' about that flood and all."

"Yeah, the *'and all'* stuff is the part I was referring to."

"Sir-r-r-r?" Crowder asked, in a tone that elbowed his way back into the exchange. He lifted a can of beer and gulped heartily, charging himself for what he was about to say. "We were just – like wondering why we kept going, after the water started coming."

"Kept going? I suppose you knew how deep it would get, and how extensive an area it would cover? *And* exactly where dry land was? Your test was to see if I could figure it out on my own, huh? If keeping on *'going'* was bothering you, you think *staying* would've been better? Where exactly? Back closer to the river?"

"But," Mounds interjected, "it was past our waists before we started doin' anything. By then, everybody was about to flip out."

"I didn't see anybody flipping jack shit. Name me a single dude who thinks waist-deep water is going to do him in. Besides, we were moving *out* of there – away from the river, from the time it was half way up our boots. Weren't we?" He didn't answer. 'Is he questioning his confidence in me? His comments imply it, but I can't believe it's all coming out of *this* event. I've earned their confidence over time, tough situation by tough situation. It's probably lost the same way, incident by incident. A single catastrophic event can do it but Xa Khoi was just one more tough situation.'

"Mounds, we've been in plenty of scrapes hairier than that. Remember last week, when that pair of dink snipers put us in a crisscross? That was hotter than anything we were in tonight. If one of those dinks hadn't fired prematurely, it would've been even hotter. Bullets coming right at you are always more dangerous than a river just sitting there."

'My problem's Mounds. A few things about him've been irking me, but they've been swallowed up by this war's daily ration of annoyances. This stuff here though, has the feel of real hostility. I can have him replaced, but not without generating heartburn. He's a career NCO with friends in the battalion. Recrimination might be one of his strongest talents. His finding the sympathetic ear of Major Tinderberry is *all* I need.'

I leaned on the bar with both elbows, thinking, while the others joked about the comic aspects of their guys clambering into the choppers. 'Why haven't I dealt with this before now? Simple, it's easier to put crap like this out of mind. Recon's details need my attention every minute. Usually I'm too hot, too thirsty, too bone tired to deal with unwanted bullshit for longer than it takes to walk away from it. The bush is too lethal for bullshit. But what if the bullshit gets so deep you can't walk?'

I looked the three squad leaders over, assessing them in a way I'd never done before. 'Until now, it's just been a matter of can they do the job? Can I get along with them? I'm feeling I need to measure them in terms of trust, like I had to do it with the Tiger Scouts – but they were total enigmas who hardly speak English *and* former VC. Now I need to do it with NCOs already tested in combat with me?'

The other half of South-side Chicago Mounds was redneck hillbilly Crowder. These two had to be the most unusual pair in the battalion. Voluntary segregation had replaced forced segregation, but not for Mounds and Crowder. These two were with each other all the time.

'What has them sticking together? They don't even seem that friendly to each other. Is their common denominator *me?* Trouble is, having to keep a closer eye on my platoon sergeant and first squad leader doesn't fill me with a single good feeling.'

Starcup was here with them. I couldn't sense anything beyond his being okay. I knew him best because I moved with his squad when we were in the field. That practice had evolved into my assigning certain men to him simply because I liked them. They were handier with their weapons, an advantage in our line of work. Carefree Starcup, a natural in the field, was perfect as their squad leader. I knew I could count on him.

Olivera, a Puerto Rican who'd enlisted in the Army nearly three years before, was the quietest man in the platoon. Since he grumbled the least, and since bellyaching was a normal way of knowing where soldiers were at, he was tough to read. Glancing in his direction, I thought of him in the field, following my instructions with that sharp purposeful jerk of his head, the nod of consent that he understood what was to be done. 'Is he really *with* me, or just going through the motions of following my orders? Ever since joining us, he's been nothing but a closed book. He's never done anything wrong, but I can't remember him ever doing anything remarkable either. Has he really been put to the test? Not sure.'

There would have to be some changes. Starting in the morning, I'd begin by switching from Starcup's squad to Crowder's.

While I'd been mulling over my situation and potential remedies, their conversation digressed. Starcup had gathered their attention to an incident he'd witnessed while a member of another battalion.

"In the middle of the night our company went out with just two platoons," Starcup said, "cuz they wanted us to set up a blocking force outside this-here ville. Half way there, we gets to this river, which normally we could've crossed, but this time the water's high – the middle's like eight-feet deep. Okay, so there's this fence in the water – going all the way across. It's made of thin, tied-together, up-and-down strips of bamboo. Somebody said they get fish with 'em but I don't know how...."

"It's a weir," I said. "They channel them into a confined space and then scoop them up with a net. It's easier than doing it in open water."

"Anyways," Starcup continued, "the CO decides we can cross hand-over-hand along the top of the fence, which is stickin' out of the water by a few inches. It's pretty rickety, but can be done if guys stay far enough apart. But if you bunch up, it'll bend toward you and take you under. This is what happens to a dude in the other platoon. He loses hold, and loaded with ammo and shit – goes right to the bottom. Nobody hears a single glug out of him. But listen to this, not a swingin' dick notices he's missing for over an hour – not until we was half-a-klick away and settin' up the cordon. So like where is he? Did he just go off on his own or something? They found him later that day. Check this out – dudes from his squad said when they dragged him up there was a couple of those big ass crabs hanging off of his face." Olivera and Crowder groaned. "Man, we came back to the firebase and the CO, the PL, and the platoon sergeant were like, *gone.* Nobody ever saw any of 'em again."

Starcup's tale ended. I turned to the others. Mound's expression was the stark goggle-eyed look of a non-swimmer imagining the horror of losing his grip on that flimsy fence. Or was it his grip on a slowly bending stalk of nipa down in Xa Khoi?

"Okay you guys," I said at last, putting down my empty can. "I've got to hit the rack. But I want you to remember, we're here to kill dinks – you and me together – all of us. It's what any good infantryman does. Everybody knows I'm pretty gung ho, but just because more of me is dedicated to getting the job done doesn't mean everything else is excluded. The same goes for you as soldiers. Each man is responsible for keeping himself alive, but that's far from being your sole mission. I'm a lifer. Mounds is a lifer. Crowder's leaning toward lifer-dom. Lifers, by definition, don't go home in body bags. "Lifer" begins with life, doesn't it? Staying out of a body bag though, isn't a career goal. My goal is to be the best recon Platoon Leader I can be, because *that's* what'll keep my people from getting killed – blown away, greased, *or drowned.* I aim to keep it that way."

CHAPTER 3

At 0800 hours, I walked up to Battalion Headquarters and joined a couple of staff officers standing outside. We traded disconnected comments, apropos to the dewy stillness of the indolent morning air. Nearby, a score of men pursued their appointed tasks with greater levels of purpose. Several were working on the 100 KW generators across the street, a pair of signal guys attended to a clump of pole-hung commo wire, and further down, a group unloaded artillery shell crates from a 5-ton truck. A Charlie Company platoon leader came out from behind us. He saluted the captains as he clomped over the dirt-filled artillery box that served as a step.

"Hey Janacek," I called. "What's happening down there in 'Charlotte Company'?"

"Ha," he called back. "Mommy's taking us to the zoo today. Everybody in 'Eat-it Company's going to be jealous."

Major Grizwell emerged from his quarters with a broad straight-ahead stride. We saluted. He passed between us without slowing. We followed him inside and into the staff briefing room, which occupied half of the headquarters' first floor. This hulking two-story bunker housed the Tactical Operations Center and the key players who ran the battalion. Its rooms were sweltering, windowless boxes of plywood and heavy rough-cut timbers, but its dirt filled walls and sand bagged roof would withstand the impact of a 107 millimeter rocket.

The building pulsed with activity. Staff NCOs came in and out, busy with details generated by the radio-squawking TOC across the hall. Others thumped up and down the wooden stairs that led to offices occupied by the Commander, XO, Sergeant Major and S-1.

The CO had been out in his Command and Control chopper since 0700 hours, so the day's operations were well under way. Our battalion commander, Lieutenant Colonel John J. Braccia, would return around midday, after "kicking some Cong ass." Trading places in the C and C with Major Grizwell, he'd spend the rest of the day crunching through the administrative details to care for a thousand men set down in a tropical muck hole hosted by an armed and hostile enemy.

"S-o-o-o-o Carney," Major Grizwell drawled, "I guess y'all had quite a time out there last night." He wiped the amassed beads of sweat from his forehead with the palm of his hand then wiped that onto the side of his trousers. It drew my attention to the stifling heat. That and the lack of ventilation had me feeling claustrophobic.

"Yes Sir, we sure did," I managed.

"I think it's the first time that we've had a platoon in trouble, where sending in reinforcements was the last damned thing on my mind."

"What do you think happened?" Captain Yoshino, our S-2, asked.

"I don't know." I heard my own voice answering in a way that I loathed. An I-don't-know answer wasn't the reply expected of a no-limits platoon leader who prided himself in knowing every last thing there was to know. Ever since the colonel had openly referred to Recon as his hip-pocket platoon, I'd taken to encouraging its implication. I had my shortcomings, but when nurturing an ethos, you don't brief them at battalion HQ.

I turned to the map. "Look at the area. Nothing out of the ordinary. On the ground, there's just bush and nipa like anywhere else, just thicker – and no indication that tides come in regularly." 'Except for the clues Tra spotted right after we'd landed that I never figured out.'

"If you look at the known tidal areas," I went on, "like the big one over here in the Rung Sat, they're marked as part of the actual river or with the little mangrove symbols…." The corner of my eye caught sight of the battalion's Executive Officer, Major Harold Tinderberry, in the hallway. He stuck his head in the door to check out who was there. His eyes locked on me. He took a step into the room. The corners of his mouth drew down with his continued stare, turning his normal scowl into a look of open disdain. Taken aback, I broke off the distraction by turning back to the map. "This place…" I pointed to it. "The place's called Xa Khoi, the hamlet name – except there's no hamlet – it's totally uninhabited." I tapped the map. "…just got the dark green for dense woodline – like regular jungle. But the nipa's super tall and thick because nobody's ever cut it."

I glanced back toward the doorway. Tinderberry was still standing in the rear of the room. His expression had moderated from glaring hostility to ominous disapproval. Suddenly, as if called to an emergency that only he could hear, he pivoted and strode from the room. *'The fucking Prince. Just what I need.'* We did not like each other. I wasn't alone. Most of the battalion's officers referred to him as 'Hairy Dingleberry,' on account of the high-handed way he treated anyone of lesser rank. The princely sobriquet came from the imperious, magisterial air of superiority he affected. Yet it wasn't a façade. It comprised his very core. This guy had stars in his eyes to the max, but performed his duties as battalion's Executive Officer as though it was and injustice that he wasn't General Abrams's right-hand man instead. Beyond his haughty arrogance though, lay the bedrock of his derisive nickname. Dingleberry was 24-carat *chicken shit.*

"Sir, what was the deal on us going into Xa Khoi anyway?" I asked Major Grizwell. "What the hell kind of poop did we have on that area?"

"We had some fairly reliable Arvin intel," Grizwell answered. "They confirmed recent NVA activity in there – enough to pound it with arty just ahead of you."

"Sir, they fired that mission, knowing that they weren't likely to hit anything… they even used delayed fuses. Hell, there wasn't a single bunker anywhere – you know they have dudes who grew up close-by who could've clued them in that you couldn't build bunkers in there." I left the map, sat down and lit a cigarette.

"You reported one KIA though."

"Yes Sir. But I only reported finding a dead dink. He'd been that way for a couple of days. The arty didn't kack him. Some chopper did."

"How would you know that?"

"Since no troops have been in there, and an M-60 got him..." I reached into my pocket, and pulled out the bullet. "I dug this round out of him myself."

"You what?! Grizwell asked grimacing at the thought of me performing a field autopsy on a putrefying corpse.

"Wrong image Sir. It was sticking out of his arm and I just poked it the rest of the way with the tip of my knife."

"Anyway you look at it Carney, dead dinks are positively correlated with live dinks."

"Yes Sir, but it's the *where* of it. That dink could have come floating in from up river."

"Maybe, and maybe not. You couldn't have covered but a fraction of that area."

"Humping it like we did was a good representative 'fraction' – convinced me the Arvin's little fire mission was a waste of ordinance. There isn't a single trail in that place, not even a single booby trap." Not finding a butt can, I let my ash fall on the dirt covered floor. "You know Sir, it looks like the damned Arvins are just pretending to fight this war."

"True," he said, "but around here just about anything might be true." He wiped at more sweat to keep it from running into his eyes. His act was contagious. Yoshino and I did the same.

"Yeah fucked up intel and fucked up Arvins," I said, shaking my head in exasperation. "I don't know."

"I don't know either. But explain to me why you wanted to go out on joint ops with the Arvins when we were working east of here?"

"Roger Sir, with Trung úy Mau. That dude was super hard core – course now he's dead. So much for being a good Arvin. Can we get back to yesterday's water shit? It still baffles me."

"Okay, Carney," he said, "it couldn't have been all that bad. From what you've told us, it was booby-trap free. It's not every day you get to just bop around out there."

"Dead man's float maybe. Sir, I'll bet you they haven't booby trapped that area, because they figure that nobody'd be dumb enough to want to waste their time *diddly-boppin'* around in there."

"What's important is, you got out. The slick commander who extracted you said you did a damned fine job, given the situation you had. Colonel Braccia was also pleased with how you handled it."

"Yes Sir, I appreciate that. I've got to tell you though, those chopper pilots did a damned fine job too." 'That's exactly the impression everyone needs to be left with – not how I got into the shit, but how I got out of it.'

"Take your luck where you can get it Carney." Grizwell got up from sitting on the edge of his desk. "Luck's always in short supply during a war."

"Agreed Sir. I hate using up luck though when dinks aren't around. I need it for when they are."

"Hey Mike, does the Colonel know about us getting cut to ten birds tomorrow?"

"I'm not sure, Sir," Captain Hembree, our S-3 Air answered. "I was going to check with him when he comes back in."

I'll get him on the horn right now. He might still be able to shake us loose a few more." He and Hembree went across to the TOC.

"Hey, Mondo," Yoshino said, "check out these intel reports. Let me know if you're interested in any of them." He handed me several sheets and headed out after the others. At his desk, I read their markings: 'Usually Reliable. Sometimes Reliable. Unreliable. Intel reports are so friggin' bizarre. Sure, sometimes they get us contacts. But like only by accident. How can dudes sitting in some far-away G-2 office know what's going on in a hamlet that I'm standing in? Here's one that's bound to get us sent there – more like our wandering around in the domain of evil sprites, who'd just gone to ground. But not before they leave behind their lethal spore of exploding snares.'

"Lieutenant Carney." A voice from behind broke my reverie. "Someone needs to have a little chat with you on the subject of impertinence."

"Sir?" I said, startled from the realization that Major Tinderberry was doing the asking. 'When had he'd returned? How many of my comments had he heard?' Furtively, I looked down at my boots, as though the word *impertinence* had just rolled under the table, a loose grenade.

"Has anyone ever explained to you," he went on, "that lieutenants do not question the motives of majors."

"Sir, I don't recall ever questioning your motives."

"It's a good thing for you that you haven't, but I just listened to your little performance in front of Major Grizwell – and I have to say, your cocky and presumptuous attitude is wearing thin around here." 'What's he referring to? Why does he care? Major Grizwell doesn't mind at all. I'd better get up – stand at attention.'

"You may remain seated," he snapped, in a rebuking tone I'd expect him to use if I'd persisted in staying seated.

"Sir, could you tell me what I said that you thought was out of line?"

"For one, your snide comments about not understanding why you'd been sent somewhere. That is not yours to know. Your job is to accomplish the tasks you've been given. You were in charge last night, were you not? You think the TOC's responsible for knowing when and where tides come in? They were here. You were there." Tinderberry spoke in a loud whisper that magnified the obduracy in his voice, while keeping it confined within the room.

"Sir, I *did* know when the tides were."

"That's precisely my point Carney. Only the dumbest most asinine platoon leader would be abreast of his tidal chart, while having his platoon up to their necks before deciding to move out. You ever heard of the Ribbon Creek Incident? Six men in that platoon were drowned."

"Yes, Sir, I am familiar with it, but see no parallels with last night."

"Perhaps because you're too preoccupied with impugning the motives of your superiors."

"With all due respect Sir, I would never make snide remarks to the S-3. Possibly, you misinterpreted sarcasm made in jest. What happened in the field situation was not at all as you describe." His eyes squinted. He leaned forward. His stare was so riveting that he seemed to be determining whether a freckle on my nose was actually a micro dot jammed-packed with indecipherable code.

"In my book, Carney, a wisecracking lieutenant is a wise-ass lieutenant, and a wise-ass presumes his superiors to be suspect – and Carney, I happen to have a long-standing animus for wise-asses."

"I'm sorry Sir, I was only..."

"Only sharp shooting the Battalion Operations Officer, a major, with five times your experience." I burned with anger from his onslaught, from not knowing what really lay behind it, and from not being able to defend myself. *'Five times my experience?!* Major Grizwell's a sharp guy, but he's never led troops in combat. Hell, Dingleberry's only been an aide de camp or in some staff or job his entire career. The Colonel's the only one who knows the score – leading a platoon and a company in real shit during the Korean War.'

"Sir…" I said. My jaw clenched. "I respectfully submit that it was in no way my intent. You may have missed part of what I said."

"Carney!" he interjected, his voice a renitent bark. "I was standing right there and heard it all! You think you're the fair-haired boy around here, but if you pull that crap again, I'll have you dancing on the end of a very short string – one you'll will find rather uncomfortable." 'Nice, Dingleberry jerking me around while I flop like a broken marionette on its last string.

"Sir, may I clarify something about the situation last night...?"

"That *situation*," he interrupted, "would make me contemplate your relief."

It sunk in. 'There isn't anything I can say. He's goading me just so he can cut me off and shove it back. Whatever lumps were left, I'll just have to take them.'

He walked toward the map, turned, and came part way back. I watched his moving uniform. Despite the insensible heat, his fatigues had no wedge of sweat down the back, no dark patches under the arms, and no beads across his brow. 'I can dig Tinderberry disparaging perspiration, it being the antithesis of starch but how the hell does he put an end to it by sheer force of will?'

Captain Yoshino came out of the TOC and started toward us, but one of the operations NCOs held him up with a question. Their voices caught the XO's attention. He glanced their way, then back at me with an ophidian-cold stare. I said nothing. Tinderberry abruptly walked out.

His leaving left me with an unsettled relief, the kind I'd feel after being eviscerated by some hungry carnivore that'd suddenly sense danger and bolted off into the jungle. Relieved from the prospect of being eaten alive, I could now die peacefully from my wounds. I rolled Yoshino's map pointer back and forth on the desk. Crafted from a two foot length of bamboo, one end had been jammed into an emptied-out 50 caliber cartridge, and the other affixed with its bullet. I picked it up and poked it into the planked floor. Pushing it into a splintered crack, I pressed harder until the front legs of my chair lifted. I let it down then pressed again to make the chair teeter on its back legs.

'What's motivating Tinderberry? It'd sure be nice to know. I don't have shit to go on, except he certainly isn't acting out of character. I didn't think he had any *special* disregard for me, but that crack about me being *the fair-haired boy around here,* definitely changes that. He's got me square in his sights.'

"What's up Mondo?" I turned and looked up at Yoshino. He must have noticed my flushed face.

"Well, Sir… I just got my ass chewed by The Prince."

"What'd you do?"

"It was for talking to you guys about last night's fucking pool party."

"Yeah, so?"

"Well, he thinks I was being impertinent."

"But you're always impertinent."

"All right, so I'm a little brash at times – 'self-assertive' was the word on my last OER. But to hear him, I was wallowing in insolence. Shit, Major Tinderberry wasn't even in our conversation!"

"There's a secret solution; when he's around, you've *got* to just keep it to yourself."

"Easy for you to say. Somebody's been trying to get me to shut up since my first day in kindergarten. Hell, I thought he'd gone." I handed back the intel reports. "This stuff is real scientific isn't it? Like I can understand 'Unreliable,' but 'Rarely Reliable?' Like the source is feeding us good stuff ten percent of the time just to keep us interested. Why don't we just go out and shoot *that* fucker. I'll bet the MI dudes who prepare this bunk are so far in the rear that they wouldn't know a shit-coated punji stake from one of their barbecue steak forks."

"That's why we have you Carney." Major Grizwell ambled back in. "Recon's job is to confirm or negate whatever intel we get."

"Right Sir, but I thought my job was killing dinks, not just trying to figure out whether MI or G-2 has reliable sources – whether they've got their shit together or not." I took a wary glance at the door. If The Prince had heard that crack, he'd be blowing smoke out of his ears for a week.

"It isn't any secret," Grizwell commented, "that Recon's primary job is reconnaissance, which means *finding* dinks, where they're coming from, what they've been doing and where they're going. You know the deal."

"Yes Sir, but we're still pulling as many ambush patrols as any other platoon – and lately, in some pretty strange places."

"The stranger they are, the more likely they'll be in there. So while you're finding 'em, you might as well just do us a favor and kill them."

"Yes, Sir," I said.

"Our best intel's been coming from our I-caps and Med-caps," Grizwell explained. "It's all ultimately Vietnamese. Good intel is always hard to come by. Lots of things work to undermine its reliability. We act on a lot of it, because what else have we got? If it's good, we get dinks, if not, we don't. So we try again tomorrow. Simple enough?"

"My experience does bear that out, Sir. Some days we get them. The problem is, they're out there every day, lots of them. I just can't figure on them hiding in a place like Xa Khoi."

"There's an awful lot of area out there for holes – and they don't stay in any of them very long. An awful lot of room for holes."

"They say, *there's four thousand holes in Blackburn, Lancashire,*" Yoshino mumbled irrelevantly.

"*And, they had to count them all,*" I added, finishing the lyric as best I could.[2.]

"Hell," Grizwell scoffed, ignoring our inanity, "if you want *lots* of dinks, I can always drop your butt right over there." He stuck the 50 caliber pointer at an area just inside Cambodia. "You'll have all you can use."

"You know I wouldn't mind Sir," I boasted, "but my men always turn into a bunch of whiners every time they have to face a couple of reinforced NVA regiments all by themselves. Hey, at least we'd be getting them in groups bigger than four or five VC."

"You lock horns with something even close to platoon size – particularly NVA regulars, and you'll find yourself with more than you bargained for. You'll get a good body count, but you'll take serious casualties in the process. Keep that squarely in mind."

"No argument there Sir. But remember that place last month? We greased twelve dinks and nobody even got scratched. The gunships drilled some, but that's the way it's supposed to be – find 'em, fix 'em and blow the shit out of 'em."

"Let's keep Recon focused on the first two. You had a three to one advantage that time. You want all of that and more. One to one is what I'm referring to, and to be avoided at all cost."

"Right Sir. Then how about me and Vo Nguyen Giap – one on one – in the ring – and just the way he likes it, no rules." I smacked my right fist into the palm of my left.

"Ha," he laughed, "I hope to hell you could kick some old general's ass – one in the one-hundred-pound weight class." He got up and stood in front of the map. "Okay Carney, I'll tell you what. We've gotten word that an element of the VC Five-thirteenth are holed up in here." He drew a small red circle around a darkened green area on the map. "No idea how many. There's a Loach coming this afternoon. Check with Captain Hembree on the exact time. Go out and buzz over the place to see if you can spot anything. The one-five-fives conducted a fire mission last week, which didn't amount to much. There's a well camouflaged bunker complex, but it seems no one was home."

"Right Sir. You know my reservations about blasting away at bunkers with arty, even big stuff. Napalm and bombs can do the job too, but it's all got to be dead on target. Seems everything misses by just enough to be ineffective. Grunts are the only sure thing."

"Carney, you know as much as anyone, those places are the most mined and booby trapped areas there are. That means casualties. I'd rather do it from a distance."

'Do what from a distance, be ineffective? The French did that when they were here – holing up in fortifications all over the country. They reduced their casualty rates and it lost them the war.'

"If you see anything worthwhile," he went on, "I'll send Recon and Charlie Company in there tomorrow for a cordon and sweep of the whole place. I'll get one of their platoon leaders to go along with you."

"Hey Paul!" I called out. Keneally and Lieutenant Milgrim, Echo Company's four-deuce platoon leader had squeezed between a pair of three-quarter-ton trucks. "You guys eat yet?"

"Not yet," Keneally answered. "We were just heading over."

"Good, I've got to tell you about fucking Dingleberry, and this morning's latest."

"He wouldn't have lit on you just now would he?"

"Lit?! As a matter of fact, smoke's been pouring out of my backside all the way down the road." I patted the seat of my trousers. "He took a goddamn flame thrower to my ass."

"So what little military protocol did you manage to breech this time?"

"At this point, my very existence is a breech. Just to speak to him, is a case of *lèse majesté.* I'm afraid this one only fell into the general area of 'impertinence' – his word."

"I tell you Mondo, he's gunning for you. If you say anything more than yes sir and no sir to him, you're just plain nuts."

"He contrived the whole thing, Keneally! I wasn't even talking to him at all, just having a discussion with Major Grizwell about last night's visit to Uncle Neptune – we were only shooting the shit. Everything was cool – Hembree and Yoshino were there too. Dingleberry must've overheard some of my bitching and went after me when we were alone. He even tried to jack my ass up for what happened last night – of which he knows nothing. The Prince, shit. Royal Purple Prick is more like it. I tell you, it's a damned good thing he can't affect my rating."

"You still better watch your ass with him. Think about if something happened to Colonel Braccia, right when your report was due. So it lands on the acting commander's desk, needing a senior rater's comments. He'd make it his business to jump right on that little task and would come up with some pretty choice comments. There'd be damn-little you could do. It'd be fired off to DA before you could say Hairy O. Dingleberry." I looked up from the ground and nodded.

"Yeah, as quick as that, he'd fuck my career. Crap! I'd better have a talk with the old man. I've got less than a month until my promotion – automatic new job – and automatic new OER. You can bet your ass I'll be on top of this one."

"Oh hey," Keneally said, "I think I know what happened out there last night. I'm not sure but it might actually have a name. I remember reading an article on flooding in the upper Missouri River – like in the spring when the snow's melting and they get a heavy rain right on top of it. It's not exactly the same but the principle would be. Okay, think of this giant bulge of water, bulging right up to the very top of its banks and moving slowly down stream, slow as my DROS. It only happens if the land is real flat."

"Where's this bulge come from?"

"Upstream!"

"No, the water."

"Hold on. Pretend you're upriver a bunch of klicks. Suppose there's a heavy dump of monsoon rains where all the rivers have to sluice into one of the larger tributaries – like the one where you were. The bulge is from that. The land is flat, so it can't just cascade downstream like a flash flood. The bulge is moving downstream, but getting more bloated with water, closer and closer to bursting its banks. Finally, and at just the right time, it runs smack into an incoming tide. Where's all that water going to go?" Paul spread his hands outward. It spills over its banks and the land on either side.

"You think something like that was what happened?" We halted at a mud-filled ditch in front of the mess hall.

"Well, in an area that's just a couple of feet higher than normal high tide, it's the only thing it *can* do. That also accounts for why it wouldn't happen on a regular basis. And if it's especially lower where you were, it'd flood there before anywhere else." He stepped on to the pierced steel planking and crossed behind Milgrim.

"Hey, I've got an idea," I said, stepping on as soon as he got off. "If you could slip in your *Keneally Bulge Theory* at tonight's briefing, the *X*O'd be forced to hear it, but wouldn't be able to deride it in front of the colonel."

"You really want me to?" he asked, "Dinges'll sniff out that you put me up to it – and give him an even worse case of *Mondo-itis*."

"Fuck Dingleberry! It's more important that all the others hear it."

II
The Field

CHAPTER 1

The Hughes OH-6 Cayuse whirred over the Tactical Operations Center and spun its tail around in a 180° mid-air pivot. Coming straight on, the sun glinted brightly off its bulb-like front end. The convex glass created a mirrored opacity that made the machine look pilotless. As if by remote control, it pulled into a stationary hover six feet from the ground. Aligning itself dead-center over a square of pierced-steel planking, the little craft held as if contemplating its next move. Then with a barely discernible change in rotor pitch, it set down as lightly as a dropped feather. Lieutenant Burkhart and I got up from the stack of empty artillery boxes and walked toward our *Loach,* the humming bird of helicopters.

All around us Hueys wheeled about like flights of pigeons, while a lone Chinook hauled itself skyward, a huge drab pelican, gullet overloaded with provisions for its far-away brood.

I slid into the seat next to the pilot, a typical sort, relaxed, casual at his controls. Good. The more casual the attitude, the more complete the pilot's mastery of his machine. He greeted me by displaying the palm of his right hand. He hadn't taken off his helmet or shut down the engine, so we couldn't actually talk. Burkhart scrambled in behind him. We'd be able to observe from both sides of the chopper. I pulled out my map and drew the pilot's attention to the lower half of a grease penciled grid square. He confirmed it with his own map. His okay sign affirmed our destination. Pulling back on the collective, he gave me a thumbs-up. Done.

The engine's whir increased rapidly and the little chopper responded by lifting smartly. With a slight dip of the nose, we moved forward, rising only enough to skim man-high over the weeds, accelerating all the way to the perimeter. Coming up hard on the wire the pilot suddenly jacked the bird into a 45 degree climb. We vaulted into the sky over the near woodline. Looking beyond, through the bubble-like windshield, a panoramic landscape of the Delta unfolded. To the far horizon, a redundant patchwork of rice paddies stretched out overlaid with a venation of brown motionless rivers.

The torrid sun lost its power to the cool wind whipping through the doorless openings at our sides so turned its attention to the land below. Directly to our front, it transformed the water of the paddies into a mosaic of glinting squares. To my left a pellucid sky reflected in a great sea of blue, threaded by an ancient geometry of the dikes.

We cruised at around three thousand feet. Using the easiest way to navigate, the pilot followed a road coincident with our intended direction. Just past a key junction, we descended to 500 feet and guided on a rutted cart track. Our speed steadily slowed. The route we were following degraded to a wide dike, then a meandering foot path in the woodline. Our objective lay straight ahead. The pilot reined in the chopper and leveled it out at about two hundred feet.

I reoriented my map to the ragged path wandering in the jungle below. In grid square XS708645, a thin dotted line ran straight into my grease-penciled ring. Its reality on the ground was partly obscured by vegetation, but revealed enough of itself to be confirmed by azimuth and distance from the known point of the crossroads. I tapped the pilot on the arm and pointed, then finger-motioned for him to follow the thin gray line of the path.

We reached the target area in seconds. The pilot swung right to allow for a lateral view from my side. Thick and unbroken, the vegetation seemed too dense for anything to show, but that was just the thing. The sparser it was, the less likely VC would use it. They needed places that could escape observation from eyes in the sky.

Flying in a slow counterclockwise orbit, I viewed the area from every angle, but couldn't detect anything relevant. Finishing the circle, the pilot turned inward and began making a smaller tighter circle. We were directly over the thickest jungle, the target.

Burkhart, his map clenched between his legs, bent out and stared fixedly at the ground. I tipped my CAR-15 downward and tightened the nylon webbing attached to me. Leaning into the passing airstream I got a much better view. I thumbed the selector switch to full auto. If I did see anything, I'd squeeze them a burst.

Taking this as a cue to assist, the pilot dropped lower. A variegated greenscape washed below the muzzle of my weapon. Then to help a bit more, he reduced our speed even further. We buzzed along at about twenty miles per hour. At fifty feet off the ground, he began to zigzag back and forth to let us check out likely spots for enemy cover and concealment. He struck me as a guy who'd done this plenty.

The results of the artillery mission Major Grizwell had talked about were evident. The 155 millimeter rounds had made craters that looked as though a huge clamshell shovel had bitten into the earth and come away with mighty mouthfuls of jungle. Paladins threw out heavy ordinance. The concavities of naked soil, ringed by splintered vegetation were stark evidence. But even these exposed wounds failed to unearth anything that looked suspicious. No shattered bunkers, no encampment shorn of its concealment.

I shook my head at the pilot. I hadn't spotted anything and pointed at a stand of trees two hundred meters off to our left. The chopper tipped slightly. We headed in that direction. As we came up on it, he cut our speed and altitude by half. We whirred along, way too slow and low for my liking. The pilot either had a pair of brass balls or was totally oblivious to the fact that this was *injun country*. I hadn't seen anything, but that didn't mean we needed to land and diddly-bop around until we did. I hand-signaled him to bring us up and pick up the pace.

Brats of automatic gunfire erupted behind me. I whipped my head around to see Burkhart ripping off bursts with his M-16. Spent cartridges spun and tumbled around him. Simultaneously, slugs impacted the chopper. From my side, all I could see was trees, but Burkhart had already smacked in a new magazine and was emptying it fast. The pilot brought the bird around to give him a better line of fire, dropping us to the height of the tallest coconut trees. Flying at five miles per hour, we couldn't have presented a better broadside target. The firing had ceased. I hoped that Burkhart had greased the dink who'd put those bullets into our underbelly.

Hitting the pilot on the arm, I whipped my hand in a quick circling motion and jabbed a finger upward, a signal for us to get moving.

"Get this fucking thing out of here!" I yelled. He spun the bird around, but not in the direction I had in mind. He pulled up slightly and gained some speed, but began flying back over the ground where we'd just had contact. Burkhart leaned out a little more and gazed down the barrel of his rifle. I shouted straight into the pilot's ear. "We're not a goddamn gunship! Don't know what the hell we've got!" I pointed at the open sky to get him headed in that direction. He was already on it.

We gained speed and altitude, but only enough to expose us to a wider area. A storm of small arms fire broke from below. More bullets thudded into the chopper. The sound of the engine changed, first to a vibrating whine, then to a loud asthmatic wheeze.

"*She-e-e-it*!" I screamed. "Over there!" I pointed to the nearest open paddy. The thought of coming down in this woodline was not even conceivable. If we did, it'd take only a few dinks to have us for lunch. The engine continued to run, but was clearly decelerating. I glanced outside, then at the pilot. He worked the controls with apt intensity. The engine's sound changed again. He was auto-rotating the blades. 'Do we have enough altitude, speed, rpm's?'

We were out over the paddies, but coming down fast. My mind whizzed through the possibilities, and stuck on the worst of them. Crashing. The image flashed of being so injured, that all I'd be able to do was lie there and wait for the dinks to come out and administer their preferred, immediate first aid for wounded Americans, a bullet to the head.

The pilot pulled full pitch on the blades. My stomach hauled upward in my body. The chopper stalled in midair and drove straight into the paddy. The windshield split across the middle as the chopper rose up on its nose. The blades obliterated themselves in the water and mud. Lurching back down, the aircraft settled into silence. We were in a forward cant of about 30 degrees with a slight list to port.

I stared at the pilot. He was working at something with one hand and pulling his helmet off with the other.

"I got a call out before we hit, but didn't get a response – beacon's on." He jerked his M-2 carbine out from under his seat.

"Good." Just as the word left my mouth, a slug tore into the chopper and shots echoed from the woodline behind us. "Shit. Looks like they're not going to let us just sit here and relax while we wait. Burkhart! We've got to get out of here!" I looked over my shoulder and saw him half hanging out of his side. *"Burkhart!"*

I dove heedlessly out of the door and into the watery mud then scrambled into the back seat. Bullets cut the air. Some hit the chopper and still others struck the water near the tail. Grabbing hold of Burkhart, I laid him over on the seats. Blood was leaking through his shirt. I checked inside. A bullet had ripped through his shoulder. Having entered in his armpit, it had come out between his collar bone and neck. With such a jagged exit wound, the lack of bleeding scared me. I pulled his shirt back and turned him toward me.

"Aw fuck man!! I shouted in painful disgust. The round had exited his shoulder all right, but then reentered his head just below the jawline under his right ear. There was no second exit wound. It was lodged somewhere in the middle of his brain. His eyes were still open, but as vacant as any I'd ever seen. I checked for a pulse.

"Is it bad?" the pilot called from the front.

"Yeah. He's *K-fucking-I A*." Another hail of angry gunfire affirmed my words. A bullet punctured the windshield and others zinged off the roof. "If they move in on us, we're fucking *next! We cannot let them do that!"*

I bailed out the door and charged headlong across the paddy firing bursts of my own. Splashing through twenty meters of slop

I was oblivious to anything coming my way. I had only one thing on my mind, hold them to where they were. If they made it out to the opposite side of the same dike, they'd work their way around to get us in a short-range crossfire. 'The fuckers'll pick us off or worse, play with us until we're out of ammo. With me controlling the dike though, they'll be constrained to stay in the woodline where their range is too far to be effective. This'll only work for a while. Even a little chopper is a huge plum, a juicy enough one to get them taking big risks.'

The range worked against me too. My CAR-15 was inaccurate past a hundred meters. I didn't trust anything over fifty. Burkhart's M-16 was back in the Loach. 'Why didn't I grab it and his magazines? No, those few seconds would've cost me more than the extra weapon. I'd be double stupid to try and go back for it now. Whatever, I've *got* to hold them off from here, any way I can.'

I scrunched down into the mud to make more of my body sink below the water's surface. Slipping off my hat, I scooped up handfuls of slimy muck, and smeared it onto my face. I peeked through the grass on the top of the dike to scan the woodline. There were four or five of them, barely visible in the light undergrowth. I slid my muzzle through the grass and drew a bead. 'Those fuckers... How many more are there? If there's a bunch, they'll be confident enough to already be trying something. Gotta let 'em know I'm in a good position to put up a fight. Shit, I'll be doing that no matter what.'

I grasped my upper hand guard more tightly and squeezed off a burst of six rounds. Silence followed. Then they answered my fire with bursts of their own. 'Should I wait for them to come out? A little closer and I might at least wing one of them. But if there's more than four, I'll just get myself in worse trouble.'

The pilot couldn't be relied on for supporting fire from back in the chopper. To shoot, he'd have to expose himself in the open door. Bullets zinged close overhead. I slithered along behind the dike to improve my position. 'Further down, it's higher and the weeds are thicker. Okay, now better cover and concealment. I can look without getting my head blown off.'

"Hey!" An alarmed voice came from the chopper. "Where're you going?!" I looked back to his flimsy metal redoubt sitting crunched in the middle of the paddy, exposed on all sides. All I could see was the protruding muzzle of his carbine.

"Just getting me a better position," I called out, my voice sounding like I'd used a bullhorn. The dinks heard me too, but already knew I was somewhere along the dike. A one-eye sliver of the pilot's head came into view. "Stay low in there. Don't try to shoot. You'll draw fire," I whispered, loud. "They can't flank me over here – can't get within effective range. Not while daylight holds. There's a couple more hours of it, so Mister Pilot, we got us a good old Mexican standoff – just waitin' for the cavalry to arrive."

An hour passed. 'Our mayday wasn't heard. If it had, a pair of Charlie-model gunships would've already chopped up the wood-line with rockets and machine guns, then picked us up. Shit, by now my whole platoon could've been flown out here. But with no one hearing us, we don't have fucking squat.'

Time dragged. I baked in the late afternoon heat. Without any water, I went from thirsty to parched, to desperate. Sun-crazed for a drink, I scooted over and sucked monsoon rainwater from the surface of the paddy, closing my mind to the fact that I was slurping in gazillions of bacillary amoeba and nematode spores. 'First things first. Heat prostration isn't going to be the edge they have on me! I'll worry about the microbial menagerie inside me later.'

Mindful of not wasting ammo, our standoff forced me to trade shots with the dinks, to remind them they'd want to think again about coming straight out for us. They had no way of knowing whether a gunship or a platoon of troops would be dropping in at any minute.

'It's been a while since their last potshot. At least when they try to shoot me, I know where they are. What would I do if I were them? Like Tra always says, think like them. Okay, they've assumed we're on our own, stranded. They know they have time. Time in Cong hands is a weapon. If I were them, I wouldn't wait. When darkness sets in, they'll expect us to slip away. So if I was Charlie, I'd move out of that woodline and swing way over there. Then I could take up a position behind that dike on the '*Imperialists dog's*' left. That'll expose the capitalists' chopper and the entire paddy to my fire.'

Sobered, I wondered if I'd ever mused over certain death. 'When had it ever been certain? The dinks have to go a long way around, more than a klick to get at me. That'll take them a while. Damn, they do have the time, and always have a surplus of energy and motivation. The bastards! – when they have time, it means I don't.' A decision rammed into my consciousness like a chambering round from the top of a fresh magazine. 'I'll have to take some chances, fast.'

"Hey, Mister Pilot," I said in a loud whisper, "you hear me?"

"Yeah?" he answered, his voice muffled as though he'd crawled under one of the bird's seats.

"We've got big trouble."

"How's that? You think they didn't get our signal?"

"They didn't get shit," I answered. "They should've guessed by now something went wrong and been here looking for us, even if nobody got your distress call. But that ain't even what our problem is."

"While flying down here, I got a call to swing by Tan Tru on our way back and pick up some artillery lieutenant from your battalion. That's where they think we are. If they didn't get my mayday, they'll keep thinking it."

"Fucking beautiful. But that shit *still* ain't our right-now shit."

"If you're worried about it getting dark before we get help, I've got a strobe to mark us."

"Man, it'll be marking our dead asses by dark. Those dinks aren't going to let us sit here and wait for help or darkness."

"What do you think they're going to do? They stopped taking shots at us. Maybe they packed up and left."

"My ass," I rasped, scrunching my lower torso and legs one additional inch out of the water. "They're hooking around and will approach us from the direction the chopper's facing – that dike in front of it – before it gets dark. We've got to get the fuck out of here."

"But when a team comes out to get us," he argued, "they'll find the Loach, and we won't be here. We don't have a radio. They won't know where we are."

"True, but being alive *some* fucking where else, is better than being where our guys'll find us *dead*. We can't stay here! If we do, we bite the big one, no exceptions. If we E and E from here and I'm wrong, we could still bite it. More likely, we'll just have a hairy cross-country hump."

"I'm staying here," he countered.

"No, you're not!" I demanded. "You're going to gather up all of Burkhart's stuff – weapon, magazines and wallet if he's got one. Take one of his dog tags. Then haul-ass and join me. Move like I did, but even faster. They're watching."

"You're not leaving him here are you?!" he asked, in a tone of pure astonishment.

"Yes we are, unless you can convince me otherwise. How's he gonna help us in his current condition?"

"Hey, hold on a minute. The same could have happened to either one of us."

"I know," I snapped, "my corpse would be pissed to hell too. But we drag him with us and we'll wind up just like him."

"Hey, I'm the AC of this bird. I get to say what we're going to do or not do."

"You can stay AC, if you can get it to fly away with us in two minutes. If not, this is now a ground operation. I'm calling the shots. You don't like it? Fine, I'm out of here alone."

"We'll see about that," he said. "That's desertion under fire."

"You don't come with me, and you won't be alive to make that charge."

"Right, Asshole – and my chances are better running across an open paddy? Why should I expose myself to fire, running over to that dike? – to go God knows where."

"Because I said if you don't, I'll be leaving your ass with Burkhart. And with *him*, your chances are exactly zero."

Two minutes were up. I turned my attention to the woodline. I was moving no matter what. 'Will I be deserting? Just because *he's* too stupid to comprehend the real fix we're in? How can the clear wisdom of an escape and evasion be redefined as desertion? Because of *his* faulty thinking? What if I get a klick away on my own, and hear the sound of a just-in-the-nick-of-time rescue platoon? I'd be too far away to get back before they lifted out. That would be the *identical twin* of desertion under fire.

Tinderberry'd insist on that and throw in gross dereliction of duty just for laughs.'

Staring fixedly at the silent motionless jungle, I edgily squeezed the pistol grip of my weapon. 'If I stay here to avoid the possibility of charges, I'll wind up dying for it. I'm not dying for that. I don't care if this pilot's scared and doesn't want to leave his wrecked chopper. He's thinks the longer we wait, the more imminent our rescue. He's dreaming. We've got to get out of here!'

There was a sudden splash and thud behind me. Someone grunted. From a sideways glance, I could see the pilot moving away from the chopper. Hunkered low, two weapons clutched to his chest, he veered toward me as though in slow motion. Caught up in the thick muck, he stumbled forward onto both knees. He regained his balance by sinking one arm past the elbow. Back on his feet, he was hurdling again. His eyes were fixed on me. Gunshots erupted. He went face down into the mud.

"Shit!" I cried out. "You hit?!" Falling like that had to mean he'd bought it. However, his head came up and he growled a clipped-off "Okay."

"You better low crawl-it the rest of the way. I wouldn't trust that gook fucker to miss more than a few times. He's already done that."

Lying prone, I fired a series of single shots at the woodline until he made it to my side. Gasping hard and slathered with a gray-brown ooze, he finally pulled himself up level with me. The two muck-coated weapons looked like child-made, mud-pie guns. Everything he had was so glopped with it, I couldn't tell what else he had.

"Boy," the pilot said, heaving heavily, "you sure can get out of shape sitting in a chopper all day and a bar stool all night."

"Yeah," I said, satisfied to see he still had some humor for our situation. He rolled over on to his back and blew out a long slow breath. "One of those bullets only missed me by a golldurn half-n-inch."

"It always seems that way." I put out my hand to shake. "The name's Carney, but you can call me Mondo. Yours?"

"Captain Dills," he said. I was looking right at his name tag, but the front of his flight suit was so dirty I couldn't make out a single letter. His left collar was clean, with Ordinance Corps insignia.

"Sorry about all the Mr. Pilot shit," I said. "I thought you were a Warrant officer."

"That's okay. What's this crap about us leaving? Out here? To go where? I don't like the idea of leaving my chopper or that poor lieutenant in it. By all rights, I'm in charge, even though I ain't been in -country long, and you got more experience pounding the ground. I see you got that bad-ass Ranger Tab and CIB too. But *I'm* the senior guy here. Holding out in the chopper wouldn't be a smart idea, but this here's not so bad a spot. They can't get to us while we're behind this dike, and we can still cover my bird."

I took a deep breath. "Listen to me, Dills. You and I are sitting in Charlie's back yard, with him being hot to kill or capture us as soon as he can. There's no one around to help us. No fucking one! I've been sharing this space with Chuck for the past eight months straight, so I've learned a few things about how he operates. Know why I'm still alive? …Because every day's a brand new lesson in how to stay that way. I've been paying real close attention. Now, he's about to give us a little pop quiz on what we know. I'm gonna ace it. You?"

"What the hell does that mean?"

"It means that you can pull rank on me if you want. You can stay commanding that Loach, it and Burkhart. Trouble is, it's a death trap. So is this dike. Any time now, they'll be making it one. Look, I don't like leaving him behind, but can't see the smarts in sacrificing our lives for a dead guy. Staying here's the same as giving Charlie your gun so he can kill you with it. We go, and we gain mobility and a chance at making it back."

"Okay, but my accepting your suggestion doesn't mean I'm not in charge."

"In charge of what?" I clenched my teeth and looked him straight in the eyes. "It *isn't* a suggestion. Here's the deal. I'm in command of my own infantry unit – cut in half by the loss of Burkhart. I'm its sole surviving member. You were supposed to provide my unit with air transport back, but due to equipment failures, cannot fulfill that mission. Now I have to walk. Seeing as you do too, you can tag along and provide my unit with support. Chopper pilots don't get to pull rank and seize command of infantry units whenever they happen to get shot down."

"What in God's name are you talking about?" His voice was heavy with exasperation. "Here I am, surrounded for all I know, and who do I have with me? A gall-durned lunatic!"

"Let me put it another way," I growled. "If you're willing to trust me, and that means doing what *I* say, I promise I'll get you out of here alive."

"Wouldn't a guy who'd run, be the first guy who'd break a promise?"

"Damn it! Haven't you ever heard of escape and evasion? I'll break my promise only if I get killed. And since that ain't going to.... Look, you're either going to trust me or... the only staying I'm going to be doing is staying alive. You coming with me or not? Ten seconds, Dills." His head turned slowly. He looked out to the woodline. His eyes darted furtively to the chopper.

Okay," he said resignedly. "Go on and lay it out for me. What do you think they're going to do?"

"They'll come up from over there and box us. We'll be exposed on both sides of this dike. They'll just close in and kill us." Dills looked at the dikes to our left and right, then back at me.

"Well, yeah," he said, nervously, looking around again. "Okay then, let's get going."

"You catch on fast. First, let's clean up those weapons, magazines too. Do it over there in that clearer water. We'll have to move south. Look here." I slid my map toward him and pointed to our location. "They'll come for us around this way. One dink was left over there to block us from hauling ass when they come up over here. When you were running from the chopper there was only one guy firing at you. Notice that?"

"I didn't notice."

"It means the others are already moving to flank us. This river over here," I pointed with my finger at the wavy blue line. "It goes down into this big mother river, the Vam Co Dong. That's where I'm going. Finding a sampan could be iffy – map only indicates a few hooches. But we need to cross the little river no matter what, to head south. Can you swim?"

"Depends on how far," he said.

"You're in luck. It's not too wide. But if the tide's running hard, we'll be crossing with weapons so it'll be a bitch. In that case, we'll try to find some kind of flotation. We'll cross here then hump down along the big river – all the way across this grid square." I continued to trace my finger along my intended direction. "You flew over an RF compound on our way down. We can hold up there for the rest of the night. Any problems supporting this plan… Sir?"

"All right," he said with the hint of a smile, "you can call me Larry. And no, I have no idea what else we can do."

Sliding on our bellies along the paddy dike, we moved about a hundred meters lateral to the single dink in the woodline. At the first perpendicular dike intersection, we were faced with the inevitable.

"We're going to hurtle over, alligator style, both of us at the same time." I told Dills. "That dink doesn't know we've come down here. When we go over he will, but he'll still be keeping an eye on where we were. We've got to be slicker than eel shit or he'll have enough time to get off some rounds at us." Dills grabbed my arm.

"If I get hit, you going to leave me like you did Burkhart?" He looked back at the chopper, his voice gravely serious.

"Only if the hit makes you get like Burkhart. Dead. Anything short of that, and I'm with you all the way. Come on, let's do it."

On the count of three, we sprang upward, scrambling and clawing at the grass and dirt. Our lives depended on it. AK bursts cracked from the woodline. Bullets impacted the dike behind us. More of them lacerated the air. We tumbled headlong into the paddy on the other side. I spun catlike in reverse to face the direction of the firing, at the ready for whatever might happen next. Dills flopped over among the scattered rice plants, covered with mud front and back.

"Now they know where we're headed," he said.

"We were never going to get out of here without *that* happening. Our new problem's over there." I pointed to a stretch of broken down dike. "It's too low to give us enough cover. And shit! If we don't do something fast, even one guy can crawl over and nail us like fish in a barrel."

"That sounds just fucking wonderful. You *said* you were going to get me out of here. We haven't gotten a hundred meters."

"Okay, okay. I couldn't see how it was from back there." Getting on my knees, I pushed up and exposed myself to the chest for a second, then dropped back down. The woodline responded again with bursts. Lead cracked overhead. "Hey Larry, I've got an idea. Stay here and stick your head up like I did, every half a minute just to let them know that we're still here."

"You mean poke my head up so they can shoot it off?"

"No dammit, if you move back and forth a few meters, they won't hit a thing – won't know where it's coming up. I'm going into the woodline."

"You're going *where?!* Man oh man! What am I supposed to do when you get your ass wasted?"

"Resume the mission," I said. His face turned dumbstruck. "Then, go back to commanding your helicopter. Shit Larry, we *don't* have any fucking choice. We act first, so we don't give them the chance to act last. I'm crawling down this dike here, then in." I moved in the direction that would allow me a concealed entry to the woodline. I had to be right. Even the most doofus VC would try to take advantage of our newest predicament. But that was the mistake *he* would make.

I moved as far as I thought prudent, then settled in at the base of some coconut trees. If things didn't go exactly as planned, their trunks would absorb slugs better than anything else. After ten long minutes, I spotted the first wrinkle. There were two of them.

From good concealment, I could see them moving cautiously through low brush. They were closing the distance at an oblique angle. Although mostly obscured, another peek revealed their faces. Alert, with eyes darting back and forth, they edged their way forward, right to where I expected them to, where the woodline met the dike. 'They might not, but 'I'm betting my life they do. What if they see me prematurely?'

I pulled my head down below where I could observe them. Bringing the barrel of my CAR-15 up, I delicately caressed the trigger with my finger. The muscles in my anus spasmed. 'Will my muddied weapon jam? Yeah, I've done it again! I've left Larry with his carbine, his .38, and Burkhart's M-16 – violated a core credo of Ranger-dom; *Don't fergit nothin'.* But, I just did. Too late now. If it goes click, it'll be all over. No, I got us into this. It's all on me'

Praying with all my might that they hadn't halted their advance, I came up to a full kneeling position. I pushed one eye to the edge of the tree, to see black pants and khaki shirt only eight feet away. He took my burst of six rounds square in the chest before he even saw me. The other spun around, but froze like an animal in the road, lightning quick to a fatal stop. He turned his weapon toward me, but his eyes were seeking cover. My next burst caught him in the neck and face, the head snapping backwards as if slammed straight on by a baseball bat. The rest of his body followed its lead. He flipped over. I slunk down and scrambled to another group of trees, to flank my previous position.

Scanning the foliage to my front, I hunkered into the smallest possible target, my gun barrel trained on the opening through which they'd come. My heart pounded. My awareness of it made it accelerate. I breathed deeply and forced myself to replay the scene. '*I am not afraid.* They should be the scared ones, trying to come after me, when I'm desperate.'

Satisfied that there were only two of them, and more than eager to get going, I skulked out of my concealment and dogtrotted back to the edge of the woodline. I waved Larry on. He quickly joined up with me.

"Man! Am I glad to see you," he breathed. His face conveyed an expression of pure relief. "I heard the firing, then nothing for all that time after. I really thought they got you. I was thinking of what I was going to do next. Then you finally came out. What happened?"

"Nothing," I said. "When you don't hear a single AK round going off, it can't ever be bad. There were only two of them – at least just then anyway." Still in a jittery adrenalized state, I scanned the foliage ahead in a nervous search for our next move, a circuitous route of escape.

"But where are they now?!"

"I kacked their asses. Gee-zuhs Larry what'd you think I did, go in there and yell boo?" I ignored his prickly look of annoyance. "There's still the ones who were moving around to get us in the paddy. That's all changed. They're dee-dee-mau-ing-it back to here, where they heard my weapon. They'll be careful because they don't know where we are now. We gotta get a move on. I want us inside that far woodline before it's totally dark. You either use darkness in this war or you leave it to them to use it against you. Let's fucking haul-ass."

The main group would plan on trapping us in the corner where the two rivers met. 'Given what they know, it'll be their best guess. If I was them, I'd split into two elements. Flanking us, they could seal off any slip we might try, left or right. If there's only a few of them, they might just follow us directly. Fine. They might think they own the night, but I can be just as deadly.'

By EENT, Larry and I were deep into my forested objective. I took great pains to swing wide of several hooches nestled in there. Any old rice farmer lying awake on his bed wouldn't need bats' ears to discern our heavy footfalls. 'The VC will be asking them about us, but I ain't giving them a direct line.'

We gained the stealth needed by moving slowly, but made good progress by sticking to the most well- worn trails to eliminate our chances of tripping a booby trap.

Just before we got to the river, Larry grabbed me by the arm, again.

"Listen," he whispered, "back there." I'd been totally attending to my immediate surroundings, but I could hear it now. Far behind us, in the direction from where we'd started, the unmistakable sound of a chopper drifted through the night and across the flat landscape. "They're looking for us."

"Yeah, that's them all right," I said. "Too late."

"Too late?!We should go back!"

"Only if you can guarantee that those dinks right behind us will help guide us to the quickest route. And that the chopper you hear will be still waiting there for us when we finally get back."

"What makes you so sure the VC are right behind us?"

"Because they'd be stupid if they weren't." I whispered through clenched teeth. "They aren't stupid. Come on, the river's right up ahead."

The water of the Rach Nha Ram lay black and smooth, yet with a foreboding current. We'd be unable to swim the forty meters across with fatigues, boots, weapons and ammo.

"To get across, we've got to find some kind of floatation." I said. "If there're any hooches here, we could use a couple logs from their bunkers ... if I had a squad of men to rip them out of cement-hard mud and the time to do it. We ain't got neither."

"So what the hell are we going to do?" he pleaded.

"Hooches along rivers means sampans. We've got to fuckin' find one. Come on."

Moving on a wide path along the river bank we found one hooch. It had no sampan. Like nocturnal animals, we passed by and walked on for another hundred meters without finding any habitation. Then, after only a short distance, we came to the river's confluence with the much larger Song Vam Co Dong. Flowing generally southwest, its twisted course bent in every direction. A hundred meters across, in the dark it looked as formidable as a becalmed ocean. Crossing it had never been part of my plan, but our having gotten where we were, created a new problem. The projection of land we were standing on put water on three sides of us. We were smack in the corner of the ultimate box, the very spot the dinks would want us in if I'd put *them* in charge.

Our need for a sampan was now total, forcing us to keep scouting further upstream along the bank of the larger river, right back in the Cong's direction. Even if successful, it would put me upstream to their left, when I wanted to get downstream to their right. But the smaller river had already cut off that option. The fix we were in, caused a new surge of adrenaline. Fear was like that. I felt like a cornered animal sensing its predicament and what it could mean. I grabbed Dills' sleeve and whispered in his ear.

"Here's the deal. We can't go back in the direction we came from. We'll lose too much time. They'll definitely be tracking us from that direction. We'll walk right into them. Along this bank… maybe. We're boxed in, but not completely. Somewhere along here, there's got to be a hooch with a sampan!"

"What do we do if there isn't?"

"Not sure. The further we go, the more dangerous it gets. We might be getting closed in from both directions. They know the rivers come together here. It's what I would have done if I was them. They know we've got to cross one of them, somewhere but they might not know where any sampans are either." I took off my bush hat and wiped the sweat from my eyes. "Larry, this could get pretty fucking bad."

"Damn it Carney," he growled. "You promised to get me out of here. I trusted you. I know you took care of those two VC back there, but you got us into that mess in the first place. You say you're getting us out of some kind of box then you tell me that you've walked us straight into one. And my God! Now you're about to get us captured."

"They won't be taking me alive, I can tell you that right now."

"Holy shit," he groaned in total exasperation. "That's *my* choice? I've got a wife and kid back home. I gotta be stark raving mad going with you. If I hadn't, I'd have been picked up by now."

"Yeah, in a fucking body bag – we would've both been dead before those choppers got there. Listen to me! Getting captured is my *last* choice. Getting out of here is my first. Getting greased is somewhere in-between, but I'll swim that river – the big one – buck-naked with two bullets in me – without a weapon, before that happens. You just be ready for anything – like when I give the word, you better be already doing it." I replaced my hat and moved away from him. I was done talking.

We pressed on, along a wide riverside path. I stepped with the expectation that each new shadowy clump of distorted vegetation contained a dink welcoming party. My muscles jittered and my eyes twitched as I forced them to see into the impenetrable. 'I'll try and duck the dinks any way I can. Failing that, we'll fight it out.'

After what seemed like an eternity, but less than a hundred meters in distance, we came up on a couple of hooches. The light brown of their thatch loomed ahead in the dark like giant piles of straw. Close to the river, the trail was all that separated them from its bank. I slowed our movement to the quietest possible pace, reigniting my fear that I was giving the Cong a chance to catch us from behind. 'We'll have to pass within just a few feet – while they're closing the distance at a jog.'

At the end of the third hooch, I spotted moorings. Closer in, I perceived something else, a mere line of darkness against the hint of the water's sheen. Long enough and about the right width, it had to be a sampan. Hardly breathing, I moved down to the edge of the water to confirm my hope. My life depended on it being one. My heart beat in a thumping frenzy.

Down on all fours, I groped around in the stifling darkness, an inch at a time. Too dehydrated to sweat, my throat was so painfully dry that I was losing my ability to even whisper. Larry and I had split his remaining quarter of a canteen a long time back. An obsession with thirst kept laying claim to my concentration.

My hands explored a makeshift dock of sticks and poles, and brushed across what had to be a small shallow sampan. *'Yes!'* Larry crept up beside me, as if to reach for one of its tethers. The flimsy mooring teetered. He toppled into the water. It was only a small splash, no more than his sliding into waste deep water, no more than a fat rat leaping in from the bank. But I heard the unmistakable sound of a voice emanate from inside the nearest hooch. It was only a single word. In another moment, a faint light could be seen.

We gave up stealth and frantically struggled to find and undo the sampan's fastenings. I succeeded with my end just as someone came out holding an oil lamp. The dim flame approached, flickering, a yellowish spot hanging in the air. As it neared, I squinted at the wizened chin-whiskered face of an old man. He halted just in front of us, his eyes studying us through the quivering shadows. Then on realizing that it was two Americans, his surprise almost sent him over backwards.

"Chua Ong," I said softly, exhausting my Vietnamese on the subject at hand. "We're going to borrow your sampan. Take over there. You come get later – *hiểu?*" It seemed plain enough. Larry made use of the bare light to find and untie his end.

"Không." said the old man, as a prelude to a long string of incomprehensible yammerings.

"Well, I didn't think you'd dig what we were up to but I don't care." I turned and stooped at the edge of the water. "Larry, I'll hold it while you get in. Stay still in the middle. With big guys like us, you can't even fart or they'll tip over and swamp."

"Không! Không!" the old man demanded, in way too loud a voice.

"*Vâng, vâng,*" I contradicted, but he was already barking orders to two young boys who'd just joined us. They waded into the water and held on to the boat. A woman suddenly materialized and came down to join them. A couple of others also appeared and moved up behind the old man. Even more inhabitants of these hooches were present, hanging back just beyond where I could positively make them out. Most days in the field, I'd normally be carrying enough piastres to buy a boat twice over, but I'd left my wallet behind. Not a single experience with these people had prepared me for an obstreperous old man. The extreme opposite had been the unbroken rule. Even the staunchest

VC sympathizer tended to be pretty docile when looking into the muzzles of an entire platoon's weaponry. But these folks intuited that we were in some kind of trick and had lost our powers. That and their knowing that the VC were around. From this dude's tone, I guessed he was all-too ready to have *them* sort out my needs.

"Look you old coot, just go across in the morning with another one and bring it back." I stepped into the water and tried to brace the stern so that I could get in. The old man upped the ante and protested even louder. Two more women came down and grabbed on to the sampan. "I told you, it'll take you all of five fucking minutes to get it back! Let go!" I got in and tried to steady myself. One woman started keening like I was stealing one of her babies.

Some of the people who'd been hanging back, pressed closer. Although silent gawkers, they seemed to spur the fellow on. He persisted with his objections. One woman was trying to capsize us a surefire way to slow us down.

'We've got to make a move, fast. Now, every Cong in this grid square knows exactly where we are. They're double-timing it toward us. But why are these people so oblivious to getting caught in a crossfire. Do they know something I don't?'

"Okay, you stupid old fool," I growled, grabbing his shirt and shoving the flash suppresser into his neck. *"Doi Trung* úy*."* Stating my rank, I jerked my thumb at my chest. "We are borrowing the sampan. Borrowing tee tee, *hieu?!*" I got in and started to push off, but the moronic geezer took hold of the mounting for the tiller oar.

"That's it!" I hissed. I stuck the muzzle of my Car-15 down between them and the sampan. On full auto, I pulled the trigger. Bullets and tracers exploded in an eruption of water and screams. The sampan separated from them as if propelled by my weapon's recoil.

"Guess that scared the Nuoc mam out of them," I said. Lying down my weapon, I exchanged it for the oar and began pushing it back and forth.

"Gee-zuhs man. I thought for a second that you'd wasted them all. I couldn't see a thing – like why didn't you just shoot up in the air?"

"Because that only works on folks who're afraid of the *sound* of gunfire. These fuckers got beyond that years ago. To really scare 'em, you've got to do something a little more melodramatic."

"Hey, you've got us going across the big river. I thought we were supposed to go down to the smaller one and cross there?"

"Don't shift your weight like that. We'll turn over. Then we'll be really fucked." I stopped paddling and spread my knees to steady the sampan. "We can't do it that way now."

"What the hell does that mean? This'll just take us further into the boonies."

"No it won't. We get to within a few meters of the other side and we'll turn right, to the south – head downstream. We'll be going with the current so it'll be easy. After half a klick, we'll come back across, pick a spot, and get off. That'll put us in the same area we would've been in if we'd crossed the little river – just further south. Doing it like this, the dinks won't know what our destination is. They'll assume we've just come across to *this side.* Here, reach behind you, *without shifting your weight,* and take this flat piece of wood. Paddle with it. Don't splash."

When I could finally make some visual sense of the dark foreboding mass to our front, the far side, we turned the sampan ninety degrees to the right. From there, we moved along in close parallel to the bank. Ignoring its unknown dangers, I concentrated on maintaining our course. Larry's bulk leaned in front of me, dipping and pulling, his movements Hiawatha-smooth. '*Sweet home*!'

Automatic gunfire erupted from the far bank. From where the hooches had been, green tracers cut straight across to the other side. An alternating staccato of AKs, they stitched the darkness with a vengeance and bore straight into the unseen jungle behind us. Some extinguished themselves in the river, others zinged off into the distant night. We hunched over in position, the tiller motionless in my hands, Larry's makeshift paddle flat across his thighs. We inched along in the weak current, invisible, motionless and silent. 'We made it just far enough down river to slip them. Man oh man, that shit was close.'

"I told you they'd think that was where we'd go," I whispered at last.

"Yeah," he answered, sounding of fear and wonderment. "There was a whole bunch of them."

Passing the river junction, we continued on for a few hundred meters, until it began to bend sharply to the south east. We needed to head southwest. I gave Larry the word. We maneuvered the sampan into the middle of the river and crossed back to the other side. He got out first, straight over the bow so we wouldn't capsize, then held it for me while I crawled forward. Once out, I sat on the bank and gave the empty sampan a double-legged shove. It cruised back into the open water.

"Hey," he whispered. "It's going to float downstream. They'll lose their boat."

"It won't go far before getting hung up somewhere. They'll find it – their short-term inconvenience against our long-term staying alive."

Facing both open paddies and woodlines, we set out, dead-reckoning toward where I hoped to wind up. I wanted to hit a road two kilometers away. With my map and compass, it'd be impossible to miss although following a course that was anything but straight, would have us intersecting the road at an unknown point.

"It's black as hell out here," Larry whispered in my ear. "We might accidentally turn back and walk right into them."

"No, we won't," I said. "Coming here with the sampan put the smaller river between us and them. They bought my ruse that we went across the larger river. That should keep them from crossing the smaller one and coming after us. As for the dark, just leave that to me."

'Won't the VC make some new deductions? They have a knack for crossing rivers. That smaller one wouldn't give them too much trouble. Will they? They will if they somehow sniff out our trail. Maybe and maybe. Fuck 'em, I've got to concentrate on what's in front of us, booby traps.'

The area had no wide-open main trails. It did have half-overgrown secondaries though, just the kind the VC loved to rig explosives on. Snares at night pitted our random steps against the dinks random improvisations. But, it only took the step of one boot to get you onto their trap door to oblivion.

I charted a course that kept us off trails. For half the night, we tread warily across the land. Unable to trust out-of-the-way dikes, we had to walk in the paddies, as silently as we could. We lifted and set our boots in the water and mud so painstakingly slow, that leaping peep frogs made greater splashes. We traversed a couple of waist deep canals, and one neck-deep river. Progress was agonizing. We had no choice. Even non-lethal wounds from a stray booby trap, could mean doom. No radio, no medic, no dust-off.

After five hours of dragging ourselves forward, thirst and fatigue replaced terrain and booby traps as more imminent problems. We were trudging through Charlie's back yard. I plodded ahead with an insentient determination. Not fully comprehending the ever-present dangers, Larry began falling behind. When he realized the growing distance, he found some reserves and caught back up. 'He's proving himself a worthy partner. I coerced him into subordinating himself, but he's got to prefer my leadership to his total lack of knowledge about doing an E&E through Dinkland.'

Sighting several hooches to our front, I held up. Exhaustion grabbed me by the throat. I stood there trying to decide whether to go right or left. 'We've got to avoid them. But whichever way I choose, there might be more. Okay, left looks better.'

We found ourselves mired in a nasty nipa swamp. In complete blackness, and thigh deep in muck, we could hardly move. It took whatever effort we had left to gain only the next meter. Nearly insane for a drink of water, I felt like I was being devoured inside a nightmare. Dills' misgivings reemerged with a vengeance.

"What in the fuckin-damn hell are you dragging me through here for?!" He'd jammed his knee into a sharp-edged root and gotten Burkhart's M-16 caught behind him. He yowled in exhausted frustration. "Admit it – you're lost and don't know what the fuck you're doing!" We were shielded by nipa on all sides, but he was still way too loud. In this watery air, you could hear the clack of a bolt at a hundred meters.

"Shut the fuck up," I growled, mean. "You want help, just ask for it. Otherwise I don't want to hear anything. You want to do your own thing? I told you before, just have at it. You want to tag along with me? Then you don't say shit."

"Look you goddamn, cocky, wise-ass bastard, you're not going to treat me like I'm some kind of fool. You might drag around your dumbass grunts like this, but let me remind you, I'm not one of them."

"I'm not asking you to be one. This is still a volunteer deal. I told you back at the chopper, and I just told you again; I'm getting out of here. You can either come along and shut the fuck up, or the next time your wife and kid see you, it'll be in a flag draped coffin." We stood there for a while, breathing heavily, neither of us saying anything. Finally, literally overwhelmed by mosquitoes, I decided to speak first.

"Larry, even the dumbest-ass grunt in the Ninth Division knows that there's ten times more mosquitoes in nipa than anywhere else; forget the muck and roots. Why'd I come in here? A fucking little accident is all – my trying to avoid dink mothafuckas and booby traps, while taking the shortest distance as possible. The first will kill us, this shit won't. I have a compass with a luminous dial, and I committed my map to memory before it got dark. It's all *I* need." I patted him on the shoulder. "So come on, let's go."

We stumbled to the edge of the road. Then, I figured out the direction of the RFPF compound. We paralleled the road until we reached what I estimated to be a safe distance from it.

"This is it Larry. Now we crawl into the bushes here and sleep until dawn – just a little more than an hour. Daylight will wake me. It isn't as bad as the nipa, but the deeper you go into that undergrowth, the worse the mosquitoes'll be. Smear more dirt on your face and neck like I showed you before – the thicker the better."

"You mean we aren't going to go in and call for help? They must have at least one radio. We can get onto one of our frequencies and call in."

"Sure, and we will, after it gets light. We approach that place now, and they might blow our asses away before we could say 'Hey, we're little lost Americans.' You don't snore do you? If I have to be close enough to kick you, we'll be too close to each other. We don't want to make a single target."

"A target for who?"

"Who knows? Anybody. The rule is you just never let yourself become a target, least not a double-one." To make it clearer, I thought of reminding him of how he'd doodle-bugged his dumbfuck chopper right over a squad of dinks, but held my tongue.

"Well, I don't think I'm going to do much sleeping out here," he said.

"Good, you've got first watch. Wake me if you feel yourself nodding off."

CHAPTER 2

"HEY, HEY, WHAT'D' YA SAY! Keneally called out as I trudged up the company road. "Until two hours ago, everyone was taking bets on whether you'd Chu Hoi-ed it to the other side."

"Well, despite my desire to run with a winner, when I found out that the VC didn't have any cold beer, I said fuck it and left. It's just too hard to be a communist." I stepped up onto a platform of planks, our orderly room's makeshift front porch. Several rear area dudes stared hard at me as I sat myself on a footlocker to rest. "Well, I'm not fucking dead, and I didn't fucking go over to the other side. Here I fucking am, same ol' - same ol' tired and pissed off. Specialist Delf! You haven't got my beer yet?!" My favorite target for jibes, our nebbish company clerk, retreated to fetch my order. Keneally sat down next to me.

"Somebody go and find me a shaving mirror," Keneally requested. "I want Lieutenant Carney to see what we're staring at. Man, you could stick your head up a water buffalo's ass and it would improve things. You *are* looking more pissed off than usual though."

"I am, yeah – tell you about it later. I know my face is scratched to hell – jamming it through thick-ass nipa for half the night'll do it every time." Sergeant Starcup came up from the platoon area, with Younce, Tra and Tho following. "You know, I sure could've used you guys last night."

"Yes, Sir. That shit must have been really fucked up. We heard you kacked a couple of dinks."

"Yeah. But they don't count for much, when you figure in what happened to Burkhart." I tapped Tra on his breast pocket. He instantly unbuttoned it and dumped out one of his Pall Malls. "The little bastards were trying to kill me – can you believe that shit?" Delf returned with a pair of cold cans. "Delf, in spite of being enlisted, *you* are a real gentleman. Someday, when your children ask you what you did in the war, you can tell them, with pride, that you not only rustled up the Recon Platoon Leader's beer, but you did it when it really fucking counted. Hey, Jimmy, would you have somebody check on the shower tank and make sure it's at least half full. In about ten minutes, I'm going to attempt the impossible."

Paul and I got up and walked down to my hooch. I dropped my weapon and magazines, and began fumbling through a half-empty box of C-rations. A chanced glance at my shaving mirror showed a blear-eyed face bruised with fatigue. Scores of red scratches etched my cheeks and forehead.

"Looks like a squad of Lilliputians with bullwhips took out their frustrations on my tanned good looks last night. Funny, I don't remember a thing." Finding a can of Pork Slices, I grabbed a P-38 and sat down.

"Didn't you get something in the mess hall when you came in?" Keneally asked.

"Yeah, but I straight off drank so much water that there wasn't room for food. What I got in headquarters' mess barely made up for missing chow last night. It's already after 1300, so this here's gotta-be today's breakfast." Dipping my thumb and forefinger into the can, I pulled out one of the thick round slices. I lopped the meat straight into my mouth, congealed grease and all.

"You don't want to heat that stuff up?" Keneally asked.

"My mind says I do, but my taste buds and stomach, disconnected as they are from my brain, don't give a rat's ass as long as I dump something into it."

"You might as well be eating a rat's ass."

"*Those* Keneally, you really need to heat." I took a long gulp of beer and sat down.

"Anyway, let me tell you about what's up." Keneally leaned against my table and took off his hat. "The old man's on the promotion list for O-6, right? So, he's gone up to USARV for two days. One of his classmates is deputy G-1. Tucked into some routine business, he's trying to see what he can finagle for his next assignment. That means Prince von Dingleberry is in charge of Dogpatch."

"Oh, let me tell *you 'bout it!"* I said. "Like here I come, just fresh from being shot down, and E-n-E-ing all night – bringing back, without a scratch, this Loach pilot, who's about as familiar with the field as my girlfriend back home – and only one step ahead of the Cong, who were on our scent like a pack of crazed hounds. And after all that, Dingleberry wants to bust my fucking balls, because I didn't do a two-man replay of Dien Bien Phu out there in that paddy – like stay with Burkhart and the chopper."

"That's what he expected you to do?"

"When I was up at the TOC he did. As always, it depends on what advantage he can wring out of blowing smoke up someone's ass. Talk about grandstanding. You should have heard him going on about how a *very* valuable aircraft had been lost – like I personally lost it – and how I'd left poor Burkhart – not Burkhart's body, but goddamn Burkhart! I suppose you heard the VC burned the chopper – we never knew that, being so far into the bush by then. Obviously the dinks took his body before they set light to it. Like what are those stupid bastards going to do with a GI corpse?"

"I heard we're listing him as MIA," Keneally said.

"Over *my* fucking dead body! Missing in Action means he *could* be alive. Get this, Dingleberry claimed that since I don't have the expertise to make a professional determination of death, it's possible he could still be alive, and, in enemy hands. Yeah, right. I got hot and told him that I had more than enough expertise to figure out Burkhart's heart was beating about as good as one of these pork slices. Hell, the first bluebottle fly had arrived before we'd even begun our E 'n' E."

"Was the Prince making a charge of desertion or some kind of dereliction?" Keneally asked.

"Both, but only by oblique inference. If he really had, I'd go straight to the old man. He knows his shit'd have him looking foolish. You know he just likes to score points running his mouth – about how we should've saved things."

"Like what things? The chopper? Burkhart?"

"Fuck if I know. If Major Grizwell had been there, Dinges wouldn't have been spewing any of that crap."

"Yeah," Keneally offered. "He's up in the C&C."

"The trouble is, I'm still smarting from Dingleberry's jumping in my shit over that jug fuck in the water." I unbuttoned my grime-caked fatigue shirt, pulled it off, and let it drop. "Here's the real kicker. This Loach pilot is a captain, right – and happy to be alive. So, from the minute we came in, he's telling everyone that I need to be put in for a Silver Star. Then fucking Dingleberry tells him that since he's in charge of reviewing all of the battalion's awards, Dills should write it up and send it to him personally. My mind was screaming; 'No, no, send it to the commander!' I couldn't say it out loud though. You know what that means?"

"You get a Bronze."

"No, I get jack shit. That's what his show was all about – to justify sliding Dills' recommendation right into File Thirteen."

"Nothing we didn't already know – he's a bastard..."

"Yeah that and a sententious prick. Shit, that ain't half of what he is." I began taking off my boots on the stoop outside.

"Just get in touch with that pilot" Keneally offered. "Have him send the recommendation up through his own chain of command – to division. It'd be worth a try."

"I dig what you're saying," I said, "but he's based up at Cu Chi. It'd take a month of trying before I could get him on a land line. The only way to do it would be go up there in person. I'd have to go through Long Binh, coming *and* going… take me at least two days. I couldn't get away with that, to say nothing about how self-serving it would look.... and *be*."

"Sometimes, self-serving's only a hair's width from what's called *acting in one's own best interest.* If you want, I can mention it to the colonel when he gets back."

"Man, I don't know Paul," I said in a heavy breath of frustration. "He'd suspect I put you up to it – and think a medal is all I care about. Do I want that in the wake of what happened to Burkhart? Like the poor fucker gets killed and all I want out of it is some glory?"

"Medals are par for the course in the midst of men getting killed. The award would be for your actions *after* he was already dead."

"Fair enough," I said, "but that's why Dingleberry was testing out his 'concerns' about what I *should've* done, even though me and Dills would've gotten killed. What the hell's he know about life and death decisions? Fuck it, my time will come."

"That's you all right," he laughed, "all humility and patience. But I was just thinking that you could write to that pilot. Then, I can definitely see Dings wanting to shoot himself before signing off on your Silver Star. It'd have to come up missing. Tell me, why didn't you stay with the chopper?"

"The whole thing is a blur. First these fuckin' bullets started hitting the chopper. Then we come down in this paddy. More bullets. Then I find that Burkhart has adiosed and left his bod behind. That's when it hits me like, '*Whoa! We're in some shit here. I gotta tend to business.*' You want to know what would've happened if I'd stayed with the chopper? It's what the pilot wanted. But he didn't understand what we were facing out there – the ultimate consequences of staying. Sure as shitting, the darker it got, the closer in they'd come – like tightening a fucking garrote, with our arms tied behind our backs... Lieutenant Mondo *and his Last Stand at Fort Doom*."

"That sounds like a Distinguished Service Cross," Keneally offered.

"Yeah, with a little box for the medal and a nice big box for me. And with no witness to write up that action, you know it'd be a nut-busting strain for Dingle-fuck to just sign off on a posthumous Purple Heart for my dead ass. Hey, I've got to hit the shower. Put the word out that I don't want to be bothered for the next two hours. After I get some of this crud off me, I'm hitting the rack – beat ain't the word for it – you're looking at what happens when an iron-hard jungle fighter gets reduced to a whipped dog."

After cleaning up, I hit my bunk expecting instant sleep, but tired as I was, a battle began fomenting inside me. Every time I started to doze some nerve ganglion fired and jolted me awake. Bands of phantom dinks roamed about, skirmishing among my innards. Their random volleys kept jerking my eyes open. Every time they did, they fell on my mud-encrusted CAR-15. It taunted me. What self- respecting grunt would let that dirt-caked abomination sit there looking back at him? I got up and set to work.

Cleaning my weapon, an exercise in meditation, gave me space to think. In spite of my impulsivity, I did have a reflective side. At least when I cleaned weapons I did. Maybe some introspection could give me a sliver of the tact I was said to need, particularly with my prime bête noire. 'Yeah right. Tinderberry'll *always* be a priggish chickenshit. What do I do with that?'

I sorted out my cleaning tools, popped the lid of an ammo can filled with a couple quarts of solvent then began breaking down my weapon. 'How does a guy become as chickenshit as Dingleberry? At what point in his life does he make a conscious decision to become a load of wet fowl droppings? Likely a deep-seated personality flaw, the kind that's right at home anywhere there's lots of rules. In grammar school, Dings was probably a little twerp who got pushed around for laughs. Now he's a big twerp and it's payback time. West Point would've showed him how to turn pent-up anger into condescending rectitude. The Big Green Weenie's been there for him ever since – regulations, standard operating procedures, you name it. Sublime baby! It's the Samson-haired source of his strength – 'Exceptional organizational ability' as his raters would put it. A rain of avian scat's more like it.'

'But Dingleberry ain't hardly the Army's one-and-only, martinet prick. There's more of them than you can count. Chickenshit's been part of Army life for so long it's wearing a campaign hat and Sam Browne belt. Hell, the REMFs *are* the

Army – proliferating staff and support jobs up the whazoo. At the beginning, Vietnam was a refuge from chickenshit. Then hordes of Dingleberry -types discovered The Nam's career opportunities. They've been pouring in ever since. The bush's the *only* place you can get away from them now. They sure as hell won't follow you out there. I'll take Charlie over Dingleberry any day. I can kill Charlie. But Dingleberry? All I can do is submit.'

'Keneally's right; 'the bigger the prick, the bigger the coward. They know what they are and chickenshit's a perfect cover. Fighting? What's that? Nope, there'll never be a bullet with his name on it, not that fucking poseur. Any time a real grunt crosses his path, watch out for another cloacal blast.'

Having disassembled my CAR-15 and submerged its parts in the solvent, I pulled them out one by one and wiped each with a rag. Attending to the bolt, I painstakingly inspected the firing pin and extractor. The barrel ramrodded and chamber swabbed, I was content. The trigger assembly was only slightly dirty. Despite the way it looked on the outside, it had only fired three magazines. While wiping the gas cylinder, a thump on the PSP caught my attention. Someone was coming.

"*I do not want to be bothered!*" Keneally mimicked my words. "I thought you were going to sleep? I heard you clunking around from my side and knew you weren't. Here's that Army Times that Top said you wanted." He laid the folded newspaper on my desk.

"I did *try* to get some shut-eye, but that shit from last night kept running through my head. It got a little hairy there for a while. If we'd been just one minute later getting into that sampan and down the river, I'd be *with* Burkhart now. Chuck would have our bods, and..." I pointed to the newspaper, "Our names'd be showing up on the inside back page, the week's recipients of the *Unalive Award*."

I read the list yesterday," he said. "Two guys from my OCS class were on it. By the way, a long-ass promotion list for infantry majors are in this edition."

"I'll be looking at both, column by column. Just before you came in, I was thinking how those lists are part of two different armies."

"How's that?" he asked.

"Whenever your name gets on a promotion list, the chances of it moving to a killed in action list, drops, sharply. I'm talking Infantry. The Army's got twenty branches, but this is the one where almost all the dying goes on."

"Yeah, it is," he agreed, "but it's not news that infantry lieutenants get killed second only to PFCs."

"What happened to Burkhart and my latest run-in with Dingleberry only sharpened the comparison. Some of us are fighting a war that can stop the rest of your life from happening – like Burkhart. The others, like Dingleberry, are just competing among themselves for promotions and cool assignments."

"Mondo, mulling over this does what for your overall morale?"

"It bums it out very nicely, thank you. The more I think about it, the bigger the bummer. For most dudes over here it's just a huge training exercise. They've got twelve months of stifling heat while being deprived of a few comforts of home. They're only going to get killed if it's by accident. If you're a career dude though – whatever your branch – a tour in The Nam falls somewhere between valuable and indispensable."

"What about you?" he asked. "You want a career as much as anybody. More."

"My attitudes are a whole lot different from REMF's. I'm infantry. I'm *out there* at night." This here's my… office equipment, not some fucking ball-point pen." I waved the bolt of my CAR-15.

"I get the heat, I get the discomforts and I get a chance to 'ride the pale horse.'"

"You're forgetting that Dings is Infantry."

"I'm not forgetting," I countered. "He's a REMF technocrat who chose infantry because it gives him an edge on making general. Rear-area staff work will keep his boots out of the shit. You know what's worse? When enough officers believe winning this war is less important than winning their next promotion, everything'll be lost."

"It won't help," Keneally said, "but it's not what's going to lose us the war. First, it's not clear we will. If we do, though, it'll be our national politics that does it. Secondly, self-interests have been with us since forever, but never the deciding factor and it won't be one now – not even in a few days when *you* get promoted."

"I want a promotion too, but it's not why I'm here – not to get credit for a combat tour either. I'm here to do everything I can to win this war."

"Mondo, you're being too harsh. Guys have the job they have. REMF branches get REMF jobs. What-d'-ya expect? Without support, we couldn't fight past a day. Granted, it's Bloat City, but it's not calculated to be that way. Nearly everyone here would prefer to win this thing. Who'd want a communist victory?" He got up from the edge of my desk. "Guess I'll best be heading up to the orderly room."

Irritation flitted like the solitary mosquito that kept lighting on my neck. As persistent as it was elusive, I could hear and feel it, but by the time I put down the part I was oiling and swatted, it was gone. I dropped my rag and lit up a cigarette.

'Maybe comparing Nam to a training exercise *is* an exaggeration. But even as close to the shit as our own battalion's REMFs are, how real are any of our KIAs to them? They're never seen again. REMFs watch grunts hump out at daybreak, and at chow that evening, they hear about this or that guy who's already body-bagged and stacked in some far-away Graves Registration. Like that REMF said: "*You can keep all that field shit. A dude can get his damn ass killed out there.*"'

'Dead grunts are as anonymous as dead dinks! That head shed's tote board says it all, – fucking side by side columns: KIA - US, KIA - VC/NVA. At least the soldiers in those Army Times columns have actual names. Were any of them chickenshit? No, they're the noble, mythic warriors of Valhalla. My reverence for them is growing. The chickenshits are on the promotion lists, redundant columns of Tinderberrys. That's him, knee-deep in a bottomless slue of nipa mud, standing on the shoulders of a dead hero.'

I applied a light coat of oil to all my CAR-15's parts and reassembled it with the precision of a watchmaker. That completed, I hung it on a nail and turned my attention to the mud-hardened bandoleers. Although protected in their cloth pouches, a patina of silt had filtered through. I slid out a few rounds and fingered a suggestion of grit that coated them. It might be thin enough for some to disregard, but to me anything was everything. My weapon was either perfectly clean or still dirty.

As I pulled rounds from the magazine, and laid them next to each other, a scene from yesterday flashed in my mind. With the suddenness of its baleful bark, two Viet Cong tumbled backwards as the siblings of these slugs exploded from my muzzle and hammered them to the ground. Just like they had. My thoughts also returned to that instant of queasiness where I'd questioned my weapon's reliability. 'What would've happened if I'd pulled the trigger and it went click? No backup weapon. I'd have bolted for the dike, but made it only a few yards. Dills might've fought for a while – until his ammo ran out... *No margin of error.* That's what I have to stay focused on.'

One after another, I wiped each bullet with a tender lifesaving reverence. 'Whose body will these guys tear into? Whose life will they end?'

CHAPTER 3

By the following morning, a restless sleep and plateful of breakfast generated an intense desire to return to where I'd been shot down. Burkhart's body hadn't been located. I wanted a crack at finding it.

Major Grizwell, the final arbiter, listened noncommittally as I explained that I was the only one with first-hand knowledge of the area and knew exactly where the VC encampment was.

"Sir, there's no way they'd go any distance at all with a dead body. What would they want with it? Their only motive has to be to deny us its retrieval." I pointed to the spot. "It's got to be right in here."

"Looking around for a dead body isn't reconnaissance," Grizwell said. "I'm sending Charlie Company in there, including Lieutenant Burkhart's platoon." He got up and tapped an index finger on the wall map. My eyes followed his pointer and its double poke on a Rorscach of green to our northwest. "I want *you...* to go up *here* to the Rach Cau Tram."

"The Snake?" I asked unnecessarily, seeing where he was pointing.

"Yep," he said. His head nodded slightly, but his expression read resolve. "We've got to do something about interdicting, interrupting, put pressure on –whatever, their movements up there. Short of using a dad gum tactical nuke, there's nothing we haven't tried."

"Thanks Sir, for thinking of me as the only alternative short of a tactical nuke."

"Yeah right, Carney," he said with a deep breath of indulgence. "It's more a case of getting back to basics – find out what they're doing up there – recon them."

Owing to its dense vegetation and broad area, The Snakes gave the dinks the best concealment in the province. Its proximity combined with their mobility had them firing mortar and rockets at our firebase every time they got a new supply of ammo. Naturally, battalion units had tried to bust them out of there, but inevitably stalled with booby-trap casualties or daylight running out. Night operations had always been seen as too dangerous.

"Sir, I'd agree with you that reducing our forays in there gives the dinks a leg-up. They only have to worry about Harassment from our arty, but bunkered in as they are, I think the one-o-fives just sharpens their wits."

"Yeah," he added, "the colonel summarized it pretty well when he said that , by not wanting to see our guys torn up in there, we've created an enemy sanctuary smack in the middle of our AO."

"You know I'm a believer, Sir. Recon's been to the Snakes too. We didn't take any booby-traps casualties, but the caution it took to avoid them, neutralized why we were there. And a Dink body count of zero, is especially frustrating when you find signs of enemy activity everywhere and not so much as a single live shadow."

"That's part of why you're going in again," he said. "We want you to pull an ambush tonight –somewhere in this area here." And tomorrow, find out where their main basecamp is. You do that, and I'll be able to let the Air Force know *exactly* where to dump enough Mark 82's that only Neil Armstrong will recognize it. This battalion needs to be done with that place."

On my way to brief the platoon, I mentally revisited all the angles for our going back out there. Anticipating their questions wasn't hard. Our return to the 'Snake' could change two things; we might finally run into the main body of VC and NVA who'd so far eluded the battalion, and we could hit mines or booby traps we'd previously managed to avoid. The former forewarned of potential casualties, while the latter guaranteed them.

Although other units had done much worse in The Snakes, I was disappointed with my scant performance there, in the face of so obvious an enemy presence. 'As damnably daunting as the place is, it's not bigger than me. I won't allow it to buffalo me again. Everyone else's failures could be an opportunity. It'd boost my reputation to a point where it will forever neutralize Dingleberry's opinion of me. Now *that'd* be the ticket.'

At 1500 hours, we crammed ourselves into a pair of deuce-and-a-halves and moved out. I decided to use the trucks, because choppers would cost me the stealth I wanted. On the other side of town, we diverted onto a secondary road. Then at an innocuous spot east of our objective, we offloaded the vehicles and melted into a close woodline.

To maximize our need for speed, I stuck to well-worn village paths, until I could conform our route to woodlines that obscured more of our movement. Humping straight across open paddies was quicker, but sapped energy and we could be seen from hundreds of meters away. The further we got the more stealth we needed.

With the sun plunging behind the horizon, timing was everything. I pushed the pace hard. The platoon met my expectations in stride and we hit my mental landmarks one after another.

A klick from our destination, we turned sharply left, and made our way through a banana grove. Crossing its waist-deep irrigation canals slowed our pace. 'The further we get from pacified hamlets, the greater the chance we'll encounter dinks. Right now I don't want to, even if we'd get a body count.'

We moved into a long stretch of trackless brush and woodline. VC wouldn't use this terrain because they had trails, and knew which ones were booby trapped and which ones weren't.

At 1730, our artillery battery opened up with a fifty-round fire mission, dropping salvos into the two fingers of jungle that concerned me most. They followed up with a series of single tube shots scattered across a broader area, to bunker-in dink movement while we made our way in to their periphery.

Dusk had begun to brown the vegetation as we approached our final point of concealment. The expanse we'd have to cross looked thin and bare in some places and thickly entangled in others.

'*Tu Dia*. Scrawled on a scrap of wood warned that we'd arrived at 'Land of the Dead.' The pucker factor increased, trepidation springing from the VC's lock-solid guarantee that this place contained both booby traps *and* enemy.

Finding a *Tu Dia* sign was akin to reading a captured enemy document that they planned to attack at dawn. Good to know. Prepare and get ready. The bad part was, the enemy would still be attacking at dawn. I already knew firsthand that this objective was strung with exploding mayhem, but didn't expect they'd extend this far out. I gazed out over the calm vesperal landscape.

Every leaf hung motionless. It felt like the whole place was holding its breath.

'Decision time. I can't take the platoon in on a circuitous route – too noisy – and the chance of someone tripping something increases with the number of boots taking all those extra steps.'

I knelt down and pulled out my map for one last look in the fading light, my meditation with it giving me the focus I needed. Dilemmas needed focus. I squinted at the barely discernible river and key woodlines, knowing that half of this playing-for-keeps war was a never ending series of dilemmas, every one requiring an immediate decision.

Combat at the platoon level shares similarities with the game of chess. Quasi-medieval representations on finite squares have martial origins and my world of moving from grid square to grid square sharpened that image. The enigmatic Spassky -esque mind of my opponent gave them a third dimension. Time was an advantage over me. They pondered their moves with reptilian patience, while my sole concept of anything propitious was *right now.*

"This shit's a little tricky," I said softly to Mounds and the squad leaders. "If we try and get everybody into an ambush position now, something's bound to go boom. There's too many – enough for them to pick up on us. They'll just steer clear for the night – kickin' back to let their booby traps do all the work."

"We need to get us a good defensive position," Crowder whispered. "How about a hundred meters back there."

"Right, we're probably thinking of the same place. First though, I've got to deal with the ambush." There was still enough light to see their faces. My words froze the four in an apprehension of the unknown.

"If you're thinkin' of goin' in there with just a few guys," whispered Mounds, "… that could be some bad shit." 'Has Mounds lost his nerve? Why's he cautioning me? As platoon sergeant, he knows he won't be part of any small group I'll take with me. But he's got a damned warning for every idea that comes out of my mouth. Nothing's wrong with caution in this line of work, except it's become the sum total of our interaction.'

"Well, yes and no. I agree that a small team can't stay there all night –too much bad stuff could happen – too risky. But I see a way to get in where they wouldn't waste good booby traps. We'll slip through and set up an automatic ambush. Right near the river'll be perfect for one."

"Can we at least have a barbecue this time?" Olivera asked, referring to the other time I'd tried this kind of ambush. We'd blown a wandering pig to kingdom come.

"Sure, but I guarantee you there isn't a pig within five klicks. So here's the deal. I'll take Tra and Bugabear – Nunziato. I'd better have Doc Younce along too. I'll set it up at that trail junction along the river – same place I wanted to put the whole platoon. When the dinks come down the river with sampans, they'll off-load right there. They like to work at night, so we can count on them not booby trapping that spot."

"You want us to stay here till you return?"

"Yeah. When we get back, we'll all slip back to that place Crowder mentioned."

Tra and I went through the platoon gathering Claymores, det cord and other essential items. I gave Bugabear, Younce and Nunziato two each. Less encumbered by additional gear, Tra and I took four. Tra also loaded up with the bag containing all my other must-haves. Completed, the five of us slipped soundlessly from the platoon and into the night.

If you didn't know the VC rigged booby traps in predictable places, along a natural perimeter at likely avenues of approach, entering a TU Dia area in the dark would seem somewhere between unthinkably dangerous and stone-dead suicidal. 'Moving where they least expect us to is how we beat them. They know they don't need to booby trap impenetrable bush. But it's not impenetrable to us.'

What booby traps had done to so many soldiers occupied my days to the point that I'd dream a trip-wired grenade was lodged between my eyes. It was all I could see, all I could think of. The opacity of darkness intensified that image. 'It's there right now, with no pin, and its handle held by strands of something gossamer. Maureen says I'm obsessed with sex. I'm not. I'm obsessed with that grenade handle inching upward, to its inevitable release, the point where that firing pin'll snap down onto its fuse primer.'

The evening's humidity climbed. More of the day's heat insinuated itself into the air we breathed. Viscid in its stillness and thick with the wet smell of jungle decomposition, it felt as though I could reach out and grab fistfuls of it. This kind of air lent aid and comfort to our enemy. These tethered little iron soldiers couldn't get enough of heat and humidity. The ground reeked of malevolence.

I led the four in single file. If anyone was to trip a booby trap, I preferred it be me. The whole thing was my idea, at my direction. I slowly picked my way through low branches and undergrowth that could be connected to what might tear me to bloody shreds. 'When it comes to seeing in the dark, I'm even better than Tra. I know my route, I know exactly where I want to end up, and I know how to get there. I have confidence, but I also need luck. Too bad good luck comes with exactly the same odds as bad.'

My route, through the formidable but least dangerous terrain, turned our trek into a zigzagging nightmare. Every other step, I peered intensely into my Starlight scope. Deciding on the smartest next move was one thing; taking a full-weight step into it was quite another. But more than anything I could actually see, I drew my bearings from intuition and instinct. 'Whoa, this is impossibly nasty. God, *please* get us through this.'

My adrenaline surged to the red zone. My heart jackhammered in my chest at a rate like it had when the dinks were minutes behind Larry Dills and me. I refused to let my body's nerves commandeer my mind. Every footstep felt like it was coming down on a pressure detonator, each slender branch an extension of a tripwire running straight to an un-seeable mass of explosives. My antidote was a mental celebration for every snarl of vegetation we got through. I paused each time to savor it. The effect brought my heartbeat to a canter instead of a runaway gallop.

'This is the most dangerous night navigation I've ever attempted. I can do it, but how do the guys feel? I didn't ask for volunteers. I hope they're more confident in our collective abilities than they are in just me alone. They probably see it that way. They know I chose them because they're my best guys.'

The jungle glowered from every blackened shadow and inky void. In the absolute stillness, the snap of a twig sounded like a rifle shot. With noise discipline to match the stakes, we insinuated ourselves through every obstacle.

Just shy of the trail junction, I spread everyone out among some old-growth banana trees. I paused to let the place settle in around us. Tra crouched next to me. The two of us studied its feel. I listened, smelled and peered into the night. Doubtless, Tra was adding his sense of taste to our reckonings, but I already sensed them. Viet Cong. Close as a set of wet jungle fatigues.

'I love Dink noise discipline. Even in remote areas like this, they don't let their guard down. They take nothing for granted. I've got to imitate that. But, they can't hear us. Maybe I can't hear them either – then I don't have to, not when I can feel them.'

We began our work by securing the kill zone. To make the best use of Bugabear's Starlight-mounted M-14 sniper rifle, he slipped down to the river. Younce and Tra positioned themselves where the two well-worn trails converged. Nunziato covered a third and me. After collecting all the Claymores, I began the task of setting up the ring-main to my liking.

Dragging two bags of mines and another of gear, I slithered and inch-wormed my way through the underbrush parallel with the trails. I used my K-Bar to probe and slice, relying on guesswork and fate. 'If I snag a trip wire with my head, I'll never know what hit me. These claymores will sympathetically detonate. No one will find much more of me than a dark stain marking the spot where I made my last wrong move.'

One by one, I pressed the Claymore's legs into soft earth. Sequentially connecting each with a length of det cord, I wriggled on to set the next. Progress was agonizingly slow. Salty sweat mixed with camouflage stick and insect repellent streamed down my face. It oozed into my eyes and the shadowy blackness blurred into nothingness. I was doing everything by feel and dead reckoning. 'It's got to be perfect. Shit, that fucking arty's so sporadic. When the hell was their last one? Maybe they're done. Beautiful, and here come the dinks!'

Closing the ring at the point where I'd set the first claymore proved elusive. I lost my bearings and my efforts to locate it wasted precious time. Then while crawling about in exasperated frustration, I accidentally clunked my elbow into it. I clasped it to my chest like an old lost friend. 'Okay, lay out the three pieces of commo wire. Connect the one with the blasting cap running from the claymore to the first empty C-ration can. Good. Interlock the cans' lids, nice and close but not touching… just like that. Now this second can's wire goes to the radio battery. Hook the third to the cap's negative, and that'll go back with me to the battery.'

Ten meters away, I scrunched down behind a large tree, my team having repositioned themselves a safe distance behind other trees. As I connected the wires to the battery, they held their ears against the possibility of human error, and our waste of a bunch of Claymores.

The beauty of this setup was the cans and the careful tension of wires on the trail. Anyone coming down this trail in the dark was sure to nudge something. The slightest movement would pivot one of the cans lids. In that instant of contact, the circuit would be completed, sending fifteen volts to the blasting cap in the first claymore. *Boom,* fourteen Claymores go off simultaneously.

'I know I'm right on this. The dinks'll debark sampans, make their way up from the river, then step on my wire and proceed to kingdom come.'

We tediously backtracked along the team's original route of approach, and following our link-up plan, the entire platoon pulled back to a more defensible woodline where we'd spend the rest of the night. The squad leaders reiterated the order of watch. As always, I'd be part of the first and last shifts; already awake for the first, and for the last, I'd have to get up anyway.

I found a spot for sleeping and unslung my web gear. Sitting down, I leaned my back against a substantial coconut palm and stretched out my legs. I propped my two bandoleers alongside one thigh and laid my weapon across my lap. Facing the open jungle, I stared into the black oblivion's nightly crawl. Amorphous shadows insinuated themselves ever closer. Somnolence was in among them and hard on my trail. On either side of me, lay Nunziato, Tra, Tho, and part of second squad.

Sitting in a net of darkness, I tuned my senses out to the middle distance, to the thrumming, pullulating sound of limitless tropical arthropods and amphibians. It lulled, invading my body like a soporific vapor. Short on sleep from the night before, the debt was being called in. Like a tax on a tax, it unjustly levied my mind for consciousness. The steady droning of yet one more warm aqueous night was the epitome of usury. 'Another minute and I'll be scrabbling around for little twigs so's to prop my eyelids open.'

I changed position by shifting to a Vietnamese squat. The small exertion helped. If I began to nod out, I'd start tipping over and wake up. But the blood circulation to my lower legs got cut off first. I stood up and looped my arm around the tree. Leaning close, I melted into its contours. Darkness was my friend, my body a gnarled appendage to its trunk, my head no more than a burl. 'This is it. I'll alternate between standing and squatting for the rest of my watch. I'll have to.'

"**BLAM!**" A yellow-white light flashed in the distance, followed by a massive rending concussion. I acknowledged the sharpness and size of the blast as its echo thundered off into the far distance. On a direct azimuth to our ambush, there was no doubt as to what it'd been. Nunziato tapped me on the arm.

"We got 'em!" he whispered.

"We got something. Hope it wasn't just a friggin rat. I cleaned the cans real good though, before the wires got soldered on. I even smeared on insect repellant to cover up any smell left. But where rats grow fat on strychnine, who can figure what sniffin' they'll do?"

I called the TOC and reported that our bushwhack had been sprung and requested an artillery fire mission I'd registered hours earlier. Twenty-five rounds of 105 was always good medicine for the aftermath of an ambush.

When the last salvo had finally finished shaking the forest, I put my head down on my poncho roll. They'd wake me at 0400. 'That'll give me four hours – about average these days. But it's accruing. Fatigue's becoming weariness. It's getting harder and harder to pull myself out of it. Man, when I go on R&R next month, *sleep,* in a real bed, is going to be the order of the day. Yeah, while the girl who'll be in there with me is doing what? What'll I do with those competing needs? Die of fatigue I suppose.'

CHAPTER 4

A BIRD'S TWITTER IN A tree above lit the day. It repeated. From somewhere behind, another mimicked in response. At a greater distance, a chirruping sound joined their comments. I turned toward the eastern horizon and one-eyed a sliver of pale gold. Imperceptibly, it widened at the expense of the blackened universe above. For a few moments, I watched the auric pastel expand, then turned over. It was just light enough to make out the men around me. Dull green forms lay at irregular intervals roughly perpendicular to our perimeter. Those who'd shared last watch were sitting up.

A new charge of adrenaline began to flow. I wanted to get going, to get back and assess the ambush site. But caution would be even more important now than last night. 'Charlie'll be expecting us to come and check out our handiwork. He'll have a good idea which direction we'll be coming from and be ready. He won't want to mess with a platoon of GIs and gunships and'll just delegate the work to a fresh ring of booby traps. No matter what though, we're going in there.'

"Okay you guys," I told the NCOs. Mounds and I crouched with the three squad leaders. "By now, they've discovered the route we used last night so we can't go in that way. They'll have rigged something nasty for sure. For the same reason, the other approaches on this side are out. That means we have to go around the periphery of this whole Tu Dia area." I pointed, making a hooking motion to the left. "We go to their main trail, north along the river, then use it to approach their offload site. They'll want to booby trap that too, but it's wide and bare. Trip wires'd be hard to hide. Any questions?"

No, Sir," Mounds answered. The others shook their heads. "Everybody's ready."

I did a visual 360, my final, transcendental gut check. The trees rose around us, as they did every day, holding up this foreign sky. Still a murky gray in the west, a flock of ovine clouds roamed the east. Maybe not so aimless, they looked to be dragging some unraveling fleece behind them, getting home before the infernal blaze of another day's sun.

We filed out, grouplets of friends unwinding into their squads and order of movement. The point team remained on the trail for only fifty meters before I had them veer off and slip into heavy vegetation. To reduce our exposure to booby traps, we stretched into a long file. I felt tense. My stomach made itself known. Acid churned in its emptiness, a rebuke to a breakfast of a cigarette and a slug of water. Everyone else had eaten while I'd checked gear, re-read my map and talked to the TOC. Later, I'd have plenty of time for food. There was always an endless supply of later. 'Food and sleep and everything else is always later. The VC are always now.'

Tra and I moved up and shadowed Corchado and van Wyck who walked point. They picked their way through the heavy bush. 'It's costing them half their alert skills – only leaving the other half to scan for Charlie. Not a favorable margin. Booby traps are still my biggest worry but it's damn good terrain for a hit-and-run ambush.'

We watched the jungle ahead and to the sides with narrow-eyed intensity. I kept checking van Wyck. 'He's far enough behind Corchado to be okay if he steps on something, but too far to provide effective cover. But a closer interval could gift a booby trap and take them both out. A sniper'll likely only get Corchado. Got to leave them alone.'

We were half way to the trail. The sun was well up and rising fast. Its rays poured into the jungle and burned the heavy dew into a steaming mist. Thick vegetation blocked the movement of air, while being too low to provide us with shade. We toiled in the oppression of it, our breathing labored. Sucking in hot stagnant air, gave us the feeling of slow suffocation. I dragged myself through a canal's slimy, body-hungry ooze. Gasping, my whole torso felt like it was enclosed in a giant, invisible fist. I tried to catch my breath just as it squeezed down on my chest. 'The whole world's running out of air!'

I looked behind me at Tra and Nunziato. Tra registered signs of exertion, but he was only in second gear. The extra weight of Nunziato's radio showed plainly in his face.

"I've heard that this wouldn't be such a bad war," I whispered, "if we didn't have to fight it in Vietnam."

"Where better you want fight?" Tra asked.

"Fort Lauderdale, Florida," I blurted.

"Ha, Nunziato moaned, "fighting the commies when they land in Miami. Anywhere where there ain't any fuckin' mud, fuckin' heat, mosquitoes, malaria, ring-fucking-worm, and about nine hundred other fuckin' things."

Yeah, Nunz, you just know how much nicer it'd be to get greased in a clean, crisp set of fatigues before you'd even broken a sweat."

"Never happen, Sir. Grunts always have to get anointed with shit first. And we've been baptized in whole rivers of it."

Corchado's sharp eye spotted it from ten feet away, a length of dull green monofilament line laced through a leafy branch that hung across the trail.

"You know something's gotta be there," he said, talking himself through it, "because branches don't *quite* grow like that. They bent it back to weave the line in." His closer inspection revealed one end anchored to a tree with the other tied to a US M-26 grenade. That little treat was slid inside an empty mackerel can that'd been pinioned to the ground. With its pin already pulled, the can prevented the grenade's handle from springing off. Give the line a little tug though and you un-sleeve the grenade. The handle pops and you get blown up.

Corchado cut the line and coiled it. Sliding the grenade out a quarter of the way, he worked in a spare pin, bent the ends over, and placed it in his pouch. Van Wyck moved forward, studying nearby foliage for a secondary snare, another VC trick. If a GI tripped the first, his buddies would rush to tend to him. Dropping their guard they'd set off a second explosion.

I cordoned the kill zone with Starcup's squad. Then followed Tra, who was still moving behind the point team. On high alert, we scanned everything. A crater marked where each claymore had been. Around them, vegetation was scythed down to nubs or blown to dirt. The artillery rounds had fallen wide, but I could make out the shredded voids they'd left in the jungle beyond.

I inspected the claymore sites, assessing how I'd done laying them out in the dark. Each one had blown a hole in the foliage behind it with its back-blast. I spotted a spattering of blood. Moving closer, I could see more on the ground along the trail. It'd already turned brown in the day's heat.

A Claymore had gone off on the other side, close enough to cut a man in half. I moved forward with tentative steps. If a man had been standing where I stood, as the thing went off, his dissevering anatomy would have been blown into the jungle. The claymore had bored a blood slathered tunnel in the vegetation. With extreme caution, I checked out their preferred spot for stringing high-explosive paybacks.

Flecks of dried blood mottled the broad leafed plants. Small shreds of flesh and guts mixed with bits of cloth lay slathered on the ground. Flies buzzed all around us. In a frenzy of delight, they seemed unable to decide on where to begin their dipterine smorgasbord. The VC had removed any larger body pieces. Gathering them up would've been a real fun time for his comrades.

"Trung úy!" Tra called in a loud whisper. He motioned for me to come over to where he'd been poking around. His lips were tight and drawn back, deepening the clefts at the corners of his mouth. It was his necrophilic expression, the one he reserved for moments like this. He'd found what we were looking for, lying just in front of his boots, a gob of someone's guts. Beyond it entrails and other viscera lay glopped on the ground.

"Ooo-whee," van Wyck said as he came up behind me. "I hope they don't make us bring that stuff in just to prove we got us a no-nonsense body count."

"You could volunteer Van. All you got to do is go back wearing that chunk of Cong intestine around your neck like a lei."

"Like a shit sausage you mean… Yessir Colonel, I killed me this gook with my bare hands. And when I got done, this here's all that was left of him."

Cautiously, we followed Tra, finding more spattered blood but no bodies. As cleaned up as the place was, their work had to have begun at first light. Additional shreds of clothing and fragments of equipment lay in a couple of spots, as well as a dink 60mm mortar round somebody'd dropped in the undergrowth and overlooked.

We stopped to scrutinize every square inch. My can setup was missing, along with the wires and battery. The dinks had them. I reckoned it a fair swap. At least four had died, but healthy and vengeful VC would be close.

Separated from the platoon, I had Corchado go back and bring up Sergeant Lupanski and his team from second squad. They moved parallel to us and took up positions on our right for security. We pressed on to the edge of the river. 'The dinks were using the area just like I thought. From the river, they went straight up the trail… until one of them snagged my wires.'

Further looking was too risky. I gave the word to pull back. Lupanski and his guys began to move. A huge thunderous explosion rocked the earth. Dirt and debris blasted through the leafy undergrowth and hurtled into the air. I saw Stovall go flying to the ground. My heart stopped.

"What the hell was that?!" I yelled. "Are you guys all right?"

"If it wasn't a fuckin' atom bomb," Lupanski called back, "I don't know what it was. We're all okay though."

"Hard to believe. But shit doesn't go boom all by itself. Go back and let them know everybody's okay. Tell Crowder to move to the north of whatever that thing was. We'll go forward in this direction."

Crowder's squad swung forty meters ahead and secured the area. The rest of us approached the spot where it'd had gone off, a huge gash blasted into the jungle, an enormous explosion. Its scar of shredded vegetation revealed expert concealment.

Tra motioned an invisible line from the crater to a dense clump of bush. "Yeah, that'd be where his command det wire was. Gook claymore you think?" I looked at the crater again and took a deep breath. A mine that big, catching a man straight on, could set a new benchmark for what was meant by getting *blown away*. At just the right angle, it would have taken out half a dozen men. "Lupanski, go tell Crowder to check out that undergrowth." A heads-up for friendly fire came back and a pair of grenades resounded, Crowder's guy doing a little reconning by fire. As the smoke cleared, he waved for me to come up.

Nipa palm fronds lay side by side, some stuck into the ground at angles. A rough wattle of banana leaves formed a small cave of vegetation. In its jungly context, the expedient concealment was difficult to detect. 'Why'd the dink detonated it when he did? Lupanski's team was twenty meters away, with just enough jungle in-between to absorb the blast.'

"He must've dee-deed with the detonator wires," Crowder said, gazing in the direction of the crater.

I nodded. "Yeah, them and our battery too."

"What is a gook claymore anyway?" Doc Travis asked. "I ain't never seen one."

"Most dudes who have are dead," Crowder said. "You don't want to be takin' yourself any close looks."

"Think big and nasty," I said. "I've only seen one. It had no cap or wires attached. It wasn't rigged up. They're homemade jobs, set in something like a big earthenware bucket with about five pounds of explosive in the bottom. They put in a lot of rocks, old pieces of metal, glass – anything they can find that's hard and heavy. Cover it over with mud and stick in a blasting cap. They blow them as command dets, because tipped on their side, all that shit gets blasted out in one direction, like our claymores. The little bastard set this one off, because he saw we'd turned around and started to head back. He was hoping someone was still close enough to catch pieces of it."

"Man, if we haddna turned around..." Lupanski said, staring at me with manifest realization. I looked at him and his three team members, faces etched in a somber envisioning of what might've been. Their eyes looked inward. A cold anxiety coursed through me. 'My order for them to come back was just routine – a reflex to hold everyone on line – keep visual control. I wasn't weighing alternatives, no impending danger. God, the consequences of it… These four guys are standing here in front of me, healthy and unhurt, instead of more splattered bloody messes on the ground.'

Lupanski and the others stared blankly, realizing the gravity of what a different instruction would have meant. In dozens of identical situations, I would've told them to continue moving forward.

"Okay guys," I said, "there's bad shit in here, but we're still going into the middle." I pointed. "Be super fucking careful. No trails and *a lot of separation.* I'll get arty to walk a few rounds ahead of us. If it only neutralizes one booby trap, that's one less to worry about. The dinks know we're here, but don't have any idea where we'll be going next – like they expected us to use this trail… but we didn't."

I radioed the artillery battery for a marking round. In minutes a ball of dense white smoke burst in the sky a hundred meters to our front. I called in an adjustment to the Fire Direction Center while watching invisible breezes high above us slowly tear the ball into wispy threads. We waited in place. 'Tipping-off the dinks is never good. Smoke gives them a head's-up that high explosive rounds are moments away. I don't like using it. But we're right on the gun-target line. I have no choice. The risk of howitzers firing long's at least as great as anything the dinks might toss our way.'

The first HE round hit, exploding with a reassuring whump in the near distance. I gave the signal. We moved out. 'Getting dinks to scramble for cover isn't a bad thing. Dropping rounds ahead of us will keep them from setting up a hasty ambush. They'll seek cover and not bug out as we approach.'

The platoon snaked its way single-file through a mat of thick undergrowth. It was rough going, but I felt secure. They couldn't anticipate the exact avenue of our approach. Compared to the deadliness of every trail in the area, the risk of booby traps in this virgin vegetation looked as low as it could get. But looks deceived.

"Hey, Sir" Nunziato said, "I think I recognize this place – we been to this spot before? Yeah, the place we zippoed those two hooches...."

"Yup," I said. "We came in from over there – checked a pair of stripped hooches in this clearing. The VC had taken them over and set up camp. We put a light to both."

The platoon encircled the burnt remains. Crowder's squad began a sweep of the surrounding forest. With no sign of recent activity, it was clear the dinks had moved their encampment to a less conspicuous place.

"Hey, Lieutenant Carney!" Sergeant Olivera called to me. "Come on over here!" He and a couple of his squad were checking what had been covered by a blanket of soft warm ashes when last seen. Deluges of monsoon rains had changed that. The palm logs that formed overhead support were gone, likely incorporated into a VC bunker somewhere. Exposed to the elements, the once concrete-like mud walls had been reduced to piles of blackened dirt half as tall as they'd been.

Three men pulled apart what had been the rear of the bunker. Sergeant Dean pushed aside chunks of dried mud with the butt of his M-16 revealing a small cavity, a VC secret compartment inside the bunker's wall. 'Seems small though, even for a real little fucker.'

"There's something here," Dean said, still busy knocking chunks of mud out of his way. He was right. It looked especially clever. On our previous mission, we'd burned the whole hooch down and hadn't noticed it. Even with their extensive VC experience, my Tiger Scouts hadn't either. The fifteen –inch-thick wall was too narrow for a hiding compartment, because it was just a channel to a much larger opening down below. A piece of wood coated with dried mud had served as a removable panel. That had all burned away.

With the opening slightly ajar from the start, a VC enticement was very real. To clear it of booby traps, we backed up a safe distance and Sergeant Dean heaved a heavy chunk of broken wall into the opening. It crashed through. Silence. We moved in for a look. A dark hole stared back at us, the entrance to a kind of small oubliette.

"I need to know what's inside." I handed Thanh my penlight. "Go in and check it out." With an understanding nod, he pulled off his gear and quick-checked the entrance for trip wires, then began lowering himself into the opening, feet-first. Half way, he decided that seeing his way with his not-so-tactile boots, wasn't the best idea to find something nasty. He reversed himself and squirmed back in head first. Dean and Olivera held his legs and inched him down. At the bottom, Thanh only found the fetid detritus of those who'd once secreted themselves there. As he climbed out, he pulled up a piece of charred bamboo. Three inches in diameter, it had been one of the main supports for the roof of the hooch and simultaneously served as an air pipe for the compartment. Men came over to examine this latest evidence of Cong ingenuity.

"Hey Sir?" asked Olivera, "What would've happened, say if there'd been some dink hiding in here when we torched the place?" Biggs, another member of the third squad, took a look for himself into the chamber.

"If I was in there and somebody done zippo-ed the hooch," he said, "man, like I'd be flyin' right the fuck out of that hole."

"Like a bat outa hell," Olivera offered.

"Shit, they can shoot my ass, but there ain't no way I'm gonna sit there and just burn up."

"Looks to me like the fire never got down there," I said. "Think about what really happened. Say a dink is hiding in there because he saw us coming. We set fire to the hooch. He realizes the place is burning, but there's no way he can get out, because the place is a damned two-thousand-degree inferno. In the compartment, he's safe from the flames, but every breath of oxygen is being sucked right up this pipe and through the cracks around the lid. The only thing he *can* do is sit there and die."

"Slow-baked don't seem a whole lot better'n burnt," Biggs reflected. I nodded and considered a man anticipating his own imminent suffocation. I noticed Thanh's pleased expression. His small smile reflected his having given up such a job. He'd spent time in such holes, but traded them for a life of no holes, with strange Americans and their constant stream of jibes.

Tra summoned me to follow him across the clearing. He pointed between two large banana trees. A pair of graves lay parallel behind the trees. I stooped down to get a better assessment.

"Ah, VC!" Tho said, having just joined us.

"No shit Tho," quipped Nunziato, "I thought for sure they were Apaches."

They weren't the fresh ones of anyone who'd been caught in our automatic ambush but weren't that old either. I kicked at one mound to assess its compactness. Clots of soft clay broke away.

"You know," I mused, "they've been here about a month. That'd coincide with our burning that hooch down."

"Me think same," Tra said "I go look all round. Then see here."

"You've got one step on us. We were scratching our heads over whether any dinks were croaking in place when we'd lit up the hooch." "Yeah," Nunziato added, "we were only twenty meters away and didn't even know it was happening."

"What a pisser, we keep killing dinks that never get racked up on the old tote board." Aimlessly, I poked the toe of my boot into the *corpus delicti*, then stepped on it with my weight. "It's still pretty soft."

"O-o-o-h, Sir, you ain't thinking about making us dig *these* fuckers up are you?"

"No." I knew Nunziato's half-joking question had to do with a related incident. I'd gotten a recent Hồi Chánh's intelligence that a weapons cache had been buried to look like a VC grave. We'd found a fresh one right where it was supposed to be and began digging. But, instead of weapons, we'd exhumed a grotesquely putrefied corpse. I'd called off the effort, only to be updated by the S-2 a couple days later. As a ruse, our elusive weapons cache had been hidden *under* the body to dissuade further digging. It'd worked. Armed with the new info, I took a team out to re-exhume the grave. The rotting dink was still on hand, but in our absence he'd already been dug up and reburied. The weapons were gone.

"You know," I said, "it'd be interesting to see if there's any bullet holes in them. Like suffocated or shot?"

"Sir, I was just kidding. Besides, you know they'd be full of worm holes, rot holes, all kinds of fucked up holes by now."

"Yeah, don't you just love a dead dink, Nunziato?"

"Sir?"

"Well, when they're your basic full-of-holes dead, you don't have to worry about them anymore – like, the *deader* they are the less they can hurt *you.* If we could get enough of them that way, the commies wouldn't be able to do any harm at all."

"A lot of people back home say it's us who're doing all the harm, Sir."

"Nunzie, you been hanging out with my girlfriend again? It's easy for them to say that crap when they aren't here with us in these villages. They know jack fucking shit. If we suddenly vanished, the commies'd still be here, killing Vietnamese. You know my opinion; 'kindness to the people, death and destruction to the commies."

"Hey you guys," I said, my words directed at Tra and Tho. "Take that shovel and show me it's only a body and doesn't have a little caché of weapons under it. Don't dig him up all the way. Just dig him enough."

Tra explored the soft ground by probing with the blade. That wasn't working so he unearthed some of the grave. A mud-covered arm and hand came into view. It reached out from the hole imploring us for assistance.

"Fucking beautiful," Nunziato guffawed. "He's gonna grab you by the balls, Tho!"

Tra probed a bamboo-handled steel rod, our tool for the no-mistaking feel of weapons and mortar rounds. After running under the body several times, he looked up at me.

"That should do it Tra," I said. Let's tuck him back into bed." I motioned with my hands the act of filling the hole back in. "Shit, Nunzie, reminds me of this comic book I had – they ain't been around for ages – *Tales from the Crypt.*"

Yes Sir, I had some of those too – another was named *The Vault of Horror.*"

"In my one," I continued, "this guy's being murdered and his hand gets cut off at the wrist. After the body and the hand were buried in the cemetery, the hand pushes open the coffin and digs its way out of the ground. It knows where it wants to go and starts walking like a crab down the sidewalk. It gets to this big old mansion where the killer of its owner lived – opened the door, goes in, fingers its way up the stairs and gets the guy in his four-poster bed – just chokes him… with *deadly* strength."

"Yeah, I think I remember that one. Weren't the dude's eyes bugging out – like as he was trying to pull the fucking hand off of his throat? But he couldn't." Nunziato stared at the hole as the last of the dirt was piled back onto that grizzly moment when we'd seen a whole arm trying to escape.

"*Quod* something; *quod* something," I recalled out loud. "That's all I can remember."

"What Sir?"

"Latin. I can only remember that one word. Quod means '*what*'. When these three riders come up on three skeletons in the forest one of the skeletons says in Latin: 'What we were, you are; what we are, you will be'."

"Talking skeletons?"

"Yeah, talking skeletons... Maybe just dead guys, still corpses like this dude. I doubt he'd have much to say in Latin, though."

"Well, given what he is, and what I ain't, I sure as hell ain't winding up in some hole in this place." He looked around. "It'd flat suck to die here – fucking worm food."

"Wouldn't it suck no matter where it is?"

"It'd be relative," he responded, "like if it was somewheres a lot better... How 'bout as far away from here as you can get – peacefully in your sleep – with some foxy lady – maybe one like you got. I'm just saying, if my number's up, I'd prefer to be somewhere's else."

Nunziato's bringing me back to my peacenik fiancé, Maureen, jabbed at me like a sharp stick. I could sort of see what he was on to. 'Losing my life would mean the loss of everything, including her. I almost died in that car in North Hampton. But how much worse would it be if it happened here?'

"I don't know, Nunzie. Maybe the better the situation, the worse it'd suck. Wouldn't Paradise lost be worse than losing what we've got? All we've got here is our lives."

"Maybe," he allowed. Not like you, I didn't leave any girlfriend behind when I left. Ain't even had one since I went to Basic. But I definitely never had a model like yours."

"She's not a model just a college student."

"Yeah well, Sir, I'd say she could pass for one real easy. She'd be paradise for me – enough to make me into one of those peace dudes who don't have to come to Nam. It's how we all know how hard-core you are – cuz you're here while she's there. That's all the proof we need."

"There's something to that, Nunz. Don't forget though, I only see her as this-here girl, just one person. It makes her way less important than the defeat of communism, which involves the lives of millions. I don't think about peace on my girlfriend's terms, but peace on mine."

Tra called for my attention. Behind some trees ten meters away, he'd found another grave. Dug, but empty. I looked at the fresh excavation, the soft dirt piled neatly alongside, and the bower of jungle all around. Tra's gaze wandered in his own assessing way, until returning with mine to the yawning slit at our feet. I looked at this hungry earthen mouth. It seemed to be calling out to the sky, for it to be fed. '*...What we are, you will be.*'

My map indicated that two more hooches lay a hundred meters away. Too late in the day on our previous mission, they'd gone unchecked. At the deepest point of this peninsula, they'd definitely be part of this VC basecamp.

We headed in their direction, resuming the wearisome business of inching our way through the bush. Experienced guys like Corchado and van Wyck could spot booby traps with considerable skill, but this place was almost too much, it being a truck garden for them. We'd already found several and we'd find more, except for that one we didn't.

'Damn booby traps – little, never-tiring, high-explosive sentries, forever on hair-trigger alert. Day in and day out, they just lie asleep in the undergrowth, until that moment when some fateful boot violates their domain. Then they roar out and shred some hapless dude to pieces. *Surprise! You're dead.*'

'It's a bitch I'm making decisions with only the barest of clues. Too much is chance, every step just another stochastic dice roll. I'm going with death-dealing odds on pure instinct. Our skills give us an edge, but how long will they be worth anything?'

Straight on, I was fighting communists, but their scads of improvised explosives worked for them like a whole separate allied army. With the point-blank lethality of AK-47s, they stared at me from behind every leaf, cold, insentient, and in their numbers, more deadly than a battalion of live communists.

The VC loved booby traps. Thousands upon thousands had been set, planted and strung. The entire Delta seemed like some labyrinthine web, rigged and ready to explode. Our fight against this mechanistic foe was only half the battle, the other half being the resourceful and quick-witted minds that devised them. 'They've turned the entire Delta into one colossal Tu Dia and imposed it on its population.'

In a hand-wringing *New York Times* article Maureen'd sent, it described a litany of *'indiscriminate'* bombings by the U.S, concluding that *we* were the only thing Vietnamese civilians had to fear. Despite my frustration with being associated with any accidental deaths, my being linked to *indiscriminate* killing really rankled.

I wished I could introduce Maureen to a little girl I'd talked to, who'd lost a leg just above the knee. Without a prosthesis she had to use a rude crutch and the aid of an older sister to get around. She told Tra and me that her misfortune had come from a VC booby trap then astonished us by saying it was her gift to the revolution. She said someday she'd be rewarded. The sight of a child's stoic display of a bare stump evoked more pathos in me than I'd ever known. I wanted to shoot the person who'd told her that. It was nauseating to contemplate seven-year-olds having to give anything to this despotic revolution, much less a precious leg. And all this jerry-rigged ordnance would be blowing kids up long after the last American had gone home. And for what?

Tra tapped me on the arm and pointed. A large egret ascended from the jungle off to our right. With long spindly legs hanging behind, it flapped its wide wings slowly in a steady rhythm. Stark white against the backdrop of a cloudless sky, I watched it gain altitude. Why did he call my attention to it? We'd been close enough to flush it. I gave him a questioning look.

"Bird," he whispered. "Say bawk, bawk." I focused on the natural sounds around us. The usual squawks and twitters emanated from various distances. I was going to ask, 'So?' but stopped myself. Tra'd know exactly when such a bird should yawp, and when it would yaup. One tiny anomaly in a bird's flight was all the boding Tra would need. There were VC real close. That big white bird had given them away.

I hand-signaled the platoon and they lowered their profiles. Seeing me take a knee the point team came back for a conference.

"Some VC just beat feet out of those hooches," I told them. "We know there's something going on. We'll move in there by two directions." I pulled myself up to a low hunker and went over to Starcup. "Get Mounds up here."

Although doubling my booby trap risk, I needed two elements to help protect us against an enveloping ambush.

Civilians hadn't inhabited these hooches for a while. The jungle was beginning to encroach. They seemed starker than usual, stripped even. Water ewers, the several large earthenware jugs that always stood out front, were absent. The makeshift metal gutter for sluicing rain water into them was missing. There weren't any domestic implements. It looked deserted, but didn't feel deserted. 'Is it the absence of what ordinary people give to a dwelling? Or is it the presence of something malign?'

Corchado hunkered low and softly approached the first dwelling's only opening. Entering a darkened doorway was always an unsettling move. Thatched walls provided no protection at all from bullets. He peered inside then signaled for me and Tra to come up.

"Somebody's cooking in here," he said, in a hushed tone. Tra moved up and looked in, scrutinizing the hard mud floor for signs of a mine being buried inside the doorway. Satisfied that it was okay, he went in, his muzzle synchronized to the sweep of his gaze. I went in after him. Four hammocks hung from the poles that supported the hooch. Hammocks always meant VC. Civilians slept family style on mahogany planks laid across the top of the bunker. This hooch had a bunker, but nothing else, no planks, no rush matting, no pillows, and no family shrine.

"Corchado, check inside the bunker." Tra, at a crouch was examining the cooking. The fire had gone out. Minutes before, dried nipa leaves had been its fuel. Tra handed me a pot full of boiled rice. I poked a finger into its tepid contents. "Hmmm, overcooked, just the way they like it." The pot was made of the thinnest aluminum possible. Its handles looked like they'd been riveted on by a child, its sorry quality suggesting an Albanian contribution to the enemy war effort.

"Four bowl." Tra motioned towards the small crockery bowls. A larger one held some green, grassy-looking stuff, while another vessel contained *nuoc mam.*

"You had it right Tra. The fuckers picked up on us and just dee dee maued on their chow." I passed the pot to van Wyck. "Go spread this rice all over the ground, then punch holes in the bottom of the pot with your bayonet." I clunked two ceramic bowls together. They fell to the floor in pieces. 'Hard to replace them out here – but right now it's all I can hand them.'

"There ain't nothin' in the bunker," said Corchado. "Nothin' 'cept one of those woven mats. Somebody's been spending time in there though – probably waiting out our arty. I looked real hard for hidden compartments, but didn't find shit."

"I'd like to blow the bunkers," I said, "but first I want to press on and find out where they went. I can't torch hooches today. Major Tinderberry is in charge of battalion operations." 'Right this minute, somewhere out there, he's up in the C&C playing supreme allied commander. If he spots smoke on the horizon, he'll be all over me for violating everything from Battalion SOPs to the Geneva Convention. Me being smack in the middle of an enemy basecamp will be the least of his concerns.'

Tinderberry had already begun splitting hairs over our kills from last night's ambush. His admonishing voice barked in my head; 'The lack of captured weapons Carney, suggests that civilians may have been killed.' I could see him sitting there in front of me, with his best expression of staged solemnity, and copies of MACV's *Rules of Engagement*, and *FM 27-10, The Law of Land Warfare* open in front of him, my specific transgressions all underlined. 'What do you have to say for yourself *this time*, Lieutenant?'

I settled on registering the place for an artillery mission later tonight. Twenty rounds of white phosphorous would burn the hooches and be perfectly acceptable with everyone.

"Take those hammocks with us," I said. "The thought of them sleeping more comfortably than us, ain't getting it."

Again on the move, I selected a route along the southerly edge of our fat finger of land enveloped by the Rach Cau Tram. I'd push to its furthest point. 'Getting there, we'll be able to see where the dinks bring in supplies. We get their backs to the river and they'll die in place. If they figure we're going back for a chopper pickup, they'll just hunker in the bush. Crossing and re-crossing isn't what soldiers'll do, if there's any chance they might not have to. That'll work in my favor.'

We didn't follow the exact direction the dinks had likely taken, but moved in a meander that gave us the best protection against ambushes. With no civilian presence to tend it, the flora had grown thick and wild.

The deeper into this area we got, the less familiar plant species were. New varieties had exploded from the churned ground of old artillery and bomb craters. Like atavistic cycads, they seemed locked in a motionless war of domination, everything clamped in a mutual death grip, nothing giving in. Everything survived, proliferated, and grew upward into a vast snarled entwinement of green.

Gunfire shattered the stillness. Close. Bullets tore the air around my head. I dove for the ground. Half a dozen M16s erupted from behind. Their angry bursts studded the bush. Reassurance. No one was calling for help. Corchado and Van Wyck were out in front. I couldn't see or hear them. I quick-slithered to the base of some stout palms and pulled myself up to look.

"Van!" I called out, just as a grenade went off. I assumed the arm that'd thrown it was his. Both guys lay a short distance from the explosion. It stunned the obscured jungle floor. Corchado jumped to his feet and ran diagonally forward. Van Wyck covered him with automatic fire. He bolted out of sight.

"Van!" I yelled again, "What've we got? How many?"

"I saw four of them," he called back. "Maybe more. It wasn't an ambush – we just walked right into them. I got the first one for sure."

There'd been no AK fire since the initial bursts. They were either trying to disengage, or find better cover. I crawled back to Nunziato and radioed the TOC to get us gunship support. The choppers might be able to get them on the run. Then, I called for Starcup to move his squad up.

Pain Maker 5, Major Tinderberry, came on the radio. He'd monitored my call for gunships on the battalion net. Instantly breaking from wherever he'd been, he was heading our way, fast. His *help* was the last thing I needed.

"This is Pain Maker Five. Tiger Claw Six, What's going on?! Over."

"We've got a contact Pain Maker. I'm not sure of our situation yet."

"I roger that Tiger Claw. So might there be someone else I can call to get your situation? Over?" 'That gratuitous sarcasm is pure Dingleberry, but his blaring it out on the open net pisses me off.'

"This is Tiger Claw Six. Negative. Wait one, over."

"Pain Maker Five, roger. You likely have a situation that rates artillery." Tinderberry went on, ignoring what I'd just said. "I want it used. Over."

"Tiger Claw Six, roger. Over."

"Affirmative Tiger Claw. You sit tight and I'll fire as much as it takes. I want no casualties. *OUT!*" As soon as I'd given over the handset, he was back on the horn. "Tiger Claw Six, what are your exact coordinates?" I read out the numbers amid feelings of total exasperation. Beaten, I shoved the handset back at Nunziato.

"Well, *fuck me!*" I hissed

"I think there's a regulation against that, Sir."

"Shit, shit, shit!" I seethed through clenched teeth. "I don't want to talk to him. If he calls back, tell him you can't get to me. If he persists, key the handset and fire a burst. Come on."

I slid back to the palms, desperate to reconnect with the point team. Using a gnarl of exposed roots, I crept along. In the clear, I crawled to the base of another tree. I couldn't see further than ten meters.

Firing suddenly erupted again. M-16s. It was Corchado and van Wyck. I inched myself forward and glimpsed a dink doing a fast belly-slither into thicker concealment but instantly lost sight of him. I emptied half-a magazine just forward of the spot from where he'd disappeared, then changed position to another tree. I reloaded. 'Where'd that fucker go? The dinks have their backs to a nipa swamp. They've got to hold us off until they can skirt to our left. If there's more than a few of them, my point team's been sucked into trouble.'

"Davidson!" I yelled to second squad's RTO. He scrambled out of leafy undergrowth and trundled up to me. I snatched the handset and called Crowder. "Move your guys straight left, perpendicular to our line of advance – that'd be a one-six-zero. Go fifty meters. Then turn due west toward the river. Hold up at the nipa – no idea how many there are. They'll be trying to slip out through there. Get people to the river bank, fast! Cut them off. Take them under fire wherever they try to cross. Get a machine gun on it."

I shifted cautiously beyond the cover and concealment of palms. Scooting to my right, I reached Tra. He let me know the point team and part of second squad had followed dinks further to the right. 'Shit! I've got a disconnected element that doesn't have a radio. Yeah, yell to them, so some dink will know just where to shoot.'

I motioned Tra to come with me. We crept ahead to another grove of palms. Nunziato, Davidson and Tho covered us from our old positions.

A glade-like clearing lay ahead. I scanned the surroundings from one end to the other and back. Nothing, save the crumpled black-clad body of the one who'd walked into Corchado. However many dinks there were, if they weren't in full flight, we'd whack their asses. Anxious to do just that, by not letting them get away, I hunkered down and moved through the bushes along the margin of the clearing. I kept my attention riveted on the area where the dink had crawled. Half way around, I spotted faded khakis. Grotesquely contorted legs said dead NVA, his weapon pitched to one side.

A burst of AK fire ripped the silence. I twisted downward in a mad lurch for wet earth. My mind reeled. 'Close, but from where?' I'd spun around and lost my bearings. Tra's M-16 ripped from my right side. 'Where's he firing?!' In response, bullets hammered the ground on either side of me. I rolled, squirmed and flipped in a crazed attempt to escape them. With no cover and no idea where they were coming from, I feared I was crawling right into some dink's sights. Trying to see in five directions at once, I noticed the vestiges of an old hooch twenty feet away. The crumbling two-foot high mud wall looked like a fortress compared to what I had. 'Move!' I alligatored with all my might across the ground. With a focus that equated speed with life itself, I scrabbled over and flopped onto the other side.

"Yaaaaah!" I yelled, landing right on top of a dink's back. As if jolted with electricity, I jerked upward. Freed from my weight, he twisted and pulled at his weapon. Falling back on him, I shoved the short barrel of my CAR-15 into his midsection. He wrenched at the flash suppresser with both hands. I drove the muzzle down into his sternum with all my might and grasped the pistol grip. In frustration and fear, he cut loose with a yowling appeal for the strength he needed. I pushed harder and pulled the trigger. The pent-up energy of a half dozen bullets exploded in his chest. My weapon kicked back and hit me in the chin. I pulled away from him, my face drenched with something that wasn't quite blood. It dripped from my nose and chin. My eyes burned.

"Damn!" I cried out. "Tra!" Everything blurred. A spike of fear stabbed through me. I blinked rapidly trying to clear my vision. Tears flooded my eyes. I wiped with the backs of my hands. Covered with dirt I made it worse. 'I'm on the enemy side of the wall!'

I grappled at hardened chunks and tumbled over. A sharp sting slapped my right thigh. An M-16 opened up nearby. Through watery eyesight, I barely made out Tra. Lupanski and Stovall yelled in the distance. Olive drab blobs moved up. 'Nunziato and Davidson?'

"Three VC dee dee mau," Tra called out. I sat up, pushing my back against the wall to take stock of our situation. I needed to rinse my eyes with water, but out of two canteens, I only had a couple of mouthfuls left. My tears improved things. I took a gulp and dribbled the rest into my worst eye.

"Well," I said, "I know of one fucker who ain't dee-deeing for shit." The sound of a chopper came up in the near distance. "Is that a gunship?" I yelled.

"Yeah," Nunziato called back, "a Charlie model named Rattlesnake- Two One. He's on the horn now – wants us to pop smoke so he can see where we are."

"Shit!" I said angrily, and grabbed for the handset. "Rattlesnake, this is Tiger Claw Six. I've got a little problem here."

"Roger Tiger," he cut in, "People're running around down there. Can't make out who's who. Get some smoke out so I can."

'Sure. Fucking beautiful – except my point team and half of second squad's somewhere out there with no radio. When we were close enough to yell, we couldn't. Now that it doesn't matter, all anybody can hear is this chopper.'

"Negative Rattlesnake, I shouted into the handset. "I repeat, negative. I've got people out there I can't communicate with." The Huey blew over the tree tops and turned to make another circle. "Go over the river! Grease the shit out of anyone in the water."

"This is Pain Maker Five," Tinderberry cut in. "Tiger Claw Six," what is this about you having lost some men out there?!"

"Pain Maker, we have negative casualties. We are in contact. Situation still not clear."

"Well you'd better get it clear. I need to know what's going on. I've called off those gunships and I'm going to fire arty and bring in some of Bravo Company. Remember, I told you to remain in place. I want artillery working this. You got any confirmed kills?"

"Roger Pain Maker. We have three confirmed."

"Well Tiger Claw, I hope they're more substantial than the ones you reported getting on that ambush last night."

A large volume of gunfire broke out to our right. I could hear AKs and M-16s cutting loose with everything they had. Grenades punctuated the exchange, followed by broken bursts of M-16 fire. Bundt's M-79 popped rounds that exploded fifty meters further on. Then, elements of first and third squads opened up. A dozen weapons went at it hot and heavy.

"Man! What're we running into?" Nunziato's head turned one way then the other. I dropped the handset and tried to get a bead on the AKs. "The Major is still on the horn, Sir. He heard all the shit and wants to know what's going on."

"We're in Fucking Dink-land," I hissed, in unalloyed frustration. "Tell him you can't reach me. I don't have time to bullshit with him." The firing went on in sporadic waves, quieting to random single shots with grenade blasts igniting new rounds of furious automatic bursts. 'Damn! Fucking damn! I can't use the gunship 'cause I don't know where point is – the bastard's just got pulled anyway.'

"Come on, we got to link up with Corchado in a hurry." I got up to a kneeling position. My right thigh felt completely numb. Checking my trousers for a rip and blood, didn't reveal anything. I grabbed Davidson's handset and called first squad, hobbling as I talked. Kessel, their RTO, told me that Olivera had gotten blocked by a nipa swamp and once the firing broke out Crowder's guys were just lying in place. I told Kessel to get Mounds on the radio.

"Ballenger says he saw one dink," Mounds reported, "a dude with only a pistol."

"That's all?! I asked. "The place is crawling with them over here, and you got one dink with a pistol pinning down two squads?"

"We might've moved on him, but he disappeared between the river and the nipa. He could've been trying to suck us into booby traps."

"With that gunship up, they're just trying to get the hell out of here," I countered.

"There ain't no where for us to go anyhow – 'cept into the nipa. Can't get nobody to the river without goin' way around. That's where the shit's likely to be." 'And that's why the dinks probably alligatored their way straight through the nipa. What they'll do, and what they'll do when their lives depend on it, are very different.' "Fuck it then," I added. "Keep working your way in our direction. We're moving toward where their last firing came from. We gotta get us linked back up!"

Lupanski's team had already moved out and the rest of us followed. I tried to walk but my leg had lost its ability to support my weight. I could lift it, but when I pushed down, it folded under me. It felt like I'd been stung by a one-pound hornet. 'Shit!' A dark patch of blood was seeping through my trouser leg.

"Hey Doc!" I called back to Younce, "Come up here. I've got a problem." I dropped my pants to my knees. Blood trickled from a wound in the middle of my thigh. I sat on the ground. Keyed up with adrenalin, my whole body was shaking.

"Looks like a gunshot wound," Younce said. He ripped the plastic wrapper from a compress bandage. "Wasn't an AK round, cuz that would've gone all the way through your thigh muscle or shattered your femur."

"Yeah," I said, "I've seen a few examples. Davidson! Get up there with Lupanski! I want contact with point." Younce probed around the wound. I jolted with pain. "What the fuck are you doing? My leg feels like it's been skewered by a steel rod and you're trying to squeeze it out like a big friggin zit!"

"You'll want to get that bleeding stopped," he said. "You want a pain shot, Sir?" He finished tying off the bandage.

"Fuck no, I want a goddamn radio. " I could hear one of the gunships M-60s chattering in the distance. "Nunzie! Give me the radio! Sounds like some fool-ass dink decided to swim the river."

"There's no exit wound," Younce repeated. "Hole's too small for an AK round."

"Got to be a pistol bullet. Mounds saw one of the dinks with one. But I don't remember anybody shooting me with anything. Hey, what the hell got in my eyes? It's not as bad as before, but they're still burning. Can't even open the left, the one I put water in."

"You mean your eyes and everywhere else. Chyme mostly, that and serous blood."

"What's that first thing?"

"Well, you took a bath with the contents of somebody's stomach." I looked down and instinctively wiped at the front of my fatigue shirt. Smearing the slimy bits and pieces into a ineffable slather intensified the smell.

"I better just let it dry." I wanted to rub my eyes again, but thought twice.

"Here," Younce said, "use some of my canteen to rinse 'em out. I ain't never had the occasion, but I reckon that stomach acid'd burn the shit out of 'em – fucking putrid enough to almost gross you out."

"Yeah, almost." I blinked my eyes rapidly after pouring some water into both of them. "Man, I'm getting too close to this war."

I tried to radio the gunship but failed. "You know, every time I want to call these fuckers, they've switched to another net, like UHF or something – like I can only get them when they call me! No, I forgot. The C-'n'-C told them to get out of here. Like fuck man, I suppose all I can do is call in for a damned dustoff."

The TOC informed that a Medevac would be along in twenty minutes. Then, Major Tinderberry came back on.

"Tiger Claw, I have an ETA of zero five minutes, your location."

'Damn this shit! He's coming in to take over direct control *on the ground!* Yeah, Recon's the only unit to make contact all day. He's on the scent of a medal! That radio chatter was him pulling together Bravo's platoons. Right, he'll usurp their company commander, get a bunch of friendly fire going, direct some artillery, and then get on the ground just long enough to dirty his boots. He'll have someone putting him in for a Silver Star before sundown. Too bad he scratched the gunship – gave the dinks just the break they needed to safely cross the river. How many of our battalion will be dead or wounded by booby traps because of him?'

"Roger Pain Maker," I said, "Be advised, that shortly you'll have to communicate with Tiger Claw Five. I am the sole objective of that dustoff." I gave Nunziato the handset. 'Dingleberry'll be too ecstatic to call back and find out what's happened to me.'

A few of second Squad returned from their little foray. Starcup came over to where I was sitting and set the butt of an AK-47 next to me.

"Good work man," I said. "The only problem is you got your asses too far out in front and I couldn't let the gunship do anything."

"Damn Sir, we had them off balance. We *had* to go after them – better than letting them get cover so they could catch us when we moved in."

"I understand, but if you do that shit, at least have Davidson with you. We've *got* to be able to communicate – so I know where you are."

"I just didn't think we had the time, was all."

"You probably didn't," I said, "but there was a risk of you getting sucked in. That's what the gunships are for."

"Damn Sir, we got them two right away, then three more down toward the river, before the chopper even got here."

"All right," I conceded, "that *is* pretty good. It doesn't matter much now. You guys are going to have to deal with Dings... ah, Major Tinderberry. Just concentrate on getting out of here. No dinks'll be coming up behind us, so tell Mounds to work the platoon back out the same way we came in. You can slip through the booby traps that way. If the XO tries to pull some kind of weird shit, sandbag him the rest of the day. He'll be busy firing arty at dink shadows anyway. No matter what, you're due for a chopper extraction by about sixteen thirty hours. If Mounds doesn't get back here, fill him in, willya."

"No sweat with that Sir. But I'd say you won't have to worry about nothing' no more– not with a million dollar wound like that. You going to be stateside bound with that baby."

"Starcup I'll *have* a goddamn baby before I let that happen. If I was to leave you guys, it'd be just your luck some green-as-shit, candy-ass, non-Ranger, leg lieutenant would come in here and turn this platoon into a non-dink-killing bunch of root-beer-drinking, volleyball-playing REMFs."

"Coming straight to Recon, Sir?! I doubt they'd ever do that to us. But as a long range goal, that don't sound half bad."

"Starcup, that's exactly why *I'll* be back."

III
The Fight

CHAPTER 1

SLIDING MY BAG OVER, I sat down on the coarse bedspread and took another gulp from my complementary can of beer.

"What're you going to do tonight Campbell?" I asked, looking straight at my thrown-together roommate's name tag.

"Oh, I don't know. I guess I'll just go down stairs and have a nice dinner. I hope so anyway. They're showing a movie at twenty-thirty."

"That's it huh? You came all the way to Vung Tau for a flick and some hot chow?"

"That's all there seems to be." He answered with an earnestness too intense for two guys just hanging around in a hotel room. "Guys like us don't need much," he went on, "not after what we're used to. This here Pacific Hotel's a luxury all by itself. I haven't had a full night's sleep in my whole three months in-country. Besides, I'm going on a tour of Vung Tau that leaves pretty early."

"A tour?" I asked, trying to get a bead on what kind of guy he was. "Where the hell can anyone actually *go*?"

"It's kind of a bus thing the USO puts on – for sightseeing."

"Shit, I did that getting shuttled over here from the friggin' airfield – can't be much more to the place."

"There must be," he said. "They say Vung Tau used to be an exclusive French resort, like ah…."

"The Cote d'Azure."

"I don't know – *someplace* like over there."

"Yeah, 'Used to be' sounds about right," I cracked. "Ain't no Saint Jean Cap Ferrat or Villefranche I can tell you, or they're hiding a whole bunch of it right under our fucking noses."

I watched him fastidiously folding his jungle fatigues. Easily the youngest looking second lieutenant I'd ever seen, short rations had given him a scarecrow-minus-the-straw effect. He'd exacerbated it by wearing fatigues that were too big, which made him look like a little kid trying on his dad's uniform. And with a constant expression of wide-eyed alarm, he gave me the impression he'd had the very last bejesus had been scared out of him.

"How'd you get to come here for an in-country R'n'R?" I probed.

"I'm rotating to the rear and they sent me here in route to my new assignment."

I nodded, not wanting to follow up on 'rotate.' Platoon leaders didn't get vacations as a reward for coming out of the field, getting out alive being reward enough. Three months in the field wasn't all that long. Probably he'd been *relieved* for reasons serious enough that they wanted him clean out of the area.

"Lucky you" I said. "I had to get shot in the fuckin leg to get here."

"Were you in a huge fire-fight?" he asked.

"Huge? When it comes to fire-fights, huge and tiny are nebulous concepts especially when you're the PL and the only one who got hit."

"I noticed you limping. Was it a serious wound?"

"Smaller than a bread box – a little bullet, but whichever size they are, it only takes one to put you in the cemetery – until the end of time." He nodded somber-faced, his eyes even wider than before, not with a thousand-yard stare, but it's opposite. He was looking inside his head.

"It happened a couple of weeks ago," I went on. "Fortunately, it was only a K-fifty-four pistol round – otherwise I'd be screwed, and my butt'd be sitting back in the States by now."

"How would that be so bad?"

"I'd miss out on all the free beer." I tapped my empty can with a finger. "Hey, you haven't even touched any of your share," I said pulling another can from the small refrigerator.

"I don't drink *al-co-hol*," he replied, over-enunciating the word to emphasize the fact.

"Alcohol? It's only three-two beer – and you look like a guy who could stand a couple – couple cases... God created it you know, to help soldiers decompress – what're you, a friggin' Mormon or something?"

"Yes," he said coolly. "I am a member of the *friggin'* Church of Jesus Christ of Latter-Day Saints." He measured each word with a controlled tension.

"Sorry 'bout the crack, dude." My can made a sibilant pop as I levered an opener into it. "Ever wonder why they call these things, 'church keys'?" I laid the opener back on top of the fridge. He glowered at me.

"I wouldn't know," he said.

"Well, wouldn't you agree you're kind of an oddity amongst us grunts?"

"We are not an oddity, although some whose minds may be influenced by alcohol sometimes see us that way."

"Not the religion, dude – the non-drinking bit. There's no such thing as a dry Ranger. But then Campbell, you ain't a Ranger or Airborne." I took a deep glug of my beer. "Guess I should've just thanked you for leaving your allotment for good ol' me and left it at that." He headed into the bathroom and shut the door. "Not 'influenced enough," I mumbled. "Not even if I finish off yours and mine – two cans apiece, shee-it."

I stretched my legs out and leaned against the headboard. 'Why is it that the more obdurate the teetotaler, the harder it is for them to dig the difference between alcoholic inebriation and just plain old drinking? Heard they can't even treat themselves to a cup of coffee.'

"Hey Campbell," I called out toward the bathroom. "I think you're right – only a can and a half down and I'm falling under *the influence.* Is that you in there making like you're the ol' Tabernacle Choir? It's coming from somewheres. Maybe you and this here beer's giving me spiritual inspiration."

He said something just as the water came on, but I couldn't make it out. I lit a cigarette and began sketching my own evening. 'We won't be spending any R-and-R time together. But hell, I knew that from when we said hello, *Dionysian* as my plans are.'

I nursed my beer and waited for him to finish in the bathroom. Once out he began putting on civilian clothes. I caught his reflection in a large mirror, a more informative version of the figure whose back was to me. I watched the two of them, their synchronous moves, and their simultaneous glances. While buttoning his shirt their eyes kept meeting, a silent signal of concurrence that they could proceed to the next move. Titivations complete, they checked themselves at a distance and performed their final over-the-shoulder view, a smug affirmation. Minus the standard jacket and tie, they were a pair of young well-scrubbed, identically-dressed missionaries.

"They stop serving dinner at 1900 you know," he informed. "It's almost that now."

"That's okay. I'll just stay here for a while and wallow in turpitude."

"Have an enjoyable evening," he remarked. The door closed behind him, his congeniality fading with a click. In the silence of his wake, his words seemed tinged with condescension. 'I'll bet the dude sees me as a fucking bibulous wastrel. Perceptive son of a bitch. But what the hell kind of grunt takes a walk on free beer – and the mountain of pussy waiting right outside that window?'

Bored after a third beer, I took a quick shower. Sticking to basic Nam practice, I slid my naked bod straight into a lightweight shirt and pants, and then pulled on a never-worn pair of mod boots I'd bought in San Francisco on my way over.

My own mirror image arrested my attention, this first time in civilian clothes since leaving the States. My face was deeply tanned. All the scratches I'd gotten from branches tearing across it were entirely gone. As well, the heavy-duty rack time I'd gotten since leaving the field, had done more good than I'd thought.

I watched my new boots clomp down the stairs, sharp-looking, but only half as comfortable as my high-mileage jungle boots. Finding the lobby crowded, I meandered around and ran into someone I actually knew. He'd hung with my group in Officer Basic. I was happy to run into at least one familiar face.

"So what're you up to?" he asked, a follow-up to our trading info on our units and where they were.

"Not much so far," I said, "just got in."

"Feel free to join us if you want. Us Greyhounds've got that table over there. The way we're going, we'll be shitfaced by the time the movie comes on."

"Thanks, but I was thinking more along the lines of getting laid." His eyebrows jerked and he looked off to our side.

"*Her?*" he asked, nodding toward the only girl in the place. In nondescript civilian clothes, she was standing at the cashier's window, the designated spot for legally exchanging MPCs for piastres.

"No. Why would you think that?"

"She's a Doughnut Dolly. And, I have it on good authority that she goes for a hundred bucks a throw."

"A hundred bucks?!" I had no reason to disbelieve him, but couldn't detect anything remotely seductive about her, and no hundred-dollar attributes.

"Guys are paying that kind of money? – for *her?*"

"She's not *that* bad," he countered.

"I didn't say she was. It's just that a hundred bucks is pretty steep. And she's no Raquel Welch."

"Raquel'd set you back more than a hundred," he jibed.

"More and then some. It ain't news to me that guys can get fuckingly stupid from sexual depravation, but damn… Are Doughnut Dollies just whores sent over by the USO – what, like patriotic dissemblers? I've never actually met one."

"I seriously doubt *that*," he said. "But some dudes get real home sick for a little round-eye – so much that a hundred ain't too much. Round-eye for a round number. Gotta be some who think that because they're doing it anyway, they might as well get paid. I heard about this fine looking one out at Biên Hòa who was getting two hundred!"

"Shit Dave, somewhere there's a guy who'll do anything. I took another sideways glance at the girl. "She looks too prim to me. I've heard them called '*doughnut holes*,' but just took it as grunt talk. Besides, there're plenty of girls in this town who're way better looking than her and who'll be happy to do it for five – or ten."

"Sure, Viets," he said. "Some of them do look super fine, but they're still going to be Vietnamese when you get right down to it."

"Yeah," I said, "that's the part I'm likin'."

"Hey, it doesn't matter to me." He waved his arm dismissively, realizing he was deep into a subject he wanted no part of. "I got married just before I left – so as for me, I fly my slick by day and drink beer by night. Ninety-seven days and a wake up and I'm California bound."

"I hope you get there, Dave. I think I'll head out for a while. If nothing's going on, I'll come back and join you."

"Man, the only way you'll find 'nothing going' in this town is if you've come here for the deep-sea sports fishing – which there ain't none. Anyways, take care of yourself out there – you going alone and all. I come here a lot and have heard a few wild stories. You don't watch it and the cowboys'll have your ass in a gen-u-ine body bag."

"I'll be all right. I'm used to their gen-u-ine VC cousins trying to fuck with me on a close-up level."

Moving on, I left the building and exited the security gate at the street. Although not usually a loner, tonight I wanted to be. 'Except for the chopper guys, that hotel crowd's a bunch of remfs – Campbell's probably the only one with a CIB. Remfs'd be the only ones getting to hang around Vung Tau as part of their job. A kind of semi-permanent R-and-R? Hell, I had to take that goddamn bullet before I could get any rest. But hey, whatever rest I'm short of is about to be subordinated to *recreation.*'

It was early evening. The streets were deserted. During the hour spent in the room, the helter-skelter daytime traffic had vanished. I moseyed along surveying each store front I was definitely in the right part of town. The first couple announced themselves as 'soul bars.' Wilson Picket's voice punched from the squalid darkness. There were no GIs in sight.

The next joint actually had a name, "Mimi Bar." A bunch of Australians had taken it over. From the doorway, I sized-up two pretty girls who were keeping them supplied with beer. None of the soldiers seemed to pay them any mind. In their inimitable Down-under way, they were into serious hammer-and-tongs drinking, already half obliterated.

One of them noticed me watching and yelled something incomprehensible. A couple of his friends banged down their cans in hilarious affirmation. Like rum-soaked denizens of *The Black Dog,* the whole group broke into a raucous brabble. I couldn't tell if it was derision or an invitation to join them. With a casual imitation of their military salute, I moved on.

Passing a few more skuzzy bars and several no-'count buildings, I came up to the 'Pussycat Lounge.' I leaned in and saw several long-haired girls chatting amongst themselves. The absence of males pulled me in. Heads spun and neotenous eyes spied at me from behind the backs of booths. Cute enough for a second look, I offered them the hint of a smile and checked-out each one. None came running over to me, to wheedle me into sitting with them.

I walked toward the bar, replaying in my mind the particular Asian look I wanted. It'd registered the second time I'd seen it. The first time, I'd just thought it fascinatingly attractive. Then, I'd spotted it again in another girl, a chance blend of the best traits of Vietnamese, Malayo-Papuan and who knows what else. If there were two, there had to be more.

The odds of finding one of these rare beauties seemed slim to none, but these joints were packed full of pretty girls, so I wanted to hold out for that sliver of possibility. If I didn't chance across such a plum, I had Plan B; I'd swing back and pick up the cutest I'd seen. The lounging pussycats across from me had neither the look I desired nor anything to compensate it, so I turned to leave.

"You wan buy me drink?" came a voice from behind. Sitting alone at the bar, she snagged my full attention with a prepossessing smile. The ones in the banquette had caused me to overlook her. She didn't have the look either, but was striking in her own way.

Standing there, assessing the attributes of pouting kittens, made me feel self-conscious. I had experience in eyeballing a group of girls, preparatory to asking one for the next dance; but gawking at them to select a total stranger for sexual intercourse, seemed to demand more than the ability to play Mr. Cool.

Without looking her way, I pulled out the stool next to her and sat down. Giving the place a security check, I caught sight of two GIs sitting in the dimly-lit back corner. Accompanied by a pair of black-haired girls, they spoke inaudibly. I put their table to my back and faced her. Greeted by a sultry expression, I studied her with growing appreciation. 'Damn, she's good enough to call off the hunt!'

Sitting as though enthroned on her stool, she exhibited a regal attitude, not deigning to sit among her common courtiers.

She looked me over, then glanced away as if I'd left her wanting. Then the dark amorous eyes came back to me. It had me reassessing her role in here. 'Does she owned this place?'

"Okay, you. Come please, you – me go table." She motioned to a booth in the front corner. My eyes jacked open as she stood up. All of five feet nine, she sauntered across the room with an air of blasé aloofness, a slow leonine lollop that fully advertised her prime attraction, a pair of astonishing legs. Accentuated by a glove-snug shift that was so short, she was the only one who couldn't see her panties, the vision grabbed my eyeballs and dragged them after her. Before she'd gotten up, a satiny-red patch of those panties had been yelling at me from between her legs. Her abandonment of any sense of modesty was just what I was looking for. Yet despite its tongue-lolling hemline, the dress's stiff white linen and high brocade collar lent her an understated elegance, at least when compared to the tawdry nymphets playing baby doll nearby.

She had wavy brown hair, lots and lots of it. It stood out as a solid departure from the ubiquitous straight black hair I'd taken a fancy to during my first days in country. Piled all over and hanging here and there with a touch of the unkempt, it reminded me of a chiding axiom I'd just sent to Maureen; *'Girls can never have too much hair.'* This coif though, affected a look of half-crazed sexual abandon. I liked that.

Miss Slinky-babe had made the sale, but continued to show herself off. In her late twenties, she assumed a haughty mien that definitely set her apart. I inspected her for flaws, for an overlooked turn-off that might void the deal. Since sitting at the bar, I'd been assessing her with fragmented once-overs. My scrutiny ended at her tooled leather sandals, their color matching her massive mane. It was a deliberate non-Vietnamese, quasi-Asian look. Who was her typical clientele? I stomped on that question. Vietnam was the world of the present and in this world, there were only two people, me and her.

"Come, sit with me," she invited. "You very nice – I like. You want drink beer?" An old woman brought over a small glass of turbid liquid and placed it in front of 'my new friend.'

"I'll have a Bud," I replied, catching sight of the cans sitting across the room. I pointed to them, needing the familiar to edge out the exotic.

"What's your name?" I began.

"My name is Lin- da, you like?" She laughed as if making a joke.

"It doesn't do a lot for me. Tell me your real name."

"Ngoc," she said, making the sound of a glottal honk. "Vietnam name, Ngo Thi Ngoc.".

"Nee-owck," I tried. She repeated it several times. I said it the way she did, but she just honked it again like I hadn't gotten it at all. No wonder she'd gone for Linda.

From working with my Tiger Scouts, I'd been amazed at how a tonal language could pack single syllable words with so much subtlety. Trying to extract meaning from a language people fired out in quick clips of fragmented utterances was as tedious as separating seeds from bananas.

"Too hard for you," she said. "You no like Lin-da, you can call me Kah-ren, or Nan-cy. Whatever you like."

"That's okay Ngoc, I think I'm close enough – unless I'm saying it so wrong that it comes out meaning something bad – like 'dog shit' or something."

"American can no good say my name. I make like GI girlfriend."

"Yeah, well, we all have a hard time pronouncing each other's language. Even if I got good at it, I'd still never say things without sounding… like I didn't know what I was doing, but that doesn't mean I need to call you Linda."

"I like Lin-da." She said again, taking pleasure in just saying it. "You say not your name."

"It's Wes Moorland," I said, pleased with my spontaneously adopted nom de guerre. "You can call me Wes. That's easy enough"

"Yes, I can say, Wes. Wes Moh-Lan. Now say what name you girlfriend in America?"

"Umm ah," I hesitated. 'Why does she want to know?' That brought the image of my fiancée right to the table. I mumbled her name, "Maureen."

"Ah yes! You can talk me like Mohr – reen. Maybe close eyes – see her. You tell me, I do all same her." She leaned forward to the edge of the table. "Can do anything…" Her voice faded to a bedroom whisper. "Beau coup more."

"That's all right, I mean, no I don't think so – besides you're all right just like you are." It made sense that a good whore would be a good actress and servicing a guy's fantasies would be a great way to be good. Ngoc struck me as ready to create a few I hadn't even had yet. How far would that take her? Maybe plain-old screwing wasn't enough for some dudes. I'd read about that.

I envisioned the land of healthy debauchery as a small island, just off the coast of mainland Continence, the first island in an archipelago of perversions. The last in the chain was very far out, too far for me to comprehend; and although the shores of that first one had until now been just a dark line on the horizon, its sandy beaches were coming right into view.

"Maybe you can be my mother," I said flatly. At that, her eyebrows jumped, drawing her small nose up with them.

"I like better Mah – reen. No do dinky Dao." I laughed out loud clunking my beer can down on the table.

"You're okay Ngoc. Like I feel better that the kinks are only skin deep. I can dig it, you know." She continued looking quizzically, either getting it, or not getting it. "No! I make joke, Ngoc. Like funny ha ha – only *talk* dinky dao."

I'd also read that every man wanted a virgin with the touch of a whore in her. With this one, maybe I'd found a whore with a touch of the virginal.

"I do anything you like," she said, so earnestly it set me back. 'Nothing virginal here, that's for sure. Can't deny it, the whole deal's been sitting right in front of me, but hasn't sunk in. She's softening, acting more demure – that staged coquetry dropped, she's less aloof. Or with her guard down, she's lapsed into natural Vietnamese? Maybe she's trying to seduce me from another angle. Hell, she doesn't have to do anything.'

"Where you stay here Vung Tàu?" she continued.

"I'm at The Pacific Hotel."

"Oh, you officer!" She said, in a way that made me think it might not be a common occurrence for her. Or was it just an impulsive registering of bigger dollar signs?

"Trung úy," I said, giving her my rank.

"Wes – you very nice Trung úy," she blandished. "I can do very nice for you. You want fuck girl, yes?"

"Yeah, *you*."

"*Me*! Yes, yes!" She announced like I'd just said the secret word and won her as a prize. 'Okay, if she owns this place, she would've given the nod to one of the nymphets.'

"Yeah, who else we been talking about? You already said you could do me some good."

"Yes, you go with me tonight. I make very happy you."

"I'm pretty sure you can. But I want you not only for fuck, but all night, and into tomorrow – maybe even more. Can you do that?"

"Oh, yes. I say before, can do all what you want."

"All right then, let's hit the road." I tipped my head in the direction of the door.

"Oh no, one minute wait. When go, you must give Mama-san three dollar. Four more dollar for drink."

I wanted to finish my beer, but she took my hesitation to fork over what I owed as a need to be convinced that everything was on the up and up. This set her into a pidgined explanation of her contractual arrangements with the old crone, the actual proprietor.

"Don't sweat it. You rent a bar stool and I rent you. Ain't no biggie." I laid some bills on the table. The old doyenne descended on the money with both hands, as if by entrapping it she'd prevent it from escaping.

The whole time I'd been there, the woman had been skulking around like a slint-eyed jackal. Her shadowy movements in my peripheral vision seemed rapacious. Doubtless, this repulsive creature had been a whore for the French Foreign Legion. Around these climes they started early and aged fast, and badly. In this hoary whore's case, it'd been amazingly bad. Her rugose face chronicled the conversion of Legionnaire jizzum into this bar, now an edifice for converting GI jizz into who the hell knows what. I winced at the thought of her tutorials with Ngoc and the others.

We went outside to hail a Lambro. Apprehension tugged in the way that prickers and thorns snag on clothes. I turned to look behind me, to see if we were still alone.

"Hey, ah," I began, "I've got to buzz by the hotel for a minute. I flew in with this other guy. I need to tell him I'm not coming back for a while." This story needed to cover for the real problem, which sat folded in my wallet, over four hundred dollars in MPCs and piastres. Any fool would know enough not to take the whole wad with him. I'd forgotten and almost had.

"Why him no come with you?"

"Ah, he – well, he's married and doesn't go in for this sort of thing. I told him I was just going out for a beer. If I don't come back, he might think I got into trouble."

"Him not know. GI stay hotel for drink beer – cost tee-tee. Him go bar for take girl. You must now go to tell him? I think him maybe dum-dum."

"No," I said peevishly, "he's not dumb-dumb. I just have to check on exactly when we're flying out. He's a major – you know, *Thieu Ta.* I've got to do what he wants – make sure he knows what I'm up to."

"You no fly this chop," she scoffed. "You come only today, stay three, maybe four day – ha ha." Her incisive read on my doings took me by surprise. But her disarming smile won out. I set the gibe aside.

"Well, you don't know everything," I said dismissively. "Maybe we're flying out and maybe we're not. That's the way the Army is. Everything's always changing. If I tell him what's up, he can figure that into his plans."

We walked the few blocks to the hotel, her leggy stroll pulling at my peripheral glances. ID cards had to be checked at a guard post by the front gate and Vietnamese *lady guests* were explicitly *unauthorized.* So while she waited for me on the sidewalk, I dashed upstairs to squirrel away half of my money in a lock box. What she'd said kept running through my mind.

'She's had plenty of opportunities to study American behavior. She'd be making it her business to know this kind of stuff.

But a total stranger, tracking my moves… predicting what I'll do next? When the VC have your number like that, you'll be in a serious hurt-locker, seconds from getting your ass wasted. I need to stay real alert.'

She looked damned good, standing there patiently waiting for me: her pleasant smile, the short white dress against the fallen, scattered petals of acacia blossoms, strands of her long brown tresses drifting on a light breeze, and those uncommon legs. She exceeded the expectations I'd had when I'd left the hotel just an hour before. Her dégagé sophistication helped. Although it was more likely a practiced stock and trade, I chose to see it as cool indifference to what *we* were all about.

"I know why you go to hotel," she said. With a coy turn of her head, she began looking out onto the street, as though a passing motorbike had suddenly caught her interest.

"And what's that?"

"You put money in room," she answered, her eyes cutting back to me.

"What?! I did like hell!" I objected, raising the tone of my voice to capture the utter preposterousness of my having done anything of the sort. Peeved, I slid out my wallet and flipped it open to flash the color of my money. "What're you talking about? I've got plenty of dough." I whacked the leather on the palm of my hand to emphasize the fact. "It's for you, me– *us!*"

"Maybe I think you put big money in room – keep tee-tee for me."

"Wrong. There's plenty. I told you, I had to go and talk to the major."

"No major," she quipped as a statement of pure fact. "But, it Oh Kay. I not mind. I think you take okay-good for me."

"I fuckin-ay better have."

That I'd found a whore with an interest in money didn't seem all that odd. But the sharpness of her observations put me on notice. 'She never saw how much I had. She's *that* cunning? I'm that predictable? Damn, I don't want to play chess with a mentalist, I just want to get her in bed.'

"His name's Major Robert Rodgers," I said in feigned exasperation. "I don't know his serial number, but I'll introduce you to him tomorrow. Come on, let's go."

Our Lambretta put-putted to a side street that edged along the face of a hill. Tightly packed, the houses were not of the Vietnam I knew. Modern, substantial structures in whitish stucco surrounded me as they emerged from the hillside at hodge-podge angles. Tropical trees insinuated themselves in-between from the tiniest of gardens. Although dark, I could make out that the slope steepened, and the dwellings gave way to a steeper escarpment. Above that, dense vegetation formed a black crown against the night sky.

Ngoc unhitched a large wrought iron gate which led to a short walkway, a few odd steps, and a glass door of distinct European design. The dim light inside, revealed a raw ferroconcrete stairwell with two-foot-wide, tiled stairs. As we climbed, I kept checking back behind me at what might be the only way out. The stark impenetrability of the structure gave me the feel of intense confinement. It wasn't the kind of feeling I liked.

A pair of closed doors greeted us at a landing. The place gave up neither sight nor sound of life. Un-tempered by anything positive, the narrow tunnel-like stairwell fed my brain with unpleasant images. 'How close am I to meeting up with a few of her cur-faced, business associates, who'll muscle me out of everything I have or worse?' I envisioned my pretty dragon lady offering an all-too-sweet valediction: *'Oh, him lie to me – keep beaucoup money in hotel. Not nice. Kill him.'*

Two pairs of men's shoes sat outside an adjacent door. Their size reassured. In Soul-Brother style, there wouldn't be many pairs that big between here and Manchuria. Ngoc turned the key, catching my staring at the shoes with another knowing glance. 'What does that mean?'

I followed her into a single bedroom with an adjoining bath, a sparse pied-à-terre. A low wooden platform filled half the room with three slim Vietnamese-sized mattresses lying side by side on top.

A huge armoire stood against the rear wall bursting with the clothes of someone with a penchant for primary colors.

Under a single large window, a vanity took up most of the remaining space. I looked outside at tiled and corrugated metal roofs in a mishmash of levels and angles. A metal grillwork of welded steel bars filled the open cavity. It had the feel of a portcullis that had been dropped down from above. 'To keep intruders out? Damn, it'd take an extension ladder and an acetylene torch to get in. So, its purpose is…? And that front door…? Three-inches of layered teak and two massive throw bolts? I'd need a whole stick of C-4 to breech it! Somebody's gone out of their way to fortify this place. For what? From whom? Vung Tàu's supposed to be a completely secured area. Completely? But this is Nam… forget about VC and NVA; what the hell do I know about common criminals? Maybe better bunkered in than not.'

Ngoc had thrown off her dress, and in a lacy bra and panties she fussed among other clothes. Her movements and half naked body swelled my anticipation. From the wardrobe, she pulled out a garment in each hand.

"You like?" she asked, "All from Paris – in Francois – you know this?

"Yeah, I've been there." She looked up at me like I'd just told her I'd gone along for the ride with Neil Armstrong.

"Cost beau coup money," she said, in a tone that convinced me it actually had.

"Yeah, cool," I said, "although some of 'em look like Carnaby Street meets the Mardi Gras."

"I no know this."

"Aw, forget about it. This one's nice." With one hand I picked up the flounce of something in a moiré silk while with the other, I flipped through a few more. A score of outfits hung at my feet, long pants dresses with voluminous bell-bottoms. "Hey ah, mind if I borrowed this?" I pulled out a black leather belt with a Mod-styled square buckle. It was just unisex enough. "Forgot to bring a goddang belt along with my civvies. I'll bet I've lost a couple inches humpin' the bush. 'Cuz of that, I've been hiking 'em up since I put them on."

"Yes, later. Make off all now." Her underwear skittered on the floor. "Now we do."

She laid herself naked on the bed, with her long legs spread as far as they could go. Her move kindled as much curiosity as ardor. I stared past her small breasts and sparse pubic hair, to her taffy colored skin. Splayed against white sheets, the contrast was compelling. Despite the wonderfulness of her tawny body, I couldn't escape the thought of it having been indelibly stained from the ecru waters of the Mekong. It was the exact same color.

"Come, Wes I know you want beau coup fuck." She gave me an expression so exquisitely lewd that my already stiffening cock jolted in my pants.

"Yeah, you got it, Ngoc." I removed my clothes methodically, to savor the moment. I was no novice, but no whoremaster either. Strange girls nonchalantly throwing their legs wide for me wasn't a common occurrence. But from months of longing, the vision alone let something loose inside me.

"You can do what you like me," she coaxed in a whisper. "*Anything*."

'*Anything?* What's she have in mind? What dark urges has she given vent to with others who've taken her up on it? Shit, nature's good enough for me.'

"Ooh!" she exclaimed with a wincing expression. "Very bad – I no know this – I think numbah ten." She pointed at my thigh, at the wound that had gotten me the four-day R&R.

"It's no big deal. I got hit a couple weeks ago." I inspected it for both of us, more annoyed than embarrassed. The incision was healing pretty well, although the reddened edematous area around it looked nasty. At the start of my trip, I'd taken the bandage off hoping air would help it along. It had, but the damned thing hadn't completely scabbed over. It was still excreting pus. "There's a war on, you know," I said indignantly. "And some of us are actually in it." My feelings flipped from surprise to exasperation. "Come on, it ain't a friggin sylph lesion or something!" She looked at me quizzically. I pointed a finger pistol at my leg and pretended the sound of a shot. "It's okay. You understand?! No disease. No sick. No nothing!"

"Yes, I understand everything." She smiled and put out her arms to me.

I climbed onto the bed with purpose, depravation girding my nexus. Entering her easily, I rut with the conscience of a stag in the woods. She moved sinuously, an easy supple motion, a perfect complement to cervine desire. Her cunt grasped my cock in a way I hadn't thought possible. It shrank my consciousness to an invisible dot, a guarantee that I'd be through in seconds. With an iron will, I tried to drive my mind away from what I was doing, but nothing could escape the reality of my body's reveling in hers. I became giddy with pleasure. But was it just a dream, nightmarish fragments, gnawing fears that this moment might never happen again. Pushing up on one elbow, I looked down to see myself in her. I had to confirm what I was doing, verify it was really me. '*There, mine, all the way in her – not a dream!*'

The war going on inside me raged. The zealots of never-ending pleasure battled the forces of the inevitable. In this psychic melee, entire regiments of continence were being decimated. My mental reserves were routed with every thrust. And with each one, the great final offensive gathered, to overwhelm me.

"Snap!" 'What was that?'

Damp with sweat, a sensation fell across my back, a cold shadow. Instincts reeled and jammed my brain with shards of foreboding. Nakedly exposed and weaponless in a building I didn't know where, senses went on high alert. Focus vaulted from her body to the room, the door, and iron-grated window. My head jolted up in reflex. I looked around the empty room, listening. Nothing. A shiver ran through me, a learned response to not seeing a sensed presence, an indiscernible danger. I pulled out and looked behind me.

"What matter you Wes?" she asked.

"Nothing," I said, a stupid answer given my reaction. She squeezed the shank of my softening cock, as if to say, 'what about this?' "I don't know. I'm..." Feeling her fingers, on that most basic of lie detectors, I said no more.

"You no be worry," she said, "no one can come here. There is only you me. We fuck." Her impregnable door and window supported the idea. 'But which side of the door is the safe side? Her reading my thoughts again sure as hell doesn't help.'

Locking my mind into a carnal force majeure, I engrossed myself in her body with debauched fantasies. Her cunt responded in kind, voracious, an animal swallowing whole its prey. At the same time, she arched her back and pushed it to me, as if insisting that I take it in its absolute entirety, the sum total of her very existence.

I looked straight into her eyes as she undulated in a wanton rhythm, my cock as hard as it'd ever been and as deep in her as it would go. And at that moment, the understanding of what this was all about culminated in an inviolable need to spend my entire being inside her.

Ngoc smiled serenely, with a kind of professional satisfaction, delight in a job well done.

"Ah, Wes, you popped the crutch!" she exclaimed.

"I popped the what?"

"Cl-lutch. Crush hard for me to say. You know this?"

"Clutch? Yeah I guess, but it doesn't usually mean this here. Somebody said that?"

"I learn this from American. He very nice. He talk all time about him car in America. Him love him car."

"Yeah," I said, wondering about the kinds of fantasies *that* guy might've been having.

"He nice, but maybe I think he tee-tee dinky dao – fuck only one time – only talk-talk-talk. No got American girlfriend. All him want is go home to him Cam-ro car."

"Camaro. Hmmm, he's probably got the big three-ninety-six in her. You've got to love that. Geezo, Ngoc, let's dispense with talking about Camaro-dude. He's probably wrapped the fucking thing around a tree by now."

The fact that I was pulling drag for Poon Patrol, a single-file of dudes up ahead who'd slogged their way through her slot, was obvious. 'From her comments though, there's been unaccountably long dry spells between those pairs of boots. Why think of this shit at all? Shove it where it belongs, back into the far, abstract-expressionist corner of my brain. Whatever's gone on here, hasn't. And the whomever was somewhere else. Ngoc and I are here now, but neither she nor this room ever existed before I laid eyes on them.'

I dozed. Surprisingly clear voices from the next room woke me. The wall between us had a row of apertures at the top where every other concrete block had been left out. 'For better air circulation? Air and marijuana smoke. The two black guys who own the big shoes must be lighting them up fat as two-handed stogies.' The sweet thick smell wafted through the holes and dropped right down onto us in bed, permeating the room.

"Those guys are really going at it huh?" I whispered, canting a thumb up at the holes. I simulated the motion of inhaling and exhaling smoke.

"You want, I get?"

"No, they can have all that shit they want. Probably just a couple of REMFs – thinking they've got it so bad they've gotta get messed up all the time."

"You no like black man?"

"Some I do, some I don't." I spoke more softly, although no sound had come our way through the holes, probably on account of the pair having reduced themselves to brain-numbed puddles of flesh. "It's remfs I ain't got much use for. Don't know if that's what they are or not."

"I no know this remp."

"Rear echelon mother fuckers – guys who don't fight and die – guys who're not in the shit, but just here for a little fun in the sun."

"Black man is remp?" she asked with a frown.

"Some are, some aren't. I suppose it sounds confusing – but come right down to it, at least they're here. The ones who *really* piss me off are back in the states – the ones I'm risking my life for. Fucked up as they are, they wouldn't quite see it that way, but…."

"You talk black man in America?"

"Some, but mostly not."

"Who talk you now?"

"Oh, America's got all sorts of people, but most are white. I'm talking about dudes like the ones hanging around with Maureen, my girlfriend. You know, I said her name before."

"Yes, Mah-reen."

"Yeah, even though communists have killed tens of millions over the past fifty years, her friends still haven't copped on to the idea that communists are dangerous. Getting stoned seems to correlate pretty highly with those kinds of perceptions. '*Everybody must get stoned.*' Reckon you're not into Dylan – Maureen's heavy into him."

"I no understand. You talk bad for black GI? They do boom-boom Maureen?"

"No-o-o-o! I ain't said shit about any black dudes – 'specially any who'd be saddling up Maureen – like none. No, she's into wimp-ass dudes with granny glasses. If you're into what color guys are, most of the ones I don't like are white – there's so many more of 'em. *White assholes – yeah, millions.* They like to get stoned too, and listen to stupid songs like that – *Rainy Day Women* – Doctor Seuss for college students." I stretched and propped my bare feet up on the wall. Screwing had taken some of the fire out of me. I wasn't usually so charitable about either REMFs or Maureen's friends.

"I think you should be in State too," she said, still running on her parallel train of thought.

"Back in the States? Who the hell's going to win this war if I don't? It needs me, and guys like me."

"I think, you no win," she said.

"Oh, yeah? If we don't, it'll be because dickhead politicians and REMF-minded generals are fucking the whole goddamn thing up – which they've already been steady- doing from the start. Hold on, how do *you* know we won't win?"

"I Vietnamese, live all time Vietnam."

"Yeah, no kidding Ngoc – a tour in The Nam without end – 'cept it don't mean squat. A lot of Vietnamese are fighting the communists for reasons better than mine. You know the score and they don't?"

"You no want be with Mah-reen in states? Get marry her. Make fuck her, no me?" I rolled onto my side and looked into her eyes.

"Yeah I suppose. Hell I don't know. I've got to take care of business here first. You're here, she's there. First you, then her."

"I think Mah-reen no like you with Vietnamese girl."

"You got *that* all-the-way right. But see, she isn't dealing with what I've got. She's not going to get an AK round through her friggin cranium tomorrow, or next month even... As for you, you're part of Vietnam – a genuine piece of it. Look, I'm not one of those 'If you can't be with the one you love, love the one you're with' kind of guys. It only looks that way. For all I know, Maureen might be having some dude of her own – maybe this very minute!"

"You no like – he be black man?"

"Not particularly. But with her state of mind, it'd probably be somebody who'd *really* piss me off, like one of those fucking, long-haired, Cong lovers. That whole area where her school is, is crawling with 'em. But hey, thoughts like that make it easier for me to rationalize my balling the shit out of you – paranoia working its magic." I grabbed the pillow and scrunched it under my head. "Yeah, ol' Maureen's another expert on the war too, you know. I'm convinced she gets most of her insights from reading Rod McKuen to her stuffed animals. Look Ngoc, if a guy starts thinking about chicks back in the states –girls they love – girls they supposedly love – he'll go crazy pretty damned quick. That's why I have you. I need to forget about the states, and keep focused on Vietnam – like get close to the people. Mao says you've got to swim through the people like a fish going through water. Yeah that'd be me all right, a friggin' Maoist."

"I no like Americans," she said, her head only a foot from mine. I looked into her dark eyes. 'Where the heck did *that* come from?'

"Well, I can imagine it's hard to like us when you have to love us for a living."

"No love."

"Fuck us for a living then. The question is who's the one getting fucked? It just hangs out there, never getting an answer. I had a girlfriend in France and she fucked for the fun of it, until she fucked me good. Boy, did she ever!"

"Yew, GI say, Fuck this, fuck that." Agitated, she sat up on the edge of the bed and fiddled with her underthings. "Always mean no like, very bad. Then fuck Vietnamese girl. Why you say?"

"Well, we're using the word in different ways – damn, maybe five. Sometimes it's bad, sometimes it's good. Sometimes it's so fucking bad it can be good. It's an all-purpose utility word – must be pretty-damned confusing. Yeah, we use it too fucking much, that's for sure."

"Yes, beaucoup much fuck. All thing, beaucoup too much"

"Americans are an energetic people. And we drink a lot of coffee. It adds up to a lot of hard-ons. Take it as a gift. Don't forget, girls choose to fuck or not. Guys get to only when a girl says it's okay."

"GI no like Vietnamese girl," she said, her voice plaintive, but seething just below the surface. "Fuck girl – all time say we numbah ten – say we gook girl."

Ngoc's tone became irritable. She'd veered off into a completely different subject. We'd been talking past each other, but had taken a one-eighty. My bitching had goaded hers. But I was a soldier and could bitch like hell without getting the least bit angry. She was fomenting her own self-righteousness. So, on the verge of trying to explain my motives for what I was doing in this war, I halted mid thought. 'Killing one Vietnamese and then making love to another is too-damned complex. Her short-fused ire says steer clear.'

"Geez Ngoc, I don't see you as bad. You're not a gook. You aren't just a poor substitute either, like something to tide me over 'til I can get home to the real thing." I sat up in the bed and tapped her on the thigh. "This here's *it* for me. It's all totally real, you, me and Vietnam. It's got to be, 'cause I'm not anywhere else. In the middle of a war, things are as *real* as they can get. You're a damned sight better than most, stateside, Vietnam, wherever. I hesitated. 'I want to say something about the far-out fuck she just put on me. But that'll parade the fact that she's a whore. Okay, her *casse-noisette* skills just pulled a full combat nut-load out of me with more purpose than I've ever known. How much of a backhanded compliment does that deserve?'

"GI talk beau coup numbah ten in bar for Vietnam girl. I hear all time."

"Hey, hold on," I soothed. "What do you expect from dumb-ass, drunken soldiers rapping with whores? I wouldn't expect too much if I were you."

"You no understand. GI fuck Vietnam girl, then him talk numbah ten – all Vietnam girl – same-same *Cong-Heo.* You know this."

"Yeah, Viet for *pig.* Ngoc, they – you – ain't any *Cong-heo.*" I laid back to examine the thing as a whole, so I could explain it to her. 'Shit, this's way beyond me.'

"You're really hung up on this stuff aren't you? Look, not everyone is beautiful, one in a hundred maybe. Five are great, another ten are pretty darned good – it goes down from there. All tolled there's maybe tens of thousands of mamma sans in this country who are beau coup gooky. I mean the betel nut chewing ones who dig in the mud all day. That's what most GIs see and I'm sure that's what they're talking about, not slick honeys like you."

"They no talk rice-farm momma-san. They talk beaucoup pretty bar girl, same-same me."

"Geez-oh-pete, I don't know what the hell they say," I said, giving up. "Some really do talk a bunch of stupid shit. But just remember one thing – *not me.*" I Pointed to my chest "*I,* say you're number one. They were all pretty in your bar, but I chose you, right?" I pointed at her and she nodded. "Most of the GIs you've seen will go back to the states and wind up with some girl who ain't half as good looking as you or your pals. They'll be fat to boot! And after calling you all pigs? Divine justice is what *that* is, Ngoc."

"I no know what you talk. Too much English I no understand."

"It's okay. You don't have to. You and I will be nice to each other and have some fun for a few days. That's what I'd like. I won't ever talk bad about you. I promise. I think you're wonderful. Like I said, number one." She nodded again and her lips hinted of a smile. Her body began to transform itself from pretty to prurient. My want of her grew in direct proportion. It felt as though I'd been breathing in some strange arousing vapor. She gave me a knowing look. I motioned for her to spread her legs. 'All I have to do is not say anything that'll put me among those Americans she doesn't like.'

"Remember Ngoc," I blurted, "you're *Number One*!"

CHAPTER 2

NGOC'S MINISTRATIONS AND THE ACCUMULATED exhaustion from endless nights in the field, kept me asleep until late in the morning. I seemed to remember her getting up several times to go out. But had been so stuporous with sleep I wasn't sure if I dreamed it. She woke me once, wanting money for food. Grabbing my pants, I found the back pocket was unbuttoned and the wallet stuck in sideways. But her request for cash reassured.

Once my fuzz-filled head was fully awake, I recalled the cock-eyed wallet, and her tampering. Unbuttoning the pocket, I decided to recount it. I glanced up and found myself caught by her stare. Ngoc had on one of her short miniskirts and wasn't wearing any panties. She stroked the palm of one hand between her legs. My eyes watched. Her index finger traced the lips of her slit. Then disappeared inside. Her tongue mimicked the tip of her finger, moistening her lips as it moved slowly from one side to the other. She was speaking to me in my native language, animal telepathy.

"You like?" she asked

"Come 'ere." I tossed pants and wallet back behind my pillow.

Ngoc effortlessly stepped from her clothes as if they'd been specially designed for quick release. As limber as she was long, she climbed onto the bed and me with a single motion. Then, on her knees, she straddled my legs. Her wanton acquiescence made my cock rear with interest. It jerked upward as if suddenly startled and capable of seeing for itself.

Inching forward, she moved her cunt closer until it was just barely touching. My cock throbbed, trying to reach for it in futile desperation. The acuteness of my hunger made her body seem like some wild Lucullan Banquet. I took her by the hips and slowly worked her down onto me.

Having Ngoc for nothing more than a 'Hey' was surely a big part of the illusion. She was the first real snatch-for-scratch I'd ever had, but the sexual phantasm she'd crafted, obscured that our doings were predicated on money. And in spite of her conspicuous anti-Americanism, she hadn't leaked a single drop of disdain on me. 'Maybe her antipathy's shot-through with ambivalence. A whore'd need a good helping of that. Or are her emotions just too walled off for me to figure out? Whatever calculus is running in her, she's so unbelievably obliging. All I've got to do is look at her and she's serving me up another you're-free-to-have-me-whenever-you-want smorgasbord. It's like opening a skin mag and climbing inside to own some gorgeous slut who's just lying there waiting.'

With my blood cooled, I lay on the bed lost in dreamy fragments of our recent bout. 'What the hell's going on with us? It's like she's been reaching into my brain and manipulating my hypothalamus with her thumbs. Well, sex *is* square one, but it wasn't ever going to be a fuck-'n'-run. Man oh man, I need to be with a girl a lot more than I ever thought!'

That thought brought Maureen to mind. Our sexual pleasures had been so different. Our long relationship, our mutual professions of love, and her orgasms negated any comparisons with Ngoc. Yet amid a world of brutality and killing, a mere whore's embrace seemed to be equalizing things. It didn't help that I'd always wanted more of Maureen than I could get, our intimacy seemingly forever beset with frustration. From her dormitory's curfews, to the betrayals of my rattletrap Hillman Minx, our asses frozen in Berkshire ice, and her constant fear of pregnancy, they all took their toll. But they were nothing when compared to the ultimate cock-block, my coming to Vietnam.

'Our last night together – our last time making love. It's been so clear. God, the emotions – her face as I backed out of the drive... But is Ngoc pushing it all out of my head? Aren't Maureen and I still *one?* Isn't it just the endlessness of us being apart?'

'How would Keneally look at this? Right, objectively. What does reveling in a whore say about the inviolability of your fidelity to your fiancée? Is this Ngoc *that* good? I'd tell him, no. Okay then, is your love for Maureen so weak that a little pent-up desire would obliterate it?'

'Keneally, it's about what matters right this minute – all that matters. *Survival,* physical and *mental.* And without sanity, I've got neither. Retaining it means holding onto *reality.* Maureen, our love, and our future? As far away as they *are,* how real are they? They're intangible, like concepts. The war's my reality. It's immediate – what I can see, hear, feel, smell, and taste. Fortunately, it's not right in this room. No, my reality is this bed, Ngoc, and her body.'

Ngoc's shower and toilet shared about a square meter of space. A chest-high spigot protruded from the wall with a short length of black hose clamped to it. Showering was accomplished by pressing a thumb to its cut-off end and squirting. Water sprayed all over the place, running down the tiled walls and onto the floor which slanted into one corner. There, it gurgled into a piece of bent pipe that exited through the exterior wall. I could hear its slap-dash expediency spattering water out onto the ground ten feet below.

Absent a bathroom door, I'd lain in bed watching Ngoc immodestly indulge in her most intimate ablutions, hose and all. Without a flip-up seat and lid, her toilet looked like a bidet. Yet in using it, she'd fold her lanky body and squat on top, barefoot and pigeon-toed on its rim. Posterior down between her ankles, she'd perch there for long periods, absorbed in eliminatory meditation. Her preference for sitting on her haunches had me speculating on her having peasant roots, but her hauteur gave me pause. 'Where'd she grow up? What'd she do with herself before she got here, to this?'

"Who's that guy?" I asked as she came in carrying bottles of beer and food. I sat on the edge of the bed and pointed at several framed pictures along the back of her vanity.

"Him name Bill – he in Australia –he very nice." She brightened visibly on the reference to him. "He come here Vung Tàu, stay with me for long time. When war *finis* he come back. Then I go with him to home in Ad-o-lade."

Eager to dig into the food, I moved from the bed to a little stool in front of the vanity. The beer was piss-warm, but I swallowed half of the first bottle with one go. In a separate container, she'd brought a fish and vegetable concoction wrapped in rice paper. I badly wanted to eat them, but didn't. They smelled like they'd been fried in something so rancid that it reminded me of the last bowel-bubbling time I'd indulged in such fare.

"You no eat?" she asked. "Momma-san make beau coup good."

"I only want the rice and bread. Give momma-san my regrets. That stuff's guaranteed to turn my intestines into a flume of liquefied shit."

"Oh yes, American not strong like Vietnam people."

"You got that right. Being able to wolf down fried excrement without getting sick is definitely a super-human strength. *That,* I'll have to concede."

"Yes, Vietnamese very strong." She took a bite from one of the rolls.

"You know, if you guys ever get around to choosing a national bird, it'll have to be the fly." I'd discovered that if I agreed with her and used a couple word she didn't understand, I could say anything. I needed the amusement.

With only chopsticks available, I began using a modified Vietnamese method for eating the rice. By placing both of the bigger ends together, I put the rim of the bowl up to my mouth and shoved it in. Using chopsticks with any degree of agility, struck me as a time-consuming mastery of the unnecessary.

The guy named Bill looked straight at me from Ngoc's pictures. They'd been there the whole time, but hadn't actually studied them, not to the point where he seemed to be observing us. Sandy haired and rangy, he had a rambunctious air about him. Knowing that he was an Australian, I scrutinized his face for anything that'd account for growing up on the opposite side of the planet. Nothing surfaced. He could've come from any place in America. 'Geez, of the unknown number of guys who've been here, why's he the only one who rates a picture? Several of them!'

"What's this dude's name again?"

"He name, Bill Shep-pard." She enunciated the words carefully, as if having rehearsed them under someone's patient tutelage. "He very nice," she went on, "not same like American – he give beau coup money me."

"Yeah, the Aussies have got it all over us for sure. It's a pure-tee-fact." I gulped another tepid beer while it foamed in my mouth. 'Nice how one dude paying a whore more than the going rate equates to his whole nation being better than another.' "You know, I'll bet you'd be surprised to learn that they get most of that niceness from screwing sheep. Then, when they move up to whores, it comes off as one hell-of-a special treat. It makes them more appreciative – like you say, nice."

"What sheep this?"

"You know, animal – eat grass – kind of white – make sweaters, lamb chops. I don't think you'd have any of them in the Nam. It's too hot – no grazing land either. Australia's loaded with sheep though – you know, they say bah, bah, bah."

"I know this," she said coolly. "I think you talk numbah ten."

"Hell yeah, I agree with you. That sort of stuff's been number ten for a long time. Everywhere. I don't know a single country where screwing sheep is considered real good."

"I no like this talk. Bill, he very nice."

"How he *got* nice is the thing. From what I hear about Australians, they're all big animal lovers. Guess they figure that making love to 'em's the *natural* next step. I'm just setting you straight on Aussies – like you've got to watch 'em." I chuckled into my rice bowl and looked up at her enigmatic expression. 'Does this girl have *any* capacity to appreciate the absurd? Waiting for Bill to return sure ain't much of an affirmation.'

"Hey, I'll bet you five bucks that Billy Boy's favorite thing was taking you from behind on your hands and knees – habits like that being hard to shake – not that I'm adverse to a little *faire l'amour en levrette.* We could, if I wasn't so dragging'-ass drained from what we've alr.eady done."

"'Il était une bergère. Ma fille pour penitence, Nous embrasserons. La pénitence est douce. Et ron, ron, ron.'"

"Why you talk this Pháp?"

"Yeah, French – part of a children's thing I picked up from my old Parisian girlfriend. Our talking reminded me of it...." She looked at me blank-faced. "Hey Ngoc, isn't there anything we can do around here? Like staying cooped up in this room is going to bum me out – maybe turn me into that kind of American you don't like. What'd you and 'ol Bill the Shepherd do? Don't tell me that he just came in, mounted up, peeled off a few bucks, and headed back to base."

"Bill, he very nice," she demanded. "Him take me Australia."

"No, I'm talking about when he was here. What'd you do then? I know that he was nice to you – and being Australian is a definite plus – if you can get past fucking you like a sheep." She clattered her rice bowl on the table and leveled a hostile stare. I took her hand. "I'm sorry. I promise not to talk number ten any more, and definitely not about Bill. I can see he's all number one." I gave her hand a propitiatory caress. 'My wise-assing aside, I've got to admit it definitely has to be some kind of achievement to get your framed pictures on a whore's dresser.' "Come on, let's go out and find something cool to do. Where do *you* like to go?"

"We can go *Nui Nho, little* mountain," she said. She was still sullen, but my contrition seemed to be having its desired effect. "It little mountain. You will like – very beautiful. We too big mountain got. But make long time go there."

"Okay," I said agreeably, " Start with the small and work up to the big."

We had to walk two blocks to fetch a Lambro. Every person I saw became immobilized from gawking at us. Ngoc had changed into one of her more soigné outfits, a jabot-fronted pants dress in opalescent fuchsia. Accessoried-out with a striped parasol and haute couture shoes suitable for strolling down a high-fashion runway, she had the look of an Asian girl trying to outdo Cher. We got so many strange stares that I felt uncomfortable to the point of danger. What were they thinking? 'Oh, there's Ngoc with a new GI. Look at Ngoc, she's really pimped out today. Yes, there's Ngoc again, getting richer still from her dissolute life, while we stay poor. We no like.'

Walking beside me, she accentuated the strut of her Pussycat Lounge haughtiness. 'Insulation against public disapproval? She flaunts it so imperiously, I won't be surprised if neighborhood toughs decide to snatch her for a little head-shaving session – and something more painful for me. Then maybe no one cares. Maybe she's just the most visible member of an organized community effort to harvest as much American cash as possible. Sure, fucking for your town or district, nation even. Ngo Thi Ngoc, femme de guerre, patriot whore. Shit, it's as plausible as the supposed bedroom antics of wayward Doughnut Dollies.'

Ngoc and I sat facing each other on the tiny benches of the Lambretta, jostling along as the 250 cc engine labored up the mountain. The road was paved but in grave disrepair, causing its small tires to slam violently into potholes and wash outs. We hunkered down trying to keep our heads from bashing into the low plastic roof.

The road had begun at Bai Truoc beach then wound a long serpentine course up the hill. The entire city spread out below us. With a steady breeze blowing in from the sea, I had to admit she'd been right; 'it very nice.' As we came around the hill, we lost sight of everything but close-in vegetation. The little vehicle putted through a tunnel of trees. My senses alerted to defensive instincts. A feeling of disquiet sharpened my awareness of being in the bush with unknown Viets, going I knew not where, unarmed. In this country, such a combination could be very unhealthy.

For seven months I'd slithered through nothing but mud and shit in equal proportions. Everywhere I went, flora existed as alien foliage that concealed my enemy, or with any luck just a home for voracious mosquitoes. Here though, an edenic garden suddenly unfolded around us. Jasmine, hibiscus and frangipani swayed in the breeze. Strong fragrances wafted, loosed by the dappled sunlight and stirred by the soft movements of air. 'Pretty damned nice.'

Ngoc instructed the driver to wait for us. We proceeded up an inviting path. Through parterres tended down to the last leaf, it presented a Vietnam I never thought existed. We meandered our way between the succulent horticulture, letting the trail take us where it might. Her hand in mine, we were like lovers.

We came up to the three jolliest Vietnamese men I'd ever met. Tapping and clinking with hammers and chisels, they were sculpting a grand relief from a large calcareous rock. Emerging like a massive tooth from its earthen gum line, a great reclining Buddha was taking shape. Half complete, they stood on mounds of chippings and beamed broadly at our arrival.

Pointing proudly at his work, one of them spoke and elicited a response from Ngoc. All three then laughed uproariously. 'Gut busting Vietnamese humor? An inside joke on the great one?'

"What're they laughing about," I asked.

"It nothing," she said with a shrug intended to make it so. I looked up at the men, still joshing each other and speaking loud enough for her to hear.

"You mean they just laugh like that for nothing? They said something about you right?"

"I not know."

"Sure you do. You both said something in Vietnamese, and they laughed at what you said."

"I say nothing."

"What?! They pointed at you. Geez-oh, Ngoc, you know, this place can make a guy pretty damned paranoid."

"I not know what is this."

"Oh no, not at all. No one said anything, ain't no-body laughing. In fact no-body's even here. I just fell in some deep-ass hole, and you're name is Alice, and this is friggin' Wonderland."

"You talk more numbah ten." I could feel icy testiness welling up in her again. 'Better back off.'

"Come on," I said soothingly. Heading toward the summit, I kept her distracted with amiable questions.

"Hey, what do you think they're building over there?"

"That for Buddha people." She pointed to the stone carving we'd just passed, then back to the construction to make the connection. "Pagoda – *Chùa Phật Nam.*"

I studied the barely begun edifice. With only two workmen in sight, they'd be at it for years. With the war, how much pagoda and Buddha-carving labor could this country afford?

"Perfect spot for it, Ngoc – a hillside looking out over a whole bunch of ocean." I swept my hand to demonstrate the broad swath of sea that stretched all the way from the north-east to the south-west.

Wide steps greeted us, and led us upward to a polished surface. At the far end, a huge vertical panel rose from a plinth of marmoreal limestone. Engravings of traditional oriental characters ran down the sides in columns. At the first step, Ngoc bade me to remove my shoes, it being de riggueur to not tread on the shiny square tiles. We went on up, she barefoot and me in socks.

"This *Tao Phùng*," she explained. "For Buddha people."

I asked her questions about the significance of different items. Given her sketchy answers, she seemed more ignorant than me. Whores weren't known for their religious devotion, but I expected that a lifetime of passive osmosis should've given her more than it had.

I understood a smidgen of Buddhist philosophy, but was totally lost when it came to the details of their practice. I pressed her to make what translations she could and with no small effort, we worked out that some of the inscriptions were a depiction of Buddha's *Four Noble Truths.*

Existence is unhappiness

Unhappiness is caused by selfishness

Unhappiness ends when selfishness ends

Selfishness can only end if one follows the Eightfold Path

The path containing *the eight* was also listed, but Ngoc's limited abilities only let us nail down, *Understanding* and *Speech.* Still, she'd taken to the task like a brain teaser and we'd had fun doing it.

Languorous in the sultry air, the scattered others paid us no mind. Slow-moving sightseers like ourselves? Worshipers in contemplative prayer? Assuming the latter, I imitated them.

One end of the area formed an elliptical overlook. We strolled to it. A stone balustrade hung over a declivity of forest and undergrowth. Over the tops of the trees, it presented a superb view of the harbor, the bay, and in the distance, a broad expanse of the South China Sea.

A wiry little guy with an oversized Polaroid slipped up alongside us. Camera bags slung at both his sides and carrying a tripod, described him as a professional. Pitching straight at Ngoc, he rattled on with more yammering than necessary for a guy who just wanted to take our picture. After only a single word from her, he began importuning me in English, but so heavily accented he might as well have stuck to raw Vietnamese. Acknowledging that I didn't understand, he pulled out a portfolio to illustrate what he was all about. In his samples, Vietnamese couples regarded each other with melodramatic affection. Creative double exposures appeared to be his specialty. Ngoc had one on her vanity, she and Bill the sheep fucker emerging from clouds of diaphanous flowers. I immediately wanted one of my own.

One after another were improperly exposed. I kept telling him to do them over, their importance rising with each one. Ngoc went from being indifferent, to admonishing the man for making her look ugly. I thought her uncharacteristic smile worth the price, but her face had come out as dark as a walnut. Over-compensating his light meter, he turned me into an albino.

More adjustments and there we were, the two of us, leaning on the balustrade, gazing out over the bay at ourselves. Framed with a radiant nimbus against an aureolent sky, our faces emerged from the heavens. Ngoc, adhering to custom, inclined her eyes to mine in a look of pure adoration, the finest silent look of acting since Clara Bow showed the world what "*It*" was. I loved it and made the guy take several more. If I was going to bring back just one souvenir of this trip, these pictures would be it. 'Mondo and his loving whore. Better still, No matter an army of guys, even whores are smitten by Mondo. Forget that. Make it, Mondo and this fine-looking honey he met at the town library, was so swept away with him that her morals had become indistinguishable from those of a whore.'

On the way back, I found myself studying the photographs. The more I stared at them, the more Ngoc's true identity faded. Rationally, she was still just a lanky whore. But our time together was morphing her into so much less of one that its relevance was blurring. The photos suffused her into just an ordinary pretty girl with whom I'd become intimate. Her pleasing face touching mine, her forehead to my cheek elicited a peculiar aesthetic. As different as we were, our implied union revealed something very new to me. I liked it a lot. Strange though that her Asian looks made the war feel so much further away.

Back from the mountain, I stopped off at the Pacific Hotel. Our encounter with the photographer had given me an idea. I picked up a 35 mm half-frame camera I'd left stowed in my bag, using the opportunity to keep up the charade of my elusive Major friend. I told her that he'd flown to Long Binh without me, but would be back in a couple of days. She received the information with a narrow gaze. I pressed on, continuing the pretense to at least appear consistent. Still not able to figure what she knew or didn't, uncertainties about her persisted.

Camera in hand, I decided to 'take advantage' of Ngoc's harlotry. The inspired artiste, I posed her every which way. The name of the game was peek-a-boo pudendum and she played it good-naturedly half in and out of items I chose from her wardrobe. The pleasure she took in the act of dressing and undressing had me wondering if it'd been the initial impulse for her taking up this line of work. Complying with every request, my little camera caught her in a score of lascivious expressions, from her usual benign unconcern, to cock-hungry invitations. 'These pics will definitely document my travelogue – crossing the globe to find *her*, the world's consummate slut. Evidence like this'll make any bar boast credible.'

CHAPTER 3

BY LATE MORNING OF THE next day, Ngoc's room shrank in direct proportion to my increasing edginess. Redundant bowls of rice began to run me down, mentally. I'd feel hungry, but thoughts of still more made the pangs go away. Ngoc brought in other things like chicken, but its unsavory aura of, *Caution-Dysentery-Ahead* was warning enough.

Ngoc herself, her body, taken as easy as my grabbing a bottle of soy sauce laid me out in a stupor. Like an old torpid dog, I continued to lie there in the heat, dozing, too worn down to move. Too bored to sit and watch me, she'd go out. When she returned I'd wake up and, *faute de mieux* fuck her again.

In the year after my car accident, Maureen contended I'd become such a hedonist that she'd begun referring to me as her 'sybarite boyfriend.' Only half in jest, it led to a serious argument and a hiatus in our relationship. She went off to be a camp counselor in Vermont. I topped that by grabbing an opportunity to do my master's thesis in Paris. Spitefully, I'd used Henry Miller as my lodestar, believing not only that pleasure was curative, but that a surfeit of it was an impossibility.

Maureen wasn't a poster child for sexual continence. She'd do it happily enough, when she'd do it, but always with a sense of reservation. It was like an invisible tether with the slack being gradually taken up. Our lovemaking had evolved into 'something to be kept *special,*' which became indistinguishable from something to be rationed out. Of course, I'd argued: "How could it ever be special, when it's inexhaustible? The more you get, the more you're getting." But her *special,* portended a kind of *Lysistrata*-esque reward, which she might offer or withhold depending on *my* actions. The dawning of this spurred my Bohemian interlude, and Lisette Duceau.

'Lisette the lorette' was ten years older than me. Instantly attracted to her give-a-shit attitude which I took to be the ultimate in cool, she was a care-free member of the 'Beat Generation' half a generation late. *Baise-moi* easy, she affected a toss-of-the-head nonchalance that made her utterly un-Maureen. I loved it and her. But she was in fact *so* easy I'd unknowingly been sharing her with others. Lisette was exactly as she appeared. The girl really didn't give a shit about anything.

The confrontation that followed my discovery was classic. Her transparent lies and my methodical disgorging of the evidence, sent her into a caterwauling rage. She berated me while I packed my things, letting me in on the secret of secrets; I was just like all Americans, '*Shit!*' Instead of inflaming matters, I'd just mused over how it all really *had* been *my fault.* I'd shacked up with an alley cat and been mystified when she'd turned out to be one. Laying out my callow foolishness for self-examination left me wiser. And with a bruised conscience, I'd returned to Maureen's fidelity and quasi-continence.

'How does Ngoc figure into all this? Unless measured on some kind of prurience meter, she doesn't. Conditions? There aren't any. I want, I reach, I take. The problem is, the insistence of her open slit and my cross-eyed hunger for it is waning. This bothers me. When've *I* ever experienced satiation?'

I swung my feet to the floor. My body in the vertical seemed a better complement to the stoic side of my personality, the side that'd brought me to a military life. I needed to get back in tune with it, but I felt like Dorian Grey anguishing over the wages of sin. 'Wilde said that the only way to get rid of temptation was to yield to it. Sure, look where it got him. Maybe I've done more than just yield. Have I driven my libido down into minus numbers? Which side of my nature is in charge?'

'Ngoc has grabbed me with more than just temptation. What satiation? Her pussy's a sucking vortex. I'm powerless to escape it. Why?! My weakness? Her whatever it is? Anthony Burgess' *vagina d'être?* I don't know what the hell he might've meant, but I know I'm in one! Is this what quenching the unquenchable is? And if you do, could it be permanent?'

I'd read the philosophy of Hefner in its entirety, unfolding a couple dozen Playmates in the process. Collectively, they told me that you couldn't get too much. But here I had the real, in-the-flesh reality lying right on the bed next to me, saying you could. 'What's the truth of it?'

I reposed again, taciturn with my thoughts. Not wanting to slide into another preposterous dialogue with Ngoc, and with the worm of boredom gnawing at my insides, I roused myself to get us moving.

"Hey Ngoc, isn't there a place down by the ocean we can go? When I was at the hotel, I read about an American USO deal out there – you know at the beach."

"Yah, I go before there. Name, *Bãi Trước.*"

"Well, you're going to go to ol' Bai what's-its-name again. Come on, I'll buy you a decent meal – like we'll chop-chop some real food, right?" I supposed that others had wanted to go to the beach with her too and had. But outside of Billy Boy and the Camaro Kid, she'd been good about sparing me any of those vignettes.

Again in the rattling, jouncing rear of a Lambro, we trundled through the middle of the city. I was finally able to develop a sense of its geography. The peninsula of Vung Tàu was more like an island. A huge mangrove swamp had connected it to the mainland, but a massive swath had been defoliated to eliminate it as an enemy sanctuary. This made it as secure a place as any in the country.

Arvin vehicles rumbled through the streets without concern for security, either because this was a model of pacification or their basecamp in the center of town making it so. With my VC thinking cap on, complacency always struck me as an invitation, but the lack of 'incidents' spoke louder.

I decided to pose Ngoc in the back of the Lambro, right in the downtown center. Coaxing her cooperation in the dense traffic wasn't easy, but since a whore's modesty seemed a contradiction, I took her reluctance as a challenge. Following some spirited cajoling, she wistfully positioned one leg on the bench and hiked up her dress. Perfect, a screaming beaver, rampant in midday traffic. Her beguiling expression of blasé indifference to the bustling thoroughfare around us, made the picture. That drew the frame counter to 68. I could only take seventy-two, so I decided to hold the rest for my next artistic brainstorm.

A mile or so down a dismal coast road, we hauled in at our first stop, a quasi-PX snack bar. Even without its chintzy presence, the area could hardly be described as 'the San Tropez of East Asia.' The joint seemed so far removed from Vietnam that I didn't think you could go this far into the rear and still be in-country. It served its singular mission well, so I provisioned our table with cold cans of Hamm's beer and a whole basket of fried chicken. Ngoc didn't drink beer, and only ate one piece, while watching me tear through half a dozen, plus a mountain of French fries. The straight rice thing had me so empty I felt disassociated from my own stomach, an excuse for taking gluttony to the brink of nausea.

GIs sat scattered among the other tables. In-between bites, I gave them quick look-overs. Slumped and sprawled in a torpid occupation of their chairs, they studied us. Whatever it was they saw was the topic of their desultory exchanges. Each time they took a slug of beer, they glanced at us, natural given there weren't any other girls in the place. 'Curious about how I've managed to have gotten one? I hoped we don't have troops that stupid. Ngoc's snooty un-Vietnamese attitude and high fashion clothes would alone account for it. Maybe they think I'm some sort of free-lance photographer who's dropped by the Nam to check out this whole sick war scene – and brought along his chick for a gas.'

Farther down the beach, Ngoc led me to an old villa. Anything pre-U S Army seemed to have a quaint, *fin de siècle* quality about it, old-world colonial enough that they could be the setting for some period movie.

Inside the low stucco building, we entered a large dank room. It smelled of mildew in a heavy salt-imbued humidity. Leprous paint decorated the ceiling, giving preview to crumbling masonry. A long bare counter ran along one end, with a stark emptiness packing out the rest of the place.

"You an American?" I asked, as much from the Hawaiian shirt as from his looks. He'd emerged from a back room as soon as we'd come in and was standing, arms folded, behind the counter.

"Yeah, what'd ya think?"

"I guess I didn't," I said, taken aback by his sharp gruff response. "I wasn't sure what to expect when I came in here. You could have been an Aussie."

"If I was, I wouldn't be here now would I?"

"Hell," I said shrugging my shoulders, "I don't know. Their base is right up the road"

"Well that's where I'd be then."

"Okay," I said.

"So now that we got that settled – you want to rent a bathing suit?"

"Yeah, my girlfriend here says that's what we're doing."

"So that's what she is, huh?"

"She's a girl, right? And at the moment, she's the only friend I have."

"Then mister, maybe you just ain't got no friends at all." Taking pleasure in that crack, he gave me a perverse grin and tossed a pair of trunks onto the counter. "That'll be four bucks."

"Geez," I said. "You can buy brand new ones for three."

"Why don't you go right ahead and buy them then. Don't forget, the closest PX that's got 'em is in fucking Subic Bay."

I pushed the money toward him and then opened the trunks and pulled out the lining.

"You expecting crabs to jump out at you?" he asked.

"Just checking... to see if they had a lining."

"Being a bathing suit, of course they do. And there ain't no crabs, cuz Mamma-san washes 'em real good – right after they're used."

"They look all right," I conceded.

"Well, keep em that way and don't go shootin' your load off in 'em."

"I'll, ah, make it a point," I said, intoning half as much sarcasm as I'd intended. "By the way, what is it you do here – I mean, are you in the army – like is this your goddang job?"

"I live here – U S Army retired."

"You've got to be shitting me– you can do that here – take an 'In-country Out' in a war zone?"

"I'm doing it, ain't I?" he said tersely, proud of the accomplishment.

"You gotta be the only one."

"Maybe I am, maybe I ain't. I don't rightly know. When the judge took my whole retirement check and handed it over to my ex-wife, I figured there weren't no sense in going back."

"You lost the whole thing?"

"All but twenty-six bucks a month. A retired staff sergeant don't start with a whole hell-of-a lot. She got enough to keep her and her boy friend in a nice new trailer. Anyways, I figure if I went back, I'd wind up shooting both of 'em. Only question was which one I'd take out first. Now if you don't mind, I got work to do."

Ngoc had brought her own bathing suit, a pale yellow two piece, which she'd put on while I was talking. She looked good, despite her small breasts and narrow-ish hips. I would not be embarrassed to be seen with her, not here, or anywhere.

We went outside and stood on the patio. I studied her. She gave me her usual disinterested smile and looked out on the sea, to that far-away line where it ended and became sky. A humid off-shore breeze fluttered strands of her long brown hair. I watched it swish the tresses across her back. Subtly, her lanky body moved with it, as if in a soft dance to unheard music. She was a strange one.

Watching her face, I wondered what might be going on in her mind. Sometimes that detached look seemed infinitely remote. Was it a kind of self-imposed isolation, a dissociation from what it was she did? I was probably contributing to it and it bothered me that it mattered. She was a whore. A whore was to have unqualified sex with. But when I noticed those fathomless looks and the abyssal thoughts behind them, they made me feel sad. I wanted her to tell me what her life had been like and how she'd come to such a trade, a trade on my weaknesses. But, I couldn't get a handle on how to broach such a clichéd question. Whatever... she'd made her choices. And good for me that she had.

Another Vietnamese girl in a bathing suit came out. She and Ngoc chatted warmly. They obviously knew each other. Blinking noticeably in the bright sun, I supposed she was a fellow denizen of the night, even though her nondescript body and roundish face didn't strike me as all that saleable. I expected she'd find herself with quite a few hooker's holidays.

The three of us walked down to the water's edge and waded in. Small tepid waves lapped at our legs. I tried to inspect the sandy bottom ahead, but the water was semi-opaque, the tinged with the brown of a billion dissolved turds. The same dirty color extended out several miles, half way to the horizon before finally becoming a sun-glinted viridian. The Saigon River that mighty left arm of the Mekong was ramming enough silt laden water into the South China Sea to keep the entire blue-green ocean at bay. Off to our right about a mile out, a US Navy destroyer lay at anchor.

Despite my reservations about swimming in this warm fecal bath, I followed the two in. 'What the hell – out in the bush, I'd plunge without hesitation into neck deep canals that're a lot closer to excremental sludge than this murky sea water.'

We stopped when it was chest deep. It was nearly up to the shorter girl's neck. They talked about God knows what in Vietnamese, while I watched the water splash around their bodies.

Suddenly, both girls began screaming out in pain and alarm. From a few yards away, I looked at their anguished faces as they excitedly pointed at the water. In a frenzy, they pushed themselves back toward the shore. Not needing to see gliding shark fins or the rearing tentacles of a giant squid, I bolted after them. Swimming madly for a dozen strokes, I came to my feet in waist-deep water. A body length ahead of them, I glanced back for some clue to their distress. As I did, a small wave welled up on my torso. The ocean had become one-third sea water and two-thirds jellyfish. High-stepping it in horror-propelled strides, I thundered out onto the beach with an explosion of slimy globs and foam.

The girls were right behind me, alternately whining and wailing as they vigorously rubbed their stings. I tried to console Ngoc, but was ineffectual as she fussed over a couple of fast-reddening weals on her thigh and calf. I wasn't sure if the marks came from the stings or her grinding them with wet sand. Her friend had taken the worst of it. Her short stature let them get her around the midsection. She had six or seven welts and a look of acute distress. She whimpered something then on very shaky legs, hustled herself back toward the villa.

"You no get?" Ngoc asked. Not knowing the word, she pointed to my unscathed body. I raised my arms to present a bite-free view.

"No way. Those fuckers are just another Vietnamese group that doesn't like Americans."

"They no like – why you no get beaucoup more?" she asked.

"Well, they don't like how I taste – and just stay the hell away, that's all. Yeah, especially with me being full of vim and vinegar."

"I think when they no like they make more bite." She made an ugly face and formed her fingers into surrogate tentacles stinging my arm, less a joke than a demonstration for me to get her point. "I get. You must get. Vietnam must not make bad for me – then make nothing for you. No good I think."

"Okay, okay, it's only paradoxical, not geo-political. Just forget it. I don't know what these fuckers think in Narragansett Bay, much less here." She ignored me and stood up, straightening to her full height. Distracted, she looked out at the sea with a vague, ulterior gaze. "They don't even have any brains, I said superfluously, my own mind going back to a day when I was twelve years old. One scorching summer's afternoon, I was fishing off of a dock on the lee side of Jamestown Island. Out of boredom, I'd scooped up a jellyfish and laid the glob on a griddle-hot plank nearby.

I passed the next several hours watching boats with an eye for unattainable teen-aged girls and helping a friend try to start his ancient outboard motor with its non-retracting pull cord. Then I caught a fish and noticed what remained of my jellyfish. The sun had baked it to a mere mark on the wood. I had to look at it from just the right angle to see where it'd been. So there was the proof. Jellyfish were made of water and something as close to nothing as you could get.

"I no more feel these," Ngoc whispered, as if having willed away the pain just to spite me.

"Hey great!" I said, taking advantage of the moment, and re-validating my childhood belief that jellyfish were mostly made of nothing. "I thought those bites'd get better pretty fast. How 'bout we go down there. I want to see what those guys are up to." I pointed to four navy types about two hundred meters away.

Just beyond the high tide line, they appeared to be working with a large piece of equipment. Without a word, Ngoc began walking toward them. She limped so I knew the stings still hurt. Our silly conversation had deadened the mood again, but I took her acquiescence as a positive.

"What you guys up to?" I asked, looking over their heavy steel cased machine.

"We're measuring wave motion."

"So you found out they move up and down huh?"

"Yeah," he said, with the depth of condescension reserved for such comments.

On top of the machine, I watched a metal arm scribing an irregular zigzag line along a slow moving roll of graph paper. From the bottom, a fat cable emerged and ran down the beach, disappearing into the water. It lay on a line that headed straight for the destroyer. I couldn't tell whether it went along the sea bottom all the way to the ship, or just twenty feet out.

"All right, so I dig that waves are of some special significance to the navy." I looked out over the silty brown sea, searching for something familiar. Sailboats? Sea birds? There were none. Dung-stained waves curled and collapsed in a heedless splashing against the shore.

Of the four sailors, two were wearing unzipped wet suit tops. Those two stood closer to the water, ankle deep when each new wave ran up onto the wet sand. They stared at Ngoc. They had from the moment we'd come up on them. She lingered back a few feet behind a pile of frogman gear. Demure, if not bashful, she seemed in stark retreat from the hoydenish character I'd been with. I went back to her.

"Your leg still bothering you?" She looked down at the reddened marks and I stooped to get a better look. "I don't know how long it'll last – I never got... Oh forget it. Come on." I took her by the hand and led her down to the monitoring equipment. I wanted to take a stab at explaining their doings to her, in the hope that she wouldn't just assume this was the 1969 version of Emperor Ming's Death Ray. In the context of my war, measuring little ocean waves struck me as being as useful as screen doors on a submarine.

The two sailors who were operating the thing gawked at her along with the others, while looking like they were tending a machine that was content to trundle along on its own. Between furtive glances, one sailor watched his EKG of the sea piling into a bin, while the other pretended it was his job to keep an eye on calibrations.

The two wet suits became attracted to the foam around their legs. When the surf sucked back into the concave of another little breaker, I saw it too. A greenish eel-like creature tumbled forward. Crashing water shoved it ahead on the sand. It squirmed with a strange gimpy movement, writhing and ill- suited to its new environment. Without an eel's hyper-flexibility or a snake's effortless belly-slither, it tried to hump and flip itself back toward deep water. One of the wet suits sloshed over and picked it up.

"Hey! What the hell is this thing? It's weird – half eel and half snake." It wriggled and twisted in his grasp as he carried it toward us. "Check this out – critter's shaped like an eel but got no fins or gills. The skin's not slimy or scaly – kind of soft and rubbery."

"Fucking gook snake, that's all," said one of the others. "It's gotta be weird if it comes from around here."

I studied it from several feet away. Out of the water and up close, its color looked black with a yellowish belly. I took an instinctive step back.

"You better get rid of that thing before you get bitten," I said in alarm. "It's a goddamn sea snake!"

"Like I got it that it ain't no pond snake, man. This here's the South China-mother-fuckin' Sea you know!" He pulled on its flattened tail and stretched it to nearly a three foot length.

"They're *deadly* poisonous!" I warned.

"You think I'm afraid of poison snakes – rattlers, moccasins, copperheads? They don't faze me none. In Alabama, they come a lot bigger than this guy. He ain't even got fangs like they got."

"Not all poisonous snakes have fangs, I said. "I tell you that son of a bitch is beau coup poison – way more than anything back home. Doesn't the Navy teach you guys about shit like sea snakes before they let you do all that Mike Nelson stuff?"

"Shit. I sure as hell know more about the ocean than some ground-pounding army dude."

"I don't know about ground," said one of the others, "but I'd say he's been pounding something."

"Alls I know of is Cecil the sea serpent," another of them guffawed. "Like alls they did up at Great Lakes was show us cartoons for our training."

"Yeah," said the other, "that's it. It's my little buddy Cecil, come home to 'ol Beanie."

The snake squirmed with persistent determination. It extruded itself through his fist. No longer held directly behind the head, it used the additional couple of inches it'd gained to whip back and forth, the tiny mouth snapping at the air around it. Then the body doubled back on itself and pushed against the heel of the guy's hand. This action drew its head down inside his fist. I watched him fixedly as he readjusted his grip and tried to secure its head again. Somehow though, it bit him.

"Ahhhh!" he yelled jumping back, the snake's razor-sharp teeth still clamped to the soft flesh between his thumb and forefinger. He swung his hand up and down several times in a vain attempt to shake it free. Cursing vehemently, he whipped its whole length over his head and walloped it into the sand. It broke loose.

"Fucking bastard!" he rasped. "Looked like it didn't even have any teeth at all – but them bitty jaws got some power!" One of his companions pulled out a sheath knife and chopped the snake, first in half, then into quarters.

"Die you little fucker, die!" The pieces twitched and flipped on their own. He gave each of them more hacks.

"Ain't no fuckin' biggie – barely went through my skin." Massaging the bite mark made blood run out. He sucked at it and spit, in the stoic manner of a snakebite victim in a cowboy movie. "I'll wash it off with salt water, that's good for lots of stuff… not even stingin' or nothin'."

"Hey!" I yelled. "You've got to do more than that – like put a tourniquet on your arm. Right away!" His frogman partner inspected the bite then followed him down to the water. Ngoc and the guy with the knife remained oblivious, fixed to the fading spasms of half a dozen snake chunks. I went down after the two frogmen. As I got there, he began a concentrated clearing of his throat.

"Hey Rick, you all right?!" one of them asked.

"Yeah, I'm just trying to hawker up something. This fuckin little bite ain't gonna make me cough."

"You shouldn't wash it in this water," his helper advised. "You could get some kind of weird-ass infection."

"Maybe you're right. What's weird though, is my eyelids. They want to shut and I don't even feel tired at all. How can that have anything to do with this here?"

I hustled back up to the equipment. "Who can you get on that radio?" I asked.

"The ship."

"Get them on the horn," I commanded. "They need to call somewhere for a dustoff."

"Dustoff? They can send the launch. We've got a pharmacist's mate on board."

"Like he's got all kinds of different antidotes for exotic toxins? You fucking numskull! He needs a dustoff to get him to a hospital. Immediately!"

"Hey, eat shit you mother fucker," the guy snapped. "We don't need you telling us what to do."

The three others came back to the equipment. Mr. Frogman was looking pretty bleak.

"I feel all right," he gasped, "but it's sort of getting hard to breathe. Maybe it really was a little poison. Hey Ron, did you call the ship? I'd better lie down."

"Shit man, it's probably some kind of neurotoxin. Give me the phone!" I growled, reaching for the handset. He pulled it away from my grasp. "I'm an officer damn it."

"Sure you are. Aye-aye Mister Beach Blanket. I already called and they're going to come in with the ship's boat as soon as they can get under way."

"You stupid fuckin' dumbass," I snapped, "He can't wait. If he's gonna be taken back to that ship, he'll be done for."

"Oh yeah," he derided, "I forgot you're the big ocean expert. Well, sailors can take care of their own too you know."

"I'm gonna have your ass for this," I said, having no knowledge of how I ever could. I turned and motioned Ngoc to come along.

We hurried back to the villa. I went straight for my pal, the sarge and found him same as before, standing arms folded in the doorway of the room behind the counter.

"One of those sailors just got his ass bitten by a sea snake. Is there any way we can get help?"

"Not from here," he said languidly. "Can't they call for their own help?" I heard his tone, and his message was the same either way. It was a stupid question. The chances of finding a phone here were exactly zero.

"They did, but they don't know what the fuck they're doing. Besides, they only have commo with their ship."

"Well, that ship'll have more than this fuckin' piss-hole beach."

"Don't count on it." The snack bar would have a military line, but it was a half mile up the road. There wasn't a Lambro in sight. 'And who the hell would I call, the USO?'

Feeling defeated, I went back out to the patio and looked down the beach. The guy was supine on the sand. The three others just stood beside him, watching. I squinted in the glare. Along side the destroyer, I made out some activity on a small launch. It looked to be a case of too little - too late, with my actions playing out as, nothing, never.

I walked over to one of the deck chairs and pulled off my bathing suit. While putting on my clothes, it struck me that there was nothing else left on the chair.

"Hey goddamn it!" I roared. "Where's my fuckin camera?!" I stormed back inside. "My camera! I rolled it up with my shirt and pants – and left it on that chair over there. It's gone!" I pointed toward the patio to indicate that it was on his premises that it had disappeared.

"Must have been one of the kids that stole-it. They'll take anything that ain't nailed down. Even then, I wouldn't bet against them."

"Why the fuck didn't you tell me that slicky-boys were prowling your place?!"

"You wanted a bathing suit. I don't recall you asking for me to baby-sit your stuff. Besides, if I did that, it's all I'd ever do."

"You could have fucking warned me!" I yelled. "I'm you're only goddam customer."

"Do I need to remind you that this is Vietnam?" He muttered, bending down behind the counter. "They're everywhere." He waved his hand to imply that they were outside, surrounding the place. "First thing you learn when you get here is hang on to your stuff. Guess you don't learn so good, huh?"

My insides felt hot and bulging as if from steam pressure.

"Like everybody else who's keeping these kids in business," he snorted, "you just gotta go on to the PX and buy you another."

"I don't want *another* camera," I said in a measured tone. The undeveloped pictures of Ngoc leapt into my mind, instantly gaining the value of lost art. The thought of picking up a new one and restaging my photo shoot seemed so inconceivably tedious that its likelihood evaporated. "I want *that one*!"

Without saying anything, he snatched the trunks from the counter and dropped them into a reed basket. His silence inflamed my frustration. Then I remembered what was on my film, which really got me going.

The first six exposures had been taken in the field three weeks earlier and been sitting in the camera ever since. One of them had been of Prine, PFC Allen Prine, KIA. I'd taken it on the morning of the day he'd been killed. I'd never seen the photos, but his death branded that view-finder's image on my brain.

Keneally had already sent an official letter of condolence to his family, but I'd been deliberating over whether to send them that picture of him when I got the roll developed. Would his parents want a last minute photo of him? Would they treasure him as a soldier sitting with his buddy Newquist on that paddy dike? Or would they recoil in horror, failing to escape the synchrony of the soldier and his imminent fate? I hadn't decided what I'd do and hadn't touched the camera until this trip. It infuriated me that some thieving slicky-boy was deciding the issue.

"Look Sarge," I hissed, whamming my fist on the counter. "You know who those kids are. They live right around here – surveilling your patio – watching for unsuspecting guys like me. We're easy pickings, and it's your goddamn fault! You get their little asses in here. Then we'll find out who took it."

He slipped his hand under the Hawaiian shirt and pulled a .45 from his waistband, then pointed it straight at my chest.

"Yeah, well, I don't rightly give a shit. Because it's time you and your whore hit the fuckin road."

I stared fixedly at the muzzle, trying to quiet an overpowering rage. The chances were low he'd keep a round in the chamber while carrying it under his belt. I previewed grabbing the pistol with both hands. Overpowering his single arm I could pull it over the edge of the counter. Then pushing down, I'd break his grip. He'd only be able to pound his free fist into my back or head. No problem, the gun would drop to the floor and the counter between us, it'd be over.

That its hammer was at half-cock, resolved the issue. It did have a chambered round. I'd be grabbing it just as he thumbed the hammer the rest of the way back. Jerking backwards as he did, would nicely align the muzzle with my belly button. The vision of that possibility, led me to nod my acquiescence. I grasped Ngoc by the arm and headed for the door.

CHAPTER 4

THE ATMOSPHERE IN NGOC'S APARTMENT felt more stultifying than ever. A late afternoon rain pelted the roofs outside, stirring only a minimal breeze. The air that did move just drew in more pot smoke from the other room. Blending with the thick humidity, it enervated both of us. I drank beer out of boredom. That increased my lassitude to the point where I assumed the torpor of a guy who'd been bitten by one of those sea snakes.

I'd anticipated this room becoming an idyllic refuge, from which we'd go out here and there then come back from an enjoyable day, refreshed and ready for a nice new round of copulation. So, we'd tried the mountain and the beach, and come back. The refreshed and ready part had turned into physical and psychic depletion. We hadn't done it in eight hours, but it felt like only eight minutes. Something had to be wrong, but what?

Compulsory screwing topped my list. I walked myself back through what I knew. She was a whore and screwing was what she did. It was her career, her chosen profession. As for me, 'the insentient jizz machine' as Maureen put it, gave me a mandate for screwing. Okay. So was she, like me, pondering some existential malaise? Doubtful. Was she wondering when I'd ever get up and say goodbye? Probably not. My staying for a week instead of a few days would be more profitable for her. Sure-fire money had to trump lulls in business. Enticing me to stay seemed her best bet, but that was not what I was sensing.

Was it me? How different was I from others? Ground-pawing and snorting-fresh from the woods, with a full rack of antlers, my blood may have been higher than most. I had no way of knowing, but hey, didn't Camaro-guy just do it once? I hadn't come to Vung Tau for a tour of the local landmarks. Too many nights in a nimbus of mosquitoes and cheating death on a score of occasions had run my battlefield adrenaline down below the red line. That'd brought me here, to fuck to the point of insensibility. 'How will I know when I am there? When I yearn to be back in the field? Well, I sure as hell don't have that feeling yet.'

Ngoc sat motionless on the stool in front of her vanity, staring at the photos we'd taken up on the mountain. I moped on the bed watching her with a curious mix of languor and peevishness. Struggling to justify my staying any longer, I mused over saying goodbye and hitting the bars again. The sexual provender synonymous with this town would guarantee me new possibilities. Maybe the carnal sampler of yum-yum girls displayed for the taking would stir my ebbing appetite.

'Is my wanting to understand Ngoc that outlandish? It is after all, a *hearts and minds* thing. I deeply believe in the concept, so why not her as an object lesson in its workability? I can't see myself just leaving.'

We'd had redundant love-making without love. But the acts of lying in each other's arms, bathing, and dressing had created inescapable intimacy. The more it looked like it, the more it *should* feel like it.

'I know *the deal.* At the end, I'm supposed to discard Ngoc and walk away. But every time I think to do it, something tells me I shouldn't. Why? I'm finished with Ngoc. It's just that every time I catch her vacant ennui, that constant *la petite mort,* I can't pull away. I can't be just another American bastard, the sum total of all who'd preceded me.'

Before coming to Vung Tàu, I'd entertained a Shangri La image of me and some Vietnamese girl making love. I'd thought of the characters Fowler and Phuong in Greene's, *The Quiet American.* Fowler's treatment of her distilled my interactions with Ngoc into one pure thought; I did not want to be seen as an *Ugly American.* I'd read *that* novel too, didactic crap that it was, forced on me by a high school teacher who believed that all Americans were ugly, except those select few who were as enlightened as he was.

'I'm not going to be seen as *ugly.* It doesn't matter how amoral Ngoc is, or how many boorish louts she's chanced across. I want her to know that ***I*** do care about her. Damn Ausie Bill got all the way into her heart! His lie will catch up with him. Americans aren't the *only* ones in this world who can be ugly. Hell, we're the only ones who go and die to help others. To help Ngoc, all I have is this small room and two options. I can make it worse or I can make it better.'

While I lay on the bed, a vision of the Navy dolt with the sea snake kept running through my mind. Long into respiratory arrest and coma, he'd be dead by now.

"Hey Ngoc," I said petulantly. "What'd you think about that dude who got bit by the snake? Pretty dumb, huh? I'll bet you he's croaked by now."

"I think Vietnam bad for American."

"Beau coup bad for that guy. Put this in your notebook. Any time you go home in a box, it's bad."

"You say Vietnam sea no like American?" she posited, her tone becoming more dismal. "Nothing want bite."

"Right, forget everything I said. What the hell do I know about anthropomorphic politics? Maybe jellyfish are one thing and sea snakes are something else – communists maybe. Yeah, jelly fish are our allies and sea snakes have taken up with the Reds. Every living thing's making an alliance. You can betcha-ass I'm keeping an eye out for the cockroaches."

Silence ensued. She toyed pensively with a curious item that had been lying on the vanity since I'd arrived. Along the way, I'd inspected it, but had neglected to ask what the hell it was for. A kind of metal tipped ferule, it was also scepter-like, with the top end sprouting a dragon-headed ormolu. Staring at the pictures of Aussie Bill, she twitched it back and forth in front of her face like a wand. His fixed gaze looked back at the brassy moving head as if watching a tiny puppet theater.

"Beau coup American die in Vietnam," she intoned. "Very many." I wanted to agree and to add the fact that our death count was only a small fraction of dead communists', but the tone of her voice stopped me. It emanated from down in her chest. Level and low, it lacked her normal rhythm, the difference measured in foreboding. I didn't like it at all. Although I'd been feeling enough indifference for the both of us, her inflection coated our reason for returning with a layer of ice. Ngoc's rueful disaffection was edging into an agitated despondency, redoubling my need to make it all better. By comparison, two days ago she'd seemed almost joyful. I couldn't see myself leaving her dispirited and unhappy on account of *me*, with my self-centeredness creating this desolate state in her. Since I was the one responsible, I had to release it somehow.

"Geez Ngoc, I don't want to talk about communists and people dying. It makes me sad – you too. Come on, we don't have to fuck now. Let's go out again – like somewhere decent. Let's have some fun. How 'bout we go to the most expensive joint in Vung Tàu – a real Vietnamese place." She said nothing and kept looking down at the stationary brass dragon. "Your favorite place... and it'd be really nice if you'd put on that silk dress you showed me this morning, the red one you liked so much. Remember, I've never seen you in it, but I sure would like to." Her head rose from its dilatory sulk. She gave me a nod and got up.

The club, or 'crub,' as Ngoc referred to it, was on the second floor above some indiscernible enterprises. It blared out at us as someone opened the door, nearly as dark inside as out. All I could see was one member of the band, a Vietnamese dude with a sax. Swinging his tenor back and forth in wide arcs, he mimicked the overwrought antics of Joe Houston. With bulging cheeks and closed eyes, he blew a wailing tribute to everything that was raunch.

Edging our way between patrons, we moved to an empty table on the far side. All the while, 'Wild Man' Nguyen honked up a storm. I stopped to watch. He hauled his outsized instrument up over his head, then, bending himself backwards, he sank slowly to his knees. Raspy juke joint notes jerked and stuttered in a parody of strip club bump and grind. I wondered where he'd come by his influences. Vietnam might have plenty of prostitution, but was far too modest for strippers.

As if oblivious to him, the sidemen on electric guitar, bass, and drums, whanged and thumped along in another style entirely. Duane Eddy imitators, they rocked with a garage full of junior high exuberance and about as much skill. If Eddy's twangy sound was the thing, Mr. Lead worked his vibrato stick like it was the *only thing*.

We sat down and ordered drinks. I made another hopeful check of the place. I'd been right the first time, no Americans. There were no other females present, except an older woman in a purple áo dài who looked as though she might be the owner's wife. Trying to make Ngoc feel better, I'd asked her to bring me to a Vietnamese place. I wasn't sure what I'd had in mind, but this wasn't it.

Everywhere I looked, I saw the dour faces of young Vietnamese men. Steadily, they watched my every move, their faces surly in the dim light. Their glowering eyes goaded my paranoia like the jab of a fire-hardened bamboo punji. The length and style of their hair told me they weren't off-duty Arvin military, so who the hell were they?

Self- consciously, I studied the label on my beer can in an out of focus sort of way, increasingly forewarned that Schlitz was now produced by the Mickey Finn Brewing Company. I took a small sip, apprehending the kick of a colorless, odorless, tasteless drug. Nearby, a couple of slick-looking dudes eyed me with a knowing anticipation. 'My keeling over's imminent?'

"Hey Ngoc, this place ain't quite cuttin' it."

"You no like Vietnamese bar? This, number one in Vung Tàu. You say you want."

"Yeah I know, but it's like – kind of weird." I slid my beer away and toward the side edge of the table. "You think they got any black market Mateus in here – like Mateus wine? I just got me a wicked-ass, all-of-a-sudden hankering for vino."

"No do this black market – no here."

"Okay so, honest-as-the-day-is-long Mateus then. We've shipped enough of that stuff into this country for it to find its way to all sorts of places. If it's here, I want some. And I want to take the cork out myself." I thumbed myself in the chest and did a screwing motion with my hands to communicate above the music. "Wine. Name *Mah-toose.* You get it?"

"You think beer get bad thing in? – make go..." she cocked her head to one side and closed her eyes. "Go very much sreep."

"Now where would you ever get a crazy idea like that? No, it's just that this place is getting me into a wine mood. In America, it's considered to be very romantic to pull the cork out yourself – very symbolic, pulling it out and sticking it back in. In and out – very romantic – sensual even. Some'd call it depraved."

"I think you wan-make bottle out, because you think Vietnamese numbah ten."

"Don't fault me for staying on my toes," I said. A lot of Viets do plenty number ten, you know. I've been an eyewitness to a whole bunch. And quit saying, *Vietnamese* – like it was how I feel about all of you – because I don't." I looked left, then right, assigning the movement of my head to our immediate company. "You've got to admit, these dudes in here could make anybody a little up tight. – jumpy, you know?"

"I see nothing what you see."

"You wouldn't see anything out of place if they were all half-naked VC sappers with satchel charges slung front and back. Do one thing, agree with me that this friggin' band is straight out of the goddamn Twilight Zone."

"Yes, I think they numbah ten. All American song."

"Well, he's singing them in Vietnamese."

"In Vietnam word, song make dinky dow."

"I can imagine. But they can sound pretty dinky-ass-nonsensical in English too. You want to get on that wine?"

She called the waiter over. Their discussion generated a deeper scowl as he retrieved the beer. This made me want to keep even closer tabs on my audience. Their malign expressions didn't seem to be getting any worse, but they were already bad enough. 'They're looking at me like I'd scarfed up their head dude's girl and brought her in to drink and gloat right in front of them. Maybe it's worse; I'm smack in the middle of the Victor Charles Club, guilelessly showing off the local party honcho's niece, the very one I'd been royally fucking for all to see. Funny how they're stringing me along. Of course, in their own sweet time they'll put an end to it, no doubt a highly relevant moment for me.'

I'd come here with the idea of casually working on a buzz. Having a couple sideways arguments with Ngoc, getting my camera swiped by some piss-ant kid, getting pushed around by some renegade pogue NCO, and watching that hapless dude buy the farm over, of all things, a sea snake, made for a day that certainly deserved a buzz. A day like today rated the hard stuff, but in here, it'd be total nutso to even think of it.

The bottle of Mateus arrived unceremoniously. I yanked the cork out as if it'd been greased. Swilling down the first tart glass like it'd been water, I began refilling it, self-satisfied. My stomach warmed to it and malignant feelings of my own bloomed out into my limbs.

"This drink maybe no good for you," she said.

"I think it's damned, goddamn good," I retorted. "Yeah, you just can't beat yer-ol' frizzante rosé."

"Wine make all GI very bad."

"Depends on what you mean by bad. It didn't help the French. They drink wine up the wahzoo, and they could have used a lot more *bad*. Not Aussies though, huh?! Don't tell me 'ol Bill didn't get crawlin'-ass drunk a time or two. You want a lesson in getting shit-faced? You just hang out with some Ausies, one time."

"No, Bill very nice – drink only Vietnam tea."

"Yeah right, and I'll bet he spent a lot of time sitting on that toilet of yours, with the kung fu shits. That stuff's famous for bringing 'em on."

"No, he get not so many."

"The guy sounds like a winner then... a real winner."

"Tee-tee time, Bill come Vung Tàu – take me to him home where he live."

"Yeah, you already told me. I want to tell you though, get ready for a surprise when you roll into Aussie-ville and meet his kith and kin – like his family." She nodded, imagining such a moment. "That is, if you ever get there." I said the words under my breath as I drew the glass to my mouth. I glugged down another good gulp of the warm rosé.

"You think him family no like Vietnamese girl?"

"Damned if I know. There're a lot of Asian people in Australia – lots of different folks there." I mused over how he'd go about the task of introducing her as some kind of war trophy, and then how much harder it'd be to conceal the fact that she was as well broken in as Yogi's catcher's mitt. I could hear Ausie Bill's mom now; 'Ngoc, Bill tells me that back in Vietnam you used to work at a place called the Pussy Cat Lounge, as a whore. My goodness, that sounds so interesting. Why don't you tell us all what that was like.'

"Hey Ngoc, I hate to piss in your picnic basket, but I got a feeling that dear ol' Billy Boy ain't-a-comin' back. In case you haven't noticed, we're all getting ready to leave this pastoral paradise. My first unit has already been gone for three months."

"I know all go. And then he come." She spoke with a touch of disdain, for my prediction.

"Sure," I scoffed, "but make get ready for the NVA first – by the way, what new line of work are you looking at taking up when they get here? Something a bit more agricultural perhaps? You'll probably wind up the merry maid of your very own, state-owned, collectivized rice paddy. It could be a nice change from indoor work."

"VC do nothing to me."

"Maybe. Maybe not. But I expect your present job will be on the line."

"Job?"

"Yeah, what you do for money. Your occupation – your métier. You know, my job is soldier. Your job is..."

"Yes, I know this I do," she said contemptuously. "Your job – kill Vietnamese people. I kill no American. You know what I do – I do you beau coup."

"Some might say we're even. Yeah, back in the World, they say *'make love, not war.'* What the hell, I've decided to do both... waste Commies, and fuck pretty girls." The comment didn't faze her. She took a tiny sip of her drink. "Look, I was just wondering what'll happen to you when it's all over. I don't know, maybe the VC won't bag this place. Maybe we'll prevail and there'll be enough of us Americans left for you to still make a go of it."

"You think I must stay always with GI?!"

"No, time will take care of that. I'm sorry Ngoc, I know you're missing some of what I'm trying to say, but I'm only telling you what I see. What've you got here? Look around, outside this town – you go from mid-twentieth century to damn-near the stoneage in a couple of klicks. I don't mean to speak bad of this country – in a hell-of-a-lot of ways it's downright beautiful, the people too – and sometimes so weird, it's far-out cool. But looking at the way you live, with that apartment and all, I don't think you're ready to do the rice paddy bit. You're a city girl – and like – those pretty Paris fashions aren't gonna cut it when you're knee-deep in mud. The communists won't leave you much of a choice. They lose sleep over people making personal choices."

"VC come, it mean nothing. I tell you this before."

"I don't know 'bout that, Ngoc," I scoffed. How about the NVA – the Hanoi boys? The VC aren't much of a factor any more. Communists never struck me as going in big for camp followers. Just look at Uncle Ho – now there's one blue-nosed gook if I ever saw one. Closest thing to vice he ever had would be green tea –that is if you don't count the tens of thousands of Vietnamese he's killed as a vice."

"Mister Ho Vietnamese, I Vietnamese," she demanded.

"Yeah, I think I picked up on that piece of trivia, 'round about the time I hit the first stair coming out of the door of the Seven-Oh-Seven that brought me here. Commies don't like prostitution – not on moral grounds, cuz they don't have any. Your kind of individual liberty is too entrepreneurial for their liking. Ha, the state needs to control the means of production, some crotch commissar!"

"You say gook. You say Vietnamese same-same gook – GI hate gook – kill gook." She flailed her hands in front of her face to demonstrate her disturbance. "All Vietnamese gook you – make nice to kill."

"Hey, I never called *you* a gook! I did apply it to Uncle Ho, but trust me, that'd be a tribute compared to other things I've called him." I glanced around at my brooding audience. With the exception of their incessant smoking, none of them stirred. Ngoc's waspishness had edged into open hostility. I needed to avoid a scene, but what she'd been saying really bit my ass. "Hey didn't we go 'round with this before? I told you, not all Vietnamese are gooks. You ain't, President Thieu ain't, and millions of Vietnamese in between aren't. Only those who do gooky stuff are, like the VC – living in holes in the ground, squatting around all the time, picking lice out of each other's hair and biting their heads off. Shit like monkeys do. God only knows what diseases they ingest and spread. Damn, I had to get a bubonic plague shot before coming here – that and six others! That's like turning your watch back to the fourteenth century."

"Yes, you say now. We monkeys to you. Her eyes darted left and right, as though fencing with mine. "So easy you kill Vietnam *con khỉ*."

"That's not true. I don't mean anything like you're monkey people – geez. Like I'm not into killing anybody – not right now... Not when I'm as far gone as I've been for pussy."

"You make Ho Chi Minh gook," she said, ignoring me. "He make Vietnam together – no more American – no more we gook – all Vietnamese same. No more fight."

"Fine. The only problem you'll have then is that the gooks will be running the place. It's all I'm saying."

"They no kill when all Vietnamese together come."

"You're dreaming. They love to kill. They were killing beau coup Viets before the first American ever got here. What do you think the gooks are doing to the Arvins? They look pretty Vietnam-ezy to me and the communists are killing them in droves. By the way, these guys in here don't strike me as off duty Arvins. They're the right age – what's the deal?"

"No Aabin here." She pronounced Arvin with a distinct meanness.

"Yeah, but *why* is the question. You'd think the authorities would come in here and just draft them on the spot – march 'em off for haircuts and new Arvin uniforms."

"They wan' not fight for Mistah Thieu. Aabin number ten."

"So some of them aren't the best soldier material around. It's just that they're all we got."

"Arvin will die." She said the words in a near whisper, but her tone was unmistakably vicious. I leaned back in my chair, needing a moment to reassess what I'd just heard. Her inflection had carried as much meaning as her words. Was it meant for the Arvins or were thoughts of her future playing into it? She had a drink in front of her, but had only taken a couple of sips… probably only tea anyway. I drained the last of the wine bottle into my tumbler and put it down with a chagrinned clunk. While contemplating the baroque mansion on the label, I thought about what was going on. Had a hundred Arvins been cut down by communist guns, while I'd been making love to a local commie cheerleader? She stared numbly ahead, as though peering at a vitally important speck of fly shit on the wall across the room.

Ngoc, always enigmatic, had me needing to know more than ever what made her tick. 'How can I adjust her beliefs, or whatever's going on inside her? I'm risking my life for this country, seriously risking it. That's worth something. Okay, so a whore gets mind-fucked from the daily grind. Is that how Ngoc got there? Or was she just some mind-fucked bitch, who one day realized that she and this work were a perfect fit? Well, fuck her and the horse she rode in on.'

Blowing out a long stream of smoke with my thoughts, I made another check of the nearest young bucks. The glare of a particularly puffy-faced miscreant in his forties caught my attention. The aura of his counsel with some of the others required another glance. 'Are they talking about me, about how cool it is that I've been helping the local economy by firing jizz-bombs into one of the town's daughters? From the look of them, the answer's no.'

Their heads were canted in different directions, but their eyes all cut back at me. Time to split. Prudence dictated my need to roll her mood back, to make our exit less conspicuous. My senses told me that this was not the moment for sudden moves.

"Maybe you're right Ngoc. Maybe wine is bad for me – makes me say bad stuff to you. You're much too nice for that. Come on, let's go."

CHAPTER 5

OUTSIDE THE CLUB, I FACED a new dilemma. Self-preservation gained the upper hand. I decided to just dump her and vamoose. But, there was nothing to taxi me back to the hotel, no Lambros, no nothing. We'd taken umpty-ump turns to get here and I didn't know what part of town we were in. I clicked off my options.

"Hey Ngoc, is there a curfew here?" I asked. Walking several paces ahead of me, she didn't answer. It was a superfluous question. The streets were deserted curfew or not. Which direction had we come? Was this even the same street? Ngoc turned down a squalid ruelle. I followed, glancing back over my shoulder at every other step.

In near total darkness, I had no idea which direction would get me back to something familiar. 'I can break into a sprint and cut in any direction that looks promising. I'll be blocks away in seconds, but where'll that be? Running with Ngoc wailing after me? I could wind up in some serious shit here. It's the middle of the night. I'm unarmed.'

The stark foreboding of these streets tightened my alarm. 'I'd prefer doing an E&E with Larry Dills in downtown Hanoi. Needing Ngoc to get me back, puts the kybosh on my splitting.

Is she leading me out or not? We definitely didn't go to that club by way of any narrow alleys.'

A foreshadowing snapped in my head, of a bunch of those club toughs circling around to intercept us at some prearranged spot, a place where my screams wouldn't matter. During the entire time we'd sat drinking, I'd interpreted a measure of restraint in their edgy looks. 'Was that because they all knew where she'd take me? Maybe Ngoc knows the owner. Maybe they've got to respect some other connection she has. I was vulnerable as hell in that bar, but something kept them at bay. If danger can be measured by ugly, with their faces I'm lucky to still be alive.'

I tagged along through a maze of narrow streets. In the indecipherable blackness, each seemed like a passageway to doom. 'Whoa a Lambro! Okay, I can ride back to her place. From there, I can make it to The Pacific Hotel – walk the whole way if I have to.'

Ngoc climbed in. Hesitating, I followed. We didn't communicate. She hung her head down. I was grateful, because it kept us from starting something disagreeable again. Watching the top of her head, I fell back into my wanting to understand the source of her impenetrable animus. 'With the money she makes, all she does is buy clothes – to look good enough to pick up men – to get more money to buy more clothes. Now that's a life that'll get you a corrosively bad attitude.'

A block away, she grabbed up her bag, alerting on the location as if from instinct. We came to a stop. I cast looks around the area, half expecting some of her night club cohorts to ride in behind us. It was quiet in every direction. Up the street, I noticed a jeep parked by the little café where Ngoc had bought our food. Two American soldiers stood talking. In the faint light, I could see their black and white MP armbands. Ngoc saw them as well.

"Please," she said softly, "I want you come with... I want you yes." Not quite a blandishment, it came too unexpectedly for me to know what she meant. I mindlessly followed her through the gate and into the darkened house. My going in was less than rational, but felt stronger than mere impulse. It seemed like her mood had changed to one of reconciliation. If true, it was all I needed to fix things; maybe I'd win over her heart yet, or at least change her mind. Accomplishing that, I'd feel good about leaving.

In the room, I sprawled out on my usual place along the near edge of the bed. Out of shape for putting away a whole bottle of wine, my lying horizontal intensified its effects. Ngoc sat on her little stool then began undressing, her usual signal that sex was about to begin. I turned to the wall. With the mutual burn of our ill feelings still warm in our faces, I couldn't imagine us *ever* fucking again. Our doing it now seemed as remote as some other dude telling me about it.

'Okay, she doesn't like me. But where'd it get started? Don't all whores hate all men? That hostility's bound to bubble to the surface now and then. What else can you expect from a constant debasing of intimacy and lovemaking, while doing it in the arms of callused men?'

I harbored some disdain of my own. It wasn't easy to like somebody who made her living off of my moral shortcomings. My preoccupying lust had fuzzed the edges. When she'd been at the top of her form, I'd felt I'd reached her. But now with my libido drained, we were meeting on level ground.

I looked up. The sight of her startled me. She'd put on a set of black pajamas. I'd half observed her slipping on the pants and it'd nudged me with a vague relief that I wouldn't feel compelled to get between her legs. Black pants were so common to

Vietnamese women's attire that they had no meaning, even taking into account Ngoc's usual bedizened outfits. The black shirt was different. Instinct for self-preservation kicked in. Ordinary women didn't wear black shirts.

One by one, she began removing the brown hair extensions that coifed her head. Slowly unfastening each one, she hung them on a wire stand, a collection of donkey tails. She spun the stool around and faced me for the first time with her natural hair. Mousy and dull, it hung in short chopped clumps, much shorter than any Vietnamese. She'd worn the exaggerated hairpieces continuously until now. Drab irregular hanks lay flat against one side of her head, while on the other they sprouted into the air. Her normal fluffed-up, coiffured look made her facial features small. Without it, they grew large, her nose broadening. It extended even to her shoulders. Entirely in black, she looked huge, nearly a head taller than the average Vietnamese man. The stark clothing made her more masculine than I could believe. Throw on a pair of rubber tire sandals and I'd take her for some hard-core VC.

"Hey, what the hell's the deal?" I pulled on the front of my shirt to indicate I meant the clothes. Reading the contentment in her face, I sensed that my gesture hadn't been necessary. She knew exactly what she was doing. "Look Ngoc, if you're trying to tell me something, just tell me."

"You have killed many Vietnamese people," she said slowly, speaking in the gelid manner I'd have expected of an enemy interrogator. She looked straight into my eyes and I realized it was for the first time. I'd looked at her plenty, but her gaze was always either averted or in half-second, sidelong cuts. No quick look-aways now. She stared dead on. "This not be good..." Fear flooded my gut as if a vial of corrosive acid had broken in my stomach, its emanations blossoming outward imbuing my torso with a strange heat.

"Hey, I really don't need this anymore," I said and got up to leave. "You have no idea what's going on in this war. You're right about me killing communists though. I do it for a living. It's my job. I like my job. The hours suck and so does the pay – considering any minute you can go home in a box, but if you think these motha-fuckers don't need to be killed, then you've either got your head stuck up your ass or you're one of them." I glared mean-faced at her, waiting for a response that did not come. "I'm real sorry that, at this particular time and place, they just happen to be Vietnamese."

"I think you want say *gook*," she said with an ugly smirk.

"Yeah, that's it – but you still ain't quite got it down as to who's who yet."

"I am gook," she whispered. The nasty feeling spread to my limbs. 'Why does she want to pump up this old argument again? Is she declaring herself a member of the National Liberation Front? What is she anyway?' One minute she's a beautiful woman resplendent in red silk, and the next a Commie goon dressed like a gook… One in the same? Maybe that dress's her oriflamme for the revolution, her body just GI bait.'

I grabbed the door handle. It was locked. Fiddling with the bolts for a second, I remembered that whenever we'd come in, she'd always used the key on them from the inside. Outside *and* inside. With those big heavy double-throw bolts slid into steel and concrete, the thing was as solid as a bank vault.

"Open the door, Ngoc. I'm leaving."

"You give me seventy dollar."

"Seven what?!"

"Seven tee – *bảy muoi.*" She spit the syllables through her teeth. "You no give, you no go."

"I haven't got any seventy dollars."

"Seventy dollar there you got." Unnecessarily, I looked down at my front pocket, knowing the bulge to be what I'd stuffed into it at the club. I took a deep breath. She would know exactly how much.

"You ain't getting it. I'm already out a whole pack of dough in the last three days. I let you keep the change every time you got us food or drinks – that was at least thirty right there – make that forty since you just pocketed another ten when we paid at the club. Then my Dear, every time I went to sleep, you swiped more, whittling my piastres. That's at least another fifty. I chalked that up to you makin' sure you got paid as you went. On top of that, I'm down sixty more, which I spent on both of us – food, drinks, lambros, and all that junk I had to buy you. Now you want seventy *more?!*"

"You put money in hotel. That your money. Seventy dollar mine you got."

"Stop with the hotel shit. And come on. This is Vietnam, not Paris. You don't get that much for it here. Your ninety bucks is way over the going rate. I'm okay with it, but not with seventy more! That'd be almost five months wages for an ordinary Viet! Hell *in Paris,* I didn't actually pay anything."

"Yes, gook monkey cost nothing for fuck."

"What the hell does *that* mean? I said it was Paris where I paid nothing. Paris! Yeah Lisette Duceau is looking pretty darned good right about now. Mademoiselle D was even better than you and would do it for a cigarette. Listen! You've got to knock that gook shit off, why-don't-you? It's not about you being a Viet. There's a going rate for pussy. You can't just decide to charge more all by yourself. This is a low wage economy with an oversupply of pussy. You don't need to have memorized Adam Smith to know that."

"I do very good for you – make fuck many time."

"Agreed. So that isn't our argument. What is though, is the fact that a lot of other girls could have done just as well *and* wouldn't have tried to charge me quadruple the going rate."

"Why you not go with many other girl?"

Right about now that's a class-A question. But here we are – and I don't give a rat's ass about whatever pussy is layin' all over this town, or what the fuck you think. You ain't getting seventy more bucks from me."

"I think yes." She put out her hand to receive the money.

"No."

"You take out." Her expectant hand rotated, motioning for the cash.

"No." I reiterated.

"This very bad. Yes, I think not good for you." Her gaze wandered away as though the buzzing of a fly on the window sill was so much more relevant. I joined her in studying the flitting insect.

"Like I said, no!"

"You no never go from here."

My attention snapped back to her. *'What the hell did that mean?!'* I stood in front of her regarding those words, not moving a muscle. She'd spoken with the kind of self-satisfied calm that came from knowing something I didn't. 'Is her plan to wear me down, get me to buy my way out just to avoid an escalating hassle? Maybe she aims to settle for, fifty. I'm sure she could wait me out. But those words…'

The black pajamas reminded me of ominous possibilities. She'd taken the hair pieces out and dressed like this for a reason.

It wasn't about wanting to make herself comfortable while she argued over seventy bucks. This PJ getup had everything to do with what was about to happen, something rough.

Her self-confident equanimity got to me. She knew exactly who was in control and what was going to happen. Were cowboys supposed to come along after a predetermined interval, for a final round of negotiation? Sweat beaded across my forehead. Mulling the impending threat, I felt my jaw muscles clenching. Their tension caused me to decide I wasn't going to concede another dime to her.

"You think I'm some chump GI, don't you?" I gave her a sneering look.

"You give me money."

"You're not listening. You understand who you're messing with. Gooks, a whole lot tougher than you have tried and right now they're *all* hanging out with Sid Gautama – you know, that fat bald-headed guy. You dig, Ngoc? *Dead gooks!*"

"So, you say it now. Gook like me. I am gook." She spoke evenly, vindicated, barely holding back a suppressed rage. The words came off her lips like she was trying to rid her mouth of an acrid taste.

"Come-on, I only said it because you've been steady saying it yourself. Give me the key – or do I have to take it from you?"

"Take key? I think maybe first you die."

"Like hell I'll die." The words erupted from me as I drove my foot into her sternum. She flew backwards against the wall, slamming her head and doubling over on the floor, gasping. *'Where'd she stick that goddamn key?!'* I grabbed the grill in the window and began shouting for the MPs. Futilely, I pulled at it, hoping with all my heart that they were still around. What if they weren't? I glanced back to see Ngoc seizing the brass ornamented stick. I froze in a crouch. I stared at her face, now contorted in a blend of fury and satisfaction.

"Give me the fucking key Ngoc!"

Instead, with a wild-eyed ferocity, she sprang at me straight on, teeth bared, an attacking animal. I turned to avoid her. The vanity checked my movement. She whirled the stick. I could only half block it. The winged creature bit into my scalp on the side of my head. I clutched her wrist and crashed it hard against the furniture's edge. The thing dropped free and skittered across the floor. The pause gave her another start. Empty handed, she came at me with her fingers open and curled like claws. They grappled for my crotch with amazing dexterity. I pivoted and slipped behind to fix her in a hammer lock. As I jacked up her arm, her free hand secured my testicles like a pincer. I jerked my thigh upward and broke her grasp.

"Stop it Ngoc! Open that goddamn door and let me out of here." She answered by worming her hand back downward, trying to gain another purchase on my groin. I scooped up that arm and clamped on a full nelson. If I could just immobilize her until the police arrived... Her feet flailed against my shins. I hooked my right leg around hers and took us both down to our knees.

"Give me the key!"

"I make die you," she bawled, jerking from side to side with renewed energy.

"You're dreaming." I tightened the lock and pressed the back of her head forward. She gurgled, but pushed back with astonishing strength. She heaved upward with both legs. I stretched to my toes to keep from going over backwards. We both yelled continuously. I was hollering for the MPs and demanding she give me the key. She spewed a stream of Vietnamese invective laced with words of English defiance. I hoped the MPs were still nearby, but would be more relieved if the Lotus Eaters next door would somehow spring me free. 'How's anyone going to get through that door?'

Mimicking the move I'd used to take her down, her long serpentine legs entwined mine. First one and then the other, she maniacally worked at throwing me off balance. I had triple her strength, but she exasperated me. I was struggling hard just to hold her. If she got loose, I was afraid I'd have to hurt her, to keep her off of me. Suddenly, with a terrific beast-like intensity, she reared sideways. I fell over. Pain coruscated through my arm as my elbow struck the hard ceramic floor under both our weight.

I was on my back with Ngoc on top of me. She was on her back too, but still locked in the full nelson. Her legs flailed as if belonging to a third person, one on the verge of getting loose from us. I quickly hooked my feet over her thighs to immobilize them. They began to slip. With an erupting rage, I pushed my hands forward and jerked her shoulders back as hard as I could. One of them dislocated. A small cry escaped her. Heedless of the pain, or energized by it, she slithered downward in the hold as if she'd been trained in its counter move. Her body wriggled. Her hands again free, grasped like mechanical pincers. From sheer desperation, I let go of her arms and clamped a choke hold across her throat. One of her hands immediately squirmed like a tentacle and went for my nuts. It grappled blindly and fiercely, wrenching at whatever it could find. I pulled her backwards while forcing her head forward over my forearm. Her yammering constricted to a stridulous rasp.

"Goddamnit Ngoc," I hissed, "just stop it and let go."

The huge door suddenly sprang open as if it hadn't even been latched. Two American MPs burst in. I released Ngoc. They hurtled straight at me. A clutch of clamoring Vietnamese women swarmed in behind them. My body suddenly reared up and crashed against the wall as both MPs pinned my arms to it. One of them jammed his night stick across my throat.

"Hey, cut the shit dammit!" I roared, "I'm an officer. I've just been trying to keep her off of me, and get out of here! She locked me in!"

"Yeah right," one of them said.

"Then let me get my fuckin ID card out." I had to fight under their tightening grasp to retrieve my wallet, infuriated that they didn't believe me.

"What you beating her ass for?" he asked as I shoved the card in front of his face.

"I wasn't beating her. I told you, I was trying to keep her off of me! She's as crazy as a wild animal!" Ngoc suddenly sprang from the floor and bolted at us, stick in hand. I watched the brass dragon streak in an arc. Given my inability to move, I could only hunker. Down it came and I took the blow squarely on the side of my head. She bayed incoherently in her rage and swung back for another go. "Get that bughouse bitch away from me!" I screamed. "I wasn't beating anyone. Can't you see *she's* after *me?!*" One of the MPs got between us, but the dragon kept chopping in a frenetic effort to get to me. I ducked my head and pulled away from the wall just enough to be shielded by the buck sergeant holding my right arm. The zingers began pummeling his shoulder. One of them caught him dead across the ear. He moved to escape her, but didn't let go of me. This gave her a wide-open shot, which she took.

"Soldier! If you keep letting her do this, I swear to God, I'm going to have your ass!"

"Okay, okay," he said, spinning me around and pushing me toward the door. Two Vietnamese police stood there, ineffectually controlling the crowd. Ngoc crouched, ready for another attack. One of them finally restrained her. The gang of neighborhood women shouted, some trampolining on the bed. Others with their backs to the wall, jeered. I bucked through this gauntlet of nattering harpies as domestic items walloped me from every direction. At the doorway, I forearmed a pair of them across the face and plunged for the stairs. The door of the other apartment opened a crack and two wide-eyed nymphets peeked out.

As though fleeing from angry bees, I hurtled down the stairwell. The sound of tromping and shrieking echoed after me. I hit the cool night air and rushed for the open gate as if it'd been an exit from Hell. I got to the jeep. Dread followed relief as Ngoc's screeching rent the neighborhood. Both Vietnamese MPs were holding her by the arms. Given her size, it took the both of them to keep her from coming after me again.

"We gotta take you two in," the sergeant explained. "She says you stole money from her."

"Like fucking hell I did!"

"They said something like seventy bucks." Having just caught up with us, Ngoc alerted on the word and went off in another burst of pointing at my pocket. Torrents of abuse poured from her mouth.

"*Sergeant,*" I said, emphasizing his rank. "I did not."

"Well it don't matter. We still got to bring y'all in." He motioned for me to get into the back of the jeep. I clambered in as instructed. The two MPs got into the front. Still restrained, Ngoc ranted on with a stomping tantrum. The jeep's engine started. She renewed her appeal to her squalling, yawping supporters. They poured out of the building behind us and encircled both jeeps. I took a closer look at them, a motley collection of aged-out and off-duty whores. They seemed more mirthful than angry. Armed with rice pots and cooking spoons, the sisterhood of sin had taken to the streets for all that was just and right.

We rode half a mile to the station, Ngoc and the Vietnamese police following directly behind. I prepared myself mentally for some kind of defense deciding it'd be better to go on offense. I didn't know what I'd fallen into.

"Hey Sarge, what's the protocol for matters like this?"

"We're supposed to bring in anybody who gets involved with the locals – them too if they have some kind of complaint – which she seems to have. We have to sort things out."

"Well, you haven't heard my complaint yet."

The old French courtyard was so floodlit, the place seemed like a huge crucible of incandescence. The overkill bleached my retinas so much that everything appeared tinged with white. In the electricity-free Vietnam that I knew, night meant darkness, except that inside our Fire Support Base, we had the intermittent luxury of puny little bulbs and shaky pint-sized generators. Outside the wire, an entire world lay immersed in a darkness so dense that you could pour it from a canteen cup. Having worked so hard to make the night my own, lights this bright made me uneasy. The illumination was a security measure, but I likened it to a child's nightlight, the kind of thinking that said, if you can see what's going on, you'll be safe. From a field perspective, I might want to use flares to light up my enemy but the last thing I'd ever want to do, is light up myself.

The MP station looked as though they might be vendoring hotdogs. The front of the building had no walls, only a long counter, covered by a red tiled roof. Superfluous florescent tubes bathed the interior with an invisible wash of sterile light. It gave olive drab uniforms a bluish hue and made the MPs look like members of some alien army. The Vietnamese police, in their mottled brown and beige camouflage, *'Duck Hunters'* as we called them, were already alien enough.

The six of us moved up to the counter. Ngoc had quieted sufficiently and no longer needed physical restraint, but was still fired up. She shifted to pleading her case directly to the two Vietnamese who'd brought her in. They listened indifferently to her non-stop calumniations. Their stone-faced response to her addled distress seemed to edge in my favor.

I scrutinized the obvious. The place was a combined American, ANZAC and Vietnamese National Police operation. Four of them mingled behind the counter. A Viet with NCO insignia on his collars came over to stand across from Ngoc. A studious looking duck hunter, he didn't have to declare himself the translator. An American SP4 remained seated. The only other MP was a New Zealander. I wasn't sure of his rank, but by his age, I took him to be the ranking non-Vietnamese. I slid my ID card across the counter and gave him my unit. One of the Viet police had already taken possession of Ngoc's. He passed it to an American staff sergeant.

"Well," said the New Zealander, "What's been going on with this pair?" I detected a bit of wry amusement in his voice.

"We heard them both yelling," the buck sergeant we'd come with said. "When we arrived, he was..."

"Hold it," I interrupted. "Since you weren't there until the last two seconds, would you be so kind as to allow Miss Ngoc to describe her version of those preceding moments, first?" 'If these NCOs are going to play joint magistrate, I need the right persona – soft spoken and reasonable. A show of magnanimity can't hurt.

I want out of here fast, with no awkward Incident Report landing on Colonel Braccia's desk. Letting her go first gives me the chance to rebut her – it'll let me have the last word.'

She began her explanation speaking only to the four Vietnamese. If it was a new me, it was also a new Ngoc. I wouldn't have thought her capable of such diffidence. With head bowed, she affected a face of tormented anguish. In rueful tones she whispered her story. The wad of bills still bulged in my front pocket and Ngoc pointed to it several times.

"She say she poor Vietnamese woman," the translator said at last. "She work very hard, get food for children. She say you steal all money from her. Seventy dollar."

"She may have just now dressed herself as..." I responded carefully. "Ah, a poor Vietnamese? That's not what this black pajama getup says to me. But, she's actually a fancy whore who works out of the Pussycat Lounge. Don't be fooled. Back in her armoire, she's got several thousand dollars- worth of high-fashion clothes." I looked to the MPs standing next to me for confirmation. "There's no children in that house, only whores – and I didn't take any money from this one. The seventy dollars is all I've got left. She already got everything else."

Ngoc suddenly cut loose with a theatrical tirade. I watched with calm satisfaction as she gesticulated with overwrought and self-defaming emotion. I pulled out the wad of bills and pointed to it.

"These are MPCs. The U.S. Army pays soldiers with them, not Vietnamese whores."

"Well, stealing aside," the desk sergeant went on, "you know how many scraps we have here over soldiers deciding they don't want to pay?"

"I wouldn't have any idea. But our argument wasn't about me not wanting to pay. Because, I already did. It was over her claiming I needed to give her *more.* Regrettably, neither of us had agreed to a specific amount beforehand. That was both our faults."

"How much did you pay her?" he asked, "and for how long?"

"Three days. Look, I went to her place with two-hundred-twenty dollars on me. After letting her pocket forty when she bought food, she filched 50 more a little at a time. I was okay with that, because she only took some – like paying herself as she went. Then there was expenses; her share of food was say twenty bucks, plus a bunch of personal stuff she begged me to buy her– twenty more there. Add it all up. So first she tells me she wants everything I have left – she knows how much. Now she's going that one better and saying I stole my own money from her?! What she got out of me for three days was enough."

I looked over and addressed the translator and the Vietnamese police directly. "How long does it take Vietnamese Police to make a hundred-thirty dollars? Two months? Longer?"

They conferred, then put several questions to Ngoc, pointed ones because it set her off into another performance. We all watched silently as she acted out the callousness of my barbarity. She'd been favoring her left arm, but now accused me of having torn it off and beaten her with it.

"She say you try to kill her," the interpreter informed.

"Look you guys, you know what I do here in Vietnam. You know my unit. If I'd wanted to kill her, I would have, without a whole lot of wrestling and screaming. I didn't come to Vung Tàu to kill anyone. All I was doing was trying to keep her from whacking me with that damned dragon-headed mace." I displayed the couple of fresh gashes above my right ear. "I hope you noted my hollering for the police… hardly what one does in the commission of a homicide." I turned back to the two MPs who'd brought us in. "I *still* have an issue with you two holding me, so she could exact retribution. Where's your OIC?"

"Err, umm," stammered the Spec 4, "Captain Wallace won't be in until around sunup."

"Yeah, well, it might've looked that way," the buck sergeant broke in. "We were just trying to separate them. She was pretty wild – clipped me a good one too – right here." He pointed to a raw scrape in his scalp. More words and their translations were traded around. The American staff sergeant handed me my ID.

"Aw-right Sir," the New Zealander said, "everything's all squared away. Your mates here'll bring you back to The Pacific. A little advice though. Get a couple hours of sleep then put yourself on the first flight out of here. First thing, she'll have the cowboys after you. And let me tell you, when they come tearing by on those motor-bikes, they'll cut your liver out and have it thrown to the rats before you hit the ground." I nodded appreciatively and turned for the jeep. Ngoc let out a harrowing screech and fell on my waist with her hands clawing at my midsection. Teeth flashing savagely she pulled at my pants, disgorging curses and spit. I thought I'd have to clock her one to keep her from chomping me in the crotch, but the two MPs yanked her away. The translator ran up from behind, trying to get their attention.

"She want belt! She say belt belong to her. She say he no take."

"Hey, I'm sorry," I said, remembering that I still had it on. I moved quickly to undo the buckle. Seeing it as incriminating, I was more annoyed than contrite over having forgotten about borrowing it. "It's my fault. I really didn't mean to be walking off with it." I pulled it out through the loops and tossed it to her.

"You take belt, you take money – same," she hissed, black faced with anger as though her having to pick it up off the ground was an especially humiliating insult.

"I reckon she needs to stay here till we get back," the buck sergeant said to the translator. "Lessen she wants to go off on her own. Don't matter to me."

We went over to the jeep and got in. As I did, the buck sergeant swung around from the passenger side.

"Sir, I just got to ask you something. How the hell did you ever wind up tanglin' with that big bitch? Man like she's not that bad looking, except for the hair – but…"

"She looks fucking crazy to me," the other MP interrupted.

"…Like there's plenty of ones you can get, where y'all wouldn't have to get into a duke-out over it. Trust me, I've been doing the Vung Tau thing for five months. I know you don't have to beat it out of them." He pulled out the jeep's log book to make a notation. "I can't see that you're even drunk."

"Did you guys even listen to my story?" I asked. "What was going on was not what you think. It's a long and complicated story. You'd understand, if I had the time to tell it."

"That would figure, Sir. It'd have to be, to account for that wild shit." His tone sounded like he only half believed me.

Embarrassment boiled in my face. It'd already been bad enough, back in front of that counter. I didn't need anybody to tell me about it. Ngoc had looked ugly and feral, worse than any female VC cadre I'd ever dragged out of a muddy bunker. That lamia-eyed look was the kind that would take your life without a thought.

I felt like I'd explode if I didn't explain to them about how she'd looked sauntering around in that bar, so inviting, so easy. And how she'd turned everyone's heads on that beach. In bed, she'd been so lissome, wanton, and compliant. I'd looked into those same eyes while making love to her. 'Man, it sure got screwed up from there. A real case of *'bitter poetry* ' as Flaubert described his whores.'

The jeep began backing up. Ngoc suddenly appeared in my peripheral vision, moving in behind us. Only a couple of feet away, she let fly with the belt. The big chrome buckle hummed around and boinked off the rear tire.

"Hey!" I yelled, "Goose this fucking thing. She's after me again!"

The driver stomped the gas. The engine choked to a near stall. He hit the clutch. We bucked to a stop, hesitating as if to present her with an easier target. The engine revved. The buckle glinted as it sailed around again. I ducked and it passed over my head. She lunged at the sputtering jeep in a final assault. I spotted the gleaming arc of chrome as it came around. It headed straight for my face. I snatched the leather just behind the buckle and wrenched it downward. The jeep bucked forward and pulled her off balance. She let go too late and fell down behind us. Looking back over the tire, I caught one last glimpse, her implacable face, full of pure animal hatred, and the tires spinning stones at it as we lurched off in to the night.

"Well you guys," I said, reliving my catch of the buckle, "nice of you to have all those lights on." I tossed the belt out onto the street.

IV
The Hotel

CHAPTER 1

THE SUN SHIMMERED FAT AND low on the horizon. Distorting to a molten glob in the aqueous heat, its rays quivered on the tarmac. Hot as it was, the asphalt seemed on the verge of boiling. Sweat ran into my eyes. I squinted. The mirage intensified. Steaming air billowed up over a row of cargo planes, their wings and fuselages, a wriggling liquid. The sun bore down on them like an attacking fighter coming in on an extended strafing run. It glinted off the edges and surfaces of dull camouflage paint like sparks.

Beyond this and many other flight lines, I could see all sorts of military and civilian aircraft. Two bomb-heavy F-4s, their afterburners lighted, thundered skyward. Much nearer, a TWA 707 taxied in a decelerating whine of relief. It'd been a long haul from its gas-up in Guam. The sound of jets and turbo-props swirled in every direction. Tan Son Nhut air base was a very busy place. Its ground-trembling noise had me feeling quite alive.

Passing under the wing tip of my hitch hiked C-130, I headed toward the distant terminal. The brain-bake of midday heat stored in the pavement played brick oven to my boots. 'The late afternoon stillness always jacks-up the humidity – air's too sodden to move. Nice that it contributes to my general attitude, hot and bothered. It's a pretty good attitude to have in a war.'

The further I walked, the more I limped. In my tussle with Ngoc, the wound in my thigh had suffered a solid whack. The gimped walk took an extra effort and increased the rivulets of sweat streaming down inside my shirt.

'It's time for me to rejoin my men and resume the war. But this damn throbbing in my leg could hangfire that round. The Colonel won't be expecting me for a couple more days. How 'bout staying here in Saigon? Better than spending it back in the company area getting swallowed by stir-crazy again. But stay where?'

My going hand-to-hand with Ngoc had brought me to some serious introspection. Like one of my men observed, "This place is so weird a dude's liable to find himself going home without his life." Vung Tàu hadn't been quite *that* weird, but from what I'd found… *Damn.* I obviously knew a lot less about this strange country than I'd thought.

Mentally I revisited my flight out, which had taken off six hours late. 'There isn't enough time now to catch a lift back to the fire base. Staying here isn't really a choice. Problem one, I don't know much about this city.'

Checking into a transient billet for REMF officers was a stultifying prospect. Once before in Long Binh, I'd wound up in an open-bay billet full of captains and majors. The guy in the next bunk asked me if my shoulder-holstered .45 was loaded. I told him it was, but that I always carried blanks.

I limped along. What emerged was unarguable. A city like this did need to be tasted. How many next-chances might I get to be footloose in Saigon? Maybe I could make up for my premature exit from Vung Tàu.

At the end of the flight line, two scuffed and sun bleached C-123 Providers sat, parked haphazardly, like model airplanes left scattered by a child. These forlorn little brothers of the Hercs held me up for a closer look. I thought this plane had been retired from service, but just beyond, stood a tidy row of half a dozen more. I walked past the nose of the nearest. The sun fell directly behind it, casting flat dark-green silhouette. Its shape and lines struck me as inherently graceful. Overhead wings always gave a sense of greater airworthiness.

Moseying toward the terminal, my paratrooper's aesthetic on cargo aircraft faded into nostalgia for the uncomplicated Army life in a stateside airborne unit. That was a thing of beauty: a mass of huge droning airplanes, seeding the sky with hundreds of crack soldiers, all peacefully floating down, perfect olive canopies against a cloudless sky. What I had instead was my playing pop-up target for a maniacal black-clad enemy, each loaded with full magazines, my name neatly engraved on every bullet.

The bustle of Air Force personnel, American civilians, and Vietnamese military in the terminal offered no clues to resolving my situation. I asked an airman at the counter if he knew of any hotels in the city.

"You got me, Sir," he said. "A hotel? My quarters are only two buildings away. It's air-conditioned, so after a twelve hour shift in this oven, that's where you'll find me. He pointed the way to a transient billet. I gave him a weary thank-you.

Outside the main gates, I found myself caught up in a throng of Vietnamese civilians. Within seconds, a cabby commandeered me with eager gesticulations. Compensating for his half dozen words of English, he pumped his arms piston-like, miming what one does with a steering wheel.

Approaching his car, the squat gnome presented it to me as if for sale. With a sweep of his hand, he offered me an expression of pure pride. Looking around at others looking at me, I wondered if his pride was more connected to my acceding to his blandishments, than from his battered beige Renault. In a city that moved substantially by pedal powered rickshaws and 50 cc engines, I took the guy to be at the top of his game.

"Very good," I said, nodding my consent. His head went up and down in a mimic of my own. Breaking into a wide smile, his teeth chronicled a lifetime of eating something that nakedly warned of alarming consequences. His face confirmed a devotion to those gastronomic horrors. Pock-marked and impacted by accretions of redundant hard labors, the man's look, a time-streaked gargoyle come alive, told me he knew his way around.

As the old car coughed its way out into six lanes of man-swarm, it came to me.

"The President Hotel" I blurted, the dross of information rising from nowhere. *"Ông có hieu không President?"* My man nodded by rocking himself in his seat, communicating a giddy-up to the car.

We plugged along, winding our way out of the city center. 'Who in the world had recommended The President? Some half-bullshit loose end connected to an eighth beer. Remembering it though, means I won't wind up on the doorstep of the *Hotel Wong Dong, Scum Drain of the Orient.*'

Stalled in traffic, the car's air cooled engine made my acquaintance. It shuddered as though from a bent crankshaft. Sizzling right behind me, it smelled of burning fan belts. Whining in agony, the heat felt so intense a complete seize-up had to be seconds away. Separated by only a cardboard partition behind my head, heat radiated through it like it'd been created for that very purpose. Trying to cool itself in an atmosphere it knew to be hopeless, each halt in the traffic became a contemplation of its final resting place.

The torrid sun tried to finish me off, pouring through the rear window as if magnified by a huge lens. My back seat and the engine compartment became one and the same, eight hundred degrees and half carbon monoxide. The front windows were open. The rear ones were closed with both cranks missing. My entire body was drenched in sweat. Near to suffocation, I shoved the back of the passenger seat forward and struggled to stick my head out the window. No dice.

"Hey, cabbie, I'm getting out, so I can get into the front seat." He didn't understand, but it didn't matter. We were stuck in traffic.

Around us, the streets flowed with congeries of motorbikes, six lanes wide, a river of amalgamated humans and machines. The impenetrable traffic engendered a collective intelligence, a single brain for this whole teeming stream of blue smoke and two-stroke engines. It revved with potential motion, for a destination only as far as the next cross street, and the next jam-up.

A fusion of stalwart-faced individuals crept past. I thought that trying to catch one looking at me might affect a kind of connection, a separation between one human brain and this dogged ant hive activity. Female riders, their long black hair and áo dài panels flying behind, donned elbow length gloves and makeshift surgical masks as protection from the exhaust grime of ten thousand motorbikes. Looking from one pair of forward-staring eyes, I sought the hint of a smile from just one. I failed.

The pervasive presence of Arvin began to thin. Chinese characters on signs said we were in the Cholon District. One large store showed itself to be in the TV and electronics business, but most had no display windows. We passed a number of fix-it shops, open-doored garages with men beating metal with hammers. Motorbike repair had to be the country's leading industry.

At a prominent divide, the avenue split right and left, a three-story-high billboard advertised some never-heard-of tooth paste. The huge, grinning face of an Indonesian-looking guy beamed out over traffic. From blocks away, his massive double row of teeth grabbed my attention. Its creator had choclatized the skin to greater contrast his inhumanly large, bright-white chompers. But the smile wasn't a smile at all. His eyes screamed at me for help. It was the face of a man whose unseen testicles were being jolted by a hand cranked generator.

My driver abruptly pulled up to a curb, ran around to my side, and opened the door. I scrutinized my location. The building at hand hoisted my attention up along a stolid tower of windows rising a dozen stories. As stark and grim as an East German high-rise, it sat in the neighborhood with the subtlety of a colossal concrete block. Its borrowed Teutonic charm bullied ramshackle neighbors into submission. The area wasn't really that bad, although *bad* in Vietnamese terms was a nether world for the damned.

I dawdled at releasing the cab and tried to think of an alternative plan, but just stood there gawking at the place.

"Hey Papa-san, this joint looks a little number ten to me. How 'bout you finding me somewheres that's number one?"

"Numbah one. Oh yah, President numbah one, numbah one." He motioned at the facade with twitchy gestures, most of them variations of an open palm. I paid him off and wandered into the crowd.

Crow-black heads jostled past me as I moved toward the hotel's doors. Furtive side glances, gave me a kind of *Lord Jim* feeling, even though I was late by most of a century. A daub of malevolence in one face inclined me to think of a character in *Terry and the Pirates*. Already conspicuous by height, my tiger-striped camouflage seemed garish in a rush of civilian sameness. In this strange backwater on the edge of a war, I looked as equally out of place as out of time.

Ambiguity, the mother of misperception must have mated with Vietnam. Opacity was their offspring. The inexplicable was their clan. It'd take a lifetime of study to understand. But staying alive here required the crash course. I never let up on honing my senses. Stropping my qui vive, I'd sliced through the obscuring vines of Nam's abounding lethality. So far, it had kept me alive, but in a war, dying only took one single solitary misperception.

'I've got the bush figured out, but how about life in this comic strip city? Which ones are VC, in from the boonies to pick up some tooth paste? Which ones live here incognito and knock off GIs whenever they find them alone?'

At the entrance I stopped my Xeno-man musings for another consideration of the hotel. The place was still in the hands of contractors. I entered the lobby and felt like I had just gone outside, from outside.

Straight ahead of me jungle vegetation grew in healthy profusion, in the middle of a gutted disaster. It looked as if a bomb had blown out the building's interior and created a sun pit for a hyper-metabolized plant riot. It was also a habitat for hod carriers. Their tools lay scattered among mounds of yellowy sand, torn open bags of cement, and mixing equipment. Planks and scaffolding of various attitudes completed this vacated set. Maybe the owners had suddenly realized a massive *feng shui* oversight, too much qi backing up and choking the lobby. To vent it, they'd gouged a cathedral-sized hole out of the building's core.

A huge expanse of mahogany counter stretched across the opposite side, pygmyfying the stool-boosted man behind it. Approaching it, I skirted a distinct demarcation line between the atrium, stillborn in cement mud pies, and a floor of gleaming ceramic tiles. The line's starkness spoke to me: *'Walk here. No walk there.'*

The little man looked up from a piece of paper, the only thing on his flight deck of polished wood. He gazed at me with an endorphic expression, the very look you'd expect a guy to have from Pledge-ing an acre of mahogany, with only occasional breaks to reread that single scrap of paper. His attention to me communicated he was *open for business, barely.*

'It all makes sense. They've finished off part of this place to get some cash flowing, so they can fix up the rest. It's late in the day. The workers have gone home, but shit, it's in such chaos it looks like they've gone out on a wildcat.'

Their aspiration for swank grabbed me. In this war torn land, the rise to modernity was a struggle. With most of it riddled with bullets, a sense of futility could be expected. 'Well, if this *Pearl of the Orient* is ever to become pearly again, she better be making her stand pretty soon. So why not right here at The President?'

I surveyed the lobby again. Something wasn't quite right. It wasn't actually rising at all, but just fighting to keep from sinking. I dropped my bag and leaned over the counter on my elbows.

"You wan room?!" The man's voice chirped at me with a funny uvular sound. I couldn't tell if he was Chinese or Vietnamese, but he affected a sense of stoic energy that was amusingly dissonant.

"Yes, room. One night." He seemed like a cardboard cutout with just its lips moving.

"You must pay fit-teen dow."

"Well, I expected to pay something. Fifteen dollars is fucking larceny, but I suppose I can deal with it."

"You wan Tee Wee? Fi dow more."

"You mean they're separate? Like not together – for the same price?"

"Yes, very good," he spouted, "can do together – you see TeeWee in room. Only pay more – fye dow."

"Yeah, no kidding. Never mind, I'll take both. Room and TV."

"Okay. You now pay," he demanded. I nodded, sliding twenty bucks in military script to him.

"You take these?" I asked. The bills disappeared behind the counter and Mister Desk cut loose with a burst of clipped syllables into the spare nothingness around him. "I guess you do..." Another fellow appeared from some discreet location carrying a small portable television.

"You go him," Mr. Desk directed. I picked up my bag. The guy with the TV was heading for the bank of elevators or as I quickly realized, elevator shafts. The elevators and their doors hadn't been installed yet. Following along, I looked into each one. Outsized doors leaning against slightly smaller door frames suggested the problem. One revealed a pit full of construction debris that must have been dropped from the upper stories. A lonely steel cable hung motionless in its vacant silo. A loop bent at the end gave it the grisly look of a noose.

I figured it'd be useless to mosey around and check on their progress in finishing off the 'Bamboo Room' in the 'Mekong Lounge.' Nguyen Van What's-his-face wouldn't be tickling the ivories in the piano bar, tonight.

We halted at a shaft. It was occupied by a one-person, three-sided, plywood box. As I checked it out, the TV nudged me in the back. I took the hint and got in. Insisting on more, the TV squeezed me into the corner.An unsecured control unit dangled from the wall. Our weight shifting, it boinged at the end of a spaghettied ganglion of colored wires. TV-guy wedged the set between our legs and fiddled with the buttons. We inched upward.

The box pendulumed in its outsized shaft, scraping one side then the other. Rickety and beat from use, I anticipated something breaking loose at any moment. The floor wobbled. I stared down at its slapdash fabrication, certain that it'd be the first thing to go. My companion's expression made him look as if such an event would mean nothing; you live, you die.

Face to face, I was eight inches taller and stared over his head at each passing floor. Exits had brand new steel doors, most seemingly catawampus in their openings. The last two were only barricades of scrap lumber.

At 10, we stopped. He pushed open a gimcrack sheet of plywood with his foot and got out. Adrenaline surged through me. My body sensed something of which my brain was unaware. My ingrained, paranormal sensing of imminent bushwhacks had never failed me. An inaudible snap was all it took, to click my awareness that I was about to walk into something lethal. This was it.

I glanced warily in four directions at once, down corridors of raw ferroconcrete. All was bare. Not even a discarded bent nail lay on the floor. A thin patina of cement dust coated lightly whitewashed walls. Barren of human activity, it felt like an ancient burial chamber opened for the first time in a millennium. Its tomb-like silence had my arteries thumping as though I'd sprinted up ten flights of stairs. It was the very same silence of the jungle, when the birds all held their breaths.

Still holding the TV in his arms, my companion jabbered awkward solicitations to my halting. An unaffected part of my mind reassured me. Maybe further on I'd find a nice finished-off area where all honored guests were brought. My body followed his TV-carrying duck walk.

Violated senses repeated their alarm. 'Why are you doing this? Why willingly go to some end room on a vacant floor, where a brace of hot-eyed Viet Cong are eagerly waiting to torture to death a screaming, heard-by-no-one, stupid, American lieutenant, lured to his fate by the promise of watching a little TV? No Cong in Saigon? How many soon-to-be dead guys were saying that just before Tết last year?'

TV-guy opened a room. The door handle hit the wall with a sharp crack. I jerked backwards. My eyes sought the elevator. I'd dash back to it as hands and arms shot from the room to grab me. I'd have that box going down before they got half way. Looking back at TV guy, their little accomplice, I suddenly felt exposed in the empty corridor. I drew to the security of the room, as if it were the interior readout of a citadel, where this hapless defender could mount his final stand.

"You no like?" the guy asked reading my hesitation.

"Yeah, it's great. It gives me the fuckin creeps – just the way I like." I walked into the center of the room. "Has anyone ever stayed here before me?" He looked at me uncomprehendingly and put down the TV. "Forget about it."

The room was bare, except for a few sticks of elfin furniture, chair, table, bed. I felt reassurance in these items of ordinary habitation. My edginess began to subside. I checked the bathroom in a blink, porcelain-white tile, clean, with a solitary liter-size bottle of potable water on the sink. Everything seemed decent, except the grime-smudged window still X-ed with masking tape. That drew me for a closer look.

Another desolate wing of the hotel looked back at me from a few yards across. I pushed open the stiff metal frame and peered down, at construction debris lying on the bottom. An icy thought froze an image of me spending the last few seconds of my life, tumbling in that windless air to become part of the flotsam below. The door shut. I whipped around. My companion was gone. 'Like he's hardly the thumb-busting goon type. If it ever came to it, he wouldn't even be able to hold down one of my legs. NVA dinks are another story. Compared to TV guy, they're as hard as fire plugs. I'd be piss-mean and sinewy too if I was driven on by fanatical commanders, backpacking a ruck full of mortar rounds over hundreds of miles of mountainous jungle, all on one ball of rice a day. It makes them ornery enough to suck up half a dozen slugs before croaking.'

'Here in the south, we've got too many hotel bellhop-types – muscles of a girl – recreants letting foreigners fight for their country. Shit, if you can carry a TV, you can carry a 105 round.'

Before he left, my little friend had plugged the set in and propped a rabbit-eared antenna on top. Since he'd shut the door I'd just been standing there staring at the blank screen. An irrepressible expectation gamboled across my thoughts. 'Mr. Victor Charles'll be dropping by any moment now. I just know he wants to show me some of his favorite rope tricks.'

'Ruthlessness and compassion are as irrelevant to the communists as good and evil. And there won't be many differences between Saigon VC and their mosquito-bitten cousins in the bush. Style maybe. Guaranteed, City Commies won't be found living in rat infested back alleys. They'll be ensconced in a place like this. Sure, the "Hotel Ho," cenotaph to the great uncle. Hell, they probably occupy the entire floor below.'

I switched on the TV. Up came an in-progress episode of Bonanza. Catching up with the plot, I relaxed and stretched out on my doll house bed. In minutes, the program ended and AFVN signed off the air. I got up and whirred the dial. Only one channel had anything on it.

A Vietnamese man and woman ranted at each other. Their faces contorted in anger, they chewed on sparks. I watched, fascinated. The two clumped around noisily on a makeshift set. The guy halted for a moment and spit out a torrent of invective. She seethed in silence. Then stomping away to opposite ends of the room, they wheeled around like duelers. He let go with a volley of rage that struck her as she turned. She jerked one way, then the other, her long hair slinging back and forth across her face, a self-lashing. Again and again the hair whipped around, struck by his vituperation.

The woman's expression darkened to the blackness of the disheveled strands hanging in front of it. Grasping the back of a chair to steady herself, she worked up some ire of her own. Slow and low it came, methodical and ice pick sharp. Syllables marched from her in a clipped cadence. Like little squads of bayonetmen, they trod across the table and plunged into him.

The kinesthesia of their tirades vaulted any need for translation. A family affair: Her brother was a slime-rancid, murdering VC saboteur; while his brother was a blood sucking, black-marketing, parasitic-capitalist Roader. Or was it that his sister had become a fancy whore with an eye for American lieutenants?

Suddenly, the door opened with a single rap. My little friend darted in and pulled the plug before I could even tense.

"Hey! I was watching that." He collapsed the rabbit ears then looked at me obtusely as he picked it up.

"GI Tee-Wee finis Six O'Crock. You no understand Vietnamese. I take now."

"What?! Five bucks for ten minutes of Bonanza? I ought to be able to watch the AFVN test pattern all night if I want."

"You no understand, GI tee-Wee finis. Only Vietnamese now."

"No shit, but who says I'm not into that there Luke the Gook Show?" My words followed him out through the open doorway.

I paced fitfully in front of the empty table, feeling like I'd just watched my own TV being ripped off, while arguing with the burglar. 'Yeah, they just don't want it to get broken when the goon squad arrives to play four-wall handball with my head. Hell, I even left the door unlocked for them. Fuck this! I don't need any instruction about staying alive. Like I've told my guys a hundred times, *You've got to out-gook the gook.*'

Truculent notions prickled through my nervous system as I ticked off my options. Zipping open my multi-pouched bag, I grabbed for the sheath of my double-edged, Sykes-Fairbairn knife. I slid it into my waistband under my shirt. Before leaving base camp, I'd vacillated over whether to bring it or my Star 9-mm. In the end, my intentions for this short R&R rendered the automatic unnecessary. 'Shit, how could *I* ever think that a gun might not be necessary in a war?'

I moved to the door and reached under my shirt to unsnap the hilt. Stepping softly into the corridor's perfect quiet, I again sensed the palpable threat. Unmistakable menace oozed from the walls like an invisible vapor. A substitute for air, I inhaled its confining stuffiness. "Why didn't I notice this before?'

I moved cautiously to the four corners near the elevators. My total noise discipline accentuated my breathing. Each breath sounded like wood being sawed. A marathoner couldn't run the length of this dust-rimed sanctum without becoming a panting, wheezing asthmatic.

At the first elevator, I edged open the plywood barrier. A yawning maw gulped a steel cable into its tenebrous gullet. My internal warning sounded again. I swung around and looked down each hallway. Nothing.

Imbued with a strange opaque light, the place became more ominous. There wasn't any way to call for the elevator, no stair-well in sight. I stood there. 'What're my options? What good is my knife? Anybody's bound to have a pistol. As bad as shit can get in the bush, I've never felt claustrophobic. Outdoors, I've got the freedom to move in multiple directions.'

In the faint dust on the floor, I could read tracks. Clusters of rectangular tread-marks spelled out my jungle boots. The bell-boy's seemed implied, more a product of my knowing he'd been there. I scanned for others, but couldn't be sure.

With my back to the wall, attention riveted, I absorbed the place. Then I heard it, down to my left, a distinct sound echoing up the hall. In the total soundlessness that followed, the recognition seemed too fleeting to be certain. I focused on the distance, on that something that might have been. I needed to hear it again. 'The building's plumbing? Some VC fuck?'

"Crrr-unk" That's it. It scraped with a peculiar quality that colored it both metallic and human.

I moved silently in its direction. At the third door I listened, annoyed by the sound of my own breathing. It was loud enough that I might not be able to hear something barely audible over it. I held it, but my lungs rasped even louder when I gave in.

Something moved, faintly. The noise had changed. I couldn't discern a thing. Now what? Rush in brandishing a knife? Surprise some old papa-san reading his newspaper? Take a dink bullet in the face before my first half-step inside? More likely I'd pile up against a locked door.

I wanted to knock, to bum a cigarette just to see who it was, but a vision of the door opening to a gun barrel arrested my arm. ' Sure, invite myself in for a test of wills – share a few bits of information about myself, like what's the exact tensile strength of my bones or what's the exact total volume of my blood, or over how wide an area can it be spread?'

"Crrr-ink." There, again! It was his being there at all that bothered me. I was either alone or not, but this was both at the same time, an ambient oppression where the air itself was maleficent. The longer I stood there, the more I wanted to figure it out. My rational side worked overtime to reassure me that the joint was as abandoned as Anasazi cliff dwellings, and that this susurration of the undead, was only me, *me* and their latest bit of ingenuity, incorporeal guerillas. But their sounds were unmistakable, as real as a Minotaur sharpening his horns, or as unreal as my wily foe, cleaning his weapons.

I struck my knuckles against the door. The sharp sound reverberated down the hall and faded. The building fell into a silence more profound than ever. Moments followed moments. I felt totally deaf. My eyes scanned the corridor to compensate for the nothingness. They caught something odd. 'The doors of all the rooms have no numbers. What do they do, memorize them all? Is mine the fourth one on the right after turning left, or the fourth on the left after turning right?'

I stole back to my room, thanking myself for leaving the door slightly ajar. The key lay on the bed. I checked the tag. It was blank.There had to be one more screwy piece to this. I went across the hall and tried it in the lock. 'Bingo. What a stupid place!'

It was a room identical to my own, but had no air at all. My chest cinched tighter as my raspy wheeze felt like it'd kicked headlong into emphysema. I wrenched open the window and hung my head and torso out over the sill, more concerned with immediate relief than defenestration. I sucked deeply of the warm redolent air, content with the mere act of breathing. A stale breeze touched my sweat dampened face. Fleeting whiffs played at my nostrils, smells too strange to identify. As if swimming in an ocean of watery air, odors glided past my nose like eely threads.

I was hardened to the special scents and flavors of this fetid land, but conceded that Nam might be the eviscerated underbelly of the world. In front of me, it spread out, a vibrant archetype of the teaming unwashed masses. I watched them below, tromping into their historical imperative, in this stifling mindless inescapable heat. With all their collective steps, they exuded the ineffable fug of their organic existence.

The whole country amounted to a massive confluence of intestinal tracts, the Mekong itself, sliding along as a colossal aggregated bowel movement for the whole of Southeast Asia. 'And here I am, smack in the middle of it, rectum for half a continent. Captain Hemorrhoid of the Orient, at your service... lord of my very own Serbonian bog.'

A city this vast and raw would have to own the kind of excretions it did. From my window I could actually see it. The fug. Rising in an albuminous expanse, it billowed like some gigantic yellowish apparition. Yet at the same time, it just squat there, motionless, a wafting, mother-lode of gastric gumbo. But was it that bad?

I recalled a Kipling quote that, although there is vice and iniquity all over the world, the concentrated essence of all the iniquities and vices of all the continents, could be found at Port Said. So as bad as mud, jungle rot, and mosquitoes in steaming heat could be, I'd take him at his word that a sand-surrounded hell, comforted only by its mirage-flickering lake, might well be worse.

'Why do I love Vietnam the way I do? Running with blood and ridden with Cong? Because it's so damned cool, and skilled as I am in the ABC's of war, it's a perfect match – to the point I can't really see leaving when my tour's up? Everybody else's ready to leave from the day they arrive. Leave to what? Some boring-ass job back in the States? *This* sure as hell isn't boring. Thank the communists for that. And they aren't about to quit. Our taking chess pieces off the battlefield, gratis, isn't going to help either. There'll be some tough times ahead for those of us who stay on.'

Dusk gathered itself into darkness. I studied my quadrant of the city with a raptor's deliberation. Directly below my man-made fastness, a stream of traffic flowed on, a mesmerizing antiphonic chorus of Mopeds and Lambrettas.

I looked around the room, now twice as dark as outside. My immersion in its indistinct features formed into an idea. Stealthily, I slipped across the hall and retrieved my bag. A few small recessed ceiling lights had come on. This eerie little trick changed the ambiance from bleak emptiness to shadowy desolation. Depleted of any useful light, they dotted along barely pointing the way in the dark. 'All right you bastards, let's play hide and seek for a while, among a couple dozen rooms.' I slid back to my new room, closing and locking the door with less sound than a butterfly fart.

I lay on the bed, revising my remembered images from that reading of Conrad. I dozed, a blend of fatigue and fitfulness. 'No, this joint could only have sprung from the mind of Sax Rohmer.'

A knock startled me in such a dreamlike way that I couldn't be sure I'd heard anything. But hadn't I been expecting it? The sound rapped again. I jerked to my feet in a crouch, dagger blade bared at the ready. The luminous dial on my watch read '23:17.' The door knocked again, this time with a note of insistence. 'Would the goon squad be so polite as to knock? Shit, even *I've* got a master key!'

With the knife held down against the back of my right thigh, I pumped myself and moved to the door. 'The first one's mine, automatically… Bull into the hallway, spin while they grab at me. Get another. Then . . . I'll probably be in trouble.'

'Fuck it, I ain't ever getting marched off to die, in their good time, at their pleasure. No, we'll get it all done right here. Yeah, and the ones who survive'll have an indelible memory of once having met one mean son of a bitch.'

"Knock! KNOCK!" 'Right, just when they've come to kill me – here I am, pissing them off by making them wait.' I swung open the door.

"You wan-I can come in?" she asked. I registered the emblems of her trade, carnality laced up snug in red and black. Her hair seemed woven with the idea that the more it was worked, the sexier it got. This one had pushed the power of suggestion to its final frontier. I stood there, speechless with a bemused embarrassment as she offered me a cutesy flutter with her eyelids, all the better to show off her face with its this'll-cost-you-twice-as-much Eurasian look.

"Yes?!" she asked as her eyes opened for show, glossy and big with anticipation. Mysterious in an impasto of makeup, they seemed like dark planets in the nether reaches of space, at once mercurial and saturnine. *'Hong-Kong-eye'* was only supposed to give her an occidental nuance, but her plastic surgeon looked like he'd been toying with creating a race of his own. "You wan nice girl yes? I very nice. I know you like."

She pushed her pneumatic breasts upward, trying to nudge them into saying something for themselves. They strained inside their escape-proof fish net. By reflex, I wanted to set them loose, but from the moment I'd opened the door to this girl, instead of half-a-dozen executioners, the psyched-up adrenaline had poured out of me. That related juice called ardor had sluiced away with it, as if drain plugs had been pulled from the bottoms of my feet. Another wincing recall of Ngoc came over me, a mix of exhaustion and weariness.

"Yes, you're very nice, Baby-san," I said, "but *xin lỗi*, not tonight."

"You aw-alone?" she enticed, both ignoring what I'd said and trying to look past me, checking to see if one of her colleagues had beaten her to it.

"Hey, how'd you know where I was?" Without saying a word, she pointed inside my room and I turned around, to acknowledge the wide open windows. "Shit, ain't I the smart guy."

"I very nice..." she began again, "make very happy you –beau coup boom-boom. I girl you can do any-sing you rike."

"I don't want to do… anything with girl, okay." She stepped back and gave me a quizzical look.

"You wan boy?" she asked, with sympathetic resignation.

"Hell no!" My first instinct was to haul her in by the arm and redeem myself in the only way I could, but took it to be another of her ploys. The notion of her as a kind of Trojan horse lingered, but my stronger hesitation came from a natural aversion to closing doors in pretty girls' faces.

"Hey look, I'm really beat."

"Ah, you wan' beat?" She made a lascivious whipping motion across her behind. "You wan' beat me? You like, I can do. Must pay ten dow more."

"No – *không!*" I repeated, as she tried to insinuate herself between me and the door jamb.

"All I want to do is sleep."

"Yah yah! I shreep wit you, you shreep wit me – very nice – numbah one."

I smiled at her, amused at her implacable struggle to find that one word, the key to her entry. Moving to within a concupiscent inch of me, she gave me what was likely her best cock-hardening look, a practiced blend of erotic alacrity and supplication. The capillaries in my scrotum jangled with acknowledgement. I felt the incipient stir in my groin. She pressed one of her breasts against my arm.

"You wan' suck?" she asked in a low moan. Her nipple coursed heat into my arm with broadening warmth.

"I want always, Baby-san – except not right this minute. I told you I'm beau coup tired – you know, nite-nite time." I tipped my head to the side with palms together, to mime the act of going to sleep. She jolted backwards, stuttering syllables of Vietnamese and as wide eyed as a frightened lemur.

"Damn!" I'd absentmindedly brought up the knife I'd been holding behind my leg. I stood there frozen, the hilt clasped in both hands, the blade pointing at her throat. She vanished. I looked out toward the elevators and a dim emptiness. In the other direction, stippled shadows blended into complete blackness.

CHAPTER 2

THE SUN BLARED INTO THE room, its hot brassy rays feeling like it had shattered the window to get in. Entering my sleep as though with broken shards of glass I opened one eye. It was like a crowbar prying up an old floor board, to expose a menagerie of crawling things to the merciless surprise of daylight. A dream dissolved, one collaged reality melting into a disconnected other. Maureen and my midnight visitor were both in attendance, both inflamed with tendentious anger.

Instinct jerked my head left, then right. The goon squad had overlooked me. They weren't known for staying executions, so I got up and checked myself for credible signs of life. A tactical reassessment seemed in order. I sat down on the chair. Staring into each empty corner, I contemplated my stark cell with the narrowed focus of a hungry gecko.

It was five 'til eight. The city outside bore into my head at full throttle. It pissed me off that I didn't have anything to be pissed off at. Having come to a symbiosis with the jungle, I had acquired a way of greeting each new day. It took an easing into, a motionless wakening that roused my brain cells at the exact speed of the retreating night. Lying on the ground, enveloped in strange flora, I didn't just let dawn break. It had to be treated as subjective reality, coaxed with no more effort than the flick of a reptilian tongue. In Saigon though, a bird's peep in heavy dew was a far cry from roaring blue smoke and hot asphalt.

Having slept in my tiger-stripe trousers, I mulled over taking a shower, but blocked that idea. Rational reassurances eluded me. Vestiges of an outraged Maureen still occupied my consciousness. In my dream, I'd been trying to explain to her how critically important it'd been for me to fuck some girl. In fact, Ngoc and I implored Maureen to understand. Ngoc was synonymous with the war and fucking her was an inseparable part of the whole thing. The fucking was an act of war! You didn't make love not war, you made them both. This kind of love was on the battlefield.

Ngoc had joined in on my side, pleading that everything I'd said was true. But it was her reason for wanting me dead. She pointed at the bulge in my pants, not the wad of money she so wanted, but my cock. "There, look!" she wailed, telling of its detestable doings, the acts of a true Imperialist Roader. Rapaciously it'd violated her, like a foreign army entering her country. Maureen, bursting with hostility, would have none of it. She was against *all forms* of war.

I hauled on my boots and began lacing them. The thought of being taken, naked, had a special aversion of its own. Besides, before I'd gone to bed, I'd run the shower water. Its brown-tinged dribblings came out reeking of hydrogen sulfide. A direct connection with the Saigon sewer system tilted the scales. My funky state beat out coating myself with the President's rotten-egg scented body wash. As a twenty-five-percent remedy, I stripped off my shirt, then with help from the potable water jug, went through some quick bush-style scrubs.

I hit the corridor with the blithe purposefulness of any ordinary man checking out of any ordinary hotel. It hit me again, the feeling of something imminently lethal. Morning had vaporized the notion that the place was a secret hive for urban VC. But the close labyrinthine walls goaded my instincts all over again. I could feel them trying to pass themselves off as mere concrete slabs in this musty, mausoleum of a hotel. My antennae were sensitive to dink deception and intuited they were hiding something. It was their specialty making everything seem like perfectly nothing. Fall for that, and you died.

It made me think of Murf. I stood there remembering him. Back when I'd been pretty green, the two of us were leading rifle platoons in the same company. One day, we'd been on a sweep and were supposed to link up on a road outside of Cái Bè. Pete Murphy was not only my friend, but the best platoon leader in an otherwise unremarkable battalion. After a long slog, it boosted my spirits to get the call to move up to his location.

As I imagined walking toward him, I could see his face clearly again. Passing his men, who had deposited themselves in staggered groups along the road, I nodded my recognition to the ones I knew. They were eating Cs, smoking or resting. The only one still standing, he'd watched my approach from the middle of the road.

Murf and I chatted while wandering across to the other side, to sit by ourselves on a tree-shaded knoll. I needed my RTO with me, so I walked back a ways to call down the line for him.

A blast behind me split the air with enormous force. I felt like I'd been skewered by lightning. Stunned, ears ringing and on my hands and knees, I turned to look back. One of the coconut trees tumbled end over end from atop the smoke and crashed to the ground. Murf had sat on a booby trapped 155 round. It'd felt like a bomb.

I ran toward the crater, knowing he'd be hurt bad, hoping that by some miracle the tree had shielded him. Until I was right at the edge of the hole, I couldn't tell. I saw his fatigues and boots lying there. The bloody cloth looked shredded. Somehow he was smaller. His head and hands weren't visible, his body twisted around. I fell to my knees and scrutinized the unscathed boot, still joined to the legs. Was this him? I called out his name as if having been blown clean out of his uniform, some other version of him would answer from off in the weeds. Sound had no sooner left my mouth than a horrifying reality set in. My friend Murf had literally been blown away.

His men hurtled into action. One barked instructions. Others followed. I just stood there, slow-walking my mind back through what just happened, those few insignificant footsteps that had led to this. That single half-minute span of time had been so benign I couldn't see where the mistake had been. Nothing so innocuous could possibly have done anything like I'd just seen. My perception of what happened *had* to have been in error.

When Murf's medics pulled up the poncho and moved what was left of him, his still connected boots, dangled freely like a loose-stringed marionette. Their swinging back and forth mocked me, me and my having failed him. That sight distressed me more than the revulsion of his death. It's what I kept remembering. The image clung to me, of how inviting that little knoll had seemed, how harmless, and of how ingeniously some dink bastard had set it up. I couldn't escape the thought that for one tiny sliver of time, the two of us had walked side by side, directly toward it.

I couldn't let anyone anticipate my predictability. And not wanting to face the confinement of the plywood elevator again, I scouted the direction into which my night visitor had disappeared. Near the end of the corridor, I found an unlit stairwell.

'Hadn't she seemed a bit breathless at first? Did she come this way to also avoid the elevator? Why? She was hardly the discreet back-stairs, assignation type. But what do I know about the protocols this place'd keep?' I started down the stairs.

The stairwell was a crepuscular pit. My first few steps into it were fine, but the further I went, the darker it became. My advance conjured up visions of trip wires and booby traps. In this concrete vault, a grenade blast would attract about as much attention as a cat's sneeze. There weren't any handrails. I moved cautiously. Dry scorching air vented upward against my face, as if from an open boiler room door far below. At the bottom of the second landing, I detoured to check out the ninth-floor's corridor.

Demonic figures rose up at me like a disorganized column of rearing anamorphs. I hunkered back a half step to refocus on the place. My eyes adjusted to the gloomy uncertainty. A scene of mid-construction chaos emerged. Vague light filtered from an open doorway at the far end. It silhouetted a moraine of clutter piled in between, giving the appearance of a great motionless legion of terra-cotta soldiers.

The next flight down glowered at me, as a formless stygian abyss. I allowed my eyes to become more accustomed to the dark. As they did, I began to make out that these stairs were littered with a lot of builders' crap, although the inside wall looked pretty clear. I moved downward some more. 'This had to be the way she went.'

After a few more steps, I shouldered into a long length of steel conduit that was propped up at an angle. I froze, but could hear it rolling along the wall above my head. I grabbed for it too late. It keeled over. Catching others that stood propped-up on steps below started a chain reaction. A huge conglomeration of pipes crashed into a fathomless void. It ended in a clanging coda of tubular, metallic disharmonics. 'Shit, that ought-a get their attention.'

A thick billow of invisible cement dust erupted in its wake. It rose up and enveloped me. I wiped the powdery residue from my lips with my sleeve, but it coated the insides of my nose and windpipe. The temperature felt hotter than ever, as though I'd just created some yet-unknown catastrophe. Sweat broke from every pore. 'What the hell're the next eight flights going to have for me? How the fuck did that little whoring bitch get out of this hellscape?' I wiped my bare arm across my forehead. It loosened the gummy caking of fine grit which then streamed into my eyes. The heat suddenly seemed more humid, as if I was standing in front of some gigantic being's hungry exhalation. 'Maybe a gang of dinks really did kill me, and I've gone straight to hell. So here I am, reporting for duty.'

Halfheartedly, I prodded at the next stair. The vision of my stepping airborne into an open portion of an uncompleted stairway, halted me. 'Now that'd make for a cool scene, a grouping of Viet and US military police standing around a colluvium of rubble, guessing at what inexplicable circumstances had brought my broken and stiffened corpse to where it had come to be.'

I knew what was going on. This diabolic building wanted to have me for its own, to swallow and digest me into its intestinal tract of a stairwell, me and a load of other detritus. I turned and trudged back to my room.

Room hell! It was mutating too. I was hot enough to hallucinate. The sterile cool white tile in the bathroom struck me like a refreshing spa. After taking a long gulping pull from the potable water jug, I dumped the remaining dregs over my head. With a dampened towel I cleaned myself up, then paced around, re-invigorated from the agitation. I was fed up feeling like some furtive rodent with nothing to do but explore his maze, while in a far corner a coiled krait waited, patiently.

I threw the towel on the bed, grabbed my bag, and headed outside again.

Down where the hallways converged, I halted and adjusted my knife. I stepped around the corner and walked in front of the elevators. Nothing, no one, dead silence. But there it was, my plywood box of an elevator just sitting in wait. Parked with its door open, it invited, a phantom presence. *Tu Dia*! That warning for mines and booby traps reverberated through my need to di-di-mao out of this ghost hostel. I hesitated.

It made me recall a recently encountered booby trap. Where two trails intersected, they funneled to a log bridge. Its upper surface appeared oddly weathered, not polished by the recent scrub of bare feet. This halted my point team. Then we discovered that the middle of the log's underside had been pre-cut, so as to break under the weight of a traversing foe. We'd get to fall and impale ourselves on submerged, steel-barbed punjis. We writhing victims would unpin concealed grenades that had been trip-wired to the stakes. VC ingenuity garnered respect. They made me appreciate that my enemy had a flair for killing, as an art form and as amusement.

I got into the elevator and took hold of the control box. A sign that had been at my back the night before read, DINING ROOM 11. The sign spoke directly to my gastric system. Having been forced to gnaw on itself for the past sixteen hours, it pulled rank on me. I mashed 11. The box jolted, but didn't move. Stomping my finger into the button twice more only jarred the plywood. I ground my thumb into the cavity and held it there. A slow stuttering upward motion followed, causing an uncertainty reminiscent of being in that mortally wounded Loach with Dills, my brain screaming to rise, to just keep flying. Staying aloft meant we were still alive, but my feet had demanded that they be replanted on good old mother earth. Feet logic said you can't fall out of the sky when you're standing on the ground.

My tethered craft, closer to being a cheap coffin levitating itself out of an undesired interment, was carrying out some kind of penitential rite. It painfully scraped itself along the concrete of one wall. The higher it got, the more lopsided it became. I hadn't noticed it struggling *this* much on the trip up. Suddenly it juttered to a stop. I kicked open the slapdash plywood barrier with the claustrophobic energy of a man about to be buried alive.

'Whoa!' The sight of a massive room containing half-a dozen full size pool tables astonished me. Completely finished and beautifully appointed, the place seemed as sepulchral as a billiard parlor for departed kings. At the first table, I picked up a cube of blue chalk. It may have been used once. On an adjacent one, a pair of cue sticks lay tight along the rail. I studied each as though artifacts from a long dead civilization. Had Specter and Wraith been in here running a few racks? I could almost hear the evanescent pair, the telltale clicks and soft bumps in the small hours of a mephitic night.

At the far end of the first row of tables, another dining room sign arrowed me down a glassed-in corridor. The right side overlooked a vast tract of the city. I turned left. A half-completed, rooftop swimming pool baked in an inescapable sun. It billboarded the same old array of projects in progress, everything just waiting for workmen to return. Their ambition filled me with a curious optimism. 'This hotel's owner has got to know a hell of a lot more about this country than I do. He's seeing the future and is investing in it! Does he comprehend what I can only hope for – that we can somehow pull this war off?' Studying the scene in front of me, that hope suffused deeper into daydream.

'A Korean-style truce is the only way we're going to salvage this galumphing jug fuck. I can live with a stalemate here – the way Korea ended. But back then, Ike had just moved into the White House – enough warfighting credibility for the Reds to call it a day. A truce'll require the North Viets to quit fighting. Like they're going to do that when we're withdrawing anyway? We've needed to pound them into signing such a truce ever since we got here, and haven't. You don't break their will to fight then you get what you get – they just keep on keepin' on. And they're going to cry uncle because we're pulling out?! Where the hell's the future in pool tables and swimming pools with that?'

My thoughts in the middle of the disrupted construction subconsciously revised my observation. The rubble and scattered tools hadn't been left behind all that recently. They were as weathered and forlorn as bleached desert bones. I looked closer at the haphazard items and their aged industry. They seemed as frozen in time as the quarries on Easter Island.

CHAPTER 3

THEY ALL STARED AT ME as I entered the dining room. Half a dozen ladies of the evening stood along two of the walls. 'Gee-ee-zus, breakfast whores. So *that's* where she went, *up* the stairs, not down.' I eyeballed the group expecting to see my little night visitor among them. 'They probably work in shifts. She'd be tough to spot in that line-up anyway. Sure, pick out the short, dark-haired girl dressed in ultra-tart.' I turned away.

A pair of American soldiers, the only customers in the place, sat at a table in the far corner. One had his back to me, but the other caught my arrival with a sharp jerk of his head.

"Hey, well look at who's here!" Captain Mark Ruddick garbled through a forkful of food. "If it ain't ol' Mondo Carney himself." His partner, SFC Albert Wiggins, twisted around to look. The two were Arvin advisors in my battalion's AO. Recon had been out on numerous joint operations with their Ruff-Puff unit. I pulled one of the diminutive bent wood chairs from the table, dropped into it, and sent the waiter off for duck eggs, bread and coffee.

"Well, well, Sir, you didn't forget we told you about this place," Wiggins remarked, "but how the hell'd you know we were here?" A broad grin spread across his large black face. With a gate-mouth smile and teeth fully exposed, his eyes squinched nearly shut. A sheen of sweat being a permanent feature, Wiggins forever beamed with amusement, his own.

"I didn't," I answered. "I got some in-country R&R in Vung Tàu and I was just passing through on my way back. Was it you who told me about this place?"

"Shit yeah," Ruddick said, "this is our Saigon basecamp. Hey, I heard you got hit – in the leg I suppose, with you doing that there Chester thing."

"Well Mister Dillon," I drawled, "it didn't trouble me near as much as yesterday when I was shovelin' horse manure in the barn. Miss Kitty came in and took off that there purdy dress of hers – petticoats and everythin.' Then she lay down naked in the hay and said, 'Come on Chester, put it right here.' So durned if I didn't. I gave her the whole shovelful."

"Booby trap?" Ruddick chortled.

"No sir-ee, Ol' Miss Kitty done shot me – with a K-54 pistol. Seriously though, I didn't know what it was until they took it out. Small bullet – small hole."

"You get the gun?"

"Fuck no. I might have, except I was in the middle of kacking this other dink and his stomach blew up in my face."

"His what?"

"Stomach. I got distracted 'cause I couldn't see from it, and that's when I got hit – stung like hell, then went numb. We were restricted by dense vegetation and beau coup booby traps – couldn't use a gunship because one of my elements was out of contact – worried I was getting suckered into an ambush. We got a few of them, but their officer got away, after he shot me." I'd known Ruddick since he was a first lieutenant like me, and his recent promotion hadn't required a change in our familiarity.

"Hey, what's with all the boom-boom baby-sans? Do they really expect business at this time of day?"

"You got me. Maybe they're hoping 'The Lost Battalion of the U Minh' will reemerge and drop in for breakfast – two decades of hungry."

"It'd be their call to duty," Wiggins added.

"If you ask me," I said, "this whole place doesn't make any sense."

"Don't you know yet Sir?" Wiggins groused, "If it don't make no sense, that's how you know you're still in the Nam. Remember that one about the breakfast cereal called 'Pros tee tooties? It don't snap, crackle or pop. Nope, it just lays there and goes *bang*. The breakfast of champions. That's the President Hotel all right."

"No shit Wiggs," added Ruddick, I saw it on the menu. 'Cherries, only in season.' Around here, that'd be like waiting for the next snow to fly. Hey, so where the hell were you last night? You couldn't have slept through that blowout we had. I've got to tell you, there haven't been times like these since soldiers wore sandals. What room were you in?"

"Nowheres near you that's for sure. Where *were you* guys?"

"Where you think? *The VIP suites* is what I call it – second floor's the only part of this big fucking gray mother elephant that's open. Far East oblivion is its charm. Only place I know that's cheap and has air-conditioning. There ain't much in-between joints like the Caravelle or Continental and some friggin' hell-hole – places about as air-conditioned as Wiggins' ass – just blowing a hot-'n'-steady stink."

"Well shoot, this here ain't no Bangkok mind you," Wiggins interjected.

"And it ain't never gonna be either."

"Like it isn't hot there, and doesn't smell?" Ruddick asked. "Besides, what was wrong with those poonanies I got for us last night?"

"Nothin' in the least." Wiggins answered. "It's just hard to beat what you'll find on Pat Pong Road. Last time I was there, I had me a sweet-lil' pair of baby-sans tag-teamin' me – Ha! That is 'til they couldn't take no more. I didn't even notice about there bein' no air-conditionin'."

"Only two, huh?" I asked.

"I'm gettin' older and it don't take so many as it used to. Yessir, them Thai baby-sans have to be the most obligingest things I ever seen. Yeah, real pistol-poppin' poon."

"Mondo," Ruddick bragged, "we did have one hell of a time last night – what with the premoes I got us – naturally, from *my* top-secret, crypto-fucking-confidential source. Expensive, best-you-can-buy. Brought 'em back and ran into a bunch of chopper pilots who had some of this house stock." He made a finicky expression in the direction of our silent audience. Those dudes had their tape deck blaring until about zero- three – put away a slew of Haig and Haig. They'll be dead to the world for a while."

"Damn Ruddick, how often do you come up here?" I asked.

"At least twice every time," he snorted.

"Yup," Wiggins sighed. "So many poon patrols to get done, and me the only one around to help out. Reckon we might even be fallin' behind a bit."

"Sergeant Wiggins, we'll just have to pick up the pace," Ruddick announced. "Remember, keeping our weaponry well oiled remains a cardinal rule of combat readiness – appreciate your outstanding assistance."

"My pleasure, Sir. You know, last night, my gun got so hot that LSA was shootin' right out-the muzzle – who-o-o we-e-e!" Wiggins' grin spread to its maximum size.

"You still haven't told us what happened to *you* last night," Ruddick persisted. 'Still wondering myself, like why'd the hotel dudes hide me like they did, with everyone else all squared away? But holy shit! I thought my time with Ngoc was satiric…? These guys make me feel like a cinched-up prig – a first-time feeling for sure.'

"I just flew in from Vung Tàu," I said. They gave me a vacant look. I hoisted my tumbler of tepid coffee and took a glug, hoping the act would distract from my truth bending. 'I'm sure as hell ain't playing the guileless naïf to this pair of free-wheeling whoremongers!'

"You staying here tonight?" Ruddick asked.

"Nope. I need to hitch a ride with you guys and not be stuck in Saigon. I'm not much for hanging loose by myself around *these* parts. I did it in Vung Tàu and it got me feeling like I was surrounded. Makes me edgy."

"Lighten up, Mondo. Stay in one of the rooms on the second floor. Guaranteed, it'll take that edgy stuff right out of you – and who deserves it more than you? Hell, just think of the remfing pogues who're assigned to Saigon. They're on permanent vacation. And, as it happens, I can provide you with some *special* company, top drawer."

"Yeah. But if I stay, I'll have to go out to Long Binh to hook up with a flight back. I did that once before – a total pain in the ass. Little going south, and what was, couldn't take me – so those remf-ing dickheads said. Took me two days."

"Aw LT, now you not wantin' to stay, means Ol' Sarge'll have to take care of your passed-up business *and* mine when I come back. Yeah, while you're out there humpin' the bush, I'll be here double-humpin' another kind-a bush." His usual grin relaxed in complacent satisfaction. I nodded with a sarcastic smirk. I glanced to my left. We had company.

The bravest of the little whores stood alongside our table. I ranked her as passable, her best feature being an uncommon lack of painted-on allure. Some of her colleagues had worked their Cleopatra-esque eyeliner to an asp-frightening extent. Maybe she was just a trainee, this solo assignment being the next phase of her apprenticeship.

"You wan *pussy*? I got for you." She emphasized it as though it was out back and she'd be happy to bring it on in. Although she addressed me, Ruddick and I both shook our heads.

"So much for the subtle sales approach," I said.

"I've been wondering why they hadn't gotten around to bothering us," Ruddick undertoned. "They've been standing there watching us for half an hour."

"Must've heard it through their grapevine that we got taken care of last night," Wiggins commented. "But, ain't this now today?"

"Shit," Ruddick derided, "last night *was* today. Since when do they ever take a break from trying? She's all yours, Mondo."

"Well, she ain't Suzy Wong, and I'm no struggling, starry-eyed artist." I turned to the girl. "Hey, no can do Baby-San. I'm just about ready to chow down – you know, chop chop."

"Choa anh? Chop chop?" she asked.

"No, not hello – *eat*!" I moved my lips as if eating with my mouth open.

"Anh muon lon?" she whispered, with a demure bat of her eyelashes. *"Toi can."*

"Yeah, I like – and eating snatch for breakfast has got to be the *true* Breakfast of Champions. Put a hold on that too, willya.

I'm not much of a decathlon man this early in the day." She stared at me with an intense scrutiny as if, by divining a meaning from my slang, she'd pick up something that would prove useful as she moved along in her career.

"I, you – sit with…?" She pointed to the three of us, then to herself.

"Yup, us is the deal," Ruddick said. "Don't let me stop you. It's still a free country."

"Thank you very much, Đại *úy*," she said deferentially. Almost before her butt had hit the seat, the waiter launched himself at the table. He slid a tiny snifter of an ocherous liquid in front of her. Stepping back, he stared into the middle distance, his countenance so wooden that I'd seen more joie de vivre in the faces of dink corpses.

"Đại *úy* must him give three dow."

"For what?" Ruddick squawked.

"Drink." She looked at the glass, then at Ruddick with an earnest bemusement over the obvious.

"I never ordered any drink, much less that thimble full of water buffalo piss. And three bucks?!"

"Ya, me sit – me talk you – you buy drink. No?"

"Naybo hotchee my little boom-boom bunny, I only told you I didn't care where you parked your business. My colleagues and I were talking just fine already."

"Đại *úy* say okay me sit," she persisted. "Me sit okay, come drink. We talk very nice – maybe go room for short-time." Ruddick turned toward me.

"Check this out, Mondo. Watch me get it for the three bucks."

"What? It's already three. Isn't that what she's arguing about?"

"No asswipe, I'll compromise on the drink and get her to throw in the pussy for nothing. I cover the drink; she owes me the pussy. We've got a glut in supply, so let's see what happens if I crush the demand – like I don't even want her poon even for free."

"Ruddick, there's a separation between whore and whore-house I think you're missing." Our waxen waiter was lingering just out of reach.

"I'm not missing it," he scoffed, "I'm counting on it. Hey Baby-san, did I hear you say that the pussy came with the drink, or did the drink just come with the pussy? Explain it to me. See, I could give two dollars for the drink and one to you. Better still, I could let you have two whole Yankee dollars." Bewildered, she glanced around the table for some kind of clue. Ruddick took out three MPC singles and laid them side by side. The waiter moved to grab them, but Ruddick barked in Vietnamese, he froze. The girl wide-eyed the money, then Ruddick.

"See," he said to me with a sneer, "I'll get her to agree just so she doesn't have to cover the drink herself." He turned back to the girl. "What are you, Chinese?"

"Yes, I chi-nee – you like? Chi-nee shor-time can do better for you – no no Vietnam girl no good for you."

"Seems there's a little ethnic rivalry going on that I didn't expect," I said.

"Look past the makeup," Wiggins said, "and we might be fa-cin' a full squad of the Chinese Crotch Corps." The girl gave both of us a look of anticipation and settled on me.

"Chi-nee girl good for you," she said. I took another look at the string of girls still standing along the wall. Some of them did look a little rounder in the face. And this was supposed to be their part of town.

"Are they all Chinese?"

"No, but they'd tell you they were Norwegian if that's what you said you were looking for. So, my little Suzy Wong, what'll it be? How much will it cost me for a few pirouettes on the working end of my Tom-Terrific trouser tool? Let's say the short time is real short. We'll use a stop watch – how's that?"

Ruddick leaned back, his gloat staring the girl down. The spindly legs and glued joints of his chair cracked in alarm. He was a bulky guy. Neither fat nor muscle, his roundness made me think that if someone could be stuffed with kapok, it'd be him. His jungle fatigues were filled to the extent they looked like they'd been upholstered to his body.

'Watching Ruddick yank this girl's chain, is about as amusing as a bully teasing a child. When we were out on ops together, I never noticed he was so fucking cynical. Is this what Nam does to you, eventually? Is it impossible to love a people, while killing them? Maybe he'd agree with Ngoc on that. I never got it through that cockeyed bitch's head that they aren't the *same* people.'

'This whole country's a swirl of contradictions – start straight from this one's aura of innocence and eagerness to please – pretty girls happily serving themselves up at the snap of the fingers for the price of a couple of cold beers. In five minutes, they've got you forgetting what they are – vicious little tigers inside facades of demure reserve – debutante dragon ladies – soul-sucking, fledgling Ngocs.'

"Hey Rudd, you're the expert, where do whores come from? – like from what mental state."

"From what *state* do they come from?! Man, this whole country's a fucking state – the Commonwealth of whore. It'll sell out for anything."

"Be serious. None of them strike me as getting to it the way you'd expect."

"Like *who'd* 'expect' LT?" Wiggins asked. "Ain't you noticed yet? These people're poorer than mouse shit. Things get bad enough, you do what you can."

"They don't all come from the poorest of the poor," I argued.

"They all poor enough," Ruddick instructed. "It's looks. If they don't have 'em, they don't have nothin' to trade – and poor they'll stay. Wiggs and I are experts – connoisseurs if you will."

"I'm talking about their mores not their looks.

"Like why they're fucking for money? Man! So they can get some. Better they look, the more they get. Mores? They don't have the same cultural hang-ups we do back in The World. End of story."

"It can't just be looks and money," I challenged. "What separates these here from the hundreds outside – all those vestal bottoms whizzing by on their motorbikes? Poor, very pretty, and not whores."

"There's some personal choice involved – same-o same-o back in the world – everywhere."

"But what triggers *that* choice?" I asked. "*Her* for instance?" I turned my head and nodded at our novice whore. "Does she look like somebody who has no other choices?" The girl gave me a fetching sidelong glance, still patient that her time would come.

"You got me," Wiggins interjected, "but it's good that some of 'em have chosen. It's the only thing making this war tolerable – that 'n' *beer.*"

"They're only a miniscule percentage," I said. "You actually have to look for them."

"Shee-it" Ruddick scoffed. "Come-on, they look for *us!* And we're sure as hell not hard to find."

"I'm talking about the villages and hamlets. There's none there."

That's because the good looking ones all go where the business is, like Saigon. And the real gems aren't just found, they're procured. That's where *my* contacts come into play." He boastfully poked a thumb into his chest, to emphasize his particular craftiness. "Saigon's off limits to anyone not assigned or on official business, right? With some exceptions, like us."

"We work with the lucky few Joes over here who ever get to touch a girl," Wiggins interjected with a laugh. Ruddick shot him enough of a reproving look that I reran Wiggins' words. 'He disclosed something he shouldn't have, but what?'

"Wiggs means we're taking care of your *tiny* population of the best, ourselves," Ruddick corrected. I nodded, but inside was shaking my head. 'Wiggins didn't mean whores. He'd commented on Ruddick's reference to a small slice of *soldiers.*'

"The vast majority of troops over here are restricted, to firebases and compounds," I said, wanting to get us back to something unarguable. "They don't have free reign. If they did, the Army'd have some real problems."

"What do I care about a bunch of tight-assed generals' problems with whores?" Ruddick motioned his hand again to dismiss the subject.

"I don't know," I said," It's just that when I was in Vung Tàu, I had a problem with one – a bad fucking experience...."

"Did I ever tell you about my *worst fucking* experience?" Ruddick interrupted. "It was wonderful. But shit, some people think we're supposed to play bridge with them on the verandah, if you get that far."

"Not me – no this one got way weird," I explained, "I stayed with this real slick babe for a few days. But then we got into a god-awful fight – I mean like a friggin' brawl. It was all so convoluted – my wanting something more I guess – *what* I don't know. Problem was, the more I tried, the worse things got."

"It's obvious she didn't have whatever the hell it was you wanted." Ruddick pulled a cigarette out of a pack and lit it up. I watched his bushy eyebrows rise as he drew the smoke in as though the muscles of his forehead were essential to the effort. "Not getting laid in Vung Tàu…? Now *that's* a dude who needs some serious help."

"No-o-o-o! Ruddick. She gave me more of that than I could've had with a pair of dicks. I just wanted some kind of emotional connection. Sympathy? I don't know."

"So you decided to beat it out of her?!Did you ever think of offering her a few more bucks? Sympathy can't be that expensive."

"And you got to fightin' over *that*? Wiggins asked. "Ain't you ever heard of, *make love not war?"*

"I was kind of stuck… and couldn't leave." I mumbled.

"Simple thing, Sir, you just up and leave. You hear all this talk back in the States about *pullin' out and leavin'* – Ha, it's all I've been doing since I got here!"

"It wasn't that simple, I derided. "It was only with luck that I got out of that jam. Worse, it was a bad miscalculation. I've trained myself to anticipate potential traps. So, miscalculating like that worries me. In my world, relax and you die."

"I'm not following you," Ruddick said. "Sounds like you went on patrol with her. Lots of things can get you killed in *this* country. As for these girls, you're over-thinking them. It's *not* a cerebral activity. And in a war zone, there's all kinds of shit going."

"So, the ones hit by the war in some particularly bad way become whores?"

"Man, you back on that again? In a war, nothing's ever one thing. It's a little of this, a little of that, and a bunch of this other. Nobody's got the same situation. This one here got talked into it by her big sister. I can tell." We all looked at her. She smiled. "Money or easy money. Work like a dog for a month for thirty bucks or make the same in a few hours of pretending you're a bitch in heat. No moral dimensions exist – just labor-saving efficiency taking over.

"They are incredibly blasé about it."

"Spend a little time with them," Ruddick said, "and you'll find that most have the carefree nature of androids. There's workings inside, but nobody can follow the wiring and there aren't any schematics."

"Hey," Wiggins guffawed, "What they got to care about? – doing the buckin' bronco on a dude's johnson for a few minutes, ain't somethin' they're needin' to worry themselves over. Nah, that can't be it, can it little honey?" He turned back to the girl. She looked up at him, our conversation being no more than a drawn-out negotiation over which one of us would be first.

"I don't care what comes along," said Ruddick. "Carefree, sympathetic, whatever – you just take the best looking ones you can. And don't look past that top layer, like *you* did."

"I guess I had to. I wanted to be sure I had a real girl."

"Gee-zuhs Mondo! I never thought you were that naive. They're brainless whores. They don't care if they're disposable. It's what they're selling. You want more? You've come to the wrong store."

'What the hell am I doing? A day out of Vung Tau and I'm still locked on my rumble with Ngoc. And letting these two into my confidence is idiotic. They're so content stewing in this flesh-pot they can't hear me. Why do I still need to make sense of not getting along with a whore? Okay, she fooled me. I let her – trying to get solace from someone whose humanity was all fucked out. She was *real* all right, all of her, the catty tart in the Pussy Cat Lounge, and the caterwauling termagant chasing that jeep.'

'Man, I've got to clear my head of this or I'll come out of the field and be glomming onto their jaunts to Saigon. Shit, on Wiggs level, I'll be navigating with a dick for a compass. You can't just sip at the pool of debauchery. You'll keep wanting to lean further and further out, until you fall in. My army career'll be the first thing I'll lose. *That's* not going to happen!'

"Come on you guys," I said. "Let's hit the road." I shoved my chair back.

"Aw," Ruddick moaned, "and leave her cryin' in her little tincture of delta doo-doo?"

"She drank it already. Didn't you say you had business to attend to?"

"I didn't," he answered. "But as a natural fact, we do." Ruddick said and pushed a pile of bills toward the waiter as he got up. "Yeah... I reckon it is about time we hit the Puzzle Palace."

"Hey, Baby San," Wiggins offered, "next time I'm back, whatsay we play a couple games of *'hide the hot dog.'* I think you'd be good at it."

As we picked up our gear, the girl's face expressed something I'd seen before, desolation. It dragged my mind back to Ngoc again. Can you actually debase a whore? Yeah, you can. But before you do, you're sure to debase yourself.' We ambled out in a heavy-booted clomp toward the hallway.

"It's gonna be more than a little tight in that elevator with the three of us," I said.

"What're you talking about?" Ruddick asked.

"About that crappy-ass plywood box. It's only yea big."

"What'd you come up on that for?"

"It's the one they showed me," I said. "The others are just empty shafts – you can see right into them."

"Yeah, the first two are. Then there's that wood thing. We always use the one around the corner – a regular elevator. Why not?"

"Right," I said reticently, receiving the information as just one more insult from this building.

As we went out the door, another member of The President's rooftop *filles de joie* was entering. She stepped back to let us by. Passing, she looked directly at me. Her startled open-mouthed expression was exactly the same one she'd given me eight hours before. Ruddick and Wiggins halted at the imploring motion she made with her hands. Her mouth was moving, but lacked sound, silently rehearsing the words.

"Hey Baby-san!" Wiggins exclaimed. "I remember you – a couple months back, right? How you doing?" He turned to me with a triumphant grin. "This here used to be one of my favorite little Saigon buddies. One time she was anyway – what's your name again?"

"I My-Lan."

"Yeah, Lan… I remember."

"Last night," she blurted, pointing at me. "I wan' give nice boom boom him. Him take big knife. Him wan me kill. Him numbah ten – numbah ten mill-yon!"

Our eyes fixed on each other's. In the light of day, her enormous pupils looked as vacant of life as cabochons of clear crystal. Already huge, they appeared to be expanding, beyond what was anatomically possible, beyond what was human. As I stared, I felt like I'd be sucked bodily into them, to tumble through a lightless hole in an abandoned stairwell, and to free-fall into the remote interstices of this catacomb for the oldest profession.

"Wa-a-a-ay to go there, Mondo," Ruddick leered. "So if you can't beat it out of them, you use a knife?" He was giving me his pig-eyed look, staring at both me and the girl at the same time, while not seeing either of us. In the next paranormal second, I saw and felt this entire land, distilled to its seductions and perfidies. It rushed straight at me.

V
The Look

CHAPTER 1

OUR JEEP WEAVED ALONG IN traffic toward MACV headquarters. Like broken-field running, Wiggins cut and swerved through swarming vehicles with nonchalance and a speed three notches past my liking. I forced myself to believe the delusion that he was a man of extraordinary skill. That was hard. Our careening lurch around an eighteen-wheel flatbed truck spiked my unease, its mountainous load of concrete block making the mismatch all the more menacing. The kind of hands on the wheel of an M-151-A, whether nimble or careless, really didn't matter. Lesson one taught that pushing it too far was always closer than you thought. Its high center of gravity, wide-open body and an unaccustomed tight steering ratio had bought the farm for many an unsuspecting soldier.

Images of olive drab metal, wrought into origami, had me re-envisioning last month's jeep-borne splattering of our battalion's Commo Officer. It morphed Saigon's streets into Hockenheimring, where Wolfgang von Trips' demise shortly'd be mimicked by me.

Jostling in the rear seat, I positioned myself to blast out like a missile an eyeblink before impact. The execution of a parachute landing fall onto pavement at forty miles per hour would be suicidal. 'Right, killed by instant smushing is worse than being abraded to the bone marrow and thumped to death by a score of eight inch Lambro tires?'

Wiggins drove on, indifferent to Ruddick's mordant observations about the passing cityscape. With nothing to add, I leaned back against the rear tire and tried to change the subject of my gory daydreams.

At MACV headquarters, a security detail pointed Wiggins to where the jeep needed to be parked.

"That's our cue, Mondo," Ruddick said, abruptly swinging his legs to the pavement. "We'll meet up over there, Wiggs." I jumped out and followed him toward the doorway. He stopped.

"I've been thinking..." he said. "Yeah, since we were back at The President. It seems you've got an interesting way with the girls."

"Meaning?" I asked. "If you're implying something about that fucking big-eyed whore who said I tried to kill her, you don't know dog shit."

"Your unusual style of foreplay *has* come up a couple of times.... Look, if you stick with me on a few things, I might could set you straight – like be of useful assistance to you."

"Assistance with what?" His whispered confidence suggested no chance of it being on the strict up and up.

"Girls," he said, "certain girls.... Like I mentioned this morning. But don't worry about that now. I want to discuss something else. Remember last time we operated together and our units had contact in that ville?"

"Yeah," I answered, my mind still stuck on what exactly he'd meant by *girls*.

"You and I both did a real find job out there, exactly the kind of performance that ought to be written up for an award."

"If anyone's deserving of anything, it'd be Thieu uy Quang, and that'd be your area to put him in."

"Fuck Quang. I'm talking about us. How do you think this shit happens? Award opportunities don't fall into guy's laps, they're created, taken. You *must* know that! I've seen it plenty."

"So what are you saying?"

"Do I have to draw you a picture? I take care of you. And, you extend me the same courtesy. It's done all the time. We're in totally different commands, yours going through USARV and mine MACV. Perfect, no one notices."

"But Ruddick, we didn't do anything – nothing particularly special."

"You're telling me that write-ups and citations aren't exaggerated? Shit, they decide what award, then describe the action to fit it. They're *all* like that and you fuckin' know it."

"Well, maybe some are. What kind of award are you talking about?"

"Silver Stars." His tone was flat, communicating their insignificance, as if they were just Boy Scout Tenderfoot pins.

"Silver Stars?! I exclaimed. "Are you nuts?"

"Cut the crap, Carney. I know you don't have a Silver Star. Are you telling me you don't want one?"

"No, I'm not," I said.

"Being a lifer, of course you do. This is your chance. You're no Mister Straight Arrow. You know the score. People fuck people, and people take care of people. And in a war, where people die, you take what you can get. In twenty years, you'll be somewheres thanking me. I'm getting real short and this is one loose end I need to take care of. I'm staying away from hairy places these days, so I'm not likely to get another *opportunity*. So…"

"I don't know Ruddick," I said, shaking my head. 'I do know... But then even Ngoc couldn't distract me from thinking about Dingleberry's bayonet that was still stuck in my back. That E-E with Dills was a sure fire Silver. Yeah, Ruddick, *people do fuck people.*'

Ruddick spotted Wiggins heading toward us. "We'll talk about these things some more later," he whispered.

Pentagon East was a gray, multi-story building. It sat alongside Ton Sun Nhut with an air of unassuming functionality. Inside, it housed the operational nerve center of the war. Tagging along with Ruddick and Wiggins, it struck me as an odd land of crisply starched jungle fatigues, Plasti-Lux coated jungle boots, and mirror-shined floors. Ruddick asked me to wait outside the office he was looking for.

The J-2 area was crammed with desks and busy men. Field grade officers were the foot soldiers, their mission objectives lying hidden in mountains of operational and logistical data. It was tough going. Frontal attacks straight into briefing rooms, the pile by pile rooting-out of quandaries and dilemmas were clearly taking a toll. It read on their grim faces. Statistical analysis could be a ruthless foe. They were tied to measuring the war as a viable substitute for winning it.

I thought of Maureen's pals, as besotted with this stuff as these staff drones. 'MACV's got its numbers and the anti- war types say they've got better ones. None of them matter. Only one thing does; we either break the communists' will to continue waging this war or we don't. They can measure anything, but if we aren't breaking their backs, we aren't winning. And if we aren't winning, what the hell are we doing?'

I sauntered into the disdainful glare of a brigadier general who stood in a doorway speaking with two officers. I edged around them, taking note of his name tape, 'Potts.' Looking sourly at my salt caked Korean-made tiger stripes, he extended the inspection down to my boots. They hadn't felt a lick of Kiwi since I'd put them on eight months before. I braced myself to be brought up short.

'I'll just tell him that these boots spend ninety percent of their time slogging through rice paddies and ten percent drying out. And that superfluous polishing time would be at the expense of mission prep. Yes sir, I'm more intent on being a soldier than just looking like one! Sure you'll say that, Carney.' I hoped that with no collar insignia and an unassuming posture, he 'd take me for a nobody. 'Right, this being the last place in Vietnam where some funky E-1 would be hanging around wasting time.'

We drove into what passed for the city's outskirts. American cities transitioned from urban to rural through miles of residential suburban sprawl, but Saigon traded its downtown chock-a-block for rice paddies in the distance of a rifle shot. My first sighting of banana trees gave me a feeling of comfort. 'Maybe you get a sense of security from the familiar; but finding it in jungle foliage says what about where I think *safe is?*'

"I was surprised when you told me you'd never been to MACV before," Ruddick said at last. He hadn't spoken while we'd driven across the city.

"Most of my time in-country's been down in Dinh Tuong. What line officers would have the need or opportunity? I doubt even Braccia's been up here. Everything goes up the chain, you know, Brigade, Division…"

"What'd you think of the place?"

"You'll never get killed working there," I answered. "And that being the J-2 section, I suppose we can attribute it to their superior intelligence."

"Ha, yeah," Ruddick agreed, "The VC targeted it during Tet last year, but screwed up. Their launch points should've been closer. With only a slightly larger force, they might've decapitaded us.

"I ran into what must be the Assistant Chief of Staff for intel, some BG named Potts, but slipped pass him. The last thing I need is a discussion with a general and two majors on what I was doing there – like nothing, and looking like a skode."

"You'd at least be telling the truth, Mondo. You don't much care for staff pogues do you?"

"No, not since reading the book, 'The Scum Also Rises.' That's 'Major Crème de la Crème meets Lieutenant Canaille' by another title, which is a take-off on 'Tinderberry meets Carney'."

"What's it with your XO there?" Ruddick asked.

"We don't like each other.

"Your S-2, Yoshino, told me he's a real prick."

"A royal purple-headed one... and Yoshino would know, he works for him." Ruddick nodded and turned back to the front.

Wiggins pulled off a narrow side road and killed the engine. We were facing what looked like a private dwelling, but signs suggested a store. In the quiet, near distance, a bell tolled. Notes drifted up with a soft ringing, the thick humid air dampening its resonance. I'd never heard the peal of a bell in Vietnam. Looking down the road, I spotted the source, a squat campanile. At its apex, a gold cross glinted in the sun.

"All right troops!" Ruddick exclaimed. "Time for lunch. You hungry?"

"Very," I said.

"You better be because this here's one of the best places I know for local chow. You know the bit about armies traveling on their stomachs."

"Yeah, armies and snakes," I retorted. "And lately, all the places I've been to don't know the difference."

"Trust me, this one does."

"When applied to the Army," I said, "the saying ought to be, '*Have stomach, will travel.*'"

"That's your Army, not mine. The way I see it, no jaunt to Saigon is really complete unless your two main appetites aren't satisfied. One down, one to go."

"Hey, wait a sec," I said. "Is the jeep going to be okay out here? An unattended jeep anywhere outside of barbed wire is a brainless move."

"I'll pay a couple of boys to watch it for us."

"Who you gonna pay to watch *them*?"

"Me and my friend Colt," he said, patting the clamshell holster of his .45. I considered the tenuous firepower of the two sidearms between the three of us.

"Right, Kemosabe, I see we're loaded for bear. You going to expect a couple of boys to betray the VC – like they'd anticipate no consequences after we're gone?"

"Come o-o-o-o-on," Ruddick soothed, "don't sweat it. You're always thinking we're in the middle of Injun country. It's not like that everywhere."

"Sorry," I said, "but you'll have to convince me. When you're not walking-it one step at a time and studying it over the front sight of your weapon, its pacification status is *unknown*."

"Pacification's not even relevant here," he said. "It wasn't ever in a situation where it needed to be de-gooked – not since Tết last year – maybe not even then."

The restaurant smelled negligibly of food, as unusual in Vietnam as was its cleanliness. 'A good start no invisible clouds of what-the-hell-is-that-smell hanging in the air.'

I attended to the décor, generic Southeast-Asian provincial. Murals extended over two walls, depicting a panorama of pastoral life. Painted in black and half-a dozen shades of green, the scenes of water buffalo and rice farming made sure I didn't forget where I was.

"Yeah," Ruddick went on, "we don't need us any boys to watch the jeep. I can see most of it from right here." Although all the tables were empty, Ruddick and Wiggins took the one closest to the door. As I sat down with them Ruddick sprung up and went back to the doorway. A severe-looking Vietnamese man came in. They walked to the other side, both speaking in Vietnamese. As if on cue, a girl appeared with three cans of cold Schlitz. She placed them on our table and I got up to search for a latrine.

Coming up behind Ruddick, I caught sight of a huge wad of MPC changing hands, with the dough ending up buttoned in Ruddick's breast pocket.

"I can see what you like about this joint," I joked. "Three beers and you get paid a fat wad to drink 'em. Tastes like Schlitz, but smells like black market." He glared, unamused.

"Fuck off," he said derisively. Obviously, my presence had been neither anticipated nor wanted.

"You gotta admit that's a pretty big pack of bucks – and me unable to recall any situations where Viets pay *us* for anything." The Vietnamese guy gave me a sinister expression. 'A truculent scowl is probably the most pleasant expression this dude's capable of.'

"You didn't see any pack of anything," Ruddick instructed.

"Hmmm, then I guess I must have *mis-translated* what you were saying." He looked hard at me. 'He's reacting too fucking strong for it to be nothing. What the hell's going on here?'

By the time I returned from relieving myself, the Viet had gone. Ruddick was sitting at the table, with a just-ate-the-canary look on his face.

"All right Mondo, about this black market shit." He lifted his can as if to demonstrate something. "I prefer calling it a *beer market.* The only thing black about it is my Afro-American Vice President for Sales, that is, SFC Wiggs." Wiggins didn't appear to have heard anything. He was moving in an abstracted lethargy toward the waitress. She was in the rear, talking to a long-haired girl.

"I can't believe what you're telling me," I said. The pocket below his name tape pouched noticeably with the hundred or so bills crammed inside. "Man, you guys are going to get your butts in a serious sling."

"I told you," Ruddick said in a heavy whisper, "you didn't *see* shit, so that means you don't *know* shit. Besides, if we didn't trust you, we wouldn't have brought you here. You owe us." I glanced around.

"Don't worry about me. I'm just thrilled with the fifteen-cent beer I haven't drunk yet, the food I ain't even eaten yet and the tab you ain't paid for yet." I swept the back of my hand dismissively. Both girls disappeared into the rear. Wiggins ambled his way back to the table.

"Yum-m-m Yum," he said, grabbing the back of his chair. "I just seen something I'd like to eat that ain't no-ways gonna be on the menu." Neither of us paid him any mind.

"Jeez Rudd," I said, addressing them both. "Against whatever risks, how much can anybody possibly make on beer? Like it's just cans of beer that hardly cost anything in the first place. Who the hell buys it? Us grunts get all we can drink."

"That's the thing man, *we* do."

"Who's this, *we*?"

"Soldiers, the troops – everybody."

"Come on, it's already our friggin beer in the first place. Why do we have to buy it back from ourselves? Why would we want to?"

"We want to so we can drink it."

"What is this, Abbott and Costello? You're losing me."

"Okay, hold on. You need another little lesson in economics, the free market, and the beer market."

"I know they're the same," I said skeptically. "Didn't I attend that class over breakfast? – the one on beer and free pussy."

"No, nothing in the free market is free."

Yeah, so I've noticed," I said, "neither beer *nor* pussy."

"You're catching on. Neither's free anywhere this side of heaven. Over here in Viet-land though, they're both pretty-damned cheap." He sounded like a teacher having to repeat the obvious to that one kid in the class who still didn't get it.

"Listen up, I buy it by the pallet – eighty-one cases per – at twelve cents a can – it starts cheap for a couple of reasons. What we're getting over here – in case you haven't noticed – is beer in steel cans. When the industry back home made their move to aluminum tab-tops, they didn't want these less-preferred cans competing against their new ones. We're dumping whatever's left down our gullets, so the military's getting it for next to nothing – probably cost less than a penny a can to ship across the Pacific – chump change in this war. There're no taxes on it, and no wholesale distributors' and retailers' cuts stuck in either. I sell it to the Viets for fifty cents. They sell it for a buck. I've seen it in a couple of places for two dollars a can!"

"Yeah," I said, "the Pussycat Lounge in Vung Tàu sells it for three."

"The higher the class of tail on hand, the more the beer costs. Sounds like you started out at the right kind of place anyway."

"Started out, yeah," I agreed. "I don't know Ruddick – it sounds crazy. Back at the fire base we can drink all we want for fifteen cents and still have a bunch of money left over for a company fund. Goes to supplying the guys with a dozen cases of free beer just before payday."

"Sure, you can do that all you want," he scoffed, "while gazing out over concertina, sand-bagged bunkers, and mud – daydreaming about the best pussy you never had. And you're still paying for it too! When you go into some Vietnamese bar, you wanna glug down *Ba moi ba* and nurse a formaldehyde hangover in the morning? Or, sip on a cold American one, brewed with water that didn't start out laced with cholera, typhus, and shit like Ethylene glycol."

"I'm – Wiggs and I are only a couple of middle men beer distributors, getting it to where the customers want it. We're just seeing to the welfare of the troops – making sure they don't have to drink rot gut, protecting them from hellacious bouts of the shits. The Vietnamese don't get it like we do – don't even have a slang word for it."

"A word for what?"

"For *The Dysentery that made Vietnam Famous.*" He hefted his can of Schlitz and tipped it toward me. "You know, I ought to get a fucking Legion of Merit for this."

"All they're likely to give you Ruddick is free lessons in the *Leavenworth shuffle.*"

"No-o-o-o, I keep myself as far from the merchandise as I am from Kansas. Besides, the CID has bigger fish to fry.

"I've heard about some heavy dope coming in," I said, "from the Patet Lao – rock something or other."

"Brown Rock heroin," Ruddick amended. Wiggins's head jerked like a half-sleeping dog who'd heard his name and 'ride in the car' in the same sentence. He looked at Ruddick with a wary expression.

"You know how it comes in?" I asked. "Like through the highlands – right through the middle of the war? It makes no sense."

"Yes it does," he said, emphasizing his patience with the child pupil. "The war's irrelevant. And it isn't always the Patet Lao. Ever heard of the Ruak River?"

"No. Where is it?"

"Burma. It flows right into the Mekong. Even you can follow it from there. Lots of folks are involved, Shan people in Burma, Chinese, Thais, Laotians, even the NVA in Cambodia – then to Arvin intermediaries. Presto, it's here."

"You know any such Arvins?" I asked.

"No," Ruddick answered evenly."

"Seems to me you've met enough Arvins to have gotten a feel for it."

"I've worked with lots of Arvin officers," he explained. "Some are outstanding, some are incompetent, and a small few are secretly on the other side. This is a very poor country. Even some of their half-way decent officers are grabbing what they can – trying to set their families up while the going's good, because nobody knows how long the good's going to be. Some Viets just want to hedge their bets, so they won't be S.O.L. when this whole fucking merry-go-round stops."

"There're a lot of Arvins out there in the field dying right now!" I said, bewildered with what I was hearing. "What're *they* hedging? All this is undermining the war. And you're right in there too – floating among the turds?"

"That's an opinion not a fact. Look, there's so much shit going on – so much money around, who's going to be flipping out over a few piddly-ass pallet loads of brew that's only being *re*-distributed? That ain't shit, and nothing to do with the course of this war, which by the way, ended last June when *your* Ninth Div guys began our withdrawal back to the world."

"Piddly-ass would be exactly the reason the CID will go after what you're up to," I pointed out. They ain't going to be dicking around with the upper levels of heroin operations involving NVA and senior Viet officers. No-o-o-o. Black marketed PX booty? Now, that'd be their game. Man, they'll be on you like stink on shit: one, it's easy. And two, it involves our guys."

"Lemme clue you in, Carney. There are hundreds of deserters living all over Saigon, right here in Cholon. White or black, they don't hide real well. Don't have to either. They're out in the open, living on nothing but scams. Prime among them is PX booty, truck loads of it. All the big brass are also right here in town. If they cared, they would've dragneted their asses out of here, but they haven't. That means they could care less. I took a glug of beer, as Ruddick raised his can. 'Great, I just toasted his activities.'

"This is a big-ass place," he went on, "big enough to absorb a whole lot of action without putting anybody out. You haven't noticed any shortages of beer have you?"

"No," I answered.

"You have no idea how much beer is coming into this country – enough so nobody'll ever get upset. Beer's not treated as part of the food ration, like say milk where some QM fuck determines how much a Soldier should have, per day times how many men, etc. Beer's like ammo. The more you use, the more of it they ship."

"Now if a unit can't get any, it goes up the chain and some general makes a call. In twenty-four hours they'll have all they can drink. But, thousands of cases a day just get lost. 'Slippage' is what they call it. How much is that? *An acceptable amount.* Excellent, no further action needed. Ultimately, they know where it all goes. It gets drunk. By whom? Viets? Not hardly. What was it brought here for in the first place? For GIs to drink! Mission accomplished."

The Vietnamese man who had given Ruddick the money returned. He didn't come to the table, just stood in the doorway. I looked him over. That same malefic gaze struck me as integral to a certain livelihood. 'His kind of ugly always means no good.'

"Hang on a sec," Ruddick said. "I've got to see a man about a horse." Both he and Wiggins went outside. The three of them stood in front of the jeep talking.

I leaned forward to get a better view of them huddling over the vehicle's hood. Ruddick was tracing his finger on a sheet of something they'd laid out. 'It's a map. But of what? We're way to the north of their district. Maybe the guy's giving them intel on something down there. If that's the case, they'd want my input. Intel from the Viet who gave Ruddick all that cash? Hardly.'

I sat alone at the table, dead-ended, musing over Ruddick's big-ass place. 'The immense rear echelon our military had built up was definitely big. The tail did wag the dog. Why wouldn't it? They've made the tail ten times the size of the dog. But the sprawl and labyrinthine environs of Saigon alone could swallow a small-time beer scam. That's no reason for Ruddick to let me in on their thing. Why didn't he just say nothing and stick with his 'fuck off." He knows I don't know a damned thing. He's co-opting me into a lot of stuff. That Silver Star's still hanging. And his references to special *girls*.'

The two of them returned to our table.

"I still don't get it," I offered cautiously. "I'll bet this here place can't move a six pack in a week. There aren't any US units around. No GIs'd be coming in – would they? Where's the beer come from?"

"Would you believe, The United States?" he answered, mimicking Maxwell Smart. He looked at me like he always did, bypassing my head, first over one shoulder then the other, as if forever checking out someone who was wandering around behind me. "It's why *we're* here, Carney" – the perfect blend of obscurity and... peace. How'd it physically get here? I have no idea. But, this place's always on top of things."

Ruddick slipped past my question and motioned for the girl to take our food order. I looked over the menu's rough, handwritten translation of the main ingredients penned next to each item. 'How obscure are we? Who needs the English version?'

"It's all first class here. You don't need to be squeamish about anything."

"It'll take more than your reassurances to get me to come around after some of the delicacies I've had put in front of me."

"What, you want me to take you into the kitchen to see their refrigerator? They've got a big one!"

"Trouble is, with the electricity going on and off throughout the day, half the time it'd be doubling as a metal closet. Over here, the difference between good and bad is the difference between barely acceptable and deadly. But if food was all I cared about, I'd be a Navy pogue. So you ain't told me yet, Ruddick. Who the hell comes here?"

"Vietnamese, those with a buck or two. Didn't you notice the neighborhood we're in? It's part of why I can leave the jeep out there."

"It's safe because Vietnamese come here?"! I asked. "Safe to me, begins when I can see at least a dozen armed GIs. What am I missing?"

"A lot," he said, "starting with understanding the particular Viets who live around here."

'Right, the very same ones who need the menu translated into English.'

"Viets need help knowing the English for what's in their own food?!" Tired of his playing with me, I held the menu toward the girl and pointed at what I wanted. As I did, a boy of about thirteen came up to the table. With an uncommon lack of hesitation, he just sat down and joined us. Then without an exchange of recognition on anyone's part, the kid broke out a deck of cards and started dealing them to Wiggins.

"Yessir," Wiggins said, as though speaking to his cards, "excuse us, 'cuz we gonna play us a little gin rummy." They commenced with a wordless game. At precisely that instant, I noticed her. The girl who'd previously been talking to the waitress, the one Wiggins had spoken of with such lickerish description, reappeared from the rear. Facing me, she moved about idly in a lingering supervision of our lazy goings-on. She had ***The Look*!**

CHAPTER 2

UNSELF-CONSCIOUS OF MY STARING, I studied her features. She was gut-wrenchingly beautiful, her face mesmerizing. She had *The Look* at a level of perfection I didn't believe could exist.

During my time in Vietnam, I was drawn to scrutinize many things. My job demanded it. But when in any sizable town where things were relaxed, females rose to the top of my list. I scanned the busy streets for pretty girls as I would anywhere, but after discovering *The Look*, this phenotypic strain from an unknown ethnic group, I stayed on high alert for it. On the few rare occasions I'd spotted it, I'd been riveted. When their eyes caught mine, the connection seared into permanent memory, angelic expressions a reflection of their personalities. I'd preserved these fleeting images by treating them like a pouch of precious stones. Dumping them into the palm of conscious thought, I could relive the unique way they glittered in the sun. Yet as fine as they were, they paled in the face of the one now standing ten feet from me.

With a quiet compulsion, I attended to every square inch of her. The shape of her eyes, eyebrows, cheek bones, nose and lips were all just right, perfect. The totality was so sublime that I couldn't stop staring. She had to be the most beautiful girl I'd ever seen, *anywhere.* 'What's she doing *here?* This place's better than okay, but far too ordinary to employ a girl who can tear the breath out of you. A golden pagoda in the clouds might suit her, but hardly this restaurant.'

Although dressed in a plain white blouse and common black silk pants, her body was as good a compliment to her face as I could imagine. Lacking the spare Twigginess of most females in this country, she was providentially round where it mattered. 'How is she making her shape do that in such formless, commonplace clothes? She'd have caught my eye dressed in a burlap rice sack. Tie a length of rope around the middle and there it is. Lord, the way her waist goes *in* like that!'

She exuded earthiness, her body as subtle as it was explicit, moving without effort, sylphlike and capable of inhabiting the air itself.

Yes, *that was it!* Back when I was fourteen, I'd gone alone to New York City to spend a school vacation week with relatives. Permissive to a fault, they let me wander midtown Manhattan at will. But with the city's iniquities beyond my comprehension, I discovered Brentano's. This enormous, 5th Avenue bookstore allowed customers to sit at tables and read, free from taking the boot of some sour-old floor walker. Caught up in their pelagic art section, I chanced across a large format how-to book on drawing the nude female. In 1958, my exposure to naked women amounted to brief peeks at semi-nude models in some kid's purloined men's magazine. *Art* however, had its own rules about what could be revealed and, this book showed all there was to show.

In a sparse ballet studio, the same completely naked girl posed, un-salaciously stretching, bending and raising her legs at all angles. Yet it wasn't just the graphic nudity that had gotten me, but the girl herself, her face, her startling curves, and massive mane of dark Rapunzel-length hair. Each page was a further confirmation of her perfection. One stunning pose showed her blithely reaching up on her tiptoes. It swallowed me in a fantasy of her leaping into my arms. The stark pictures awakened something in me.

Time lost to goggle-eyed concentration, burned that insouciant girl into my memory and made her the standard by which all would be measured. And in the eleven years since, many pretty girls had come along, but none had surpassed her.

There it was though. Right in front of me a get-out-of-the-way challenger had shattered the art model template in my brain. She had the same physical attributes, lighthearted spirit, and aura of kindness. But combined with *The Look,* she was the equivalent of a homer smashed three rows beyond '*the red seat*' in deep right at Fenway.

I watched her, benumbed as I'd be peering through a hedge at a real-life *September Morn,* a bona fide David and Bathsheba moment without the marble column to conceal my trance. She atomized my inhibitions as though blasting them with a 500-pound bomb. I couldn't stop staring. 'This girl's got to be a final contender for the *most beautiful female in the world,* God's own all-time standard for female perfection. It's *The Look that does it* – lofts her into the realm of demigoddess.'

She went about several trifling tasks, in the middle pausing to push her black waist-length hair aside. As she bent, a thick skein swung like a curtain flowing in a light breeze. Her subtle ballet transfixed me. 'Hell, I'm cataplectic! All I can do is stare. Okay, her sensuousness is magnetic, but this's like something burrowing inside my body.'

She puttered around and fiddled with a samovar, to the point of pretending to work. Her eyes darted in my direction. Other glances followed, like the reaction of any girl who'd become aware of being minutely inspected, except she didn't pretend that I was invisible. Instead, she took wiling looks back, to check me out. Using her hair as cover, she spied sideways through it. Each time she did, her eyes met mine.

Suddenly, she stopped and stood there staring back, eyes locked onto me. It was my turn to look away, but I couldn't. Then something passed between us, from her to me. It was an arrhythmic sensation in my chest, that wriggling alive thing again. It was working its way deeper. 'What in the world am I feeling?!'

She smiled, a big cheerful, open-mouthed expression. Blood shifted in me so fast it felt like it'd become full of bubbles, fizzing to the point I could hear it. With that circuit of recognition, her face acquired the supernal summit of anything I'd ever seen. Despite the sanguinary foam coursing through me, I sat there like she'd turned me into a block of stone.

She abruptly spun about and went into the back room. Her leaving broke the trance. Severed with a snap, the sinews holding my heart in place felt like they'd just been snipped with a pair of wire cutters. The rush of my blood stalled. I turned back to Ruddick. He'd been quiet the entire time. Wiggins and the boy were still dealing and drawing from the deck of cards. All that'd come from them was occasional Vietnamese numbers and low groans from Wiggins.

"Holy crap," I blurted. "Did you guys check out that girl?" As the words were leaving my mouth, I wanted to retrieve them, to protect and hide my staggering discovery.

"I tried to orientate you to her before, Sir," Wiggins said in an I-told-you-so tone, "but you didn't cop on. Yeah, 'I taut I saw a *pooty tat*' – tol'-ya I could eat that stuff with a spoon."

"You got that right," Ruddick joined in. "From what I saw, she's the best thing I've seen in my whole seventeen months over here."

"But from what I seen," Wiggins offered, "looks like Lieutenant Carney and her were tryin' a no-blink, stare-each-other-down duel. I've seen some big smoky eyes in my day, but I don't believe I ever seen a girl have 'em mixed with goddamn hypnotism. I tell-ya, she flat got that shit goin' on."

"She could damn sure numb-up my head," Ruddick agreed. "It's funny we never saw her here before – and wouldn't have missed *her* that's for sure. There's something beyond Vietnamese about her. I can't put my finger on it, but it's– some kind of...."

"Some kind of wonderful," Wiggins soulfully tuned. "Nice set of tee-tahs for the Nam too."

"My old girlfriend in France told me there's a town in Algeria called Tit," I offered.

"If she says so," Ruddick said. "But speaking of France, that there Eurasian is dimes to doughnuts French – right where that Brigitte-Bardot bod came from."

"It's your *essence* thing," Wiggins cut in. "I can't put my finger on it neither. But then I usually start things off by putting my finger *in* it – Aaht aaht, I best be careful 'bout what I say – being that Tuan here is her number one lil' brother. They don't let on 'bout how much English they're pickin' up. But she does look like she'd be from some other country – no tellin' where."

"*My money's* saying it's here... something special all right." Ruddick took a definitive swig of his beer.

I nodded. 'He's right, but only close. He doesn't know he's sitting across from the cognoscente of *The Look*. He's no idea that it sourced from a collection of rare and enchanted genes. They can see it, they might like it, but they'll never be able to dig it like I can, with layers of recherché appreciation. Wiggins thinks it's hypnotism, Ruddick's numb with it, and it's given me… Stendhal Syndrome. When a girl reaches the realm of demigoddess, there's no equivocating. A dude'd have to have lapsed into straight-jacketed, rubber-roomed psychosis not to see it.'

The kid brother struck me as too vigilant for my liking. Whenever he looked at me, it seemed like he was collecting information for later use, anything from absolute nothing to extreme pain and a merciful death. 'He's a handsome kid, but there's no resemblance to the girl. He's all Viet too.'

The girl reemerged from the back her gaze already on me, now a contingent part of her movements. With a smile, she repositioned a package of chopsticks on the next table, moving them an inch to the left of where they'd been. 'Exactly, all chopsticks should be precisely aligned at 60 degrees to the right edge of the kitchen door. That activity is either terminally anal or just an excuse to come back out, and come closer. My God, that face!'

'If all the men on this planet could be brought together to decide *who's the fairest of them all*, in a hundred rounds of straight elimination, they'd get through the world's entire girl population. And this girl'd be right there in the last bevy of the ne plus ultras. When the final stupendous ebony beauty and blonde nuclear bombshell finally had to sit down, this one'd still be standing. Yeah, and I'd called her from the start.'

"Hey Rudd," I directed, "ask the kid if he can go get her – to come over and sit with us – if she will…."

Ruddick mumbled something in Vietnamese and the boy's blank-faced countenance tightened. He cogitated Ruddick's words, weighing them. The kid didn't move. Ruddick smiled and spoke again, this time pointing to both the girl and me. I jolted. 'Is he setting me up for a practical joke – to earn him a chuckle from Wiggins, at my expense? If she bugs out the back door, I'll be going over this table for his throat.'

"Errr..." A fragment of an unknown word escaped my chest. It didn't matter. The kid was out of his seat and half way to her. It shifted my attention to the two of them. They spoke amiably, both regarding me as they did. Yet their back and forth went on too long for my simple request. She appeared to be asking him a lot of questions.

A chair stood off to my right at an odd angle. I hooked my boot under a rung and dragged it next to me. The motion re-spoke the invitation. We looked at each other dead on and traded the barest semblance of smiles. Then she just walked over and sat in it. There she was right next to me, nearly touching, still looking at me, her expression reading 'yes,' and 'now what?'

"Chào cô. Cảm ơn," I said, politely.

"Không sao đâu," she replied, with matching demeanor.

I felt the prickly sensation of a sudden perspiring. My eyes began to well with tears. No one in my life had ever had the power to do this. I wiped them with my sleeve while grabbing for my beer, an effort to keep the others from noticing.

"I... I... Do you...?" I was caught up in some kind of a viscous force field, the air as thick as syrup. My words came out, but their sounds had to struggle through it to get to her. "*...Biết nói tiếng Anh không?*" I asked, taking my Vietnamese to the breaking point.

"Yes, I can a little English. I can more French speak. *Vous pouvez parler français?*"

"*Oui, un peu,*" I said. "I spent some months in France, but I already have a feeling that your English is better than my French."

"You go Paris?" she asked.

"Yeah, it's where I lived, and picked up my pettit French." My mind flashed on the image of Lisette painstakingly tutoring me in her apartment. I snatched the intrusion in the same instant, crumpling the unwanted remembrance into a wad.

"I so much want go Paris my whole life" she said.

"No problem. Next time I'm headed that way, I'll give you a call." 'Lord, why did I say something so inane?' "Hey, I can understand you knowing French but where'd you learn your English?"

"I learn English when I in school. Marie Curie Lycée, you know in Saigon?" I shook my head. She continued. "I was for time, in university. Friends in Saigon, we together French speak one-time French, one-time English."

"You mean sometimes you spoke French and sometimes you spoke English. Both?" She pronounced the word 'Eng-rish' and I thought her tongue's attempt at the L to be super cute. "Yes," she said with a vivacious laugh. "Both! One day only French, one day only English. We make fun time." I shot a glance at the others. Their eyes were fixed on her, Wiggins, sunken in a heavy-lidded interior study of her, looked way too sly. His tongue wet his lips in a slow salacious motion. Given the breathtaking beauty of this girl, it would've been to no effect that he'd spent the whole previous night getting his ashes hauled. She'd be able to put life in a cock that'd just been shot through its head with a 45.

She looked up at me pleasantly. 'How much English does she understand? Maybe not enough to stay at it for long. I've got to connect with her – do something that'll keep her sitting here. *Yes!* the cards.'

"Hey you want to play cards?!" Before the first word had left my mouth, I was scooping the idle pack from the middle of the table.

"Be my guest," Wiggins said. "Ol' Tuan here's already whipped my ass six games straight."

"You gin rummy can play?" she asked almost in a whisper, her face down-turned, eyes looking up at me through her lashes.

"Sure, not much to it. Three of a kind, four of a kind, right?" Her eyebrows went up and I hesitated. "Yeah, it's one of my old favorites. I played it back home, with my sister." 'Isn't it a kid's game like, one rung up from Fish? Gigi and I did play it, back when we were about nine or ten.'

She dealt out the cards, while I thought of how the game might have gotten to this table. The name conjured up other names, like Beefeaters and Captain Morgan. Adventurous Brits of a couple centuries ago had brought gin and rum to the far corners of the world. 'How'd that get turned into a card game? And how'd it get here? Maybe by now it's evolved into the Viets' national pastime, a cultural abjuration of Chinese checkers?'

Feeling like a drooling fool, I tried to act as if it was a revered custom, one loaded with symbolic meaning. But my demeanor of respect only stiffen my posture. 'How do I do this – jack myself up to some non-verbal plane of honor in her eyes? But God, how can I ever know what to do in *those* lambent eyes?'

Ruddick broke out of his reverie and ordered more beer. It cracked my own spell and I shifted about, around feeling like I'd been lashed to my chair and just been cut loose. Our waitress brought three more cans.

"Way-da-go Baby-san." Ruddick said. "More beer for the troops – and ain't we all 'bout that." The teen-aged girl gave him an expression of partial understanding and smoothly delivered herself into a chair as if she'd been part of the order. Her interest in the proceedings made her look kittenish, although in her case everything she did seemed kittenish. Ruddick ignored her.

Wiggins persisted with his predatory staring at my opponent. While she studied her cards, he reminded me of a reptile lying patiently in wait, not moving a muscle. The boy continued to apprehend the both of us, in his silent, penetrating watch.

I dealt and re-dealt. With astonishing rapidity, she beat me three in a row. I'd no sooner decided on what numbers or suits to go with, and she was laying her cards down, three of these and four straight of those.

"Where in the world are you getting these cards from?" I asked, affecting a pained expression. Her short-sleeved batiste blouse offered nothing in the way of possibilities. "This isn't any fun – like it's not some kind of mentalist brain-game or something."

"They got me a-believin'," Wiggins said.

"Mandrake the Magician must come in here regularly," I offered. "...Free lunch for staff tutorials."

"In game," she said, "one win and one lose. Is not so?"

"Yeah, it's so all right, but not just – wham, the *same* one. That's not really a game."

"In a game, one person must win," she said methodically. "It better when person be you, not me? This would make the fun for which you want?"

"No, it doesn't *have* to be me."

"Then it is not."

"No, no," I said, "I'm talking about it being the same *whoever person* every time."

"Only three time same person. Why it – when I am same person, it make bad for you?" She posed the question to me with such earnest compassion that I believed she thought it important, something even beyond this game.

"That's not really it. You whipped me *too* fast. It's about what fair is."

"I not mind," she said softly. "It is you who say first of it." Her demureness affected me like a powerful drug, one that tranquilized and agitated at the same time. It was as if curare was diffusing through my blood stream, right after having gulped down a handful of amphetamines. Seemingly powerless to affect anything, I settled into a benumbed, mind-racing apprehension.

I had to get us off this stupid card game. As to *what,* I pondered the small rectangles as though they were tarot. Surprise burst in my brain as if the pictures had suddenly become animate. I dissected them for confirmation. 'Whoa!'

The cards' reverse sides depicted a collection of stylized flowers. From the largest one, a single petal had fallen, but on each card, a different petal, and in a clockwise rotation. At a glance, each garish bouquet looked like identical splashes of color, yellow bleeding into orange and then to red. But with exactly thirteen petals on each, it wasn't hard to figure. Four different flowers coded the suits.

"Hey, Rudd, check this out. They're playing with marked cards! It's in the flower petals." I laid them in front of him.

"I'll be dipped in sweet shit." Wiggins muttered. He grabbed up a few and laid them down for a comparison. Our beer-retrieving soubrette tittered.

"You dinky dao," she said, either referring to my reaction or trying to contradict the obvious.

Turning back to my divine opponent, I was hit with a smile so evocative that all thinking ceased. *The Look* suddenly became palpable. Pulchritude irradiated out at me in pulsing waves. Her equanimity had me believing that she could just will gadzillious rhoentgens of it, as if from some kind of internal generator. A dizzying effect suffused my entire body. I forced myself to turn away, to clear the weird rocking sensation I felt in my head. My chair felt like it'd been set in a pint-sized rowboat a mile south of Block Island, its pitching a replay of great North Atlantic swells rolling under me. 'How can minute adjustments of lineamental bone and skin have such an effect? She's not only got *The Look*, she can *do The Look!'*

"No wonder you win!" I blurted, "you cheat."

"Is cheat – time I win?" Her words were again subdued and patient, a simple clarification. "I think no."

"Well, yeah, cheating to win. Playing with marked cards is always cheating. It's not what fair is. Card games have to be fair. Fair to win is good. Cheat to win is bad."

"Flower card give help to me," she said. "I know nothing what help you. Now you know the flowers. When come in your mind," she pointed to her forehead, "you take this from me. I take nothing from you. I think maybe you make no fair to me. I take no cheat from you."

"But I don't have any cheat to take!" I exclaimed. "I don't have anything to take, no cards, no nothing – though exposing your cheating is sort of a tacit victory."

"Oh, I no know. You talk-talk much. Maybe this make... *un tour*."

"No, I ain't tricking anybody. Not by losing every game that's for sure. You don't understand...." I stopped myself, suddenly aware of the morass in front of me. I could see myself sliding effortlessly from this argument on elementary fairness, to my standard treatise on the fairness of depositing bullets into dinks. Doubtless, that'd set into motion her transmogrification from a demigoddess into a half-sistered Madame Nguyen Thi Bình, a seamless slip from a Helen to a Clytemnestra. My disaster with Ngoc was now an all-purpose lesson.

'True that the plots of Aeschylus and other tragedians could be found imbedded in the predations of this land. But not *this* time! Is she the most beautiful girl since Helen? Only Aphrodite could decide that. But I still want to carry her off – take her where it's just the two of us – no matter who comes after us. I'll *teach* her about fairness – about what constitutes cheating – about what a sporting chance is. We'll go to Fenway Park – the perfect place for explaining how fairness works. First thing we did after fighting the Japs was teach them baseball – worked like a charm. Taking her is the thing though – a win into infinity... this stranded Venusian princess.'

As for an actual place where I could secret her away, my aunt's cottage on Block Island came back to mind. The consummate hideout, I fantasized the two of us lying in its snug upstairs bedroom, the old wooden beams just above our heads and a cool, salty breeze blowing in through the dormer window. The little waitress scurried off for our food, returned, and dealt our plates with the same spare efficiency Tuan had showed when dispensing from his deck of cards.

Ruddick and Wiggins dug in, eating like hungry soldiers. She remained, watching me eat. It had me treating the food as if it was a solemn offering, each morsel a rich benison. I was more than distracted. *The Look* was one thing, but she really did seem to be using it on me. She'd wrested my thoughts and was now spinning them into a vortex. 'I'm obsessed with her!'

Ruddick and Wiggins traded random utterances about Viet food, rating this as good, with others variously described as putrid. Repeatedly, I tried to slice off a separate conversation with the girl, but Wiggins kept interjecting himself with suggestive comments. It pissed me off and I dredged up my tattered French to wall him off, worried that Ruddick's penchant for playing verbal yo-yo with girls, hadn't been fully satisfied at breakfast. They'd had a few beers and it was beginning to tell.

At my finishing, she put her hand on the back of mine and held it there. It felt as though every physical process in my body abruptly ceased to operate. My brain still functioned, but it was consumed with whether I'd discovered a time passage or a wormhole in the universe. 'How else could I have gotten here?!'

Content with my response, she calmly got up and went into the back room. And on that cue the waitress cleared our dishes and little brother snatched up his marked deck.

"Man, did I fuck that or what?!"

"Not while I was sitting here," Ruddick said. "I would've noticed."

"No damn it, she's gone! That's what I meant. Did anyone say something stupid?"

"You were looking stupid," he said, "if you want to include what you didn't say." Something indecipherable played across his face, vanishing as quickly as it appeared. "Hold your water, Mondo. We'll get her back."

"Okay," I said, agreeable to the goal, but not liking the sound of the '*we*' who'd be doing it. "I don't know what the deal is, but this chick is something else. You know the one where you'd crawl a thousand meters through barbed wire and over broken glass, laying WD1 just to hear her fart into a canteen cup over a field phone? That's her, totally. Man she's better than the last five Playmates of the Year rolled into one."

"I ain't seen that much of her yet," Wiggins said, "but if she'd be givin' me those eyes, I'd be kickin' Miss Foldout – *out!* Yessir, she'd have no trouble makin' ol' Private Junior J. Wiggins, stand up at attention – all ready and rearin' to give her his best one-gun salute."

"Wiggs," Ruddick said, "You summed it up nicely. And speaking of private, Wiggs and I still have to see someone. Mr. Chu's gone to get him – a local intel thing – a couple of buildings down. He has something – and he knows us, and not you. So like I said, it'll have to be *private*."

"So while you're making friggin' beer deals, I'm supposed to stay here alone? I don't know where the hell I am – which I don't like… with no weapon – which I *never* like."

"Who said it's about beer, Mondo? And who said you're alone? You can rap with the chick – like you're going to have a problem with that?"

"No," I said. "But you just saw her bug out. And, I don't deal well with being unarmed, anywhere. You know me; '*Cogito, ergo armatum sum,*' I think, therefore I am armed. Hell, I don't like hanging around with just forty-fives when Charlie pisses with AKs and shits RPGs."

"That's you all right – can't tell the inside of a Saigon café from a VC basecamp. So-o-o-o, say bye-bye, Baby-san."

"So fucking nothing," I growled. "Gimme one of your weapons if it's so goddamn safe around here. And tell me where you're going and for how long."

"You candy ass," Ruddick ragged. "It's just three buildings over. I thought you fucking Rangers could kill with a toothpick. Take one of these here chopsticks and you ought to be able to hold off a squad. But not you I guess." He ducked his head under the holster's strap and hefted the gun toward me. "Here, you REMF-ing-ass bed-wetter. We'll be back in an hour or two – probably'll find you fetal with the jimjams, sucking your thumb, and having visions of being the last man at Dien Bien Alamo."

"Thanks," I said sourly.

"Don't sweat it, Mondo. This place is jake-a-loo. I'm not even gonna bother moving the jeep."

The two got up and I surveyed the empty room with fragmented attention. 'Why're *they* so eager to go somewhere else, and so ready to leave me with this girl? If it's about enemy poop, they'd want me there. But we're too far out of the district for relevant intel. So, it's got to be beer – or something dicier – something a lot more lucrative. That'd change things all right. Fuck that shit. Like I want to become an accessory?!'

"Hey, Ruddick," I yelled after him, "You said you'd get her back."

"But it was you who wanted her. And ah, didn't we just hear her speaking *English.*" He followed Wiggins out the door.

CHAPTER 3

Casually, I slung Ruddick's leather clamshell's strap over my shoulder, shrugging the weight of the .45 to settle it comfortably. His goad amused me. 'No, I don't need a challenge. Not with *her* I don't.'

I knocked on the door to the rear. The stern-faced Tuan spied from a narrow crack. He said nothing. Over his head, I glimpsed part of her face. She was trying to see who it was. I wanted to kick in the door to get to her. I motioned for him to open it wider. As he did the waitress began yammering. I stepped aside in case there was something going on that they wouldn't want me to see. She came out.

"You friend, they go?" She asked, her eyes searching beyond me, but settling on my new accoutrement, the gun. My eyes were locked onto her clothes. She'd changed, and was wearing a stunning red áo dài. The way she stared at the leather holster made her unaccountable change of dress seem no more relevant than if she'd just gone out to get a glass of water. "Why you got now this?" I gritted my teeth. 'What significance is she putting on the gun? It's the last thing I want to come between us.'

"They went down there." I jerked my thumb where they'd gone. "As for this, it's a rule that I can't be alone without a weapon."

'Yeah, like my own personal SOP. Why *did* she change into this cool áo dài?'

"You think VC come?" she asked. I shrugged my shoulders. 'Not this crap again. Not now.'

"Can a man in this country ever be certain?"

"There are no VC here," she went on. "They are far away, no?"

"I'd really like to think so." I almost offered her that it was smart to assume there was always at least one double-dealing fucker around. Her face though, was a reminder of what was at stake, and acted as a quiet caution for my hostilities. "Those guys I'm with told me there aren't any VC around here."

"This you can be most sure," she said. We not like the VC here." '*Whoa!*' I thought, 'that definitely isn't a Ngoc-ism.'

"Why aren't there any?"

"Many reason. All people here fight Viet Cong. We make war to them. Want American come, Vietnam soldier come, help kill *de communitt.* There are no dangers for you here." She broke into a faint but unmistakable smile. "Only *I* here for you." I nodded with unrestrained surprise. 'Her malediction on the Cong would've been enough, but that last bit? *She's here for me?*'

"You changed – you put on an áo dài," I said.

"You like áo dài? I make on... for *you.*"

"Yeah, I sure do... Does your family own this place?" I asked, tangentially, my eyes still taking in her gorgeous dress. 'She said she dressed up *just for me.* For me! But how'd she know I was going to stay – that we wouldn't just get in the jeep and drive off – that I'd be here alone?'

"No, I have not family," she answered. Here be friends to my family."

"I thought Tuan was your brother."

"No, he is brother of Lan." She motioned toward the girl who'd served us.

"How about that guy Mister Chu? Who's he?"

"I know not so much this Mister Chu. Sometime he come here – talk to man, Mister Phan. I think he friend you, no? He come here now – to talk with you." She looked around to make sure we were still alone. "I no can say."

"He's not any friend of mine. I've never seen that guy before today. Those Americans aren't my friends either. I just have to ride back to my unit with them. But they're doing… business in the district. I'm not part of it. I'm in a different unit and… just along for the ride."

Her tone and expression intimated an opinion on Mister Chu's unsavoriness.

"You have no family here?" I refocused. "Where are they? Where are you from?"

"My family live no more. I am from Cholon."

"You don't look all that Chinese," I remarked.

"Oh no," she laughed, putting her hand to her mouth, "Many Chi-nee in Cholon, but not all." She pronounced the word 'Chinese' in the same way as my Tiger Scouts, as though they were extraterrestrials.

"Okay, then what are you?"

"You no believe I Vietnamese?"

"Well, sure. But you've got some..." I hesitated to say there was something in her from outside of Vietnam. 'Like how do I explain to her that when it comes to looks, racial mixes often have a synergistic quality that works heavily in favor of girls. This beauty though is in a category all her own, a perfect Gestalt from a genetic dice throw against the many hundreds of millions of other young females on earth. Probability'd have the number rolling over every millennium or so: Helen, maybe a couple of others, then this girl.'

"There are things in your face that are very different – very beautiful."

"Perhaps you see English part of me. This you think nice?"

"The *English* part? Geez, in your case, all the parts are maxed out."

"Maxied out? I know not this."

"Yeah, the max – maximum. Like it's so filled up with beauty, you can't fit any more in. So, your father is English?"

"No, father of my mother. Mother of her be from country, *Birmanie.* You know this?"

"What the French call Burma?"

"Yes, Burma. It west from Vietnam." She pointed in the direction of the door.

"How did they get from there to you being here?"

"They not come. When Japan soldier come – Burma *envahi*, they kill my English grandfather. After Japan soldier go away, much new trouble come to Burma, much fighting with Burma people. Same Vietnam, *communit* want take country. They kill grandmother of me. This for she marry to English man."

"But wasn't he dead by then – already killed by the Japanese?"

"Yes, but they care for nothing. They say she were marry to colonialiste. *Communit* all time say this, in Burma, in Vietnam. My mother then alone, afraid. She come to Vietnam, stay with other Burma people in Cholon. Very soon, she marry Vietnam man, my father. I am their daughter."

"Heck of a story. I'd assumed you were part French."

"You no like French?" she asked.

"Why wouldn't I? Remember, I told you about my being in France. It's got a lot going for it. It's like anywhere else; some

French you like and some you don't. I never even met de Gaulle and I know I don't like him. Most Americans don't care about where someone's blood comes from. I know some do over here – Being a *Tay Lai* meaning something bad and all. But it doesn't mean a darned thing to me. Besides, having French ancestors doesn't make you French – not when you're Vietnamese. Hey, if you told me you were half Maasai and half Eskimo, all I'd say is: 'Cool!' It's what I see. You're a miracle, an angel." She lowered her head.

"I think I not so angel. I make bad with flower cards, no?"

"Like cheating?"

"Yes, this not what angel do," she whispered.

"I can't believe you're admitting it," I said, surprised at her total turnabout. "Actually, I thought it was pretty funny – see, real cheating would be serious, like if you'd taken me for half my paycheck."

"Oh, I see you understand." Her lips made her look impish, while her eyes still expressed self-deprecation. "I now know you understand in Vietnam," she went on. I *Tây Lai*."

"Yeah, it's pretty hard to hide," I soothed, "but trust me, in your case it's paying off big."

"You say before you no like some French, but I tell you, I also have French blood. Sometime in Vietnam this bad."

"Not with me it isn't. Not ever." 'Some French' aren't *the* French.' "Mon Chéri, if you were de Gaulle's daughter, it wouldn't matter. We have a saying that the sins of the parents should never fall on the child. You understand?"

"My parent make no sin," she said adamantly. "This I am sure."

"No of course not – they made a royal straight flush. It's even worse because of that."

"How no sin be this – worse?"

"Whoa," I said, "forget all that. No sin is always number one – really good. Everybody knows that. That's why you're an angel. See, cheating at gin rummy isn't really cheating anyway. And French blood can only be bad when it's in the French." I abruptly stopped. 'What the hell am I talking about? She's hanging onto every word though. That's got to be good.'

"Look, I believe that we're unique individuals, different from every other person on earth. Identifying us with a race is self-limiting and attributes things to us that are just made up by others. Whether those things are good or bad doesn't matter, because they don't apply to any one person. You understand?"

"Yes, I think this…." She said hesitantly. *"Je ne suis pas comme n'importe qui autrement."*

"That's right, you got it. You're not like anyone else and neither am I. That's what unique is. It's even a French word. It's what we are."

"Yes," she said.

"So your father was in the French Army?"

"No, no, father of my father was in French Army. This make my father also *tây Lai*. His mother was all Vietnam woman."

"That'd be your paternal grandmother. She and the French guy were your father's parents." Saying it out loud helped me keep her amalgamated family straight. "When were you born?"

"The twenty-four day in August month. My year, forty-six."

"Your parents? They wouldn't be that old."

"My father, the VC make die."

"They killed him? Geez, when did that happen?"

"Oh," she said, her face expressing a winding back of time as she tried to remember. "It in time of Diem. Monsoon time begin, before president *assassiné*." I nodded my understanding.

The Kennedy assassination had come a few weeks after Diem's, so the event was branded into my mind. I'd been a sophomore at UMASS. She'd have been seventeen then.

"Your mother, she's..."

"Mother of me have very bad sick. She die since long time."

"I'm sorry that all this has happened to you."

"This, and much more happen, but it is not for you to be sorry. I see you... you... *vêtements.* You wear the lines of the tiger." She traced her index finger down one of the irregular black stripes on my camouflage shirt. "You go to fight the VC, to kill the VC."

"I do my best," I said, hesitating in spite of her shy yet matter of fact acknowledgment.

"Too I see, you are *hors de combat, no?*" She pointed to my left leg.

"It's only tee-tee," I said, trying to remember when she'd ever seen me walk.

"There is one VC who die for do this, no?"

"Yeah one. But, unfortunately, not the one who did it."

"One good," she said with a slight smile. "For one who hurt you, there must be other day for him to die. For save us, for save Vietnam, we need everything of your best. I pray you be like tiger." She looked at me with a palpable earnestness. I was dumbfounded. *"Je prie toute l'heure."* She took my right hand in both of hers. "Now, you like I can sing to you?"

"Sing?"

"Yes, I want sing Vietnamese song for you. You no like Vietnamese girl sing?" I felt the radiation again. A great storm of some undiscovered cosmic ray passed through me. Subatomic particles in my being began careening and ricocheting. My torso felt warm, chest and back dampening with sweat. My collar bones felt hot. 'Am I doing this to myself when she looks at me like she does? Or is she doing it to me when she wants me to agree?'

"Yeah," I said, "I'd like that a lot – especially if it's you." She turned and went back into the room. The removal of her presence made me nervous in an instant. More than just the breaking of a dreamy spell, it felt chemically induced. 'Did I really hear her right?' Then, in a matter of seconds, she put it to rest by returning. She had a small guitar with her.

She began plunking at the gut strings. Oddly tuned, disconnected notes on a five-tone scale, sounded a blend of ukulele and koto. She tuned it, but her chords sounded like they'd come from the planet Sigma X. I couldn't really attend to anything but the cloud of obsidian hair draped across the instrument, partially obscuring her face as she leaned over to work her fingers. She frowned myopically, and her expression struck me as deliciously fetching. I drank in the entire sight of her, the draft scintillant with allure. I needed more. I had to get closer.

To get a better look at her fingering, I slid my chair forward. Close up, the color of her skin had to be hers alone. If there was any tinge of the Mekong here, it'd be from its Tibetan headwaters, back in the Himalayas, way up above the clouds, from crystalline rivulets of melting snow. It seemed a mixture of blenderized milk and bananas, swept with a barely discernible under-wash of russet. 'Palleting-out the actual hue would be a flustering chore for a conclave of Flemish masters.'

The stark black strands falling across her cheek intensified *The Look*. She pushed them aside. Misbehaving renegades slid back and she had to peek through them to look at me. Whenever she did, I couldn't help but smile. Although her face continued its visceral hold on my attention, her shape was trying to compete. Covering everything as an áo dài does, it was hardly risqué, but this one had obviously been sewn by an artist. Its snug contours and shantung silk hid nothing. A cestus on loan from Venus herself, it strained the bust line each time she inhaled. The effect cried out to me. I stole surreptitious glances at her breasts, not allowing my eyes to linger. Swollen as they were with some ineffable goodness, it was almost impossible.

In search of diversion, I looked down at her feet. Redundant perfection. Emerging from her long white pantaloons, they were slid into a pair of lacquered clogs. They fidgeted slightly under my inspection. Each toe was impeccable, and had done about as much rice farming as mine. 'And her white pants? Áo dais come in all colors, but always with black pants. Have I ever even seen white ones? They must mean something, but what?'

With a busy-fingered intentness, she picked away at the guitar. Gradually, the discordant strains formed into something unmistakably of the Far East, yet even to my western ears, catching. She hummed, insinuating her voice between the notes with doleful fluctuations. Vietnamese words emerged and curled around me in a way that only my subconscious mind could comprehend.

Her voice sounded lower than the average Vietnamese girl, almost an alto, and its breathy tone added an intoxicating heat to this haunting lament. I hung suspended on it, captivation moving over me as softly as a pre-dawn fog bank. Her plaintive wailing and the tortured emotion literally had me by the balls. She wasn't just the most exquisite example of everything female, she was its apotheosis. On that realization, she plunked a quavering single-noted coda and abruptly stopped.

"I sing of Vietnam woman," she said softly. "Woman very sad, because man she love must be far away. She not for sure he come back." She lowered her head. "Maybe in time of war... he not."

"My God, what is your name?!" I exclaimed. 'Why don't I already know?!'

"Name, Mã Thị Cây Bàng," she answered. Her sprite, run-together, inflected syllables came at me too fast to draw a bead on, but I'd go over them a hundred times if I had to.

"Please say it again for me." I drew imaginary letters on the table in front of her. "M A, T H I... Okay I think I got that part."

"Ya, Baahng. B-A-N-G. You say in English, like a big noise, like weep-pon you have. Pfoon!" she added with a percussive force of air, her attempt at onomatopoeic ordinance. "I read in American book, you know? Big noise say, Bang!"

The pairing of her velveteen voice with the sound of a grenade going off in a bunker seemed a sacrilege that sounded nothing like her name. Stuck on the moment as it was, my heart didn't notice. It pounded in my chest, an absurd mimicry of underground grenade explosions.

"What does your name mean – like in English? I know that Vietnamese like to name their children after certain things – things all around us."

"Yes, this is true. I am name for tree. I not know name in English."

"A tree. Your parents named you for a tree…?

"Yes. Before I born, we lived in house next to Buddhist Temple, it had very large tree in front, but it make cool for our house. When very hot, my mother sit with my brother under…" She gestured its branches and leaves with her hands. "My mother like this tree very much, but when I born, we must move to another place. She sad to see tree go away and put name on me for remember. I am only one I know who have this name."

'*BANG!* Almighty God, I'm alone with her.' I touched her arm, wanting to hold at least part of her, but afraid of committing some horrendous faux pas. 'Just a touch… that's all. She touched *me*, when finished eating, and again when she went to get her guitar. If she's already touched me, wouldn't it be okay for me to touch her now?' I laid my hand lightly on her sleeved forearm.

My aesthetic feelings for female beauty had never been much for keeping my erotic ones at bay. They usually fed them. But my being this close to Bang, engendered hungers that were so rapacious, they felt capable of tearing me apart in a feeding frenzy. Animal fantasies loosed themselves inside me. 'What'd she be like in one of Lisette's naughty décolleté peignoirs? Manually liberating her from one, while only inches from that gorgeous face could jounce a pounding pulse rate into uncontrolled fibrillation, and an early heart attack. Fuck it, I'll work up to it, from either that plebian cotton blouse or this elegant áo dài.'

"So, why isn't your family name a French one?" I asked, thinking of her paternal line and the clan name, Mã̲.

"Long time, she said, pointing at herself, "my father, use name of him mother family. Better in Vietnam not to make French for name."

"Yeah, I guess French is cool around here, but only up to a point." I said. I'd lost her with that turn of phrase, but she smiled to make it all right.

"French is good, but not good in Vietnam," she said.

"Being a colony is like that. America was a colony once too, and we also had to fight to get them out, but we didn't have any problem keeping everything they left us, including names."

"Your name is Cah-ney," she said, pointing at the embroidered black-on-OD nametape sewn over my right shirt pocket."

"Yeah, Carney," I repeated, careful to enunciate the 'r.' "It's Irish. My grandparents came from Ireland."

"I hear other soldier say Mon-do. This your first name?"

"You're pretty darned observant," I said. It's a nickname – not the one your parents give you – what your friends call you. It's ah.... A sobriquet. Friends gave it to me back in my first year of college."

"What means Mondo? I never hear before."

"What does it mean?" I repeated her question. "Oh, Mondo? It's Italian," I said, "for 'world' – like, you know, in French it'd be *le monde*." She looked up from the guitar quizzically. 'Like being named for some tree is not as weird as the whole world?' "My real first name is Gavin. That's the name my parents gave me."

"I can call you this, Gaa-vinh?"

"Sure, what the hell. You know, you'll be the only one who does outside of my family." I knew Maureen did, but mercifully, that long-distance connection faded as quickly as I'd become aware of it. Bang practiced my name. Her repetition and accent made it sound like an incantation over a thaumaturgic potion

"You have other name?" she asked. I frowned. 'Does she want to know if I have other nicknames?' "Name in middle, same my name, *Thị*. All people have three names, no?"

"Most yeah. All the girls in this country seems to have Thi for a middle name – you too. For a while I thought it meant 'girl,' until I read the ID cards of some who had different ones. Anyways, my middle name is *Bartholomew*. In French it's Barthélemy. Ah, I'll write it down for you."

"No," she said, with a sudden, wide-eyed mix of surprise and confidence. "This Barthélemy I know. This saint day is same day I am born."

We went on talking, interspersed between my listening to her musical elegies of unrequited love. She looked at me as spellbound as I felt, and perfectly comfortable. 'Most girls back in the states would be wondering if I was some kind of dimwit. I've never been at a loss of words before. But this question keeps pestering me; is she doing it *with* me or *to* me?'

Bang began telling me about her growing up in Saigon and her schooling. Traded details of my upbringing contrasted so starkly with hers that I felt embarrassed. Through all the years I'd been playing in Little League, rollicking with my pals at Boy Scout camp, or been on some college weekend, ski-lodge bender with Maureen, she'd been here, in the middle of this war, suffering the tragic and untimely deaths of her parents and older brother.

The war and communism had been a constant in Bang's life. She talked about numerous places she'd lived and about what upheavals forced those moves, all beyond her control. Often, when she'd had to move, it involved someone's death.

We discovered we'd read many more of the same authors than I would've guessed. I mined French literature for all it was worth, discussing impressions of Flaubert, De Balzac, and Moliere, Camus even. I told her of my liking for Dumas, and she told me of hers for Hugo and Proust. I'd only skirted the foothills of his, *Remembrance of Things Past*, a mountain range of reading. So compared to her, I felt like a dabbler, doing well just to get through English translations. 'Lord, she's done it in French. And the insights she's gleaned from these books gives her a sophistication that charms me to the marrow.'

Despite her obvious fluency and my having been there, France was still foreign to us both. 'What a weird irony. Nineteenth century Gallic life is creating a greater connectedness than a war that's subsumed the both of us. So much for my fellow officers at the fire base calling me Mr. Vietnam War.'

Even with the nudge of soreness in my leg and Bang's familial, war-torn reminiscences, the field of battle seemed further away with her recall of observations from Hugo: 'I think maybe I am like monsieur Hugo's bird. It takes rest on branch that is not so strong for it. But even when it go down – break, the bird still sing, because it knows it have wings to fly.'

Bang's entire life was solely of Saigon. Although she could fly away to Paris with help from the pages of a book, her feet were bound to this sprawling city of five million. The war and the indescribable pain of her own losses had been inseparable from her earliest memories. Wherever her English vocabulary ran short, she substituted French, the expressiveness of her face communicated emotion where the words of two languages failed. Yet, I sensed incongruities. Her autumnal recounting of grave wounds to the heart seemed inconsequential. It was as if the pain had been only an uncomfortable pair of shoes, kicked off and skittered under a bed with an oath that they'd never be worn again.

Few Vietnamese had escaped the pervasiveness of this protracted war and experience showed me how so many coped by stoically inuring themselves to its pain. Bang had this too, but without a shred of callousness or indifference. 'She's so inherently sweet that even the Grim Reaper's scythe can't kill that smile – tales of woe tenderized by time and her nature – bitterness marinated in honey. Her paradoxes are like an angel expressing hostility. Angels can't, and neither can she.'

Tangentially relating one of her stories to an experience of my own, I described how Recon had shot up a VC resupply sampan on a night ambush. Its cashe had sunk in deep water and two bodies swept downstream in an outgoing tide. At daybreak, we had nothing to show for our *success*, except our finding one of the bodies a little ways down river, unarmed of course.

Although well within the Rules of Engagement, all I had was one military-age man in a sampan, in the middle of the night. I could already hear Dingleberry's officious devil's advocacy; the body could easily have been that of a hapless civilian, who in utter desperation to seek help for a sick child, had become heedless of the nighttime curfew.

In an effort to preempt such a contrivance, I had Duc, Hagerty and Tillinghast diving into that opaque brown water for over an hour. The current and depth allied themselves with the VC, but I was able to call it off with the retrieval of a single mortar round. We'd successfully greased two VC, neutralized a bunch of 82 mm rounds, likely a pair of AKs, and possibly a mortar tube, but had nothing to show for it. It summarized this entire will-o'-the-wisp war. We scored on them more than they scored on us by far, yet the scoreboard seemed forever shrouded in fog.

"Next you kill VC," she said on my conclusion, "You kill for me?" Her words stunned. I just let it sit there. 'Did I hear her right?'

"...kill the VC for you?" I asked.

"You kill the Viet Cong, no? I think yes."

"Yes," I said, nodding my consent. I had. I'd do it again too. I suppose I'd only have to overlay her request with that eventuality.

"When next you kill," she went on, "you must cut out *coeur de Viet Cong – coeur de communitt.*"

"Cut out his heart?!"

"Yes heart," she said, placing her hand over her left breast. "With knife cut out – hold in hands. For me you can do this, no?" She cupped both her hands together and motioned them toward me. I imagined myself unsheathing my less than scalpel-sharp K-Bar and performing a not so expert ritual. Then like some Aztec priest, I'd raise the warm dripping organ of muscle and severed vessels into the scorching sun. My men, my acolytes, would be watching in open-mouthed stupefaction.

"Bang ah…" I attempted. "Americans…. we kind of don't operate that way, you know – we don't do that sort of thing."

"You can do, I know. When this time comes, I will know. Her voice became a whisper. *"Puis, je prierai."* She lowered her head and clasped her hands as if in some votive meditation.

"You'll know? And pray?"

"O-o-o, Oui. You will please do for me, no?" She gave me *The Look.*

"Yeah, I reckon…." I took a deep breath and shook my head in a vain effort to clear it. So her sweetness wasn't violets and buttercups all the way through. Somewhere in there a contumacious seam of sinewy gristle was tied to a bucket of something burning, her feelings about the war. At the bottom of it all, she'd given me a personal glimpse into a wellspring of revenge.

"Look Bang, I want to come back to you, here. I don't have much time. So I need to come back, bad, real bad." She looked at me and her eyebrows moved a millimeter closer together.

"Why it bad when you come back?"

"No, it'll be *good* when I come back."

"But, you here now." She motioned with her open palm to show the plain obviousness of it. "This – not bad for me. I am very happy."

"I'll explain. In American slang, when you beaucoup want something, we say *bad.* The wanting is so strong that not getting it is bad."

"Yes, Buddhist say this want is bad."

"Yeah, desire. It can certainly feel bad, but I think it's only natural to desire things anyway, especially when they're really good." 'Am I desiring something here that I can't ever hope to have? Is this girl beyond such a hope?'

"Yes, I also think this," she said, her eyes seeming to shoot tiny sparkles. "I want this what you say good. *Beaucoup.*"

"I can't stay much longer today so that's why I've got to think about getting back here again. Those dudes I'm riding with will be back any minute. When they do, we'll have to hit the road."

"Ga-vin, for you, there is only one road. It come back to me. I wait at the end of this road for you. She pointed to the front door. "Here I wait."

"Yeah, you bet." She got up and hustled away. Again, a cold spike augured my diaphragm and straight, into my elation over what she'd just said. The image of her standing by that door in that áo dài, waiting for *me,* was almost beyond comprehension. This feeling of craziness I got any time she went more than three feet away was even more incomprehensible. I got the same feeling out in the bush after something bad happened. I'd get hyper-vigilant, because of the portent of everything getting worse from there.

CHAPTER 4

Although she'd only gone to a table at the far side of the room, I sprang from my chair and followed after her. As I closed the distance, the feeling went away.

She picked up a large thin paperback from several books lying on the table and began flipping through the pages. While she did, I skimmed the covers of the other's, *Les Contemplations* by Victor Hugo, *Un Barrage Contre le Pacifique* by Marguerite Duras, and *L'abbé Pierre* by Han Suyin. The one that Bang had was in Vietnamese. She pushed it open in front of me. A finely detailed ink drawing of a Vietnamese man and woman filled one page. The woman looked at the man with an expression of melodramatic adoration. It reminded me of the set piece poses that the photographer up at *Tao Phùng* shrine had been creating with his double exposures. Bang pointed her finger at each of the figures then moved it from one to the other.

"You like?" she asked. I nodded. "They have much love, *beaucoup d'amour.*"

"Who are they?"

"They man and woman." She pointed at me and moved her finger to the man in the picture. She then indicated the link between the woman and herself. "I no can say it. You... me. You understand?" She moved her finger again from the woman to the man, then from me she pointed to herself. *"Homme et femme."*

"Yeah, beaucoup. I can't even explain how much." Our GI use of 'boo coo' in every other sentence, had reduced it to a meaningless measure, but coming from her it seemed like a massive amount. *"Extrêmement ainsi."*

"*Voila*! Now I know you come back to me. Forever I pray."

"Forever?" 'Does she mean she's been forever praying for *someone* to come back, or praying that the two of us would be this... *homme et femme,* forever?'

"I pray we together be, forever."

Yeah," I said, it being the most profound expression I could utter. Her instant answer to my unspoken question struck me like a blow. I had to shift my feet to keep from tipping over. 'What kind of inexplicable fantasy is this? I'm not short on self confidence, but I ain't the Hercules unchained of swagger either. How can I be exuding anything that'd make this girl feel what I think she's feeling – what I'm feeling? Is this some kind of mind-game spider's web? If so, I'm already Dog-tag deep. I've fallen too far to get out. Fallen hell, wallowing. *Please, just devour me alive!'* Another vision of me, arms slathered in blood, kneeling at the ripped-open chest of some bullet-riddled VC, brought me up short. *'Does this girl have a screw loose?'*

The shortcomings of my better judgment had me flashing back to six years earlier, when a friend of my father set me up with a summer job down at Folly Beach, South Carolina. At a large dance hall built out on pilings, it specialized in rambunctious rhythm and blues. To a timber-rattling beat, my sole duty was drawing sudsy beer into big Dixie cups as fast as I could get it out of the taps.

One night while Doug Clark and the Hot Nuts juked the joint, I spied a pretty waif. I'd noticed her wandering around before, an attractive non-conformist blend of beat and hippy. Always alone, her detached, far-away look seemed the identical twin to an aimless, existential ennui. I thought it very cool.

After watching a couple of guys fail at conversation, I positioned myself for a try. Choosing a quiet spot near the entrance where we wouldn't have to shout over the band, I engaged her when she headed out. To my genuine surprise, she took to me as if I'd been an old friend. And although she spoke in non sequiturs, her too-small, black leotard shirt and matching bathing suit bottom that could have passed for black panties, convinced me she was as hip as a girl could get. It was a sweltering evening.

Strolling to the end of the concrete boardwalk, we descended down to the sand for a walk along the water's edge. By the time we'd gone two jetties, and unable to communicate in riddles, I suspected she might have something askew upstairs. Referring to herself in third person was a big clue. Suddenly, she started to undress me. My mind running a moment or two behind, I just stood there. Frustrated with my not helping, she tossed off her tiny garments and pulled my half clothed form down on top of her, resuming her fumble to undo my belt.

Despite her weirdness, my head was locked on her looks and naked body, which had just rung up as three gold bars. Although the cause of her frenzied behavior had been baffling, no amount of rational judgment could compete with what I had in my arms. Holding such an enticing girl, who at the same time was so totally deranged for my cock, made any thinking at all impossible.

As I was about to enter her, she stopped me, imploring me to say that I loved her, and that I would always love her. With my rampant cock arrested in her hand, I'd stuffed one of her gorgeous breasts into my mouth. I hoped it would distract her, but it only kept me from being able to say what she wanted me to say. She began to emit a feral sound, her voice squeezing down to a thin hysteric squeal. Her eyes rolled with reflections of distant lights, the same swimmy movements that glinted on nearby waves. A foray of incipient schizophrenia, her high keening drifted off on the night breeze like the cry of a distant gull. It became one of my less noble moments. I'd told her everything she wanted me to, and more.

I looked into Bang's eyes. All I could see was warmhearted sincerity. There wasn't the faintest hint of the Cimmerian foreboding that lately seemed to glower at me from every corner. What else could she be but genuine and pure? She being the royal straight flush of *The Look*, and everything of an angel inside. But what could I really discern about her true mental state? What the hell did I know about the minds of angels? How could I tell the difference between some wigged-out camp follower like Ngoc, and a girl with the steady-handed rationality of a Vietnamese Anna Freud? 'Because I can, that's how! Where's even the suggestion of schizo beach girl here? Nowhere. What does it matter anyway? With a girl this dazzling, you take your chances as far as they'll go. How far's that? *All the way.*'

"You want me, Bang?" I asked, desperate for clarification.

"Yes, very much I want you!" She said it as though she'd already told me ten times. "This is good for you too, no?"

"Whoa... Good isn't the word for it. But, how come you don't already have a man? You don't, right?" 'Why is she drawn to me? No man in *her* life? It's not plausible.'

"He die," she said with a pained expression. "In year before this, I marry in *Hội Xuân* time for three month. He was *thieu uy* in army, by My Tho. Viet Cong kill – maybe Hanoi Soldier, I not know."

I nodded. She'd unveiled more depth of feeling than she'd shown before. There were a lot of dead Arvins. There'd be a lot of girls suffering like her. The flame of enmity at her core had to be the same stuff that burned in Tra. Hers might only be a smoldering ember compared to the inferno inside him. 'But how can I know? She embodies her feelings with such beatific grace.'

"I understand," I said earnestly. The communists had murdered her Burmese grandmother in the late forties, killed her father during the Diem presidency, her brother in some convoluted circumstance five years back, and recently, her husband. 'That'd be a heavy toll in anybody's reckoning. The way I feel about communists is rational not emotional. But what if they'd killed my father? And Gigi? My reasons for fighting them would definitely switch fuels, from what I know to what I feel, from what's true to what's right. Yeah, that'd sure make expedient cardiectomies easier.'

Bang looked at me with a neutral expression, the Viet's all-purpose countenance. I took some comfort that her face didn't match the dolefulness I'd heard in her words. In spite of my inability to think of what, I needed to say something more. "Bang, you've been through so much," I breathed at last. "My wounds are nothing compared to yours... I was down near My Tho too – for quite a while. Your husband, he must have been with the Seventh Division? Her expression flittered to puzzlement, so I took my index finger and drew the outline of a patch on her shoulder. "You've seen this. ARVN seven – bird here, *un aigle* – with the wing coming all the way down." I inscribed the stylized eagle that formed the numeral seven inside a patch. I pointed to the Ninth Division patch on my shoulder.

"Me nine, him seven," I said, mimicking my Tiger Scout pidgin. She nodded, smiling.

"Yes, I know this. It my husband group."

"You must have lived down there too…? With him?"

Yes. For short time I live in My Tho. Before live Đà Lạt, then go to My Tho. Only time I not live Saigon." She put both of her hands out between us. "Now I must give you to understand more, why I come to you. When I see you here – I see him."

"Okay," I said, trying to follow. "We are – were both soldiers. Infantry officers, right?"

"Yes, but you must understand, he – you are one."

"You mean we look like each other?" I furrowed my forehead.

"No, I believe not," she went on. "In my head, I say to myself that something is very wrong for to do this. I talk to myself inside. You do not look like my husband, you are American. I know American man very different. 'How can this be?' I ask. Then I understand what come to my heart. It is feeling of woman for man."

She pressed the heels of both hands against her lower abdomen, pushing inward and a little forward. It was a nervous gesture, an unconscious kneading of her uterus. It affected me like I was the last man on earth and had found the very last woman standing before me delivering the pain of her own craving. I knew Bang didn't mean it that way, but it bore into me like she did.

A new round of physical agitation erupted. The yearning in her eyes and animal display of her fecundity didn't help. My capacity for rational thought was dissolving as if fragments of my brain were breaking free and swirling away into my bloodstream. Soon, I'd be convinced that little motes of gray matter were recomposing in my groin as phlogiston, as if an ignited thermite grenade had been dropped into my lap.

"Before..." she went on, "I feel this for my husband only. It is the *reason....*"

"The reason... What reason?"

"It is like I say to you," she said. "Inside myself is feeling. *Il est grand – vaste.* It can only be good for me, because I feel same as I did for my husband. I have this only for him, no other man. I – *Je ne peux pas dire...* She struggled to explain her thoughts. It returned her expression of melancholy. Suddenly though, it came out. "I have for you a coup de foudre!" she exclaimed. "This is reason. Yes? I must come to you, to make both us be together."

I stared at her totally mystified. 'Is she a disturbed Asian version of the girl at Folly Beach, or something a whole lot worse? Is it possible for such a face to be used as a weapon of war? She seems more like an instrument of black magic, some kind of succubus, taking me as its host, to use me for diabolic iniquities. Like what? But if my plain-old destruction is what they want, I could've been dragged out back and shot already.'

I looked square into her eyes. The more I did, the more her powers encircled me, a writhing cockatrice. It begged for some earthly explanation, but only morphed into a vague foreboding. Was there preternatural good inside her or was she just a guileless tool for cunning archons of the Cong?

She'd make quite a classic dragon lady. Outside of old movies, I didn't have much to go on, but certainly she was more beautiful than Anna May Wong. Bang's innocence was so seductive that it was tying me up in bonds of irresistible desire. 'Isn't this the kind of thing that leads to dangerously compromising situations and terminal events? Do I care? Not at all. I've just been proposed to by the world's most beautiful woman. That's what femme fatals do, entice you to the point where you're incapable of making rational decisions. *Cherchez la femme.* Sure, just look for the woman. Fuck it! I'll sweat out all the small stuff *some other day.'*

"Why me Bang? That's all I want to know."

"Why you? I tell you again. I have *coup de foudre* come into me. I know not English for this – you not understand this?"

"A stroke –of something… fire?"

"No, that *feu.* What is fire from sky? Make *beaucoup... un bruit fort.* Bang!" She covered her ears for the sound and laughed merrily.

"You mean like gunship rockets?" I simulated the sound of such ordinance being fired, traced its flight with my finger and mimicked it exploding onto the table.

"No, no, no, she said, as if I'd suggested something as tangential as *Lucy in the Sky with Diamonds.* Sometime it come with rain."

"Oh, lightning."

"Tonnerre et foudre, oui? Yes, thunder and lightning. This I have. Lightning is love that come very fast – first time I see your face. Lightning is very strong."

"Yeah, very. But it ain't even as strong as what I've got. Look Bang, you are the most beautiful woman I've ever seen in my entire life. I've been lost in Goo-goo-eyed-ville ever since I first saw you. I'll bet that for your entire life, men have been after you. I have no idea what the hell Vietnamese men like in a girl, but no way they wouldn't find the whole deal in you. Aren't I right?" Her eyes dropped with a shy modesty. It was the first time that I'd seen a Vietnamese blush.

"I am *Tây Lai.* You know this."

"Well, Bang, this country might have some weird racial hang-ups, but they can't be friggin' blind with it. There isn't any denying what men can see plain as day."

"Yes," she said, "many man have want for me." In a quick blink, her eyes came back to me. "But all man cannot have. Only one."

"So far so good. But..."

"Only husband can have."

"Okay, right, but I'm just an average guy. If I'm anything above average, it probably ain't by a whole hell of a lot...."

"No, no, you very much more! Very strong – *fort et beau.*" 'Compared to whom, her dead husband?'

"What I'm getting at is – it's totally understandable for *me* to be flipping out over *you*. But you can't possibly feel the same toward me."

"I can very easy feel same – because it is so. Many things we want to not believe in our life, are things we must. I not want to believe my husband die, but it is so. For more than a year, I see no man, I look no man. Long time I very sad. I think I can not feel same for American man. They not same Vietnam man – speak much English I not understand. But what come to my heart for my husband, now come again in it for you. I see you for first time and I must believe. *Because it so.*"

"Yeah, but you said you thought I was him. How do you mean?"

"I know you cannot be him. He die. He *dans le cimetière Militaire*, by Biên Hòa."

"Yes, up on Highway One."

"He no reason. You... this is reason I say before." She spoke earnestly as though I should not only comprehend, but believe and never forget. "When he die, I think him âme go out – out to..." She made a slight spiraling motion with her hand, indicating that the poor guy's soul had escaped his chest and buzzed off into the vague beyond. "Monsieur Hugo say I – my *âme* be, go not in ground with body. Not stay in *le cimetière.* I think his *âme* come to you in My Tho."

"Hugo's take on the soul is pretty standard Christian stuff, but whoa, Bang, that other part... You mean like reincarnation? We were probably around the same age. But doesn't that sort of thing have to start from when you're born?"

"I do not know," she answered. I thought hard about what she was trying to get at. I'd read about a religion somewhere that was connected to that kind of belief.

"There are many thing you cannot know," she went on. "I pray for long time for my husband to come back. I know his body cannot return, but then you come. I know the reason now." Her logic astonished me. 'Love at first sight is one thing, even a fall that include aerial pyrotechnics, but is she proposing there'd been a transfer of souls, and that it could only have happened between him and me? Does she think there's been a transfer *because* she's fallen for me?!'

"Is this part of your religion? You're a Hindu or something?"

"No, no, I am Catholic."

"So am I, Bang. But geez, I've taken a few steps off the path in the past, but you're not only straying from the flock, you've gone off into the mountains and joined the goats. Hasn't his soul gone to heaven? That's what we Catholics believe. Jesus laid it all out for us – our salvation."

"Oh oui, quand tu meurs, ton âme va au paradis. I do not think it can, when it go to you. I cannot have coup de foudre, if this not so." I nodded. She believes the guy's salvation is on hold – because without my knowing, his soul has somehow gotten stuck in me? Oka-a-ay... like invisible angels have engineered my movements right into this restaurant, just so lightening could strike her heart?!'

"Bang, I believe I already have a soul. I'm pretty sure you can't carry an extra one, especially if it belongs to somebody else."

"You cannot know when it stay with you, before it go to heaven. I have hope it do only when you are old and die."

'I'm some sort of metaphysical way station, my life a personal Purgatory for some star-crossed Vietnamese lieutenant? My days and nights in this war are no picnic, but expiatory purification for the dead?!'

"So when I die, two souls will go to heaven?" I wiped the sweat from my forehead. 'Yeah right, Carney.' I could see me and him arriving at the same time, and my slapping him on the back in sympathy, for my being the beneficiary of his singular bad luck.

"*Peut-être.* You no like?" she asked.

"You have no idea how much I do, but..." I thought for a moment, trying to fully grasp her double soul conundrum. "Bang, you don't know anything about me." 'You stupid clod, talk her out of it why-don't-ya. It's got to be the absolute last thing in the world I ought to be saying. I don't know *her* either, but she's long-since made that irrelevant.'

"I know you, Ga-vin." She said. "I know all you are. We talk for long time here. I see inside you." Her intense gaze bore into me with such sincerity that I had to accept it as true. 'This bewitching girl has to have some kind of metaphysical back door to my existence. How else could she have done it; been in there, kicking around, checking in closets, snooping in boxes and drawers? And, she's come out apparently satisfied with whatever the hell she's found.'

"Nothing matters, Bang. I'll be him, he or your husband. Both. I'll be whatever you want, for however long."

"Yes. You understand. You can no want for it not be. Thank be to God it so. The *âme* my husband go to you. The *coup de foudre* in my heart tell me this. It bring you to me. No person can say it not so." Her demure passion, her sweet earnestness, her total faith in something so fantastic was more than enough validation. 'I've got to chew on her notion of it bringing me here – that little homunculus of a spirit inside me hauling on my internal tiller.'

Reconsidering her convictions, I recalled that other religion's belief, where on a person's last breath; his soul would travel to another person. 'That sets up the quandary of some people running around without souls while they wait for those who have them to croak. But hey, I don't have to make sense of it, I just need to accept it.'

"Well my sweet Bang, if you want to believe in the transmigration of souls, I'm willing to play archbishop to that devotion."

I got her to bring me a pencil and paper to write down her address. I gave her mine. She told me she knew where it was.

"I can come there?" The thought almost sent me reeling over backwards. 'Ker-ryst! To come in from the field and have *her* waiting for me. Hell, I'd never go out again.'

"What if I found a house for you," I blurted, "in the town?"

"No, is not good for Vietnam girl to have American in house."

"I'm not sure how else to pull it off... It's not all that unknown in these parts."

"Cette ville not big like Saigon. People know all, say many bad thing. Also, I am Catholic, people there Buddhist."

"Aren't there plenty of both all over," I asked.

"No, not all place. *Vous oubliez également, cela que je suis de course mélange – Tây Lai."*

"Geez-oh, not that race stuff again," I said, not one millimeter closer to understanding why she'd never be considered a whole Viet.

She shook her head trying to come up with a solution. "VC come this town?" The question popped with the echo of an AK resounding across a rice paddy.

"I don't know much about the ins and outs of the religious friction, or God-knows the racial stuff, but the VC part I can explain. It's a district town. Right in the middle of it it's as secure as you're going to find. But the VC can carry out assassinations anytime they see fit. Unfortunately, connected to me, they'd put you near the top of their list."

"*Assassinat?*"

"*Oui.* Ah, no," I stammered. "You're right. There's no way that town can work. Saigon maybe, but not there."

"American place you live?"

"Our fire support base? No, that wouldn't cut it either. No way on God's green earth. It's not like an Arvin compound – no hooches inside, filled with mama-sans and baby-sans – just hundreds of GIs."

"Many Vietnamese girl work for Americans in this?" she asked.

"In the fire base? A few, yeah. But they don't live on the base. They go home in the late afternoon. We don't even have regular buildings, just sandbags and bunkers, and barbed wire – and mud. Most of the girls work in the mess halls. A few work in the laundry-store, barber-shop thing we have. Others clean up around the troop areas. None of that'd be for a girl like you."

"I never before go to this town. Maybe I come on bus to see. I look, no? I can talk to people." 'What the hell will I do if she just shows up? She'll create some impossible dilemmas is what.

Fixing her up with a diddly-fuck job is possible, but too ridiculous to even think of.'

"Geez, Bang, even if you found *la ville* workable, you can't fix the problem we have with the VC. I'm out in the field most of the time. The base is a total absolute negative. You aren't just another Vietnamese girl. Cripes, I'd have to leave a squad behind just to guard you, another squad to guard them, and my only other squad, to guard that squad! And they'd wind up shooting each other over who got to talk to you next. I'd be out in the field all by myself?!" I laughed at the ludicrousness of it, but the mere thought of the Queen of the Universe in the guise of a charwoman slammed any further consideration behind a massive iron door. 'But what do we do? My God! I don't even care if she's a V-fucking-C double agent. At least *that'd* keep her safe!'

I hoped she didn't know the extent that she had control over me. My mind flitted over even more outrageous options, like an in-country desertion. 'Shit, I'd do it right this minute if I knew of a sure-fire way of vaulting us both out of the Nam. To where, Sweden? *ME?!* Man, get a grip on yourself. Get control. Rule One: Discipline. Rule Two: Simplicity.'

She was like an immense treasure that I'd stumbled on, a sea chest brimming with gold doubloons and jewel encrusted gewgaws. 'There's no way I can make off with it without losing it. I'll have to leave it behind, hidden here, and return at a more propitious time. That's what I'll do.'

"I cannot come to be with you?" she asked.

"No… *yes!* But not just yet. I've got to figure out a plan, a good way for us to be together – where there aren't any problems."

"I must come be with you."

"Correct... That's the whole idea. We need time, that's all. Anything else'll be just too crazy – like *trop fou.* We're not... We can't just..."

"Yes," she said, nascent pain touching the corners of her eyes. "This we cannot. We not be married. Not good."

"Don't worry," Bang. I'll come back." It sounded so clichéd, like my telling her that I'd phone her sometime. My making excuses for keeping us apart seemed even crazier than us shacking up. I needed to leave her with no doubt as to my intentions. Telling her I'd figure it out somewhere along the way wasn't a pledge of consequence. I *had* to give her a promise she could believe in. "I *must* marry you, Bang," I said, with gravity.

I wanted to have the ceremony right then and there. She looked up at me with a countenance so imploring and seraphic that sweat flooded from every pore of my body. Her beauty swelled still further, second by second. Its unearthly powers slipped over me like a membranous body bag. It enveloped me with my subservience to her complete.

My pledge of marriage sparked something else. At the threshold of awareness, an obstreperous gang had begun fomenting a rebellion inside me. Was I handing over my entire person to someone I hardly knew? This eruption of self-preservation addled me. Did I have an innate biological mechanism that alerted on femme fatals? I would either have to succumb to her or bolt. *Bolt?!*

"Je vous épouserai aussi." She said calmly.

Okay, I heard – that you'll marry me. Like you'll marry me back?"

"Oui. Je suis dans l'amour avec vous," she whispered. "Comprenez-vous?"

"Yeah," I answered, stunned. "Uh, my French isn't as good as your English. But I totally understand. I love you too."

"Au delà de tout autrement?" she persisted.

"Beyond even that." Her words were doing it. She was there.

Bang's English, rudimentary as it was, got across everything, but whenever she felt something deeply, she'd switch to her accented French. 'Good that it isn't Vietnamese. All I can do there is intimidate detained VC suspects. My French is miles ahead, but too halting to trade volleys of it with her. She breathes French, and expresses love with such heartfelt urgency that I can't deny it.'

We looked at each other from inches away. 'Only a fool would run from this girl. I have to stop questioning myself and her. I just have to stop.'

I'd been infatuated before, even wildly so. I'd been in love before. I'd thought I was all-the-way-in love with Maureen. My God, Maureen. I didn't know shit from Shinola! Bang's magnetism swept away every belief and attitude I'd ever held on the subject of anything.

Bang's face held me fast. I studied it piece by minute piece. Without a single flaw, there wasn't anything on earth capable of complementing it. The finest makeup would be a rude insult, a defacement.

I moved to the point of touching, to feel that her skin was blessed perfection, so smooth that it seemed to be without pores. Her small nose was an indecipherable delight, transitioning to her cheeks in its Asian way, without an actual point where one became the other. I studied her unmolested eyebrows, angelic, without even a single -haired attempt to improve on nature. I stared into her eyes, her irises, narrow bands defined only by a smattering of pyritic flecks. They seemed like the barely discernible tips of dancing flames, each one a far away oil lamp, a yellow spec prickling the opaque darkness of a Delta night.

The close warmth of her breathing made me weaker still. She drew me in to revel in the whole visual entirety of what promised to be mine, forever.

"To marry," she whispered, "you must come back to me. When will you?"

"Yeah, you're damned right I will – like as soon as I can."

"I will stay here. I will do all you want."

"Okay, only for two days. I'll figure something out by then. I will come back. Damn. If I have to go to another part of Vietnam in a few weeks, you'll have to come along. Could you?"

"Yes, I come," she answered.

"Bang, you must stay here for now. You must stay safe." My mind went around in that circle again, unable to land on any solid ideas. "No matter what, I'll be back in two days." Not touching her made me believe I might keel over and die. Death by self-discipline. I took one of her hands in mine. Waves of galvanic energy surged up my arm. With my touch she coalesced diffuse ions into a turgid river of heat. With her slightest move, her breasts stirred as though wanting to touch me in their own right. They swelled as they got closer, taunting me, mocking my propriety.

The recrudescent insurrection against my enslavement boiled over into open civil war, the forces of foreboding reeling to the fanatics of passion. As the conflict soaked my brain with androgens, I felt like I could be on the edge of a lycanthropic shapeshift.

"Hey, Mondo! Time to hook up." Ruddick's voice bellowed from the doorway. "We're waiting on you. Let's get rolling."

Although I'd been expecting them back at any minute, their return hit me with the surprise of a mortar round bursting through the roof. Half a dozen plans were suddenly crushed, like delicate blown-glass angels pulverized under a drop forge. They expected me to just jump up and *leave?* Not now. *Not possible!* My insides screamed for an alternative, but all that emerged was natural impulse.

"I'm staying," I growled.

"Suit yourself, but I'm not leaving without my forty-five. What you do after that's your business. I'll be waiting for it out at the jeep – and I'll be expecting it in exactly zero one minutes." He headed back outside.

The thought of staying here unarmed went through my spellbound state like a bayonet into meringue. 'This might be the most pacified and secure place around, but by whose reckoning? Ruddick's? Even if it is, you don't escape nasty shit in a war. It's always there, and my presence alone'll be the perfect catalyst, unarmed? That'll guarantee it. Word always travels fast. I'll be at the receiving end of an AK barrel by midnight. There's no way I'm going to risk her life – certainly not by my own reckless actions. Nam-rule One: Any kind of shit can go down. Rule Two: It usually does. Damn it! If I'm going to marry her, we've at least got to stay alive!'

I'd just handed myself over to her, but I still retained some rational control of events, like digging up buried treasure. Getting back here in a couple of days seemed the smallest of problems. With my leg wound not quite healed, I could grab Tra and Tho as discreet bodyguards, and pull off an easy two-day disappearance, say a medical consult at Long Binh. It'd be all I'd need to seal this thing for good. My mind kept racing around thinking of ways to get her out of the country. 'First things first, Carney.'

"I'll come back to you, Bang, or die trying, damn-it."

"You will not die," she said calmly. "Please wait for one moment." She whisked off into the back room, quickly returning with something clasped in her hand. "No, not die!"

"Bang, I just meant that death would be the only thing that'd be able to keep me from coming back."

"He say this too," she said sadly. I nodded. Despite her own amaranthine qualities, this war made the rest of us pretty-damn perishable. "You please take this for me," she continued, "and you will not die."

She offered up a small silvery ovoid object. I took the walnut-sized thing in my palm and stared at it. Faint traditional characters roamed the surface in what seemed scattered order. They might as well have been the sigils of some proto-civilization, one of their shaman's profundities. Whatever they were, the vague sketch of a butterfly was inscribed across its bottom. A seam ran around its middle. What it meant seemed as relevant as what it was.

"Looks like a locket of some kind," I mused, "although it doesn't have an eye-hole for a chain. Chinese writing? What's it mean? What is it?"

"Not Chinese. This *Chữ Nôm* – Vietnam writing – from old time, come from Chin."

"Looks like it," I said, recalling the stone carved characters Ngoc had read to me up at the *Tao Phùng* shrine. "Confucius say man with butterfly get…." I stopped, having no desire to complete the joke. Her face was dead serious.

"Boo-tre-fr…" She cut off her attempt to pronounce it in English. "*Un papillon* be same *une âme.* You know this?"

"Umm, a butterfly is a soul? I can sort of see the artistic symbolism." I inspected it more closely, looking for a place to insert my thumbnail.

"No! Not do." She put her hand over mine to stop me from trying to pry it open. "You must never do this. Only stay closed. Keep with you, and you not die. Then you will come back"

"I take it that your husband didn't have this with him when..." I hesitated, measuring Styxian-dipped invulnerability against the power of rabbit's feet and other lucky charms.

"He could not take."

"Okay, I can. It doesn't matter. I will be back, Bang – with it in a couple of days." I unbuttoned the flap on my left breast pocket and dropped her strange little amulet into it. "No matter what, I will be back." I buttoned the flap and thumped the pocket for emphasis. The horn of the jeep sounded. In reflex, I turned to leave, but halted in mid-stride. I yanked my wallet from my pocket and slid out the last of my 500 piaster notes, rolling eight crisp blue bills, the equivalent of about forty dollars, into a tight little cylinder. Then I pressed it into her palm. 'My God, can I actually leave her?'

I pushed my face against her waist-length hair until my nose and cheek burrowed deep into a mound of sidereal tresses. Long ebon strands went into my mouth. Their taste created a sensation that took control of me. Her essence drew into my nostrils and a euphoria that made me want to breathe her in. I wished I could just inhale her incorporeal sylphan form into my lungs to carry her away inside me.

A-swirl in that thought, I took her in my arms. She turned her head upward and kissed me on the cheek. It smoldered there. I'd been branded by her lips. My own lips pressed lightly to her cheek. She tucked herself against my chest. Her breathing became heavy and sustained, increasing with each breath. She turned her head back up and kissed me full on the mouth, her body molding to mine. My cock pushed embarrassingly between us, her desire dissolving my control. '*God help me. Not like this damn-it!* Not now, with bellyaching Ruddick about to come stomping back in at any second.'

"Je me sens comme je peux entendre mon propre battement de Coeur." Her voice trembled.

"My heart's doing the same, Bang.... Look, we are already married." I blurted. "As of this very minute – you understand? We are married, *now!*"

"Oui. À outrance." Tears welled up in her eyes. *"Je t'aime de toute mon âme."* Tears began filling my own and I kissed her more hungrily and with more feeling than I'd ever kissed a girl before. She responded in kind, hugging me tightly.

"Yes, heart and soul. Two days then. We will get Vietnamese papers for the wedding, right?" She nodded just as the horn beeped again, with prolonged, strident blasts. "Today – tomorrow, please go to the church and make plans for this, Okay? *Je t'aime!*"

"Je vous aimerai pour toujours," she breathed. I quickly kissed her cheek, and tasted the ambrosial tears that were spilling over and running down her face. *"Je suis maintenant votre épouse."*

"Yes, that's it, my wife now. And I am your husband." I clutched her special gift inside my shirt again, wiped my eyes, and headed for the door.

CHAPTER 5

WAITING IN THE JEEP, RUDDICK and Wiggins lolled in a languid sprawl, the sun having turned them into soft putty. Slumped sideways in his seat, Wiggins looked like he was dead. His head was cocked over the back of the seat like his neck was broken But it was only a case of extreme GI relaxation. A boot was propped up on the steering wheel. He'd been pushing the horn with it. Ruddick stretched more supinely, hat brim down over his face, both boots up on the dash. It was the kind of heat in which flies take delight.

"All right you malingering goldbricks!" I shouted. "You've got your way." They stirred as I ambled down the road toward them. In a futile attempt to catch some shade, they'd moved the jeep alongside the thick trunk of a dying tamarind tree. Bare limbs reached to the sky like huge supplicating arms. There were no more red-streaked yellow flowers, no brown fruity pods, just a few feathery leaves. High atop its sparse branches, they flittered like tiny pennants, either pathetic vestiges of all that had been, or obstinate proclaimers of that which survived. I wondered how Tra, my geomancer, might read it.

Several boys of about eight or nine stood alongside watching us. Not begging, they were either unfamiliar with GIs or Ruddick had given them the word that we had nothing to give.

In the glaring sun, their white shirts seemed so bright they made me squint. Back in the bush, with no clean water much less bleach, any color lighter than mocha was unknown. The novelty of it made me attend to them. I read the name of their school embroidered along the edge of each shirt pocket.

"Boc Tre, huh." Silently, they sized me up. The smallest one rated a chuckle. With each straight hair standing separate from every other, he had the fuzzed-out look of a newborn duckling. The kid standing next to him had him beat. His bristling cowlick stood as resolute as an aigrette. I smiled at the little one. For a split second, a tiny twitch quivered across the top of his nose, otherwise he remained as still as a woodcarving.

I wondered what Bang's star-crowned, black-as-the-cosmos hair would be like, framed against a fresh New England snow. That sublime pleasure would be denied me in the coming winter because I'd still be here, but pure elation was borne on my absolute certainty that it would happen in the one to follow.

"I knew you'd change your mind, numbnuts," Ruddick groused, as he climbed out of the jeep. "And here I thought you were supposed to be the Cong's greatest nemesis."

"It's still valid."

"Well, come on, we've got to haul fuckin' ass!" He gave me an exasperated look and started to lift up his seat. I already had my foot on the rear bumper and I pulled myself over the back. "Our shit took much longer than I'd thought."

"We've got plenty of time," I groused back. I knew and they knew exactly how long it would take to get to the fire support base and how much daylight was left. Wiggins started the engine with a stomp that was one part heavy boot and two parts sour attitude. They'd only been lounging out there for five minutes, but the afternoon sun had kicked their irascibility quotient up a notch. 'What else's new? Everybody in Nam's got something to piss and moan about. But the way Wiggins is acting says… maybe whatever nefarious shit they're into, didn't work out. Fuck 'em. I've got more important things going on – like locking in a mental treasure map.'

As we pulled out, I concentrated hard on the buildings and neighborhood, desperate to get a bead on some kind of landmark. Every structure seemed unmemorable. Anxiety shot through me like a current. I'd been in this exact situation before.

On my return from Europe, I'd spent time in Manhattan. Still on the outs with Maureen, I'd met a girl down in the East Village. A Puerto Ricana sitting alone in the Night Owl was unusual enough but this 'cultural renegade' was also electrifyingly pretty. Taking to me from the time I'd grabbed the back of a chair next to her, she set the hook firmly in my jaw. We'd talked until 4 a.m. By the time I escorted her on the subway to her home in the South Bronx and kissed her goodnight in a grimy stairwell, visions of our future life together were dancing in my head. She wrote her address and phone number on a scrap of paper and put it in my shirt pocket.

Back in Rhode Island the next day, I'd absent-mindedly tossed my clothes into the washer. Discovering the horror of what I'd done, and totally unable to recall anything of what I'd turned to mush, I immediately took a train back to New York, where I searched in utter bewilderment. Which direction had we gone after coming up from the subway station? Had it even been that station? I jogged from corner to corner looking for something familiar. Addled, I asked a hundred people if they knew her. All I could think of was her waiting on my call, my solemn promises still fresh in her ears hardening into a lie. My inability to find her had me feeling like Holden Caulfield in full manic tear. Exhausted, heartsick and depressed, I gave up on the third day.

That loss had me swearing to the depths of my innards that I would never repeat such a disaster. I really needed to burn the faces of the little boys into my memory, but from only a block away they were already blurring. I looked around in every direction. Their school? Boc Tre. That was it. That'd be the place to key-in on. People from at least a klick away would know it. The church's bell tower came to mind and I felt even better. With its simplest description, people would point the way.

As we turned onto the main road, we passed a large metal fabrication shop. I locked that in as a solid landmark. Then there was Bang's address, written down and sitting buttoned in my pocket. Burning in my mind like a picture that needed to be stared at, I took it out for a study of her handwriting. *She wrote this,* I thought, remembering her hand and careful penmanship. The paper fluttered in the wind of the open jeep and I grasped it tightly. Then after committing it to memory, I carefully slid it into my wallet and relaxed. Given the sublimities of this girl, the nightmare of returning to the island, to find that I'd lost where **X** marked the spot, would instantly reduce me to a blithering Ben Gunn.

"I'm sorry I took so long in there," I said. Ruddick passed his hand in the air dismissively.

"I expected you'd have trouble breaking yourself away. That is one smokin' baby-san. Yeah, we'll definitely be dropping by here more often – like on next week's snatch-hunting safari."

"Like every next week," Wiggins added. "Yeah, I can feel li'l' Private Wiggins already givin' me the nudge. That's his way, you know, of volunteerin' for a mission. He just starts-a-nudgin' me."

"Oh no you don't," I demanded. "I claim her right here and now, you got that!"

"Sure, sure," Ruddick countered, "Right after I just said I was coming back."

"No! Back there when I was with her. I'm dead serious Ruddick."

"Hey, check out this bullshit," Ruddick exclaimed. "I take him there once and he thinks he owns the damned place and everything in it."

"You got half of it right fuckstick. I don't give a shit about that place, but I flat-out own *her.* I'm warning you guys. You mess around with her and so help me, I'll put a goddamn LAW in your fuckin ear!" Wiggins turned back and glared at me over his shoulder.

"Sir!?" he exclaimed, Wiggins was grim-faced, obviously, not taking to the threat and my cold invective.

'So fucking what! They aren't going to misunderstand me. Good that he's seen this in me before, when I'd had a loaded CAR-15 in my hands. They know I've used it as easy as lighting a cigarette. All the better for them to link what I'm telling them, with death. *She's off limits.* My marital plans? Tell them? I've got to.'

"I'm going to take her back to the States with me. It's already settled."

"Ha! Listen to this bullshit," Ruddick scoffed. "Yeah Mondo, sure you are. No problem. Shit, when Bob Hope was here last February, same-o-same-o. I got leave and took Ann Margaret home with me. She's waiting for me back in Jersey right now."

"Lieutenant Carney," Wiggins chided, "you ain't got your own ass out of here yet. Fixatin' like you been, on that stuff, will get you in a bad way. What you got like three hearts already? Who's to say the next one won't have a CMH to go with it? And I don't mean no Congressional Medal of Honor. Nope, a *'casket with metal handles'* will be the only CMH you gonna get."

"You talked to her for two hours, and it came to *that?*" Ruddick asked. Either the minx is some-kind-of mover, or you've been in the field way, way too long."

"What?! You think it's pussy depravation? After just being out in Vung Tàu? You saw what she's like! You don't believe she's worth it?"

"Worth...? Now you might be talking my language. Hmmm, damnedest-looking baby-san in Nam."

"In this whole world," I interrupted, "and even nicer on the inside."

"I'm not ready to go *that* far," Ruddick continued. "But even supposing she was, it wouldn't mean shit. *The World* and getting back to it is what Wiggs was on to. You've got to see this place like I do, these people, this war – everything. I've been here more than twice as long as you. Look, we're just here for a year, except fools like me, who in a fit of temporary insanity, extended, twice! Those two dumb-ass moves make me a qualified expert, since the *only* goal a grunt has is getting out alive –infantry being the only ones where it isn't all but guaranteed."

"So, while you're here you take all the poon you can – hell, we deserve it for fighting their war for them. Haven't you noticed that, never mind how beautiful some of them are, *nobody* takes Vietnamese girls home with them? No matter what – not even if they're ten times prettier than anything they'll ever have, they just don't. There's a reason."

"Yeah, because the Army's death on it," I said, "and won't let anybody… If they could, they would."

"Of course, but you think the U.S. Government wants dumb, stupid GIs bringing poontang back as *war souvenirs,* just to dump them a year or two down the road? Nope."

"Poontang *war souvenirs*?! Why would they be either? And governments don't own people, here or anywhere."

"All that's arguable," he said. "Governments only have to think they do, to act accordingly. And didn't I just hear you say *you own* her? So you think."

"Shut the fuck up." I thumped the back of his seat with the heel of my hand. "I'll be getting her out of here, in spite of all your government shit. She ain't just a piece of *poontang* either."

"Great and wonderful poontang then. Look, war is hell. I shouldn't have to tell *you.* You take one of them home and you'll be taking a piece of this war with you. Why would anyone want to wake up to a piece of stinking hell every morning?"

"That's an idiotic analogy and you know it," I fumed. "You're sick. Fucking crap, 'a piece of this war… a piece of stinking hell…' Fucking crap. Poontang – *crap!* She's not just a pretty Vietnamese girl. There's plenty of them. She's way more than that. Way more than half of what's good about her is on the inside."

"I told you before," he corrected, "she's far and away the best I've seen here. But, they're all the same inside... gooky. That's how they got that tag in the first place."

"There's nothing gooky about her in the least. Zero."

"That's because you're just looking at the French in her."

"English and Burmese too."

"Fine, whatever, but that's *all* on the surface. Just from living here, she's pure-tee gook in the middle. I've got X-Ray vision. I'll bet, that in her more private moments, she'll be squatting and shitting over a carp pond, then having fish for lunch."

"Aw, smoke my prick. Better still smoke Wiggins's. I'll bet you she doesn't even shit. That chick lives on sunlight alone."

"Sure Mondo, sure. Hey, I'm sorry as hell that you'll be pounding the paddies, but that can't be helped. It's a fact that you might not be able to get back there for ages – and with your battalion fixing to move west, maybe never. So why should Wiggs and I sit around with our respective thumbs stuck up our respective asses? Just because you said so? While the likes of *her* run around loose?"

"You got it Ruddick. Bull's eye. *Because I said so.*"

He remained impassive. I wasn't sure that he'd heard me above the jeep's engine, but knew repeating it would only gain me another round of guff.

Off to my side, I contemplated the passing green of coconut and banana, the monotony of growing rice and the redundant nipa palm hooches. For all that it meant, and all of it that I loved, I repeated my vow to Bang and to myself. I swore it as a blood oath. I would be back ahead of them, even if I had to crawl every foot of these twenty klicks on my stomach over broken glass. The eidetic vision of her face, that look, hanging in front of me, would surcharge my last living breath. Her words swirled in my head; *'Ga-vin, for you, there is only one road. It comes back to me. I wait at the end of this road for you.'* I could see her standing at that restaurant door, just like she promised.

"Hey Mondo," Ruddick started up again. "I think you're getting all bent out of shape for nothing. You're obviously not digging the big picture over here. The way I see it, all the pussy in this country's for *us!* It's my philosophy. The whole place's a great big cunt. What could be plainer? It's even shaped like a vertical slit – real fitting too that it's a little crooked. Ha, and now we're pulling out – *coitus interruptus belli.* Can you dig that?"

"You're sick in the head Ruddick."

"No, Mondo, I'm just ultra-tuned-in to what's going on."

"Like we're hardly going to use it all up," Wiggins said. It's a physical impossibility. It just keeps on a-givin.'"

"Yeah, give it up Mondo," Ruddick added. "You had your chance."

"Had my chance?! I didn't have shit."

"So it was your first chance. It isn't my fault you couldn't get any. Better luck on your next try – oh sorry, there won't be one with you poor fuckers headed for the Bo Bo Canal. Yeah, she won't be closer than fifty klicks – more if it's further north. You might have to settle for some Cambode culo. Your turn there, our turn here."

"You don't *get* a turn here," I growled.

"Man, I don't know what the hell's wrong with you. I shouldn't have said anything. But fuck-it – I'll put it to you straight. That restaurant is one of our little ops bases– and like I said, we've never seen her before. So, I want to bring her into my ... my orbit."

"What the hell are you talking about, Ruddick?"

"Hang with me, Mondo," he continued. "I know you've got a special thing for Viet gals, and obviously a whole lot for this one. See, we have a string of gals around town, premos we supply for a price. This one's ripe for recruitment. As good looking as she is, we're talking *top* dollar."

"Ruddick, I said you were sick in the head. Make that criminally insane."

"I'm not finished. You work with me on that little problem I told you about when we were outside MACV, and we get to work something out with regards to her. But how you do that from way out in The Plain of Reeds, I don't know."

"I'm getting promoted in less than three weeks. I'll be coming out of the field. Who knows where they'll send me. But she's coming with me, even if my ass gets put up on the DMZ."

"Coming with you? Damn Mondo, I'll bet you don't even know her name."

"It's *Bhang*," I said, stressing my best pronunciation.

"Whoa, she can light my pipe anytime," Wiggins gibed.

"Not Bong. It's b-*A*-n-g," I corrected and regretted just as quickly.

"Oh, even better! Ruddick hooted. Wiggins pounded the steering wheel with his fist while emitting a high-pitch whoop. Ruddick matched him by slapping his knee with his hat. "Perfect. Beautiful. You know they usually name their kids for some kind of attribute they see in them at birth. Hal-lay-fuckin-looyah, they were seeing the future."

"It's Cây-Bàng, turd brain. She told me it was some kind of tree."

"Yeah," he said, I've heard of it, like it's called the 'poison fish tree.' They use its sap to stun fish, and has nuts that're useless. What the hell were her parents thinking about?"

"It had something to do with giving their house shade during the dry season," I said.

"Ha!" Wiggins let out. "I'm tendin' more to that cereal I told you 'bout this mornin'; It don't do nothin' 'cept lay there and go…"

"Fuck you, *Sergeant* Wiggins," I seethed.

"Forget about it, Mondo," Ruddick soothed. "It's bigger than all of us."

'I'm not about to forget anything, not you Ruddick and not this war – which isn't hell or stinking. How can it be if it brought me to the exact spot on the planet where its most beautiful girl lives? Maniacal-fucking-insidious though, bringing me this far, delivering her into my arms, then separating us by twenty klicks, and maybe triple that when the battalion moves. Now it's scheming to substitute them for *me?*'

Fast-breeding mental turmoil grabbed hold of my edgy fitfulness and turned it into a welter of anger. It was one thing to feel like Bang had 'body snatched' me and another to be obsessed with her all too real physical absence. Now, my need to rescue her, condemned me to a mental Tartarus. 'Having to eternally crawl, thirsting and starving for her with Ruddick and Wiggins luxuriating in my anguish, is the true epitome of *a stinking hell.*'

My thoughts of Tartarus made me think of Orpheus journeying to reclaim his love, Eurydice, from the underworld. I recalled a grueling, late-night labor of trying to translate Rainer Maria Rilke's sonnet to Orpheus for the sadistic pleasure of my forth-year German prof. That was hellish for sure. 'Well, I won't be replaying that tale, not one second of it. I'll never look back in forgetfulness to see if my Eurydice was still behind me. I have complete faith in Bang. She'll be there. I'll stay focused on the light ahead, our way out.'

"She's not going to do jack-fucking nothing for you," I said evenly. "She's no whore and you know it."

"Well, you have her parentage – French soldier and Viet whore – any Eurasian her age... Beyond that, it depends on what kind of *jack* you're talking about."

"Like everything else, Ruddick, you got her lineage wrong." His crack got to me, but I forced myself to stay controlled. "Just because life's cheap over here doesn't mean you can buy anything – not people – not people's souls."

"I never said anything about buying anybody," Ruddick countered. "Souls, shit, what the fuck is that. Your problem is you spend all your time beating the boonies and not enough of digging the general Viet scene like I do. They don't have to be a whore to pop their eyes open over a little jack, say four months of their wages for twenty minutes of work. A bit of beau geste in the face of their impoverishment can go a long way.Whore schmore. Call 'em recreational specialists will-ya. These people don't have much – and big-hearted me's into helping them out wherever I can, which includes... ummm, developing employment opportunities."

"Talkin' 'bout eyes popping," Wiggins interjected, "she-e-ee-e-it, jack or no, hers'll be jumpin clean out when they spot their first length of rearin'-up Alabama black snake headin' straight-'n'-true for that curly curtain. I wanna be there for that."

"I'll see you eating rat shit first, Wiggins!" I shouted. "And hear you begging me to feed you more. Goddamnit, I told you, I own her."

"Whoa, Lieutenant. Ain't anybody ever told you that nobody owns nobody no more?"

"Yeah, tote that fucking barge and lift that fucking bail, Wiggins. She's the one who says I own her."

"Sounds like we need to save her from herself then," Ruddick said.

I grabbed the back of his seat and pulled myself forward, wanting both of them to appreciate the toxic venom that had replaced the saliva in my mouth. The vision of their returning to that restaurant sickened me, despite the fact that I knew Bang's sincerity to be absolute, and that her virtue could never be defiled. No matter what blandishments they'd toss her way, she wouldn't be entertained. Her own words had spoken to that doubting insult; '*Not all man can have. Only husband can have.*'

I couldn't stake much of anything on the abstruse mores of this country, but was willing to risk everything on the honesty I felt from Bang. The depth of her appeal wasn't even a question. The thought of it brought back her breathy words, *Tout que j'ai seul est vôtre et à vous.* 'The French sure know how to communicate love. No, nobody's ever going to defame her, her sincerity, her *Look.* Besides, *I'm* now the carrier of her dead husband's soul.'

Ruddick's cock-sure attitude was the real catalyst for my hostility. Put toward military business, I respected it. Put toward this it made my intestines feel like a hungry constrictor, coiling around in a slow predatory stir. 'Bang isn't going to give them the time of day! But their thinking that she'll fall over and turn tricks for them is vile beyond words. Their just thinking it enrages me.'

"Hear me out Ruddick. It's you who don't really dig this scene –the one we've got right here in this jeep. So, I'm going to help you. Listen up! There're a million girls around here, and you can have any one you want – every last one, except *that one.* You can fuck *all* of them for all I care. But you just think about talking to that one and I'll see to your ass being wasted... Don't take it as a threat or even a promise. Take it as a cold, stone guarantee."

The jeep droned along with the three of us staring at the road ahead, no one saying a word. I mused over my threat and viciousness of tone. 'Do they think I'm crazy? All the better. Let 'em wonder just how screwed up in the head I might be. I've got to make him sufficiently unsure about going anywhere near Bang. Life's cheap in this country. Untimely deaths happen all the time. What treasure isn't worth fighting for?'

Anger simmered inside me. An imagined confrontation flittered through my mind. It was a nightmarish fantasy with the two of them deciding to teach me something about intimidation. On cue, they'd suddenly drawn their 45s, but my knife'd beat them to it. In a blur, it taught them the last lesson they'd ever learn. I imagined dragging each of their wretched, stripped corpses into the jungle. Maggots would render them to clean bones in a matter of days, which some incurious farmer would find and bury in an unmarked woodline grave. The jeep, abandoned in a dicey Saigon alley would exist only as parts in an hour. By then, I'd be back with Bang, for the assignation of all time.

Such rattling thoughts shook me back to reconsider the affect she was having on me. I recognized the contradictions, but couldn't make sense of them. 'She's irreproachable– so why am I still worried? It's her relative value. Precious as she is, any threat at all's going to be major, inexpiable. I've got to keep them away from her.'

'Suppose Bang actually is the most beautiful girl in the world – not just according to me and not just on the outside, but inside too. Such a girl's got to exist. Okay, so she's her. Suppose too, she's the complete protean woman, able to embody my every dream. And it's *mutual*! I'll do anything to keep her!'

I put my hand across the breast pocket of my shirt. Clutching the hard little egg of a locket to my heart, I stared down at my boots, first at the burred and cracked leather, then at their mud-stained and sun-bleached canvas sides. Thoughts trickled on images, of cases of beer by the pallet load, and of treachery and betrayal.

VI
The Return

CHAPTER 1

A SHORT STRETCH OF ROADWAY connected the town's main road with my fire support base. Walking along its slippery laterite surface to the entrance, I faced off against a pair of deuce and a halfs. In unison, they gunned their engines in low range and crept toward me at one mile per hour. Wiggins could've driven me all the way in, but not wanting to back out, he'd just let me off. It suited me just fine. I'd been ready to get out of that jeep from the moment I'd gotten in.

The trucks edged closer, taking their half of the road out of the middle. To keep my boots from getting any muddier, I walked them single file inside a wheel rut at the far margin. The front tires of the first truck gingerly squished passed me and I gave the driver a casual wave.

When first laid, our firebase's roads had been wide enough for two vehicles to pass. Then successive monsoons turned them into quagmires. Undaunted engineers fought back, with layer on layer of crushed stone and gummy laterite, the surface becoming higher and more convex with each load. Now, vehicles had to carefully straddle the crown, or suffer a pitched slide into one of the abandoned rice paddies and the thickest wheel-swallowing muck in the history of motorized warfare.

Approaching the portal to the base area, I paused. As I typically exited and returned by chopper, I'd never taken a close look at it. A large overhead sign spanning the roadway read, "1st Battalion, 43rd Infantry." The supporting mullion on the left held a large painted plywood replica of our regimental unit crest, its wreathed muskets and bayonets on a field of flames, with the motto, *"Animosus et Accinctus."* Graffitists had markered underneath: "*Say What?*" "*It's Greek to Me*" and "*Pig Latin = Ain't Sinked Us Yet.*"

The other mullion had a more in-country sign emblazoned with '*Death From Above.*' Under the words, a ghostly black eagle with a Huey gunship superimposed on its chest, plunged to the attack. Its wings were stretched high, mouth open in full cry. At the same time though, the big raptor also looked as though it could've been reaching upward for a takeoff. This had given flight to a rogue artist's inspiration and a massive penis and attendant pair of hairy testicles now dangled beneath the talons. Dripping blood illustrated recency of separation. "First of the forty-third. Or Worst of the warty turd" was scrawled underneath.

A bored guard surrounded by a parapet of sandbags and sand-filled barrels watched me. An EM from Headquarters Company, he was an unfamiliar face.

"It sure is nice to be home," I said. His eyebrows jumped to alert as if I'd just announced myself as the battalion commander's assassin.

"I don't know 'bout this place being home to anybody," he said slowly. "You must be from some bad-ass place to wanna call this here home."

"It's all relative," I responded. "Wherever you live has to be some kind of home. This firebase makes a whole bunch of things seem relative."

Walking on, I mused over how my concept of home had changed during the past seven years. For most of my life it'd been the house where my parents lived, *our* home. But when Gigi left for college, they'd sold it and moved. The psychic bonds to my boyhood home had been further loosened by a long string of impermanencies generated by college and the army. Short-term roommates and temporary addresses had squeezed out my instinctive feeling of where home was, to the point that it was now wherever I was. 'Where else is there, when there isn't anywhere else? Going by talk at the platoon bar, there're only two places on earth, *here* and back home. I suppose that compared to the precariousness of combat, anywhere back home probably does seem pretty idyllic. Yep, relative.'

For me, Vietnam had simplicity. I'd been in love with the place from day one, but the life and death intensity of the bush forced everywhere else into unimportance. It'd shrunk my life to an archipelago of mental realities, a string of small places where I felt okay, relative to everywhere else. It was how the asperities of a firebase could exist as an oasis of pleasures. Hey, I had a dry mortar-proof bunker, lots of friends, and plenty of beer. Outside the wire I had hundreds of square kilometers of bush, with uncountable dink fucks trying to kill my ass. Life doesn't get much simpler.'

'*Bang's* causing things to be simpler still – doing it by making everything else irrelevant. And she's not just physically here, but intrinsically here, as much as the jungle, the Mekong, and the war. Inextricably so? No! Because I'm going to make off with that treasure – have her or die trying. How's that for simple?'

Spellbound with the idea, I thought of one of my favorite songs, Screaming Jay Hawkins' *I Put a Spell on You.* Mentally, I mimicked the overwrought voice of Screaming Jay, yelling over and over, "*Because you're mine*!" 'Yeah, Jay, you got that right, except Bang's the one who's put a spell on me. I am hers. Either way, Bang *will* be mine.'

Maureen's image sprang at me with the unwelcomed suddenness of an ambush. I stopped walking and put down my bag, partly to wait for a repositioning 155 mm self-propelled Howitzer to pull back off the road, and partly from the perplexity of the thought. My conscience was in a nagging mood again. I looked out over an acre-size pond of accumulated rainwater. Its surface rippled in a soft breeze and I took off my hat to cool the sweat on my forehead. At the water's far end a half-submerged roll of concertina was only visible as an oblique row of prickly parallel loops. Submerged or not, the single coil was elongated to the point that it wouldn't even slow a sapper down.

Framed by similar haphazard entanglements, a little Vietnamese cemetery stood oblivious to the war. Pale yellowish markers mounded up inside, higher than its rectangular, casted-cement immurement. Identical to the many thousands that dotted the Delta, these diminutive enclosures always seemed overfull, stuffed as they were with all the Vietnamese who'd ever lived.

The realization that Bang was the key is what flushed Maureen out in front of me. *Key* stuck in my mind. Key. I recalled the several dozen orphaned ones I'd amassed as a kid. There was a mystery about them. They opened things that small boys weren't supposed to access. There was intrigue in needing the right one and value because adults kept close track of them. So, throughout my early boyhood wanderings, every time I chanced across a lost key, it joined the unrelated others in my battered Whitman Sampler box.

When I was eight, a group of us ruffians while playing along a nearby railroad track were surprised to discover a caboose parked at a siding. Despite our best efforts to look inside, the windows were too high so our curiosity grew. Then, I'd remembered my keys. Strung on a ring fashioned from a length of coat hanger wire, I brought them down for a key-by-key try at the caboose's locked rear door. My third grade pals gave their rapt attention to my bragadocio, scoffing when a couple went in but refused to turn. That is, until one key did. As if from sleight of hand, the door swung open, my genius now incontestable.

Despite the odds, the fact of my having that right key backed my contention that in the entire world there were only seventy-two different keys. Being the exact number I had, I boasted that adults had lost their ability to lock *me* out of anywhere.

The parallels were right there; Maureen's key went in, but couldn't turn. Bang? An orphaned key found by chance, tried in a random lock, magically turned. Everything was perfectly aligned, the unknowable probability bettering all the keys in the entire world.

How had it come to this? Maureen and I had never stopped expressing love for each other, but I could finally see that we'd been just rolling along with a heedless momentum. A recent photo of her told the whole story. Sitting cross-legged on the floor, she'd posed as the centerpiece among a group of pointy-headed Northampton and Amherst intellectuals. It said to me, 'This is where I belong. This is my place. These are my *people*.'

'So they'd been in *a friends* rented farmhouse outside of Hatfield. Whose house? And who's the dude snuggled up against her? Yeah so cool, holding his guitar like Dylan, with his other arm surreptitiously around Maureen.'

While I'd been hanging around waiting for my leg to heal, I'd looked at that picture too many times. All my thoughts of her now passed through the filtered haze of that hemp-toked moment. 'All of her letters say it. She's involved with that guitar-strumming, draft-dodging douche bag. It's glaring out at me. I've got that dude's number. I can see it in his eyes. He's looking right at me. I can hear him too, wallowing in his casuistries on *my* war.'

'There's no denying it. My love for Maureen has a mortal wound. That picture is an x-ray of the damage. It's an exposure of everything, the bullet's entry and the resulting path of visceral destruction. It's showing all the old wounds too, all the ones inflicted during my assignment in Georgia. Gangrene'd set in way back then. It's been festering ever since. How had I not seen it? Making love to her is how – the perfect drug to numb me into a disregarding of every danger sign.'

We hadn't always disagreed about the war. Her campus antiwar activities began a month after I'd arrived. Since then, it'd become a second front in a war against my eating, sleeping and breathing the Mekong. Ever since then, we'd been deepening our defensive positions, reinforcing them with overhead cover, and constructing interlocking trench lines. From these static positions, we'd initially fired our letters like volleys of good-natured illumination flares, but gradually escalated to barrages of high explosives. While I'd comforted myself that it was all just academic sparring, our love had been steadily bleeding to death.

As for literal bleeding, while hospitalized in Saigon, vivid dreams came around to pay me visits. I was always out in the bad bush, places infinitely worse than 'The Snakes.' Menacing, impenetrable jungle wrapped around me. Vines and creepers transformed themselves into webs of trip wires and det cord. Maniacal Cong closed in and surrounded me. I was alone, with no one at my back. 'A soldier's got to have someone at his back – got to know someone's there. If it's his girl, he's never alone.'

'Maureen's been too busy making excuses for Hanoi to ever have my back. Shit, only two days ago, I thought Ngoc had delivered us the coup de grace. Not even close. She'd only switched on the lights. A corpse with ten bullet holes is lying at my feet and I'm still determining the likely cause of death? The murder weapon's right there, self-delusion, the belief that my oh-so-pretty Irish girl from Boston would be utterly invulnerable to whatever it was that had befallen her. 'Why's she still perpetuating this farce? Who betrayed who first?'

'Why do any of these questions need answering? Maureen and I are over. The coffin's already nailed shut. Bang's everything now. Her power's beyond her sublime beauty. She's right here, breaking through to my doomed one-man Bastogne, my liberation from enemy encirclement, and taking a position at my back – while Maureen's providing aid and comfort to the very ones who're gunning for me.'

I picked up my bag and limped on down the road. 'I'm standing with Bang now, to fight whatever we have to, together. Two days to our reunion. That's the horizon. I'm not letting Ruddick and Wiggins drag me down either, down into a welter of paranoia. I'll get my Tiger Scouts for bodyguards. What an irony! My fiancée's in bed with a Marxist, while my most loyal protectors are ex-Viet Cong. Ha! Too bad we couldn't drop by one of those 'Teach-Ins' Maureen tells of in her letters, to learn 'em a few lessons about The Nam.'

Taking stock of my new situation, I mentally stared at the collection of grid squares that comprised my world, our AO, the chunk of this piteous delta on which my fire base had been located, and the moving square meter of ground over which I was absolute Suzerain. 'That's another problem Bang solves. Bent on retribution, she's more of an anti-Communist than I am. This war's personal now. I'll be avenging my wife's family. Every dead dink will make her revenge just that much sweeter.'

One of Bang's Hugoian paraphrases about thoughts being prayers interrupted my train of thought. I only understood the last part; *l'âme est sur ses genoux;* the soul is on its knees. 'She's got a lot to say about souls and prayer. It's not that esoteric, because only one thing matters; she's mine now. An hour ago I was holding her in my arms swearing to the depths of my soul that she is. And in equal measure, she gave herself to me.'

"Hey Mondo!" a voice hollered from up ahead. A three-quarter ton truck had halted at the turn coming out from battalion headquarters. Paul Keneally leaned from its passenger side window, his arm waving. "Come on!" he shouted. Closing the distance, I threw my bag into the back and clambered after it. Keneally hopped out of the cab and climbed in with me.

"What the hell are you doing back?" he asked. "I didn't expect to see you until maybe Thursday. Why'd you cut yourself short?" I looked at the dial of my watch.

"Yeah, *MON* – that's Seiko for Thursday."

"Well, what's the deal? You said you intended to fuck your brains out. You did it in only four days flat? You know what that means?"

"Yeah, nothing. That's cuz it's got less to do with the amount of brains you think I started with than the rate of flow. At the rate they were, it only took three."

"I've always had you pegged as a real task-oriented guy."

"Perseverance and fortitude – turned into, redundant fucking. It hurt so good. It's a long story, and it'll take a good few beers to get through it."

"I've got to tell you something," Keneally said, his tone changing to serious. "Your platoon got hit the day before yesterday. They got ambushed. Two KIA's. One other got wounded."

"What?! Who?!"

"Dean and Andresen."

"Shit, damn shit!! I stomped a boot onto the cargo bed and slammed my fist into my thigh, anger collapsing into exasperated frustration. "Who got wounded?"

"That Tiger Scout named Duc. He's in an ARVN hospital. I haven't been able to get word on how he's doing but don't think it's life threatening."

I grimaced at each name. They came at me borne on bullets as fat as M-79 rounds. It felt like they'd torn through me, taking my entire volume of blood with them.

Sergeant Jeff Dean, a team leader in the third squad, had transferred from Charlie Company a month before. So far, he'd impressed me. During my initial interview with him, he'd said that things had become too routine in a regular rifle company, and that he wanted the kind of action Recon was always getting into. All he needed was my okay. I flash-backed to the all-too-casual scrawling of my concurrence for his transfer and what my signature had come to mean for him.

Specialist 4 Robert Andresen had been with Recon longer than most of us. I had to think to remember his full name, because everyone called him Spot on account of a half-dollar sized splotch of pure white growing in front, slightly to one side. He'd been a damned reliable soldier.

Duc spoke the least English of my four scouts, causing him to hang back, always taking his cues from the others. His face was so expressive he really didn't need to say anything. Whenever I spoke directly to him he gave me the look of pure credulousness. I had no doubt that with a single word, he'd follow me to hell and back. I always wanted to share with him that he'd probably forgotten more about the VC than I would ever know.

"Andresen," I said grimly. "It sounds almost like it's somebody else."

"I know," Keneally said, "He had 'Spot' embroidered for all his name tags. I couldn't ever tell if he was always smiling or just squinting in the sun."

"I think the sun made him smile a lot."

The truck pulled into the mortar platoon's area. We jumped out and took long deliberate strides toward the orderly room. I pushed the pace. Keneally caught up with me when I halted in the doorway.

"Are they in?" I asked.

"Not yet. They air-mobile out early this morning, just for the day. When I was at the TOC, they'd just decided to bring your guys in before dark."

As we entered the raw timbered and sand bagged office, Specialist Delf, the company clerk, looked up with surprise.

"Geez Sir, you ain't supposed to be back for three more days." He laid a pencil in the gutter of his *Field and Stream* magazine and folded it over to mark his place. Sliding it aside, he watched me intently. I dropped into a metal folding chair in front of his desk and stretched my legs.

"Kinda hard to believe isn't it?" I asked, "That a grunt would leave a course of serious fucking and drinking just to get back to his ol' unit. We grunts are often torn, first one way then the other."

"If you say so, Sir. Then again, you*'re* a lifer. I'm a Seventy-one Lima with one-hundred and six days and a wake-up."

"Ain't denyin' it Delf. You got any info on my platoon coming back in?"

"Not exactly, Sir – except that they're supposed to be coming. Don't know the when of it, but I heard Top call over to hold some chow for them."

"You know where they've been?" I asked Keneally.

"West. That's where everything's heading lately."

"Sir, like..." Delf started. "I reckon the CO's told you about Dean and Spot..." He hesitated with a sheepish glance to Keneally, on the thought that he hadn't yet mentioned it.

"Yeah," I answered dully. "What the hell happened with that?" I looked to Keneally for the answer. "You said they got ambushed. You know how?"

"I don't really have a picture of it. Recon didn't come back in 'til the morning after, and nobody was in the mood for talking. I had Sergeant Mounds come down to my hooch to go over the whole thing. He wasn't very descriptive. Afterwards, I had to write those God-awful letters you know – and I hope to God they're my last. Not having been out there at the time, doesn't make it any easier. You can't ever write what really happened anyway, because you have to use the Army's form. Putting my signature on it, I couldn't help but imagine what it'd be like to be a parent reading those words..."

"Those strung-together euphemisms and generalities," I offered. "I thought of writing a letter of my own when Prine got it. Family members'd have a lot of unanswered questions – especially after getting that official letter. Something in me wanted to answer them – give some actual details. But I know, if they got them, it might make things worse. That's why it was standardized it."

"Anyway," Keneally went on, "Dean and Spot got shot up pretty bad – goners even before the dustoff arrived."

"They get any dinks?"

"None they could count."

"*Shit.* Tell you what Delf. Why don't you zip down to the cooler and get me and Lieutenant Keneally a beer – better make that two for me."

"You're putting me in a bind Sir. Top told me that I couldn't go more than two feet from the phones and radios until he got back. If he catches me coming up here carrying three beers, he'll think I'm fraternizing with officers and go crazy."

"Damn Delf! All the beer is for *us.* Besides, it'll take you less time to go down there, than it would to take a piss. You've been holding it all afternoon, right?"

"Well, not quite, Sir. But…"

"Delf," Keneally interrupted, "Lieutenant Carney has just come back here from Vung Tau, obviously weakened – from some very *draining* events – to find out that three of his guys have just been blown away. He's probably so parched he's ready to suck gasoline from a generator, through a piece of old rubber hose, and you're standing there with your thumb up your ass." Delf reflexively glanced down at one of his thumbs.

"You're such a dumb ass Delf. You think I'd just sit here and stare at my own company's commo – leave it squawking until you got back?"

"Uh, I was just joshing, Sir," he said. Halting at the doorway, he came back and grabbed a pack of envelopes from a tray and handed them to me. "This here mail's been waiting on you, Sir." I could see by the color of the envelopes that there were two from Maureen, one from my sister Gigi, and one from a friend in the 101st. I tapped the letters on the edge of the desk while noting the same day postmarks on Maureen's envelopes.

"Thanks Delf, I appreciate it." Acetate sheets on the wall distracted me and my eyes ran down the columns of grease-penciled names listing the company's personnel. Recon's third squad still listed Dean and Andresen, but two boxes in the status column were marked KIA. I reckoned we'd probably continue to carry them as "assigned," until the end of the month, a sardonic way of easing a man out. A soldier could be home safely tucked in his coffin, while at the same time he'd still be showing as a member of E Company back in Nam. I maundered over the concept of an *unofficial* death. It implied that one might be able to come back from it. Due to some bureaucratic snafu, it could all have just been a mistake. '*Yes Sir, I was mis-assigned as dead. Sure glad they got that shit straightened out.*'

"Get anything good from the world?" Keneally asked, trying to restart some conversation. He'd been watching me stare at the platoon roster.

"Oh, ah yeah, a couple of beauts." I separated out the two pastel envelopes and tore them into several pieces. "Maureen Donegan, R I P."

"Whoa, you didn't even read them yet! Wait, you never told me she sent you a Dear John. How do you know those weren't kiss-and-make-up letters?"

"She didn't dump me at all. That was *my* Dear John to her." I motioned to the trashcan into which I'd just dropped the pieces.

"But it's too late to say you're sorry.
How would I know, why should I care?
Please don't bother trying to find her.
She's not there."[3.]

"Huh?" Keneally said.

"From that song by the Zombies – one of my all-time favorites. Yeah, *she's not there* all right. Weird when you find yourself living out song lyrics."

"Okay... But something tells me she's not going to be giving you a big 'Roger, Lima-Charlie' for that Dear John." Keneally pointed at the trash can. "Besides, chicks might dear-john soldiers every other day of the week, but nobody-but-nobody over here does it to his girl back home, especially a heavy-duty fox like her. Now what have you got to look forward to when you get back to the world?"

"Plenty. Things have happened," I said. "There's been a change. Besides, those letters are just more stuff about her recent doings in this or that anti-war shit and how it's all so great. She's always trying to convince me that quitting and pulling out of here, is the best way to get me home safe and sound. Man, I didn't even tell her I got wounded. The fatter envelope probably includes some pinko tract she picked up at another one of those teach-ins. She's always wanting to *expose* me to the *real truth* – like you know, set me straight. I'll show you this classic one I've got in my hooch. It's actually titled, THE REAL TRUTH ABOUT THE VIET CONG. I read part to Tra. He said if it'd been like *that,* he'd still be one. Like it friggin' makes me dizzy – my girlfriend in Massachusetts cluing me in on the VC."

"Aw," he appeased, "that stuff's just the fashion. It sounds good when you don't know anything else. When she's out in the world and has to make a living, she'll leave it all behind."

"She might not," I retorted. "Maureen's been accepted to several graduate schools – political science, Ph.D. programs. She's settled on Brandeis. She won't ever leave some campus or another for the rest of her life. Man, when I graduated, I was already gone. My parents never forgave me for skipping my commencement. That was two days before I got in the car accident."

"But hey, I wasn't there to work for a cap and gown. I was there for Second Lieutenant's bars and an Army uniform – had to get a degree to get there. Then I went back for my M.A. Fucking painful. Now the assholes are trying to kick ROTC out entirely. UMASS isn't Smith, but they're all the same – the pinkos she hangs out with – the same mindset – all of Hampshire County – Smith, UMAS, Mount Holyoke, Amherst College – Hell all of Western Mass for that matter. The whole place is crawlin' with 'em."

I reached across the desk and glommed onto a cigarette from a pack lying next to Delf's magazine. "Now for the good part. You think Maureen's good looking? Well, compared to what I've got going on now – on a scale of one to ten, she'd drop to about a three. And if you figure in all this Peace Action Coalition junk, she's a *point three.*" 'Damn,' I thought, 'stacked against Bang's feelings on the war, Maureen'd be into negative exponents.'

"Good God, Mondo… I don't fucking believe you. Everybody knows you're crazy, but this is so certifiable, it'll get you checking-out of the army."

"What are you talking about?" I asked.

"Like you're not going to tell me you've fallen in love with a whore in Vung Tau are you?! And throwing off your fiancée, who's back home faithfully waiting for you?"

It's not like that" I said, his words causing Bang's voice to echo in my head again. 'Come back to me. *Revenu à moi.*'

"Not like that?! How then?"

"Ah, this here, uh…" I stammered, "Maureen and I have been going down for a while. Our engagement simply dripped away. I was lying on my bunk after I came back from the hospital and its demise felt like these fat rain drops that were falling from the overhang outside my hooch. When the rain began to stop, the dripping slowed, the intervals between the drops got longer and longer, until that very last one. That's where Maureen and I are at this point. The last one has fallen."

"Along came the little whore, and dried up all the rain. Isn't that part of a song too?"

"It's a long story, Keneally."

"I'm sure it is. The shrinks should get a real kick out of it."

"Willya shut the fuck up?" Delf had reemerged with the beer. This wasn't the kind of conversation that I wanted to share with the company gossip. "Let's go down to my hooch and I'll tell you about it. You won't believe it."

"I already don't," Keneally said with an indulgent sigh. He got up and followed me to the door.

"Hey, Sir, I wanted to hear about Vung Tau. I think I'd like to go there sometime."

"Let me tell you something, Delf. In this battalion, you've got to get blown up or shot before you can go there. Kinda weird 'cause otherwise the place is actually full of REMFs."

"Yeah, and it'd be just my luck, if I ever did get shot, it'd be right in the dick – so's I couldn't do nothing with it." I stopped in the doorway and turned back to him.

"Delf, I can almost guarantee it."

CHAPTER 2

Keneally and I ambled down through my platoon's area, picking up a few more beers on the way. At my hooch, my bunker-for-one, I unlocked the door and pushed it open.

"Ah yes," I said wrinkling my nose, "just as I left it. Sour and fusty are the two best smells this place has."

"Putrid piss seems like the most dominant one to me," Keneally added.

"That's because the piss tubes on the other side of *your* hooch are so saturated, they're leeching into that stagnant water behind us. All the dudes coming back from chow see the tubes as useless so they just take their leaks straight into that water. I'm sure though that our *company commander* has a remediation plan all ready to be implemented."

"This whole fire base is a goddamn toilet," he said, ignoring my crack. "It's one never-ending, un-flushable outhouse – without the luxury of the house."

"It flushes a little when a good monsoon comes in. Trouble is we've only been catching the edge of them lately." I punched a pair of holes in my can and tossed the church key to Keneally.

"Well, there she is," he said, looking at my thumbtacked photos of Maureen. "You've got to admit it's going to be tough to say good-bye to those headlights coming at you – now, not coming at you."

"Like that same song goes," I said:

'Let me tell you 'bout the way she looked.
The way she acts and the color of her hair.
Her voice was soft and cool, her eyes were clear and bright.
But she's not there.'"[4.]

I quoted the words gravely, as though a somber poem. "Yes and no is how tough it'll be. More and more she's been thinking that guys can't see her for what she is, because they can't take their eyes off her knockers."

"They do have, hmmm, just that kind of saliency."

"That's only natural, right? And it's definitely true when you first meet her. After that, they kind of blend in. I gotta tell you though, for the past few months, she's been writing a lot of weird stuff about how her looks are actually barriers to men seeing the *real* her."

"Sounds like a couple of toads have gotten to her," he ribbed. "Jealous ones."

"I don't know. Like she wrote me – it got back to her that some guys had referred to her as '*Jugs Donegan.*' Right, like *that's* a term of derision? Then this 'breasts-on-the-brain dude supposedly went for the *crowning insult* and tagged her, 'Jug-a-thon Don-a-gon'."

"Ha! I can assure you my wife would love to have it so bad."

"It's nutty. You'd have thought they'd been calling her 'The syph-slut of Smith. Geezo, she doesn't get it that those guy'id give their left nut to be her boyfriend. Two years ago, she would've thought it funny. I was always trying to get her to accentuate what she had, but even then she was modest. I tried to coax her into dressing like a Bill Ward illustration, but never got her half way."

Evanescent memories of Maureen fluttered away, replaced by her purposeful change of looks. 'Love *me,* Gav, not some superficial way that I look,' she'd chided in one of her letters. My correction that she and her looks couldn't be separated had gone nowhere. Bang made such notions seem ludicrous, accepting her sublime looks with nothing but humility; all things as they are, being as they should be. Maureen though, was taking what she'd been blessed with as a mark of shame, God-given gifts only worthy of guilt. From my perspective, the whole thing was a nonsensical contrivance.

'Sure Maureen's smart, smart as hell. That quick-wittedness got me the day we met. But all those straight A's that she used to be just proud of, is nothing but hubris. Bang has humility. Lord, she's got the heart of a *Little Dorrit.* All that reading in French says she's plenty smart enough. But how much of that intelligence is from her occult powers? *Damn!* I have to stop thinking of her like this.'

"Yeah, Keneally," I added out loud, "Maureen'll just have to find some guy who isn't into big high-riding tits – with nipples as hard as pencil erasers."

"Oh, stop," he said shaking his head. "If he isn't, there'll be a serious defect in that boy. None of that would ring true for you though would it?"

"Not now, no. "I told you, I'm trading up. Oh and, check this out. Maureen wants to be called Mo now."

"Moe?"

"Yeah, short for Mo-reen. She says her *friends* started calling her that – and she likes it."

"Like Moe, Larry and Curly?"

"Could be…" I riffled through a box full of papers and envelopes. "A couple of 'em in this photo make Nina Khrushchev look like Sophia Loran. But get a load of Maureen here, wearing one of those wooly-ass serapes – just the thing when you want to hide everything. And look at the short hair – and the fucking dull-ass brown she's made it. Now, check out the dude next to her."

"The two of them do look a little lovey-dovey don't they?"

"Has to be why she sent it, a subtle message."

"The guy's definitely got an all-too-serious look about him – that Trotsky look they all seem to like. The rest are just regular hippies."

"Yeah, the dude's super earnest, but I'd say it's more the ascetic look of a Dzerzhinsky. See the cold, singled-minded intentness in his eyes?"

"You've got me there, Mondo. Remember, I majored in business."

"Felix Dzerzhinsky was head of Checka, the Soviet secret police during the Red Terror – right after the Bolshevik revolution. He specialized in mass summary executions –tens of thousands of them. He became the prototype for his successors: Yagoda, Yezhov, Beria. Each in turn ran the NKVD. Implementing Stalin's orders, they were responsible for the deaths of millions."

"On a smaller less-organized scale," he said, "I saw it played out in Africa. And, we're seeing that legacy again right here."

"I've read countless books on the subject," I said, "and still can't conceive of how they get people to think it's good. 'Hey yeah, let's slaughter as many innocent people as we can get our hands on! It'll be good for everyone. Let's do it!'"

"They don't figure good and evil like we do. It's about having power or not, then when you have power, it's about gaining the ultimate power. When you can order summary mass executions, you have ultimate power. That's their idea of good. Without fail though, it breeds fanatics. And among fanatics, you get psychopaths, your Heinrich Himmlers and all those you mentioned. Don't know the equivalent in China. They murdered so many millions- Mao must have had his boss henchmen too."

"Yeah," I agreed. "I've read a couple of books on the Chinese revolution but not enough of it to remember exactly who Mao's murder-machine men were. With the sheer size of the slaughter, there were probably a bunch." I paced to the end of the room and sat down on the edge of my bunk. Placing my beer on the floor between my boots, I pulled out a cigarette, lit it, and took a long contemplative drag. "Look, I already know I can shoot some NVA trooper – a guy who maybe hasn't gone past the sixth grade, but grown up in a hard-core totalitarian system stoking him with commie propaganda every minute of his life – to the point that it's all he knows. But what do I do with some guy who's had the best education in the world, unlimited access to all the facts known, the wherewithal to make an informed choice – like discerning the actual truth and, *still* comes up a friggin' commie trying to do America in?"

"Depends on the when and where of it," Keneally answered. The ones in the jungle who're active threats to you, are fair game. The ones back home are subversive threats, but not an imminent danger to your life – not yet anyway. All you can do is..."

"Call them what they are," I said, finishing his sentence. "Real powerful."

"That's about it." He looked down and scrutinized a different picture of Maureen, then tapped it with his index finger. "You know, those whamo-mamos could get me to overlook the new haircut."

"Okay, we have a consensus – they're excellent. But, I can do without, very nicely, even if she was looking the best she ever did – and red white and true fucking blue – instead of just goddamn pinko pink. *That's* because of what I've got *now.*" I took the first picture from in front of Keneally and looked at it again. Then picking up a loose M-16 round from the table, I poked the bullet through 'Dzerzhinsky's head.' "Wow, the dude just got his head blown off by a tank round... at fucking point blank range!" I tossed the picture back onto the table.

"Please don't bother trying to find her.
She's not there."[5.]

Keneally looked at me with an earnest expression and drew another gulp from his can.

"So-o-o," he began, as if about to tread on a delicate subject. "Tell me about this beautiful whore with whom you've 'traded up' – err, fallen in love with. I'm sure it was reciprocal too, *love* being their main business, right?"

"I swear Paul, she *isn't* a whore. And for the record, the main business of whores, isn't love, not even a close facsimile of it."

"We could argue the similarities of the mechanics Mondo, but I'll concede your special expertise in that area. So this – this – person, gave it to you for free? Like she's just so incredibly grateful for all you're doing for her country. She's kind of a magnanimous, high-minded slut?"

"Repeat after me. No whore, no screw, no Vung Tàu. I didn't hardly even touch her. Okay, we did kiss."

"Whoa. You went on R&R for that? What was she, Nguyen Cao Ky's daughter – and you were afraid of getting secretly rubbed out by the National Police... for doing more?"

"It was on the outskirts of Saigon..."

"Wait a minute. Back in the truck, you said you screwed your brains out in Vung Tau. Wow, you really do have shit for brains. A case of diarrhea must have done you in. You mean I'm talking right now to someone with the IQ of one of those peep frogs chirping out back? Only smart enough to chirp and mate – definitely be you all right."

"Come on Keneally, it was a total unexpected coincidence. I did go to Vung Tàu and did get plenty of a whore there, but after three days, got into this out-and-out brawl. Then I had to get the fuck out of Dodge, like fast – so I headed back to Saigon, and wound up in this hotel straight out of HP Lovecraft. But while there, I ran into those two advisors from district headquarters, you know that captain Ruddick and a black E-7 named Wiggins?"

"Yeah, I've run across them a couple of times."

"Well I hopped a ride back with them and we stopped at this little Vietnamese place – not all that far off the main road. That's where I met her. There's just no way to describe her. I mean she's Eurasian – part English, part Burmese – and French too – she's all-the-way fluent in it."

"She's not Vietnamese?"

"Yeah, of course. She's been in Saigon her whole life. But the thing is, she's physically flawless and her face has this special mind-blowing look – partly in the way she looks at you – *me!* I ain't shittin' you Keneally, you would not find one thing even minutely off on this girl – not from top to bottom. Anybody'd be bowled over by her. Ruddick and Wiggins definitely were. Man, all three of us were fucking drooling. On top of that, she comes across like she's some kind of an angel."

"So how old is she?"

"Twenty-three."

"Good, I thought you were going to say fourteen. But doesn't twenty-three mean at least four baby-sans – with maybe the fifth's on the way, huh?"

"You're off by five. Look, this one is in a total category of her own – like every segment is perfect.

"Oh, she's segmented too huh? Like a praying mantis – you know right after copulation the female tears off the male's head and eats him?"

"Gee-Zus, Keneally, you know what I mean! If she does have such a *physical* quality, it'd be a wasp waist – maybe twenty inches – I shit you not. With her other two measurements, it makes your tongue hang out. Just conceive of her as perfect perfection! I'm talking better than anything you've ever seen in your whole life – here, back in the world, anywhere."

"Okay, okay," he sighed. "So you're going to marry her, right?"

"No shit Uncle Ken. Like there's no way in hell I'm not. She's the kind of thing that for mere mortals doesn't come around even once in a lifetime. The odds against it are so massive, there isn't even a number that goes that high! Our paths crossed by total accident. I ain't ever letting it get by."

"Oh-kee-dokey. I was just wondering where you two love birds might be honeymooning. Or, might you just be sticking close to our local, err… Tatterdemalion comforts?" He tipped his head in the direction of my funky mosquito-netted bunk in the corner. "You might get away with bringing her in as your own personal house mouse – for a couple of hours anyway."

"You don't bring royalty to a fucking, floating outhouse. Scratch that. This girl is so sweet she lives on sunbeams, and shits strawberries."

"I knew a girl who once shat a Twinkie," he said.

"That wasn't the girl you married, though, right?"

"No, she married some other guy. My wife was my second choice."

"*See!* You've got to move fast with these kinds of girls." Finishing my beer with a final glug, I spun the empty can onto the equipment table and grabbed up the other. "Come on, Paul, you need to help. First, I'm going to marry her, and then I'm going to get her out of this country, whatever way I can."

"Damn Mondo, what the hell can I do? I'm stuck here same as you."

"Think, basically. Remember, I fucked my brains out, and you didn't. Man, I don't even have an idea of where to start." Fitfully, I walked to the end of the hooch.

"Well," Keneally began, "why don't you tell me why in God's name she's going to go anywhere with you? Then again, there's bound to be some who'd find the idea of getting out of here more than bearable – and hitching a ride with an American officer, perhaps even appealing."

"That's not it at all," I demanded. "I forgot to tell you about the part where she's in love with me so coming with me wherever I go is a given."

"Oh boy," he said, skeptically raising his eyebrows and exhaling. "When I said certifiable, I wasn't kidding. I'd better check the supply room for straightjackets. Hmmm, maybe a flak jacket put on backwards could work..."

"Cut the shit, willya?"

"So, Lieutenant Section-Eight," he resumed, "all this happened in a couple of hours? She'd have to tell you that though, wouldn't she?"

"No, because she could also say it if it was true." 'All this does seem hard to believe: Like I've just met the actual most beautiful girl in the world, fell headlong in love with her, while a lightning bolt skewers her into falling for me. Then we both swear a blood oath to run off and marry. *And* what about me being a recipient of metempsychosis, while she exercises some sort of Circean power over me? If Keneally thinks I'm nuts now, what'll he think if I tell him that part?'

"She doesn't know yet, that I'll be taking her out – like back to the world." I went to my equipment and began rummaging through it, trying to come up with a tin of C-ration cheese. "I've got fucking crackers, but no fucking cheese! No fucking peanut butter either. Did I tell you she's also a wicked-ass anti-communist…?" I let that item lay there for a moment, reassured by just hearing it said out loud.

"No, you didn't," Keneally said. "I'll put it in the plus column."

"Look Paul," I've got big problems here. One, I've got to get back to her fast – like within a couple of days. Two, my leg has gotten a lot better, but I could still malinger with it for a while. I don't want to be out of sight and out of mind of the Ol' man though. Now isn't the time for me to be seen as some gold-bricking, supernumerary LT. Because when I put on my tracks, I don't want any of that carrying over to my being seen as a supernumerary captain. Time's too tight. So I go back into the bush? That'll put me back in the operational side of things, but remove me from where I can strategize as to what my new job will be when my promotion forces me out of this one."

"You could go up to the TOC," he suggested. "That'd put you right in the middle of where you need to be – and for only a month."

"Actually, its nineteen days now. Don't forget, my promotion is a week before yours."

"Mondo, when have you ever let me forget? I only meant that a short month at the TOC would give you the time and location you need."

"True, but the TOC means twelve-hour shifts, seven days a week. Where's time for *her*? You eat, sleep, drink a beer, take a shit – and that's it! Besides, I'd be square under Dingleberry's nose. Yeah, there he'd be, standing right behind my chair, listening, watching. Wouldn't *I just* love *that?!*"

"No," he conceded. "The guys up there now don't, so *you* wouldn't times ten."

"Okay, nineteen days to bide time and position for my promotion. I don't see any captain slots opening here, so I'll have two bad options: Go up to brigade and be an assistant jack-off to some staff major or get transferred to the Twenty-fifth Div."

"You, Mister Infantry, might get a Rifle Company, somewhere. You wouldn't want that?"

"*HER,* Keneally. You're not listening. Her first, then my career. That's the new order of things."

You ever see the movie *Sayonara*?" I shook my head. "Your loony-tunes shit reminds me of it. It's set during the Korean War and this guy, played by Marlon Brando, is an Air Force fighter ace, West Pointer, son of a four-star, and fiancé of a generals daughter. He gets sent back to Japan where his future inlaws have gotten assigned, and have their daughter with them. Brando meets and falls in love with this Japanese dancer. She's the most beautiful girl in this huge show – filled with beautiful girls. She falls in love with him too. And just like you, they both have to decide."

"Decide what?"

Well, Brando has to decide whether he wants her or his career. She has to decide if she can leave her culture, which she's very wedded to."

"My girl'll come home with me. I'll have both." I said the words with conviction and swore again that I'd make it happen.

"I'm not done with the story," he said. "It's what the title is all about. Ever read James Michener?"

"I read *Hawaii* on my way here. It was okay."

"I read Sayonara a couple of years after I saw the movie. But see, they end very differently. In the book, it turns out to be just too big a deal for them. The guy says 'sayonara' and heads home to the States and promotion to lieutenant colonel. The girl was deeply imbedded in traditional Japan and had a lot of apprehension about a new life in America. Our war against them had only ended a few years before. So, she goes back to her dance troupe. But in the movie, Brando says 'sayonara' to everything *but* the girl."

"I'm with Brando," I said, "but since I love the Army, I've at least gotta try to have both, before giving up."

"Michener was driving at the fact that having both is too hard – too many complications."

"It might've seemed that way to Michener," I countered, "but from what you say, the screenplay writer didn't see it that way."

"That's debatable," Keneally argued. "He had Brando say goodbye to the Air Force instead of the girl, in keeping with the notion that he couldn't have both."

"Why couldn't he?"

"Well, that was another theme in both the movie and the book – the difficulty an Air Force officer might have in gaining acceptance – having a Japanese wife... prejudice."

"Society's changed a lot in the past twenty years," I said. "Racial prejudice? Countless military guys've married Koreans and Philippino gals. How many would marry Viets if the brass'd let them? Like we hate them so much they have to keep us from loving them. Our authorities are the miscegenists, not us. Besides, Vietnam is more western than Japan. No, I won't be saying, *Chào em.* And neither will she. Hey, I know! I'll just have her speak French all the time. Yeah, like she's this French girl, who only happens to look Asian."

"Look, I say go up to brigade. At least that'd keep you here in the Ninth. You could set her up in downtown Tan An and see her all the time."

"I know I need some staff time, but if I go up there, sure as shittin', I'll get some total chicken-shit, candy-ass Dingleberry for a boss, resenting all my field time. Naturally, he'll want to teach this young captain a thing or two – take his alligator mouth and stick it up his hummingbird ass. Man, I'm so wild right now about how stupidly we're fighting this war, I'll wind up punching somebody's lights out."

"Aw, come off it Mondo. You're exaggerating. I know you can behave yourself when you want to. If this chick is as great as you say, your motivation ought to be as high as it can go."

"My motivation's got contrails, Keneally. Sure, I'd be cool and STRAC ninety-nine percent of the time. Then some friggin' chickenshit'd come along with the whole war hanging on his petty-ass office shit, as if the real life and death goings on out there doesn't even exist. Bam! Next thing I'd know, I'd be assistant sandbag officer in a log depot somewhere in II Corps, with a lost career, and even forcibly separated from *her.* I can deal with a staff environment, but can't put up with people like that."

"Tinderberrys are a lot less common than you think," he suggested. "I still say Tan An's your best bet. Brigade will give you the kind of sham time you need to fix everything up. Secrecy will be your biggest problem though. It won't take long for everybody to find out about her."

"If they saw her, they'd understand."

"If she's like you say, understanding isn't what you'll get. Jealousy and envy are a lot more powerful and a lot more common. Hey, this is just a thought – you haven't taken a regular R&R yet. Why not fly her out on a parallel flight? I'd shoot for Hawaii. It's inside the US. If you run into trouble getting a visa from our embassy in Saigon, you could try getting one from somewhere else, like Singapore or Hong Kong."

"Now you're cookin' Keneally!" I said excitedly. These are exactly the kinds of ideas I need to explore. I wonder how hard it'd be to get her a Vietnamese passport."

"In this country?" he said rubbing his thumb against the index finger of his outstretched hand. "A little baksheesh and you're on your way. Corrupt systems can be pretty damned efficient – if you've got money. And you do."

"Right," I said, turning toward the sound of choppers out to the west of our firebase. "Sounds like them."

"Somebody all right, but Alpha and Delta were out today too."

We continued ping-ponging the problems I'd face in getting Bang to the US, until R&R in Singapore rose as a real solution. I decided to put in for it and work out for Bang to rendezvous with me.

'Legally married it'll be easier for her to get a visa to the States. I'll just get her a ticket out just ahead of my DROS. Gigi'll help take care of her until I arrive. My head reeled with the imminence of Singapore, from the heart-pounding rapture of meeting her when she got off her plane, to sitting in Raffles bar with her dressed in an oh-so-cool outfit, to my getting her pregnant in our plush hotel room.'

'But our wedding ceremony's coming even before that! She's getting it together right this minute. I wish it could be in Saigon's Notre Dame Cathedral, but given our circumstances, a discrete wedding mass in her local church might turn out to be even better. Geez, I think I know what strings I've got to pull to make it happen, so why am I so uneasy about getting back to her in two days? Is it just because I want her so bad? It's the same weird edginess I was feeling in the café, when she left me for a moment. Then in the jeep coming back, the further away we got, the worse it felt. Now, it feels like a fucking fire. Geez am I obsessed!'

Keneally and I both alerted to the sound of footsteps outside. Picking up on familiar Recon voices, I pushed the door open with my foot.

"Hey Stovall! You guys didn't come in on those choppers?" Four members of the second squad, with Stovall in the lead, turned and looked toward my door.

"No, Sir. We came from out front. We had to walk our asses off, then they picked us up with deuce-'n'-halfs about six klicks south of here. Casswell stepped on a toe popper and got dusted off. His foot wasn't too bad though. The way things've been going, I guess you can count that as lucky. You heard about all that shit from the other day?"

"Yeah... Hey, do me a favor huh, and go tell Sergeant Mounds that I want to talk to him."

In a moment, Mounds and Crowder hauled themselves into the bunker. A heavy coating of sepia colored mud extended half way up their legs. Above the knees, it had dried to a dull gray and went up as far as their breast pockets. They nodded to the presence of Keneally with stolid, heavy lidded expressions and jointly leaned their butts against the edge of my equipment shelf.

"Gee, Sir," Crowder began, "we didn't expect you back. I sure can't imagine Vung Tau being like a bummer."

"No, Vung Tàu was… very interesting," I said. My cryptic reply produced dead silence. "So, I heard you've been out for a little stroll in the country this afternoon."

"Shit, Sir, first they said choppers were coming out to pick us up. Then 'cause it was doing a monsoon somewhere, they got grounded. Then, they told us there wouldn't be no choppers, and if we wanted to come in, we'd have to hump-it two klicks to the road so trucks could get us. Of course we wanted to come in – like it was already getting dark. We weren't ever supposed to be stayin' out tonight. If we didn't make it out in time, we'd have to stay put for the night – no claymores, no machine guns, no water, no food."

"They could've found one chopper to fly that stuff out to you," I said.

"Well, why should we stay out pulling an ambush, just cuz they couldn't get their shit together? So, we humped our asses off. Just before we got to the road, Casswell stepped on that toe popper."

"Stovall told me he was lucky," I said. I'm not sure what kind of luck putting a bullet through your foot is, unless you're comparing it to stepping on a mine."

"Luckier than that, Sir. The bullet went through his foot, about right here." He touched the muzzle of his M-16 to where his bootlaces ended and the leather began. "Clean through, right between the bones. Probably would've tore up his whole foot if it had been a quarter of an inch to the right or left."

"Yeah, that sounds like luck all right," I went on, "because in the dark, it could have been something a whole lot bigger. Were the trucks sitting out there, waiting for you?"

"Not really, they were parked at that little Arvin compound for their security. There can't be nobody liking a ride in an open deuce-in-a -half, in the dark – not down *that* goddurn narrow-ass road."

"Tell me about the other day, Mounds, the day Dean and Spot got it."

"It was fucked up, Sir. You wouldn't have believed it even if you was there." He stared at me. He'd taken my question as a reminder that he had been in charge.

"Where were you at the time?" I asked, making a conscious effort not to sound stern.

"They put us in to the west of that place called Dinh Tru. We swept through a group of hooches and some woodline, and then moved all the way out to the river. We didn't see a thing the whole way – no signs of nothing. You know out there's a nothin' place for dinks. After a while, the colonel got me on the horn and said the choppers'd be picking us up in an hour. I figured we might as well go back to the village – to break for some C's. We were heading back up the trail...."

"The same trail?" I interrupted.

"Damn straight, Sir!" he insisted. "That was the only one we knew for sure wasn't booby trapped."

"Sergeant Mounds is right, Sir," Crowder said, jumping to his defense. "That place down there is loaded with all kinds of bad shit."

"He just referred to it as a 'nothin' place for dinks' – but okay, go on and tell me what happened next."

"Well, we'd only gone about a hundred meters," Mounds continued, "when, it happened. A bunch of gooks opened up on us from inside the bush."

"How many?" I asked. Mounds looked to Crowder then at me.

"Three that we saw, and from the sound of it, maybe a couple more. They emptied a magazine and just dee dee mao-ed. We fired back and chased them, but I was worried they might be trying to drag us into a bigger trap. I called in gunships, but they didn't spot...." He hesitated, hearing the sound of the word, unavoidably reminded him of Andresen, and of his being killed that very minute. He paused. "Ah, they didn't see no dinks. I'd already called in a dustoff."

"Were they still alive?"

"Me and Travis got to them first," Crowder said, "They were already done for. Dean took rounds in his chest. Spot only took one, but it went through his head." Morosely, he looked down at his boots. "Man, it was fucked up. Even Duc. He made it out, but got hit in the leg – had a piece of goddamn bone sticking out through his pants. Travis put a tourniquet on it, cuz he was bleedin' like a motha-fucka."

"Where's he now, Paul?"

"Saigon, in the Arvin hospital."

"It's probably the same place Xuan went and almost died," I said. "If Duc ain't doing well, I'll ask the Colonel to get him transferred to third Field. Fuck-it, I'll do it anyway. Shit, they might've cut his leg off by now."

"I think those gooks just walked into us, Sir," Crowder said, not leaving the subject alone. "Like they were walking down the trail from the other direction and didn't know we were there. Remember that time when we were working out of Dong Tam, and the same thing happened. That lead gook got so surprised he tripped his own tripwire and blew himself up with his own bag of grenades."

"Yeah. But you described it as an ambush, meaning they saw you first. Hey, you guys better head for the mess hall if you're going to get anything." The two NCOs nodded and got up. They were uncomfortable and I could sense their relief in my letting them go. The unspoken presence of Keneally, their company commander, made them feel like it was an official inquiry. "Hey, bring me back something will-ya – like a couple of sandwiches."

I stood at the door watching them tramp obliviously across the rickety PSP catwalk. On each of their steps, it bowed in the center and plunged below the surface of the water, an inadequate rinsing of their mud-laden boots. 'I'll have a talk with my Scouts to fill in the blanks. They don't have any particular loyalty to Mounds or Crowder, so I'll get a clearer version of what happened.'

"Now what do I do?"

"About what?" He looked up from a copy of *Girls of the World.* My *Count Belisarius* and a paperback copy of *Herzog* had been lying on top of it, but the magazine's partially exposed cover had become irresistible.

"You're supposed to be happily married," I said, "put that down."

"I love my wife dearly," he said matter of factly. "But what's that got to do with this girl here being even better than your, um-m-m, former fiancée?" He nodded at the pictures of Maureen on the wall. I looked over his shoulder at a full page black and white picture of a very pretty, buxom, naked blonde. I read the terse caption, 'Kaia Bjorklund hails from Sweden.'

"Our lovely Kaia," I improvised," spends her free time relaxing in Stockholm coffee bars, discussing the works of her favorite communist poet, Pablo Neruda. She's also enjoys spreading venereal disease among her many friends and acquaintances. Look, Paul," I went on, "I've been out of the field almost three weeks. The first week, Ballenger got wasted. The second, Newquist bought a ticket home with his leg ripped off at the knee. Now this with Dean and Spot, and Casswell too. Three dead and three wounded. Maybe Casswell will be back, but with a foot wound, he might be out of the field for a long time – maybe permanently. I don't want to sound like I'm blaming Mounds – I wasn't there, but shit. I can read between the lines. They were too complacent. Nothing was out there before, so they just lollygagged their way back up that same trail."

"I don't think it happened quite the way they said either, but then we weren't there."

"I don't know," I sighed. "Those dinks weren't surprised like Mounds was trying to tell us. They'd come in by chopper only a little while before. The dinks were probably shadowing them and were set up and ready. Dean took it point blank, a classic ambush. They wouldn't have gotten the drop on our guys any other way. When everybody dove for cover, the dinks just dee-deed. They aren't stupid – they know how lazy GIs can be, inclined to do things the easy way. Compared to them, damn! They'll sit in a place with the patience of a rock, neck deep in muck, breathing mosquitoes, just waiting for that single moment when they can press the detonator. My guys wanted to avoid encountering booby traps – and where did it get them? Another thing – about tonight. They should have stayed out there. Humping over unfamiliar ground past dusk is asking for it."

"Isn't that what they were trying to avoid on the day they got ambushed?" Keneally asked.

"That's just it. Mines and booby traps are hard enough to deal with in the daytime, but when you can't see at all, you don't have any idea what your next step is coming down on. I can do it myself, but its super hairy and can't ever be done on a trail. They just wanted to come in for the night, and were willing to risk serious casualties to do it – at least Mounds was. That's my problem.

"They know the deal out there, Mondo."

"Yeah, well enough. But it's hit me a few times. Left to their own devices, it's the lazy judgments they're prone to make. Disciplined judgments, where you have to constantly do it the *hard way* are what you have to have."

"You're going back out there with Recon, aren't you?"

"I've got to."

"And what about Miss Vietnam?"

"Miss Milky Way Galaxy! I corrected. I'll take care of that first – short term goal number one. I'll just shoot up there to see her – day and a half is all I need – shit, eighteen hours in a pinch. I've got to – or go totally nuts. I'll need the three-quarter ton. Tra and Tho will come with me. That way, nobody outside of you will know shit. If the head Shed asks for me, I'm up seeing to Casswell– and yeah, Duc – which I definitely will, but just not as long as it'll take."

"Okay," Keneally said with a slow deliberate nod, his face having the expression he wore when running through problems with unknown complications.

"Ah, no more beer," I said, realizing both my cans were empty. I went over to my foot locker and fetched a bottle of Jack Daniels. Swilling it around revealed a couple of disappointing mouthfuls. I poured it into a canteen cup and added water to make it seem like more. "All I've got to do is keep things cool for about two weeks, right?"

"Depends on how cool you keep things."

"The field's the only place where I've got any real control. I'll just go out there and do my thing – keep 'em alive."

"I always figured you'd be the last soldier in this country to sandbag the mission."

"I'm not! I'm just talking about keeping the guys okay – like I always do. With my new girl behind me, I'm personally going to kick more Cong ass than anyone in this battalion. Then, right when I get promoted, and haven't yet gone to my new job, I'll ask the colonel for another Vung Tàu in-country, then manage to.... No, scratch that – I'll tell him the honest truth, just not every tiny detail – that I want to take two days and a night in Saigon to check on Duc. With a smashed femur, there's no telling what they'll do with him. And while I'm up there, I'll be needing to see this *friend*. That's the friggin' ticket, man."

"The ticket to what?" Keneally asked.

"The ticket to my getting married. That's when it'll be happening. And you dude, are my best man, so that means you'll have to cut loose and join me – couple hours is all."

"You've lost me back a ways, Mondo. You said that if you return to the field, it won't give you the opportunity to wrangle a new job."

"It'll just be harder, but I'll hang out at battalion every extra minute when we're in. I'll feel out the ol' man on the possibility of sending some captain who's been around for a while up to brigade instead of me. Then I could take his job and stay here – and be miles closer to *her*. See, the Old Man might decide to leave the platoon with Mounds for a couple weeks if he thinks my leg isn't okay. But, I'm fixing to tell him I'm ready right now. Goldbricking with this wound would give me the opportunity to slip up to my celestial honey, but what if in the meantime more guys get hit, KIA-ed? I couldn't deal with that."

"Mondo. Some of this has just been bad luck. You've had some too – what was that PFC's name who got killed a while back? – right before I took over as CO."

"Prine"

"Right. It happens. And to Recon Platoon Leaders themselves. You're the fourth one we've had since I've been in this battalion.

Your predecessors were all fine officers, but that wasn't good enough to keep their asses out of the way of a bullet or booby-trap blast."

"Let's talk about Prine, the only KIA I've had since we moved into this AO. The day he got it, the platoon was in two elements. I had one and Mounds had the other. Prine was with him. Look, I know that the greatest Recon platoon leader who ever lived wouldn't be able to guarantee anything. It's a high-risk job – a bazillion booby traps – everything from homemade dinky shit to rigged-up, eight-inch arty rounds. Nobody can control where each one of sixty-plus boots are stepping every minute of every fucking day. Now there's a lot more NVA coming in, full of esprit to put my guys right in their sights and pull their triggers. Who says every one's going to miss? As for booby traps, you walk around out there enough, and one'll eventually make your acquaintance. No, the Dinks aren't going to kill my guys one by one while I'm still in charge, but too busy playing goddang *remf!*"

"God forbid *you that,* Mondo."

"You got it. I can't do that, even for her."

"So she's *not quite* the number one deal."

"Well yeah... when you're going for both, each has to trade off with being my top priority. "If I get back to her right away, it'll be no big deal to wait a couple weeks until we get married. By then, I'll have come up with a longer-term plan. Remember, *no* Sayonara."

"Hey, how come you haven't mentioned her name?"

"I didn't mean not to... It's Bang," I said.

"Bang?! Like B A N G?"

"Yeah, but they don't say it quite that way. They pronounce the A like when you say ah with a tongue depressor in your mouth." Keneally tapped his can of beer and slowly shook his head.

"Bang." he repeated, almost at a whisper. He was staring at the bullet lying in front of him that had taken out Maureen's Trotskyite friend.

CHAPTER 3

An hour later, I headed along the hundred-meter road that connected the rifle company's living area to the battalion headquarters' compound. More a track than an actual road, it alternated between being a series of sunbaked, cement -hard wheel ruts and a slimy excuse. But its prime feature was weakness.

Strung with helter-skelter barbed wire on either side, I saw it as undefended space, smack in the middle of our fire base. As I walked, my mind alternated between the defenselessness of our midsection and dreamy thoughts of Bang. 'At least these center ruts are firm enough that I'm not slogging like I was in the field. You know something's wrong when you can't tell the difference between your fire base and a rice paddy. *"Je t'aime de toute mon âme."* Yeah, with all her soul. *"Passionnément!"*'

Pitch-black darkness keyed up my awareness for sight and sound. Continuous ambush patrols in a nocturnal jungle made nighttime itself synonymous with hair trigger instincts. Vigilance being the key, going anywhere after twilight without a weapon, made me feel like I was strolling buck naked down a crowded city street. I'd once heard Crowder tell an FNG in his squad that the dinks owned both the jungle and the night. I'd interjected that it'd be true only if you believed it and behaved accordingly. I didn't and we wouldn't.

'Shit, this battalion's defenses are so bad, how could it be defended? If hit, we'd try, but with so few defendable positions, a well-led company could overrun us. The more nights I spend inside this give-a-shit barbed-wire corral, the more claustrophobic I get. In the field I can at least maneuver... Yeah maneuver my way back to Bang... Maneuver my whole situation. *"Je vous aimerai pour toujours."* You got that right, Bang. *Forever.*'

Movement to my front sharpened my qui vive. I slowed and heard several footsteps scuff the ground ahead. Indistinct forms began moving from the black air toward that point where a friend-or-foe identification *had* to be made. 'And I do what if it's dink sappers?'

From the barest available light, a sweat-dampened sheen on a pair of white faces emerged.

"Good evening, men," I said, speaking with a tone of authority.

"Oh! – Yeah, I mean right – How ya doing, ah, Sir?" They stumbled over each other's words. I'd startled them and my sudden presence had spiked their surprise. We passed silently into each other's dissolving wake. 'There's another lesson about being a grunt LT over here; you can't ever be too paranoid. How can you be with a hundred-thousand dink fucks sitting out there looking to kill just one more *me.*'

I passed the darkened mass of our solitary M-42 Duster. Immobilized in a sandbagged parapet, its twin 40mm guns lay locked in a flat trajectory, trained on a distant woodline. From its position it could sweep 200 meters of open terrain, a formidable defense against the least likely avenue of approach. 'Now if I was a dink commander, I'd want to penetrate each of the undefended spots where thick woodlines are growing right up to the concertina: "Yes, stupid American have only three roll form their perimeter. Make nothing for my sappers. So while these foreign invaders sleep well in their rocket-and-mortar-proof bunkers, they have no defensive berm, no strong point, no machine gun emplacement, no interlocking fields of fire.... Make much joy for my infantry." Not so fast you dink fuck. With my wife Bang at my back, all you're going to get is one of my CAR-15's bullets right between your commie eyes.'

I breezed through the bottom floor of the head-shed, slowing only to wave at the guys on duty in the TOC. At the top of the stairs, I knocked on the Colonel's doorjamb, unnecessarily. His door was open and he was sitting at his desk looking right at me.

"Hey, Carney! Come on in – sit down." I wasn't actually reporting to him, so while moving to a chair near his desk, I offered up a casual salute. He returned it in like fashion. "Man, by the sound of you bounding up those stairs, I reckon that leg of yours is in pretty good shape."

"Yes Sir," I said, giving my thigh a smack to confirm it, taking care to strike next to the wound. "You'd be surprised how beneficial a little sun and salt water can be."

"You think that's what did it, huh?"

"Well, Sir, I did get a bit of physical therapy from this girl, to help things along."

"Funny how *that* helps. Care for a beer or soda?" He motioned to his runt refrigerator.

"Thanks, Sir, a soda would be fine."

Lieutenant Colonel John Julian Braccia, West Point, Class of '50, pushed back from his paperwork, fully prepared to give me whatever time I needed. Iron- haired and built like a galvanized trash can with an OD tee-shirt stretched over it, he had the well-dented look of one used for twenty years. But his gaze gave away his primary composition, steel. I went across the room, knelt down, and opened the fridge to sort for a Coke.

"You know," he reflected, "getting dusted off in a medevac is one hell of an improvement over the way it used to be. Back in Korea, I took a round right through my butt cheek. The Chinks were laying down machine gun fire so low I was begging the ants to move over and give me more room. The hard part though was the six-hour ambulance ride on a road rougher than a dry creek bed. Every bolder we hit, felt like getting shot all over again. So, what's on your mind?"

"Sir, I was just thinking on my way here that this compound is..." I hesitated. 'It's his battalion, so I need to be cautious.' "Ah, if we got hit, there're some weak spots in our defensive perimeter."

"That's what you came up to talk about?"

"No, Sir, I just got to thinking about it."

"Carney, it doesn't take a great military mind to critique one of the least defendable fire support bases in Vietnam." I raised my eyebrows. I'd never heard a commander condemn his own compound. "When I saw it for the first time," he continued, "I almost shit a brick. Those 'Dollar Ninety-nine' guys who chose this spot and built it were a bunch of sorry-asses. I've been requesting engineer support ever since, but now that we're OPCON to the Twenty-fifth, and the focus is west towards Cambodia, they don't want to commit resources to a place we're going to vacate. So, we stay vulnerable until we do."

"Any idea when we'll be moving, Sir?"

"Somewhere between imminent and soon. Right after we arrived, my boss came out and the first thing he said was, 'Don't get comfortable.' He did promise me a one-week heads-up, so we aren't going anywhere for at least that long."

"Won't they have to scratch out a new fire base for us?" I asked. "Nothing's out there."

"Once they decide, they can do it in a week."

"What they really ought to do, Sir, is put us on the Cambodian border so we'd be right there to greet them as they come across."

"They'd greet you all right, Carney, with a regiment – roll you flat and be back on the other side thumbing their noses at us in the morning. We're going somewhere out there, just not as far as the border." Our repetition of *'out there,'* resurfaced my concerns about the difficulties it would create for Bang and me. "Hell Carney, with all your interest in our perimeter, you're not angling to get Lieutenant Spiegel's job are you?" He smiled.

'Spiegel the Beagle,' as he was known, or lately 'Barbed Wire 6,' was the battalion screw-up. Having been relieved as a platoon leader after all of a week, he'd been assigned a series of invented jobs, '*Special Projects Officer*' being his official title. I'd noticed him on my way in this afternoon, he and a pair of hapless shit burners staring at concertina on the perimeter.

"Not quite, Sir," I said. 'I do want to talk about what my next job'll be, and get him to okay my getting loose for a couple of days. But my timing isn't quite there.' "Sir my own hooch is standing at the very weakest point we have. The dumbest sapper in the Five-oh-eighth Long An Regiment'd only need two minutes to get in and lob a satchel charge through my door. When you hear my ass being blown skyward, that'll be your signal we're under a ground assault."

"So if we can slow the sappers to five minutes – we might give you a running start?"

"No biggie, Sir. It's kind of ironic though that the Delta's greatest jungle fighter is feeling queasy about being on the supposed safe side of the perimeter."

"Hah," he laughed, "greatest bullshit artist maybe. I'll have the Beagle go down and take a look at relocating your bunk outside the wire, so you'll sleep better. Now, I know you didn't come up here just to chat about barbed wire."

"No, Sir, I didn't…."

"Recon getting ambushed the other day then… Carney, I'm deeply upset over what happened. I've been waiting for you to get back so I could have a talk with your guys. Is tomorrow evening after chow okay?"

"Fine Sir. I'll let them know. But… one thing I need to discuss with you is this dilemma…. Coming back from Vung Tau I stayed in a Saigon hotel last night. And at breakfast, I ran into those advisors, Captain Ruddick and SFC Wiggins, so I hitched a ride back with them. On our way, we stopped at this café to get chow. That's where I accidentally witnessed an older Vietnamese guy slipping Captain Ruddick a huge wad of MPCs – all twenties, maybe a thousand bucks worth. I confronted him at our table. So he launches into this involved story about how he and Wiggins are black marketing American beer, to pussy bars all around the city."

"And..." he said.

"I don't buy his story, Sir."

"I take it you have some alternate theory…?"

"No clear one. I paused, to gauge his expression. "It's just that the way Ruddick laid it out, there might be money in black-marketing beer, but I can't see there'd be enough to risk going to prison."

"Do you have some figure in mind, Carney, where it becomes *worth* the risk?"

"Oh, no Sir. All I know about crime is what I've learned watching TV shows… where the bigger the potential haul, the greater the temptation – and tolerance for risk."

"It might be less than you think," he said. "I'll bet there're men in Leavenworth right now who're contemplating how much they overestimated the amount, and underestimated the risk."

"Yes, Sir. But it's really the logistics of it that I don't get. How could they run such an operation from way down here? I think it's something else, like drugs. I read in Stars and Stripes that a lot of bad shit's coming into Nam. Ruddick's a know-it-all and talks like his finger's on the pulse of everything. He seems to know too much about where heroin comes from."

"Okay Carney, you say this Vietnamese guy gives Ruddick a bunch of MPCs, supposedly for beer. But if it's heroin, wouldn't Ruddick be doing the paying?"

"Straight-up, yes Sir, but it's, ah…"

"Carney, do you have any loyalties to these two – something that'd cause you hesitation?"

"Not really, Sir. We've been on a few joint ops together. Their PF unit is pretty good – their lieutenant, Thieu uy Quang is solid. So, I was okay with Ruddick and Wiggins until today. Now though, I'm convinced they're capable of any number of illicit activities." 'But would I be ratting them out at all if we hadn't argued over their putting Bang in their sights? If I'd never met her, would I be contemplating Ruddick's *compensatory* Silver Star – and one of his special girls? Man, I need Bang more than I know!'

"We're all *capable*, Carney. The critical difference is in whether we choose to do or not do something. My question is, would you overlook a few diverted pallets of beer, if you believed they'd saved your life? Conversely, if you learned they could be middlemen in a heroine operation, and hadn't done anything for you, might you handle it differently?"

"No, Sir," I said quickly. "At the very least, I'd bring the subject up – just like I am now. I'm not really the kind of guy who holds stuff in."

"So I've noticed, Carney."

"Sir, if my suspicions have some basis, considering the seriousness, I'm duty bound to bring it up."

"But you said you don't have any hard evidence. All you could put in a statement is that you saw some money change hands, right?"

"Sir, they flat-out admitted to the beer scam."

"I like to think of evidence as more than a verbal accusation, something that can't simply be denied."

"Sir, ever since I saw Ruddick getting all that dough, I've been asking myself what legitimate circumstance would have a Saigon civilian handing over a heavy wad of MPCs? What's that Viet get for his money?"

"Have you considered money changing? I've heard it's pretty lucrative, and just as illegal. Viets accept it for all sorts of things, but they've got to unload it as fast as they can. A Viet holding MPCs on our Change-Over Day is one holding the equivalent of toilet paper. Maybe that guy's getting paid after Ruddick buys either Piastres or merchandise with it."

"Sounds plausible, Sir, but why'd Ruddick give me a story about doing something else equally as illegal?" The colonel sat back in his chair and tapped his pencil on the middle of a pad.

"Well, suppose the CID was ever to look into such an allegation – black-marketing beer. But, they can't establish anything because there's no such scam going on. That's why he could admit to it."

"Yes, Sir, I did consider that when I was thinking of the drug thing. And when the CID didn't find zip, it'd not only discredit the source of the allegation, but clue-in Ruddick on who the stoolie was – me."

"Right," Braccia agreed. "And with the CID dropping further investigation, if it is drugs or money-changing, Ruddick'd just close up shop."

"There is something else, Sir."

"*What?*" he asked.

"From what they said, Ruddick and Wiggins have a routine of going up to Saigon, at least once a week. They have a highly fraternizing relationship. They boasted of having this arrangement involving *'special girls'* – super good-looking ones, which they get from somewhere and supply to God-knows-who for prostitution. Maybe that Viet was paying Ruddick his cut."

"What evidence do you have for that?"

"Well, beyond just their bragging, Ruddick tried to feel me out on getting involved – on the girl thing not the other. Why me? I'm a field guy! But Um, I do know of this one girl they intend to try and recruit next week." Braccia nodded his understanding.

"That's not a whole lot for evidence either. What do you recommend we do?" he asked.

I frowned. 'Does he really want my help in deciding this?' Braccia moved to the front edge of his desk, half sitting half leaning.

"I'd want to contact the CID," I said, giving him an expectant look. 'Is this what he wants? What else do you do with suspected crimes?'

He traversed the room. I watched his romping-stomping VC-style dee-dee-mao sandals, strapped to the largest calf muscles I'd ever seen. I imagined him as a Roman throwback, crunching along a gravelly road, inspiring his young centurions on to face a barbarian hoard. His stoic countenance alone likened him a true son of Marcus Aurelius.

"I *could* call in the CID," he said at last, "but they'd have to use their counterparts in the National Police. However, if you've got a pair of Advisors who're into some shit with a major Saigon connection, you'd have to count on their having at least one back channel. They'll get wind of it and shut down. Then what?"

"A dead end, Sir? As a grunt in the field, I don't know squat about how the CID operates, but this sort of stuff should be just their game."

"In this world Carney, wars always attract dirt – loose money – loose everything – bad actors – a perfect situation for nefarious bullshit. And what does the average American MP know about the age-old corruptions of this country? Then look at the language barrier. In my experience a lot of MP work turns out to be little more than shortcomings in command." He looked straight at me.

I gulped. 'What if my Vung Tau blotter report hits his desk? Ruddick and Wiggins know a little too much about my *scrape* with Miss Ngo Thi Ngoc. If they come to suspect that the rat's me, will they play that card, and bring up that big-eyed My-Lan at the President Hotel to boot? Fuck yeah.'

"I'll tell you what I'm going to do, Carney." Braccia began tapping his pencil again. "I'll take the C'n'C and pay a visit to Colonel Jenks. Bob's the MACV provincial advisor. We've been friends for years – classmates. Considering how little real evidence we have, but given what you've told me, I'll ask him for a favor, to swap Ruddick and Wiggins out of *my* AO and put them where they can be watched. In that small pacified district headquarters, they could well have gotten into something without arousing any notice."

"Whether it's drug dealing, money changing, beer or prostitution, there'll be some trail of their converting chunks of MPCs into greenbacks. Then, they'll want to get the dough out of the country. Money-orders might be too obvious, but they've got to do it somehow. I'll ask Jenks to split them up. Dislocated from their present routine, someone can watch what they'll do next. Investigating money transfers though, will definitely require the CID."

"Ruddick's pretty short," I responded. "Less than sixty days."

"If he's into something, the closer he gets to his DROS, the greedier he'll get. But, if we're up the wrong tree, no one's the wiser. This means *'Close Hold'* Carney. Have you mentioned this to Keneally?"

"No, Sir," I said. "Do you think we can act on this pretty quickly? If it's drug stuff, it can't wait, can it?"

"I didn't say it could. Will tomorrow morning be soon enough for you?"

"Yes Sir," I said with an appreciative nod, and the decision to go straight into the subject of where *I'd* be going when I got promoted and the thirty-six hours I needed for Bang.

We both turned at the sound of someone hustling up the stairs. Lieutenant Dahl, the duty officer from the TOC, appeared in the doorway.

"Cobra just went down Sir. They had a Hunter-Killer team working a section of the Nhà Bè. The other, Tomahawk One-Niner, is still out there – that's who I've been talking to. He says it caught fire. They're in a thick woodline and there's no way for them to help."

"How'd it go down? Any ground fire?"

"They weren't sure Sir, but didn't see any tracers. It was descending for a run – punched out a pair of rockets, then seemed to just follow them in – drove right into the ground. It didn't explode straight off, so somebody might've been able to get out before it was enveloped."

"Were the canopies opened?" Braccia asked.

"Fire and black smoke obscured Tomahawk's view, Sir. It's cooked now. They've been hovering around close but with the vegetation and darkness, they didn't see anyone get out and don't see anyone now. Tomahawk only has ten minutes of on-station gas left."

"Has Brigade been informed?"

"Sergeant Walcott was calling when I came up."

"Tie in with Tomahawk's company. We're the closest troop unit by far. We'll get a reaction team out there. If the pilots did manage to get out, they're bound to be hurt."

"Yes, Sir," Dahl said.

"See if they're getting another fire team to relieve him. I'll need five slicks up here. Carney, go across the street and have my driver run you back. Get your boys together and move out to the road for a pick up. Ten minutes!"

It took most of ten minutes to find the CO's driver, who I located in a bull session at a far corner of headquarters company area. 'I've actually got a little time. Those chopper crews won't be at high alert and will have to get up and running, then fly out here to get us.'

I hadn't been out in three weeks, but from rote, an abbreviated *Five-Paragraph Field Order* quickly coalesced in my mind. My mental motions innerved me like a physiologic servo that opened a reservoir of epinephrine and kicked it into my system. No room for deep thinking. Excitement flooded into me. Hydro-electric-dam-sized sluice gates were wide open, deluging me in pure joy.

'This mission'll sync perfectly with a stand-down tomorrow – just enough time to head up that twenty-klick stretch of road, right to Bang's door... *and* fate putting Ruddick and Wiggins out of my way!'

"Okay guys!" I shouted, hustling into the platoon area. "Get your shit and saddle up!" In varying shades of torpid dress and undress, my men were already putting together one or another piece of gear. A few of them stood watching me, web gear on and weapons slung. I was relieved that the TOC had raised the company on the radio to get things going ahead of me. A couple of them tossed questions as I limped through their bunk area, my leg beginning to hurt again.

"You coming with us, Sir?!"

"Yeah."

"What kind of chopper was it?"

"Cobra."

"We gonna be out there all night?"

"I don't know, but let's say, yes. Squad leaders! I yelled, checking off the presence of Crowder, Starcup, and Olivera. Mounds looked completely ready, standing by for any last-minute instructions. "You got the word. A gunship has gone down and caught fire. We've got to get out there. Seven minutes to hit the wire. I want plenty of ammo and grenades. Water. Don't worry about C's. Leave the M-60s and Claymores. We'll probably be back in a few hours, but can never count on that. Mounds! We got everybody?"

"Yessir," he barked.

"Check 'em all out while I get my stuff. If anybody's been drinking too much beer tonight, I don't want them coming. You guys decide how much – you didn't know about this. I won't hold it against anybody." I hurried out the back toward my hooch.

"Hey, Paul!" I shouted as I passed his door. "We're headed out." I went in and began pulling my gear together. My CAR-15 had a few spots of surface rust on the flash suppresser, but the chamber and bolt was well oiled and ready to go. I threw on my web gear and slung three bandoleers of magazines across my shoulders.

"For crying out loud..." Keneally stood in my doorway. "What'd you do – talk the ol' man into letting you go out *tonight*?! You couldn't even wait until goddang morning? And he went for it?!"

"Not quite. A cobra just went down, on the other side of the Nhà Bè. The call came in while I was up there talking to him. So, I kind of volunteered. They called down to the Orderly Room and told my platoon to saddle up. You best find out why whoever' you got there didn't tell you." While I talked, I snatched items of equipment and tossed them into my pack.

"Ogden's on duty tonight," he sighed, "so certain failures are to be expected. Did you get to ask the Old Man what his plans are for you?"

"Dahl came in right when I was going to, telling us about what just happened."

"Well, as it also *happens*," he said, "I was next door in Alpha, and Captain Heniker told me the scuttlebutt is you're getting the S-4 shop. Spain's going up to brigade. Dingleberry informed him at chow tonight."

"*S-4?!* I don't know a thing about supply – and *me* working for Dingleberry?!"

"That's the story. Heniker got it straight from Spain and he got it from ol' Dings, who's supposed to be informing you tomorrow. That's good enough to be a non rumor in my book. Geez-oh-pete, Mondo, the S-4's just the kind of ticket you were looking for."

I didn't disbelieve Keneally, having blurted my reaction from pure astonishment. Thoughts ricocheted in my head. Like a dozen super-balls in a four-wall handball court, the implications hammered me with a blur of high-velocity bounces. 'Damn! Tinderberry probably requested me, just so he could get me under his heel, for the pleasure of crushing me like a bug, and watching my vital juices squirt out on the floor. No, it's the obvious! Bang. She'll be right within reach and permanently all mine. There's *only* one thing I can do. Rise to the occasion.'

"Keneally, I take back every word I just said. You will soon be witness to the greatest supply officer since... since the greatest one up to now. See you in a while. I've got to get our asses out on the road." I grasped the locket in my shirt as I scrambled out the door. '*Bang, you sweet, beautiful sorceress. I can feel you. I can feel you doing this!*'

Darkened figures dribbled out of the platoon bunker in a broken file. They'd been an unhappy group to come back to, because they'd anticipated a solid night's rest. But, I could always rely on them to pull it together when it counted. In their minds, like mine, they'd have the picture of those two pilots, and the help they needed. I rambled back inside to find Nunziato, to get on the battalion net and inform the TOC we were on our way out.

Fifteen minutes later, five choppers hauled us into a welkin night, into air indelibly stained with blackness, so black that the blaze of another day seemed inconceivable. Black enough that its past inevitabilities reentered my thoughts. Some astute grunt had once observed, "The reason why moving at night's always so fucked up is cuz you can't see for shit." The observations of an infantryman owed much to his succinct reality, its scope as narrow as the track of a bullet in the dark.

Looking forward, between the two pilots and through the wind shield, I imagined the ease of someone flying a chopper right into the ground. The windshield might as well have been spray painted over. Although flying in the third chopper back, in trail formation, I couldn't make out any of the running lights ahead. To my side, the black air and darken landscape were indistinguishable. Forget to glance at that altimeter, while diving toward an earth, discrete in its nothingness… and BOOM!

Sitting in the chopper's door, my legs seemingly afloat in a anabatic wind, I contemplated the tenebrous enormity that lay below, an entire country at war. I couldn't see the slightest evidence of it. Just as I cursed the cloud cover that reduced available light in the bush to virtually zero, I saw an opening. Far ahead and obliquely to our front, into the wind tearing past the open door, a great vault of stars poured from a breach in an unseen ceiling.

Closer by the moment, the gap expanded into a massive rent in the cumulostratus blanket above. A glimmering profusion began to spill out as if diamonds from a torn open bag. We could fly right into them. Somewhere up there, I thought, among those centillion stars, there had to be just one more constellation for Bang. Maybe between Cassiopeia, so prideful of her own beauty that she angered the gods, and her incomparable daughter Andromeda, the virgin. Bang was neither conceited nor a virgin, but in some classical dimension, she would be forever virginal. In this predaceous land, it wasn't hard to imagine her with Andromeda's fate, chained to the rocks, waiting for the serpent to devour her. No matter, I was her Perseus.

VII
THE QUIETUS

CHAPTER 1

STARLIGHT FELL ON A WIDE and formless expanse beneath our chopper's skids. As if sprinkling down from an astral canopy, it imbued the viscid darkness with light that illuminated almost nothing. It just sifted through, dissipating the collective light from a billion suns, only managing to bring an absolute opacity to the bare threshold of perception. The river was thus revealed. Indistinct and little more than a pallid sheen, the Sông Nhà Bè stretched below as smooth and motionless as polished basalt.

About half way across, the choppers dove in rapid descent. An irregular mass of black vegetation loomed up and marked the far extent of the placid water. Closing in on it, the choppers turned obliquely. The woodline grew in width and foreboding. It glowered at me, a black-clad malevolence. I riveted my attention to the formless veil, as if from effort alone I might gain purchase. I couldn't see it, but it was palpable. Submerged in darkness, it presaged its dangers with a kind of pulse, a land alive communicating nothing but derision. All that remained hidden was the precise measure of its lethality. Subsumed in this ocean of ink, it seemed forever unknowable.

Nunziato rapped me on the shoulder. On the inside of our orbit, he'd spotted the crash site. Scanning out through the opposite door, I took advantage of our remaining altitude and referenced the river's location with the faint glow in the jungle.

We'd predetermined an LZ back at the TOC, but it suddenly pinpointed itself with the burst of an illumination flare. No more than a silvery viridescent hole in the night, the choppers wheeled about and bore down like a flight of homing pigeons that had just made a visual confirmation of their birthplace. A hundred meters out, I rechecked our heading. 'Two nine zero degrees. Hit the ground moving!'

Our choppers flared into the wide rice paddy and settled impatiently on their skids. Everyone scrambled from the metal floor and into the water. Above us, five main rotor blades slashed the air. Unseen in their frenzied whirl, they whipped the night to a mad scream of turbines. Posed for immediate takeoff, the choppers shuttered with a kinetic intensity. They seemed edgier than usual, as if fully cognizant of the risks, that without pitch, without purchase, without immediate lift, they were hulking bullet magnets. Free of them, we strained to open the distance between us. By dogged habit, we fanned out to our flanks. If any lead was about to fly, seeking cover in a flying bladder of jet fuel was on no one's list of choices.

The greater apprehension that tagged along with any night insertion was always masked by the dark. One thought predominated; get to cover. We slogged to our best reckoning of it, buffeted at our backs by the last vestiges of whupping prop wash. Cover for some was an old dike, for the rest it was the woodline. Everyone arrayed themselves in a tentative line.

The prospect of moving a couple hundred meters in the dark, over hostile terrain had my full attention. Looking ahead into the dank featureless undergrowth, I steeled myself for the order I was about to give, the order to move directly into it. The idea made me feel as though it had given life to a ghostly hand, one that was reaching into my chest, to put a death grip on a few of my vital organs.

"Send up Mounds and the point team," I whispered.

They worked their way to insinuate themselves around me. Several others adjusted their positions. It became so quiet the light sloshing of paddy water seemed like it could attract more attention than the choppers.

"I don't like the idea of moving in there on trails –don't even know if there are any. We're going to have to work our way in, through the thick of it – could be a ball-breaker."

"You mean *way* slower, Mounds said. "Don't we need to get in there best way we can?" 'He wants the easy way out again, but I have to admit they've all been humping-it since early this morning.'

"Yeah, but you aren't walking point. Out here, trails'll be the only place they'll booby trap. If dinks want to ambush us, they'll want us to hit one first. Remember, those cobras were shooting at something."

"I wasn't talkin' 'bout trails," Mounds corrected, "...just some looser shit."

"Bustin'-it in heavy stuff's gonna make it noisier," Corchado added.

"Look, the dinks already know we're here – where we're going – and which direction we're coming from. They'll either have shot the pilots or taken them prisoner and beat feet."

"You talkin' 'bout the same ones who shot that fucker down?"

"We don't know why that cobra went down. We do know they had a target in here. There'll be booby traps, because there always are. We have to go where *nobody'd* ever go. Let's move out."

The platoon shifted slowly into its order of movement, with each squad folding back on itself to change direction. In a foot of mud covered by six inches of water, the effect was awkward. Our collective swash sounded like a stumbling gang of blindfolded men. Our inclination to bunch up made me nervous. I made my way along the line pushing them apart. The squad leaders began straightening things out.

'How much of their unsteadiness is the residue of the losses they've suffered? It's got to be affecting them. I can feel their hesitancy. But this shit here'd account for it. Half the platoon has little experience moving through the bush at night. Only a small few can gain it, most getting killed before becoming good at it. I have, but how much of my Dinkland skills've been dumb luck?'

'So I'm back in charge. They know I'll make them do things that Mounds wouldn't. They probably took Mounds' methods as a holiday. Two of their buddies got wasted under his leadership, but they might not blame it on his decision-making. I'll have to figure out why.'

I moved up within sight of the point team to follow them toward the woodline. One by one, we slid single file into an embowering curtain of black. As we did, I could sense our old stealth returning. By each softened footstep, we wound our way forward with the satisfying litheness of a centipede, one bristling with a lethal stinger on each of its segments. With sweat running down my face and the smell of wet jungle in my nose, I had the sudden feeling of being reborn. *I was back.*

After trudging through heavy undergrowth for a while, the point team held up to consider whether to bear right or left. I listened to the jungle without the overlay of our movement. Far in the distance, I attended to the crack of gunfire, its sporadic pops roughly equating to the range and direction of the downed chopper's location. I listened to the haphazard pattern of shots, imagining some half-crazed inebriate, staggering gun in hand around his campfire. As each shot rang out, another of his inner demons was dispatched into oblivion.

"Hear that?" Corchado whispered. "Not much of the Cobra's ammo left."

We plugged on toward it, sweating as profusely from mental wariness and caution as from physical exertion. Progress came in chunks. Flat hard ground, with bosky vegetation that could either be ducked under or finessed with body English, was interspersed with leech-infested canals and slues of iron-rooted nipa palm in waist deep muck. From our starting point, I'd gauged the distance to be about two hundred meters. Mid way, I refigured. It would take us another hour.

"Ka-pow!" From the depths of the darkness, a lone shot cracked the nearby jungle.

"Aa-a-ah!" cried out a voice from behind me. Stovall. Everyone hit the ground. Not wanting to pinpoint their positions, nobody fired back. 'To where? I didn't see a muzzle flash.'

Word quickly came up that a slug had torn through the plastic stock of Stovall's M-16. It'd also gone through his canteen, imbedded in his web gear, and spun him around, uninjured.

"It's a fuckin sniper all right," Starcup whispered, as he crawled up next to me. His squad lay scattered on the ground directly behind me. "Don't know how he can see us. We can't even see him with Starlights."

"I don't think he can," I said, my mouth only an inch from his ear. "He's been waiting for us – picked up on our movement – firing where he figured we'd be." Several situations whirred through my brain. We were maybe fifty meters from the crash site. With dinks on the scene, the pilots would either be dead or gone. But that single shot made me wary. 'If it's only a lone VC, why didn't he burn a whole magazine straight into our approach? Was it an SKS in the hands of a guy low on ammo? That'd make him VC, not NVA. Did he bring down a Cobra with it?! At night?! Is there really only one of them? Is this some kind of ruse?'

'I don't have the answers, but I do have solutions. I can get another gunship, one with a Minigun. Hosing the fuckers with lead always has appeal. But right now, here, I can't trust a gunship's sense of where our position begins and ends. That leaves me with going it alone. Somewhere out there though, some dink's squinting into the darkness just like we are. He's trying to line up his muzzle with a sound. Whose body will make that sound?'

My gut feeling that the pilots had been lost, returned. Their survival seemed improbable now: pilots crawling from the burning wreckage, lying seriously wounded nearby, waiting for our help. Their chopper may have struck the ground at a low angle of descent, but hard enough to explode. 'Men only leap from crashes like that in movies. So, what's my mission now?'

'Nothing's changed. Pulling back to the LZ or somewhere more secure, without knowing the pilots' actual situation's unthinkable. Risk has to be taken. It's got to be a lone sniper intuiting where we're going. I'll give him half a brain. He'll want to shadow and harass us all the way. His chances of a lucky hit are what? An arriving dustoff will give him a bonus opportunity. But staying put will only make it easier on him to harass us. Solution? *Shit*!'

"Starcup," I whispered, "slide your squad forward – over there toward the site." I drew a diagram on his back between the straps of his web gear. "Go twenty meters from the wreck and stop. It might tease him into firing again. If he does, have all your guys ready to cut loose at the same time. Empty a magazine. Follow it with a grenade."

I sent third squad to the left and pulled the rest up into the middle to create a partial cordon. Slowly, we inched forward, low and quiet.

Suddenly, from somewhere to our front, two shots split the night. I dropped my muzzle to the sound and pulled the trigger. Just as suddenly, a phalanx of M-16s to my right and left erupted into the void like a dragon's roar. Magazines empty, a score of grenades rent the night with the concussion of a small artillery barrage. As the shock of sound reverberated through both the jungle and my head, I resigned myself to having lost yet another increment of my most important nocturnal sense. But the crisp clack of fresh magazines snapping into place was reassuring.

We closed the circle around the site and pulled in tighter. No dead sniper to be found. He'd either crawled off wounded or slipped away unscathed before we'd encircled him. 'I hope he at least got my message: want a duel dude? *Two* bullets from you, four hundred from us.'

The fire in the burning gunship flickered candle-low, fueled by the last of its grease and oil. The ammo which had been going off like pop corn when we'd landed, had all cooked off. I moved in closer with the point team. My senses jangled in conflict. Although my men ringed the entire area, I stood there, illuminated, exposed. Faint as it was, the vestigial tongues of flame backlit the forest into a tableau of slim shadows, or a clutch of VC moving into position to carefully draw a bead on the center of my chest.

On hands and knees, Corchado vetted the ground for trip-wires, his green filtered flashlight going back and forth, slowly scanning each blade of vegetation. If the dinks had had any time at all, they'd have expediently strung a few around, certain that a troupe of GI feet would be along soon. The more we moved around, the greater our risk of tripping something and doing the dink's work for them. My heart was in my throat. I apprehended the horror of someone's foot finding one, riddling their body in that split-second fountain of sparks.

"Nobody move a muscle," I whispered to my right and left. "Pass it down."

At five meters from the wreckage, my grimmest premonition was confirmed.

Stark and black in a spectral light, the Cobra sat on its skids as if it had simply landed in a tiny jungle clearing. The entire aircraft had burned in place. Glass, outer skin and frame were all totally gone. What remained were the pilots and the engine. Still sitting in their armored seats, one behind the other, they'd shrunk to half size. Their cindered helmets, huge in comparison, made them look like hyper-cephalic aliens perched on some bizarre sled, waiting to slide off to God knows where. I stepped closer still, transfixed, as the charred pair flickered in an eerie chiaroscuro. '*You poor bastards.*'

"Man this is fucked up," Nunziato whispered. "What'd they do, just sit there and get burnt to a crisp?"

"Kind of gives you that impression doesn't it?" I took the handset and called the TOC.

Colonel Braccia had gone to bed, but left instructions to get him up when we arrived. In a few minutes, he was on the radio.

"I've got a sniper out here – hope that's all we have."

"You want the gunships back?" he asked.

"Not right yet. We can handle things as they stand and stay put until daylight. This place's a high risk for booby-traps, so we can't move an inch more – like the sniper wants. In the morning, we'll secure the remains at daybreak – won't know until then if we can get a chopper in here. If not, we'll move to the nearest clearing."

"Roger that – check with you later. And, be careful! I'm counting on you to bring all your guys back in one piece – out."

We pulled back into a defensive configuration. Looping around half of the wreckage, we lay in small groups that could engage a returning sniper's most likely approaches, while acknowledging how more effective it would've been with claymores. 'Or as Dingleberry would put it; "yet another failure in contingency planning." Plan hell, we weren't supposed to stay out here – and doing well just to get here. Loaded down with a bunch of uncalled-for gear and we'd still be slogging through the nipa.'

'I could've asked the old man to fly us out some machine guns, belt ammo and claymores, but apart from the small pleasure of getting some REMFs out of bed to put it together, we'll have to scramble around in the bush to gather and set it up, no better way to set off booby traps. Whatever the drawbacks, some of these fuckers just don't get it that when you're playing at night in Chuck's backyard, you better be as light and quiet as possible – the greater risks of wounds outweighed by speed and agility. Heavy means slower, and slow means easier to hit. Hell, the VC travel in PJs, with nothing more than an AK, three magazines and a ball of rice. But then, they don't out-gun us, they outwit us.'

'Maintaining a full alert for the first hour won't be so hard – we're already awake. After their Adrenaline dissipates though, keeping us at fifty- percent alert'll be a bitch. Out on ambushes for the past two nights, and busting ass on sweeps both days, is bound to have drained them to the marrow. They'll wake easily enough, but staying that way'll be Herculean. Good that we're concealed in all these trees and undergrowth, so we can stand with Starlights when starting to doze.'

Morning crept in, insinuating its tropical reality into my mind. Not having been awakened by a poke from one of my men, it came gently. If it wasn't flat-out urgent, why light up billions of gray neurons all at once? Let the jungle light them up, a mere hundred-million with each somnolent blink of my eyes. Taking only a minute of real time, my rousing in this underbrush was meditative, the experience of a watery light forming from nothingness. It washed the foliage, not at first with their inherent greens, but as a grisaille of distorted striations. Then as the nacreous sky brightened, every plant burst into its own verdant shade. It was as if a forest of mycological giants had suddenly been transfused with a flood of chlorophyll.

Daylight encouraged the platoon to scratch around the area for booby traps, and the squad leaders rearranged them into a better security configuration. Then, there was nothing else to do but wait. They looked to me. No chow and only the lucky ones with a last swig of water.

I'd given the TOC our SITREP at EMNT and at sunrise Major Grizwell came on the horn.

"We've got a small problem Tiger Claw, Brigade needs two of our companies. They'll be moving out in a little while. Six is going with them. You'll have to stay put until Graves Registration can get out there in a few hours. I'll have someone put aboard Cs and water for you. You'll be okay 'til then, right?"

'My favorite question. Sure, as long as I have ammo and can talk on the phone, I'm okay. But *okay* is indistinguishable from *still alive.* We were only supposed to be out here for a *few* hours. Right, just in case, we prepared to stay until morning. Now where are we? Ill prepared. Yeah, be *prepared for every contingency at all times* – easy to say – impossible to pull off.'

"We'll be okay," I told him, "but if you can add three cases of soda and we'll be a hell of a lot better."

"Roger Tiger Claw, I'll see what I can do — out."

The sun nudged higher in an inexorable climb to its midday zenith, that perigeal point where the whole center of the sky above us seemed ablaze. At this latitude, the sun crossed precisely overhead twice a year, in late April and again late August. We lay with this late summer's ball of flames readying itself to bore into us at an angle almost directly perpendicular to our skulls. Ernie Pyle once referred to us grunts as "the mud, rain, frost and wind boys." He'd apparently missed our kind of war, with air so hot and heavy with humidity it made you think you could trowel it against a wall.

The surrounding bush was too low to provide shade, but just tall enough to block the slightest of breezes. This made the century mark the day's starting point. The sky seemed to move closer to us, its morning blue giving way to a shimmering metallic. I soon felt as though I was sitting inside a giant cask of scorching steel. We waited with lethargic indifference, like indolent cats. Yet each languorous body belied feline alertness. A single peripheral eye twitch or ear prick could scramble the entire platoon into instantaneous action. Nothing did. It just got hotter.

Eventually the supplies arrived, despite Nunziato's predictions that we'd been left to lay there for all eternity; and with some of the others griping in terms graphic enough for me to imagine them as the subjects of Gericault's *Raft of the Medusa.* But with grunts, it only took a few cases of Coke to turn Promethean torments into a paradisiacal *Garden of Earthly Delights.*

The sodas, tied in plastic bags were dropped from a hovering chopper. My men tore into them as if sun-demented by this infernal broiler. Several evanescent chunks of ice keeping them cold, revealed Keneally's hand in our relief operation. 'It always comes down to the small things that divides those who have concern for the troops, and those who just talk about their concern.'

The cokes guzzled, the squad leaders divvied up the water and C ration meals. But along with these supplies, we were given two body bags and condolences that no one from Graves Registration could get down to our battalion. Suddenly, it became our job; *pull the pilots out of the wreckage and put them in the bags for later pick up.* The prospect of actually doing it however, produced sour faces all around. During the hours they'd lain within easy view of the two macabre figures, they'd had time to over-contemplate the pilots' last few seconds, the terror of the flames, the canopy that wouldn't open, and the heat rising a hundred degrees a second.

"Crowder. Get the bags. I need your squad to get them out. The rest of the platoon will continue to secure the area." Several of the men nearby, didn't move. They were part of Crowder's squad, the closest to me, MacAlier, Desmond and Walkins. I looked into bleak emotionless faces and thought again. "Hey Tra, come here." Everyone knew that he would do anything I asked. I expected his approach would shame them into moving. It did, but moving and eagerly pitching in were two different things. 'Screw it, I'll do it without them.'

A close-eyeball inspection revealed nothing new. 'We've been close enough for hours. Whatever's left in the rocket pods was either expended or by now cooked-off in the fire. The dinks couldn't booby trap it while it was burning.... Okay, no more delays.'

The torrid sun beating down on the corpses had been taking its natural biological course. Close up, its putrid stench caught my nostrils, as if irregular waftings were leaking out thin streams into the air. Blowflies had picked up on it. Scores of them landed and flitted on the bodies. More of them found us by the minute. 'The ghouls from Graves would have training and special tools for handling decomposing remains. We've got nothing.'

"Hey," I yelled at no one in particular, "Any of yous ever have any experience with dudes cooked like this?" Stony faces were my answer. I turned the other way and the silence spurred a couple to mutter a 'no,' with the rest just shaking their heads.

The flies were problem one. Luckily, Tra and Thanh were wearing Vietnamese black net T-shirts under their fatigues. I got them to take the tees off and tie them up over their bush hats like apiarists.

With Bowie knives and thin sticks lashed together, they began prying the charred bodies from their seats. Incinerated flight suits and flesh having become a brittle and blackened crust, the slightest movement cracked it open to the ravenous delight of the flies. 'Handling the remains of fellow soldiers is supposed to be a solemn act, but what do we do with baked perdition?'

A thick gout of stench invaded my nose. It felt as if the Grim Reaper had slipped up behind me and clamped my nostrils with the hand of death. I tried to breathe through my mouth, but almost inhaled half a dozen flies. I drew air through my teeth, so they lit on and around my lips, scurrying and buzzing up into my nose. Needing both hands to secure the bag for my scouts, I spit and used my shoulder to chase the flies, to no effect. They were driving me mad.

"Damn it all you guys!" I yelled, in frustration. "Just get them the fuck in!"

Efficient teamwork prevailing, the corpses got loaded, zipped, and pulled off to the side. The flies frenetically scattered, most contenting themselves with residue left at the chopper or smeared on the bags. The rest zoomed around among the platoon, searching for where we'd hidden their chow. But with carrion-tuned antennae telling ommatidial eyes that their delicacies had been taken off the menu, they were soon gone.

"Now what we going to do, Sir?" someone from behind asked.

"We're going to get the fuck out of here," I said, wiping a grimy hand across the sweat running into my eyes. I motioned Mounds with the other.

"This is where I think we ought to go." I showed him my map and pointed out the locations. "The spot where they dumped our resupplies won't work, because we can't load the bodies while they hover that high. This clearing over here looks big enough to bring in one chopper. We'll haul the bags over there, they pick them up and we head east toward these hooches. We'll use their paddies for an LZ. Battalion should be ready to get *us* by then."

The body bags themselves presented a problem, their nomenclature "Pouch, Human Remains" being only half right. They contained human remains, but three-feet wide and over seven-feet long, they were unwieldy. And, I could not afford four men each to carry them. So, using what we could, I had them fashion a pair of crude travois. The bodies would be dragged.

The platoon moved out, one by one. Tra and I walked slack behind point, the two of them well ahead in a narrow defile. Corchado at the lead, hunkered a couple of inches lower than usual, alert to the sniper deciding which one to put in his sights. From fifteen meters behind, I watched van Wyck visually pick apart each suspicious leaf and branch. 'No booby traps yet. We're due.'

I surveyed the lay of the land, while as always, Tra intuited its mood. 'Much wider than typical woodlines... Random trails, but no signs of human activity. Remember the rule: Look for the differences – the smaller and harder they are to see, the more lethal they'll be. This place has no civilians and no crops, but only one enemy? The dinks might have a basecamp along the river. Coming in from the southeast last night, we would've missed it by a hundred meters. Now we need to head directly away from it. Was that gunship firing rockets at nothing? Were they acting on bad intelligence? Maybe they drew tracers. From what? We've seen nothing that could've taken down a Cobra.'

A few trails meandered across our line of movement. Dry and partially overgrown, their lack of use was a warning. Waist-high, overhanging branches were perfect for the VC to thread them with green monofilament trip wires.

A hand signal went up from Corchado. I moved ahead to see what he wanted.

"Look 'ere," he said. "This one's a lot more used than those others. Recent too."

"For sure," I said, noting its surface smoothened by daily use. I checked my map. It connected the distant group of hooches with the river. "There's a hamlet up here marked Xom Ha. It probably goes from there to the river fifty meters to the west of us."

"The hooches – ain't that where we're headed?" Implicit in his question was 'Why don't we use the trail going right to them?' It came up at least once a day; shouldn't we trade the problems of ball -busting labor, relative noisiness and low visibility for the much higher likelihood of mines and booby traps?' My answer was the same every time. "It depends," I said. "What do you think Tra? This trail's getting pretty regular use – wide open too – no overhanging branches."

"Maybe papasan go down to sampan. Maybe VC come up from sampan."

"Yeah, maybe." I knew why he wasn't sure. 'Civilian sampans would have hooches and moorings together, but there's no hooches. This trail's obviously being used for something. Papasan or VC, it means they haven't rigged booby-traps.' I looked at Tra and nodded toward the east, my request for any objections. He answered with a look of neutrality, the sign of his acquiescence. I wanted more, but his role wasn't to set into motion a movement leading directly to a man being blown to shit five minutes later. *That* was on me.

"Maybe VC put booby trap in morning," he said at last. "All trail around."

"Yeah, that'd be the smart thing. Ring our asses with something on every trail in the area, and bet on us taking one of them." I looked around. The thick foliage and undergrowth interspersed with canals of black slime suddenly seemed less appetizing than the diminished but unknown risk of insentient mayhem. "Hey Corchado, spread out a little more, and keep a sharp eye. This one's on you." I nodded in the direction of the hooches. "Let's go."

The point team wended along for fifty meters, then broke out into the clearing. Just as they did, a concussive blast rent the center of the platoon. Everyone hit the ground. I looked back, right and left, but could only see a cloud of smoke. It filled the entire middle of the section. Several bodies lay sprawled on the ground behind me.

"Damn it. Damn it!" I hissed. Heads came up and craned around to see for themselves. They were okay. No one was calling for help.

"Is anyone hit?!" I yelled.

I don't know," came an answer.

"Then, what the fuck was that?!" I started moving back toward the spot.

"Some kind of booby trap," came another. "Or a mine maybe." The obvious frustrated me. Was it really all that obvious? Ten guys had just walked over it.

"Nobody's hurt?"

"No!" another voice shouted back. This made no sense at all. A command det going off on the middle of my platoon and it hits no one? I stepped cautiously over sprawled bodies, legs and M-16s. 'A command det? No, not that big of a blast.'

"What'd you say happened?!" I called directly to the ones lying and crouching nearest to where it had gone off. "Didn't anybody trip anything?" 'A pressure device on a charge that size would've torn someone's foot off.'

"I guess," Bundt said, "the dead guy did. I was just towing him along, and BOOM."

Taking a few more cautious steps, I studied the scene. At the edge of the trail, I could plainly see that something had blown a hole a foot deep and two feet across in the hard-packed clay. The first of the body bags lay off the trail in the bushes. Half of it was shredded. I reached in and slowly pulled it back out by the rope that'd been tied to it.

"The fuckin' dead guy blew it?"

"Yes Sir," Bundt whispered grimly. "And man, is he fucked up now or what?"

"He was already fucked up," Hagerty said. "Now he's totally fucked up."

Assessing the damage, I could tell that both legs had been ripped off, but felt strangely relieved it'd been that end. 'A blast that obliterates everything but a pair of legs says something about the relative value of that charcoal brittle helmet and flight suit.'

"Doc!" I shouted. "Come up here. Get out a few rolls of adhesive tape and close up the bottom of this bag, like nice and tight."

Doc Younce and Bundt quickly went to work. Pulling the open end of the bag up, then sliding what was left inside to the other end gave them enough of the ribboned material to spindle and wind it with tape. Younce folded that over, then wound more tape around the whole bag.

"That ought to do it," he said.

"Hey no," Bundt challenged. "We forgot to put the legs in."

"There ain't no legs," Younce said. "Like they got blown to shit."

"That's one there." Bundt pointed to the bushes a few feet off the trail. It just looked like an eighteen-inch-long, blackened chunk of non jungle. 'We don't leave our dead behind – if we can. What about pieces of the dead? If I was him, how bad would I want to bring my leg with me? How small a piece is okay to leave?'

I considered what needed to be done. Untaping and reopening the bag so we could slide in that one grizzly appendage, began to clarify. Several faces looked back, awaiting my decision. 'Who's crawling in there to root around for whatever's left? I'll explain to Dingleberry how the dead guy blew off his own legs how?'

I stooped down and stared into the wet leafy void at the advancing unseen army, divisions of saprophytic microbes, reinforced by brigades of gormandizing annelids. 'What's dead in the jungle, will be very soon alive again. Fuck it, I left all of Burkhart behind.'

"I don't really think they're legs anymore," I said. "Let's get the fuck out of here." I turned toward Corchado and van Wyck. With a jab in the air from my index finger, they resumed the pace.

Snaking around the outer periphery of the clearing, we formed into a natural perimeter. Most of the platoon melted into the edge of the jungle. I put in a call to battalion and didn't have to wait more than thirty minutes before a Huey came looking for us. We popped a smoke grenade. It orbited the clearing to confirm the heading I'd given them. Concurring, it banked and dropped into the middle of us and set down. The markings on its nose indicated the dead pilots' unit.

The body bags lay in the open, aligned side by side for quick loading. But after the choppers arrival, it looked like the sad forms were on display an inspection display.

The crew chief jumped out from his door gun position and stared at the lumpy bags. It was an unusual moment. Whether inserting or extracting us grunts, crew members never budged from their seats, pilots from their controls nor door gunners from their M-60s. Yet there he was, standing at the edge of the rotor wash, with a half dozen of us around him. The way he looked at those bags, I knew he had some special attachment to those guys. He stared fixedly at the shortened bag. The pained expression on his face hardened. 'He's got to be grappling with how one of the bags got shredded in half and crazily taped up.'

Accentuated by his green fire retardant suit and flight helmet, I fixated on the crew chief's strangeness among us. 'Everything's crisp and new – not a scratch on that helmet. I can't imagine how the ones in the bags, heads and all, in a single minute became just oversized briquettes.'

The other-side door gunner came around the chopper's nose and the two began the somber work of loading the dead -weight bags. They looked depressively morose. 'Hope they never decide to take an identifying peek inside.'

With the chopper's departure, we turned due east and pressed on. Soon after leaving the more dense vegetation, we plodded our way through one final slue of waist-deep muck and nipa. These stands, tall and dark from lack of cutting, stood as still as their earthen roots. Their tippy-top fronds were moving, almost imperceptibly, in a breeze too high for us to feel, making their insentience seem more like indifference. As we labored through the viscous slime at their feet, I felt their disinterest transforming into stolid mockery; *'If you think you can so easily escape us, you are wrong.'*

Sweating profusely and breathing in equal measure, I pulled myself up onto solid ground. With a renewed sense of fortitude, I thought of my having the last laugh. I grasped the locket in my breast pocket. Her face and *The Look* came up strong and powerful. 'Not only have I proven I can beat this land at its own game, I've got the ultimate dryad at my side, Bang. Borne on her magic, this talisman is going to deliver me straight into her arms. There's no doubt about it. With this thing, the VC are nothing but a bunch of feckless chumps.'

Strung out in an elongated file, the platoon moved even more cautiously through the final fifty meters of woodline. The weirdness of that last mine was having a therapeutic effect. Every step the point team took looked to be a separate deliberative act. An instant of hesitation hitched their stride just as each boot touched a fresh new patch of ground. ‘We’re all doing it, mentally willing-away a hundred pounds of ourselves. Not that it helps. Step heavily on a mine, step lightly on a mine; they blow up exactly the same. But that last blast made us all sure that a little extra caution won’t hurt.’

CHAPTER 2

EMERGING INTO THE OPEN, I could see most of a grid square of rice paddies and dikes. About three hundred meters to our front, lay the first of the sere brown hooches of Xom Ha. I surveyed the terrain at a glance as a welcome breeze blew across our sweat-soaked bodies, a nice complement to the relief I felt to be out of a potential mine field.

Corchado and van Wyck continued on, leading the way down a wide dike. Barefoot smooth and damp from recent traffic, it'd be free of booby traps. The VC could always bury a mine, but their typical expediency had never fooled my point team.

Thin pale stalks of an anemic rice crop sprouted from gray argillaceous soil. The infertility of the paddies accounted for the scant number of hooches. These rectangles of water covered mud had probably been reclaimed from the sparse Permian reed that grew naturally in such soil. But for what? All they'd achieved was a life at the far fringe of subsistence, a tenuous hold on a thin edge, where perennially they were on the brink of falling off, war or no war.

"Ka-pow!" A rifle shot rang out. A bullet cut the air. Everyone dove off the dike as its report faded in the distance.

"Sniper!" someone yelled out unnecessarily. I looked down the line at guys lying half-submerged in paddy water, all peering over the top, M-16s at the ready. The rest of the platoon lay on the opposite side of a dike running perpendicular to mine. I scanned across the faces I could see. 'No calls for help – nobody hit.'

"Nunzie!" I waved for him to come up next to me. Slithering and sloshing, he made his way over. "Let me use your radio to get Mounds." He crouched in the mud and I spun the knobs on top of his PRC-25 to switch from battalion to our platoon frequency.

"Nobody's hurt," Mounds reported, "but we don't know where that sniper's at – just somewheres back in the woodline."

"It's to the left," I said. "If he was to your right, he'd have a clear shot at you in enfilade – and would've fired at you again by now." 'Yeah, a shot at stationary men he'd be certain to hit.'

"Shit! We're sticking up here like sore thumbs," Mounds said, as if reading my mind, "a whole bunch of 'em. He'll just pick us off."

"The fact that he hasn't taken another shot is like I said. He's further to your left."

"Then he's probably on his way to shiftin' right, Six." Mounds said nervously. "We need to be moving up."

"Hold on. Don't move anywhere yet. The banks of the dike may be mined. That might've been his strategy from the beginning."

"We can slide along in the paddy," he answered, "and work our way to your dike."

"You can't until we move first," I said. "We'll get too bunched up. Stay put for a bit. Start popping a few 79 rounds out there. That'll keep his head down. I've got to flip this radio back to battalion. If you see anything, call Davidson. Scratch that. Just start firing and I'll figure it out."

I called the TOC and told them about my situation. Pinned down in the open, I couldn't move anywhere without becoming exposed. And two thirds of the platoon were about to become even more exposed just by doing nothing.

'I could send third squad back into the woodline after him, but he'd only disappear. When the squad tried to return, he'd follow them into his old spot and snipe them from there, with the rest of us too far away to cover.'

"Pain Maker Three-Six, this is Tiger Claw Six. I need a gunship, pronto!"

"You got it Tiger Claw, give him thirty minutes."

"Roger," I answered in frustration, "I was hoping to get something out here before somebody got picked off and not after." My sarcasm on the open battalion net had Major Grizwell cutting in from his distant C&C.

"Keep cool, Tiger Claw," Grizwell said. "We've got some TAC-AIR on station – a Foxtrot-Four – running low on fuel before we can use him again. Take whatever he's got left. I'll get the FAC heading your way."

"Tiger Claw-Six, roger Pain Maker."

"This is Pain Maker-Three, wait out."

While I waited for the S-3 to get back to me, I let the platoon know what was up. They all lay in place, although the ones on the safe side were taking the wait a lot more casually than the others. Wisps of cigarette smoke rose from a few of them. Bugabear, my own sniper, lay near the top training his M-14's 9X scope on the woodline. A duel between that and our old adversary's SKS was something I'd take any day.

While calculating our situation, I constructed a profile of our little nuisance. 'He's got to be the same guy who pot-shotted us last night. Why not keep up the harassment? Why not when we resupplied or when the body bags got picked up? Short on ammo – or just in love with picking his shots from total cover and concealment? Expecting gunships any second? Maybe he's just some dilettante VC rice farmer without the balls to take on an entire American platoon? Isn't he doing what snipers do, tying up a whole unit just like he is? But their first shot usually kills someone. Okay, this one's a bad sniper.'

"Hey Nunzie, why hasn't he taken a second shot?"

"He probably ain't got no clear shot, unless he moves. He might not want to show himself to do that. He could crawl, but any VC's gotta expect that we're just waiting for a gunship, but he don't have no way of knowing all the time he's got."

"Pisses me off," I groused. "It seems like I've got gunships up the ass, except when I really need them. If this dink has any balls at all, he'll move down there. Lining himself up with that dike, he can fire right down our line. Mounds and those guys won't be able to concentrate fire with everybody in each other's way. He's got to figure that. If he's smart, he'll go way back and around, without us seeing him. Having your enemy pinned down in the open's still got to be a red-letter day for any sniper though."

Until that TAC-AIR arrives, right Sir?"

"I'll say Nunz."

"Ka-pow!" Another shot rang out. Heads ducked. A few poked up, their desire to locate its origin being greater than self-protection.

"Sir, I think our guys had best be getting the hell out of there."

"Call down to Second Squad, Nunz. I want them to work their way up here." Several guys in low crouches moved our way.

"Starcup," I said, as he sank a knee into the mud next to where I was sitting, "start working your guys up to the hooches. Just follow point. Spread out one at a time then occupy those first two. Leave Bugabear for last in case he sees something." The radio squawked and Nunziato poked me with the handset.

"Tiger Claw Six. This is Spike Four Niner." The unfamiliar call-sign quavered in my ear. The thin voice emerged from a rush of static as though from a lost spacecraft suddenly reestablishing contact

"Roger, Spike, this is Tiger Claw."

"Okay, Pardner, I'm inbound your locale and hear tell you need something fixed?"

"Roger that. Got any napalm?"

"Negatory on the hot sauce, but my boy's got Mark eighty-two Snake-eyes stacked to the moon. Got to make up your mind in a hurry though, he's sucking down gas hauling all those eggs around. And I'd sure rather see 'em dumped in your yard, than a disposal point."

"Roger my 'yard,' Spike. You got the coordinates. As soon as I have a visual, I'll pop smoke on my location. When you've got your boy on station, I'll pop whiskey smoke on the target. You can put your willie-pete right there."

"Roger, Tiger Claw."

Five minutes went by while Starcup's guys, one after another, stepped over our legs and moved along the dike toward the hooches. Corchado and van Wyck disappeared into the door of the first. Lupanski, Tillinghast, Stovall, and Tho got up and followed after them. Starcup and the rest of his guys took their places. All of third squad moved into Second's original positions.

That left Mounds, Crowder, and first squad exposed, but they were crawling forward.

"Tiger Claw Six," came the radio. "This is Spike Four Niner, I'm inbound. You still out there?"

"Yeah Spike, we're just laying out here sunbathing with our gin and tonics. Look for brightly colored lawn furniture, over."

"Spike Four Niner, I'm a-looking."

"This is Tiger Claw, I'm popping smoke to help.""

"Roger Yankee smoke," came the reply. Looking in a wide northerly swath of sky, I spotted the O-1 Birddog coming up on us.

"Affirmative, Spike. Hold your course." I could hear him, the barely audible buzz of the single-engined Cessna. I could also hear a rumbling thunder off in the distance, our F-4, somewhere. I searched the partly-cloudy sky as the sound increased. On-station, it moved into a wide orbit around us. I finally spotted him, a far-away speck.

Go ahead and put out the smoke!" I called down the line. We had a rough consensus as to where the sniper had been.

One of Olivera's guys, SP4 Padget, plunked a smoke round with his M-79. In turn, the FAC fired his much larger smoke rocket right on top of it. It was a dud.

"Tiger Claw, you got any more of that Wilson Picket? Thought we could get this done with the last one I had. Buckshot upstairs saw it, but it looks to be blowing away with the breeze."

"Roger Spike, we'll put out everything we've got left." Shortly, I heard the confirming sounds of M-79s bluking their rounds. Padgett and Walkins sent our last five rounds down range. Balls of pure-white smoke mushroomed upward from the jungle, billowing into five pathetically small separate clouds above the palm trees.

"Now! Spike," I called into the handset. "Get him on it!" Just as I spoke, another breeze began fluttering the brim of my bush hat. As if willed by some dink telekinesis, the smoke began to disperse. I squeezed the talk button and ground the hand set into my ear. "Spike, can he see it?!"

"Roger there Pard, hold your water."

"Roger, Spike." I replied. The Phantom disappeared behind big puffy clouds. I could hardly hear it anymore. *'This whole thing's going to be a bust!'* Suddenly, I caught sight of it again. Dark against the bright sky it pitched in a hard banking turn. Its thundering engines momentarily quieting, it plummeted in a precipitous dive. A stiffer wind buffet my back. To my front, the thick phosphorous smoke sifted through the foliage, diffusing into nothingness. It looked like little more than a light haze in the green undergrowth. I couldn't imagine that he'd still be able to see it, yet the dark accipiter bore in dead on it. A split second before it came even with us the entire underside of the aircraft seemed to separate and come away as a clutch of bombs took flight on their own.

"Ba-ba-ba-rooom!" Half a dozen five-hundred pounders fell into a gigantic explosion. From two hundred meters away, the concussion made artillery shells seem like a string of Chinese ladyfingers. Trees and dirt vaulted upward beyond a huge billow of black smoke. The roar of the phantom reached us again, its engines powering a steep climb. In seconds it was just a dot in the sky.

"Good eye, Spike. He put them right on target!" I said into the handset.

"We aim to please pardner. Hope we did you some good."

As the smoke cleared, I had no doubt he'd done me good. A swath the size of a football field had been turned into a moonscape. Around that, a twenty-meter ring had been scythed to nubs, the surrounding vegetation hanging in shreds.

"That Nunz," I proclaimed, "is an ex-sniper."

"Fuckin-ay, Sir." He shoved his shoulders up to stretch his muscles under the aching weight of the radio. That fleeting comfort complete, he adjusted his M-16 and stared at where he'd lain, making sure to leave nothing behind. I continued looking out toward the bomb strike with the certitude of having blown the crap out of our sniper. 'And Bang wanted me to what? For me to bring her a piece of some dead dink – like a cat bringing home the gift of an eviscerated mouse. No, not like that. Her request extended only to my cutting out some VC's heart. Well hadn't I? I've just spared him the personal intimacy of my K-bar.'

Nunziato climbed up the side of the dike to assume his normal tag-along position. I turned back to check on the rest of the platoon. Olivera's guys ambled nonchalantly toward me, their faces indicating that they too had assumed the obvious about our pesky sniper. I headed in the direction of the hooches.

Delta hamlets had no precise boundaries. Where one ended and another began was vague even to their inhabitants, except when they were like this one. My map said it was called Xom Ha, five isolated hooches scattered across these remote and forlorn rice paddies. Compared to most of Long An province, this kind of bleak loneliness reminded me of life along the margins of the Plain of Reeds. Subject to the privations of bad soil and heavy enemy scrounging, that region had been decimated. Habitations had thinned to the vanishing point.

With only Corchado and van Wyck occupying the first hooch, I decided not to go any further. Starcup's squad split between the first two.

"Move your squads to the last three hooches," I told Crowder and Olivera. "Set up there, and keep an eye on that woodline to the far side." They both nodded and began shunting their people in that direction. Security dictated we keep even the far hooches under our control.

"How long you think we gonna logger in here, Sir," van Wyck asked.

"My guess is, at the end of the day's operation, the slicks will get freed up and they'll send some to get us. To answer your question, at least a couple of hours." This sort of thing was as routine as a hot day, but because we'd come out as a quick reaction force everyone was stuck on the expectation that we should've already been back twelve hours ago.

An infantryman always liked to have some reckoning as to where the end of a trek might be. He didn't really mind humping great distances. It was his lot after all. He just liked knowing how long it'd take, so he could adjust his mind to it. When he didn't know, any distance at all felt endless from the very point where the exact end became unclear.

I scanned the panorama of woodline around me, wishing I'd brought my binoculars. A seven-power look was always preferable to the naked eye, but last night's mission in the dark had made them superfluous. Tra would have to suffice. His eyesight wasn't that much better than mine, but his instincts for spotting anomalous things made it seem like two-power vision.

Ducking out of my web gear and bandoleers, I dropped them next to the doorway. Outside, I could see the two squads moving across the dikes and taking up positions at the other hooches. Nunziato and Davidson propped their radios against a dried nipa wall and stretched out in the shade. I'd just finished unfolding the antenna on battalion net when the handset came alive. *Big* bad news. Our brigade C&C had slammed into a Cobra gunship in a spectacular mid-air collision. The brigade commander, operations officer, artillery liaison and the crews of both choppers had been killed. The day's operation would continue, but more than a few things would be thrown off schedule. I gave the TOC a sitrep on our status, shared the news with the RTOs, radioed it on to Mounds, and went into the hooch.

Tra was speaking to a woman of about thirty. She stood next to her cooking fire with a coal-eyed baby propped on her hip. She observed my entrance without expression, her little one tracking me with a knowing seriousness. Tra said something and both sets of eyes cut to him. He read the mother's ID card then handed it back.

"Her man is an Arvin, right?" I asked, knowing that he'd already posed that question.

"She say yes this."

"Out here? It'd be pretty iffy, wouldn't it? I don't believe her." 'This woman isn't living out here alone.'

"I think same you."

"Do you think that sniper might be her man?" Tra looked at me and scrunched his upper lip exposing the two dark gold eye teeth. He spoke to her again, gesturing toward the direction from which we'd come. I picked up on his reference to the sniper, his odd few shots, and the F-4 strike. Her stolid reaction made it hard to believe it had been her husband who'd just gotten himself blown to bits. Her own eyes had seen what Tra was talking about but showed not a trace of emotion. By way of the predations of a war that had been going on around her since her earliest memories, she would see death differently. Death never seemed to impress them, ours or theirs. They just shouldered on, with this sempiternal stoicism, as if their lives were unaffected by it.

I perused the hooch, trying to glean something from this woman's abject circumstances, from the nothingness of her thatch-walled and mud-floored existence. How *was* she making it? If the Delta's average rice farmer appeared to subsist day to day, this woman had to be taking life by the hour.

Tra suddenly barked a series of questions at her. With a voice a couple of inflections higher, he displayed his super-nasty scowl. That opened her eyes to the point of a slight startle. She answered him in a calm confined manner, her words carefully measured. Tra adjusted his tone. This new line of inquiry unnerved her. She sputtered through a halting response. He turned to me and motioned that we should leave her and go outside. I ducked back through the doorway and into the bright sun. We walked to the edge of a rice paddy.

"Her talk beau coup shit." Looking off at nothing in particular, he grumbled, his tone harsh.

"Tell me what you said. You and she."

"I say her, where her man stay in ARVN, what him unit. Why him let be here in number ten place, let be here for VC come fuck, make new baby-San for him."

Her hemming and hawing had really begun when he'd told her that he was an ex-VC. No amount of her bullshitting was going to get past him.

"Ka-zing!" A bullet sliced the air above our heads. We hit the ground as the sound of the gunshot reached us.

"Man oh man, that bastard's still out there – still alive!" Hagerty shouted from the hooch next door. He popped a couple of M-79 rounds out in a best reckoning of the sniper's location. The first fell slightly short, but the other landed nicely in the woodline.

"You know Tra, the good news is he might be using a rifle with a slightly bent barrel. The bad part is we've got somebody drawing a bead on us and pulling a trigger. Who says he's gonna miss *every time*?" We got up to a hunkered crouch and scooted behind the hooch. "Go over and get Bugabear."

I was frustrated from the sniper's return and the logic of the situation. 'If he's the man of this house, what's he expect to gain by harassing and pissing us off? We have his wife and kid. What's he think we'll do with them if he hit one of us? He knows, nothing.'

"Come here Bugdon," I said, motioning him along. We slipped around to the side of the hooch. I lay down. "Here, set yourself up in the prone. You've got a complete view of the wood-line. Start studying it for a piece of that fucker's face. When I hear that rifle of yours go off, I want to look down there and see a glop of blood and snot jumping four feet in the air. All you got to do is walk those cross hairs from one leaf to the next until eventually they land on that fucker's nose. It's all breathe and squeeze from there."

I rejoined Tra and Nunziato in the hooch. They were leaning against the bunker, smoking. The woman and child continued eyeing us with impassive attention. She knew the score, but she'd be more likely to enlighten us on the success of the Mets than the local military situation. Pacing the interior, I moved closer to her. The baby's hard black stare followed me with a wary gaze. It seemed to comprehend far more than it should.

"What we gonna do now Sir?" Nunziato asked. "Call in some B-52s?"

"Ha!" I laughed. "Gradual escalation. It's the story of this war. And it'd give us the same results it has everywhere else.

He'd just zip himself up in a spider hole. If they don't land one in the middle of his head, he'll stick his fingers in his ears and ride the fucking earthquake out – just like he did the TAC AIR." I sat down and lit up a cigarette. Starcup and Younce entered and stationed themselves inside the doorway. "You know," I went on, "reminds me of something I read in this book once – about the Vikings. When they raided villages, they'd take babies and toss them up in the air, to catch 'em on their spear points for the sport of it."

"I bet nobody fucked with those dudes," Younce offered.

"No, not for a long time they didn't. Tra, you ever heard of the Vikings? – who knows what the Vietnamese word for them would be." He shook his head. "They wouldn't have been too relevant to Southeast Asia. They were these guys from a place called Scandinavia – about a thousand years ago. For a couple centuries, they kicked some serious ass – lightning raids on settlements along the coasts – no such thing as a lightning defense. So, if we were Vikings, we'd be out there on a paddy dike, hoisting that kid on the point of a bayonet with momma-san screeching along behind us. We'd give ol' sniper man a ringside seat and a heavy morale problem."

I pulled a couple of C-ration cans from my pack, then went over and put them next to the woman. "'Ham and Limas' and 'Beans and MothaFuckers' – You see bitch, it's the VC's deal to cut off Vietnamese babies' heads and the like. But that ain't no biggie now is it? Karl Marx himself said, 'The ends justify the means.' With that little dictum alone, you commies have slaughtered millions. But us? Naw, we sit down and have lunch with you – tabs on us."

I went back to my gear and sat down with Nunziato and Davidson. "The Vikings killed because they were barbarians, pillaging and murdering with no sense of morality as a check on it – that and no one around to stop them. Communists kill because they're obsessed with making society over – to the way they want it. That requires a totalitarian system – where they exercise total control over every human activity – and to make that easier, every human thought. However many people they have to kill to get there is just part of the deal... like the Vikings, they don't have any moral restraints – no Ten Commandments – not even one."

"If that's the case, Sir," Younce asked, "how come so many back in the world are against us?"

"They're fucking stupid, that's all," I said in frustration. That thought brought Maureen to mind. "Many are purposefully ill-informed. It's complicated. The average American can't get a real feeling for the threat of communism. Its horrors are just words. Then there's the way this war's going. We're kicking ass, but not enough, and it's in slow motion. Civilians watch the news on TV and think we're hopelessly stalemated. There's a lot of attention on our casualties and how the NVA just keeps on a-coming. People back home can't get a steady diet of that and not be frustrated. Americans don't want to keep supporting a war where its progress isn't obvious. Then there's the perfidious."

"What's that Sir?"

"It's one thing to be against this war because you're disillusioned with the seemingly endless course it's taken, but quite another when you start sympathizing with the communists. The perfidious are those who like to excuse communist aggression and always blame the U.S. for it. Every time they try to take over another country and we want to do something about it, politicians and a host of others who're sympathetic to them, swing into action to stymie our efforts. They've rallied an awful lot of Americans to oppose what we're doing here."

"The Peace Movement dudes, right?" Davidson asked. "How come they're called that?"

"They call themselves that because they're free to call themselves anything they want. It works too, like who's against peace, right?"

"I don't know anybody who's in the Peace Movement." Younce said.

"Unfortunately, I do," I said. "My girlfriend for one. She and her college friends are all in it – my old *ex*-Fuckin'-girlfriend – and everybody like her."

"Uh oh!" they all groaned in unison.

"Yeah, we're in for it now," Nunziato quipped. "LT's gotten himself a Dear John."

"I didn't actually," I said.

"Then you saying, Sir you got that sixth sense that Jody's been moving in?"

"Oh yeah," Younce interrupted, "you guy's seen those pictures of her – the ones LT's got in his hooch? Jody'd be moving in on *that* fox for sure! What's her name, Sir?"

Maureen," I snapped.

"Hey," there was this dude I knew when I was in Alpha," Davidson chimed in. "One time, he got the word from one of his buds back home that this Jody was messing' with his girl. Mor'an that, he'd left his Chavelle Super Sport with her, and the Jody was seen drivin' it! So he got his bud to find out who it was and where he lived. Then he sent Jody a letter – you know – telling him how when he gets done with wastin' Gooks here, he's coming home and going to be looking him up. He put an M-16 round in the envelope, along with a picture somebody took of a dink with half his head blowed off – brains an'-all comin' out. Like fucking cool. He DROS-ed and I never heard what happened, but man! That Jody had to be shakin' in his boots. Like, *'Yeah, I'm 'fucked-up-mental – cra-a-a-azy, and I'm a comin' to see little ol' you!'* That Jody'd never know the day or hour he'd show."

"It's not *quite* like that," I said, thinking for a second of my bullet punching through the picture of Maureen's Trotskyite pal. 'How'd the twerp take a letter like that? It'd be *Conduct unbecoming,* but it'd be damned-near worth it just to see the expression on his face.' "I'm planning on sending her a regular ol' Dear John, but haven't gotten around to it yet. It's got to happen – not over a Jody, but over the same stuff I was just talking about. Guys… I've got a girl who's cheering on that sniper right now. Real romantic, huh?"

Sounds like she's *real* complicated, Sir," Nunziato said in a wry tone, a goad to keep me talking about Maureen.

"More complicated than you know, Nunz," I said. "A lot more... even where it extends to our dropping bombs in the jungle, just to scare the shit out of birds." I looked up, first at Younce and Davidson, then back at Nunziato. "She loves taking jabs at my beloved US Army. But even love taps can get old. I've tried to explain how it really is, but she's sure I've been brainwashed by the military."

"You? Brainwashed, Sir!? Davidson exclaimed. "You're the head fucking brainwasher."

"Yeah, Davidson, we call it *training.* Anyway, she's decided that my explanations of our operational realities are actual proof of it. Like I'm *'too caught up'.* She and her friends though, have *separation,* and are always *rational* and *objective.*"

"A hundred-fifty-nine days and a wake-up," Younce quipped, "and I'm getting me some of that separation."

"Listen to this," I persisted, venting my feelings to my guys in a way I never had. "One of Maureen's friends saw a picture of me when I was a Ranger Instructor at Benning." Her friends introduced her to the notion that my black beret was symbolic of *'American neo-colonialist imperialism.'* Back then I chalked it up to her innocence about military stuff, until she started in with the idea of *changing me.*"

"That's the deal, Sir," Nunziato said glumly. "I know all about that. My Mom wanted to change my Dad. Then my Step-dad. Now she ain't even married to nobody. But, she *still* ain't figured out that you are what you are."

I nodded. My mind digressed to the doorway of that restaurant forty klicks to the north of us.

'I can't tell them about Bang and about her being the reason for my dumping Maureen. She's Vietnamese. They wouldn't understand, until those pictures of Maureen come down and Bang's take their place. But how smart is *that?* Do I really need to go out of my way to advertise things? Damn, I want to stand on the roof of my hooch and proclaim our love to everyone. *But* promenading her around Block Island's a wet dream while doing it in the Nam is downtown Nutburg City.'

I went out to a thin strip of shade, leaned against the side of the hooch and faced the sniper's last known direction. Refreshed by a light breeze stirring the air, I reclined on one elbow. 'Is that dink lining me up in his sights? Does he really want to use his or his comrade's hooch as a backstop for his shooting? Go ahead, try it again. Show just enough of your monkey-assed face for Bugabear to turn it inside out. *Whatever you please, you dink fuck. Have at it. But don't forget, I've got this.'* I patted my shirt pocket.

Gazing out over the far line of jungle was like looking at islands in the Pacific during World War II. Strips of green on a blue sea, weren't so different from strips of green on a green sea of land. Palms and banana predominating, they too would have appeared innocuous from an offshore landing craft. Inside, a hideous world of shit awaited. 'No matter, grunts just like me took those islands, one by one. We're taking these islands too, but passing through them like we did this morning, doesn't fill me with a lot of confidence. One measly sniper is all we've got and he's doing fine running that island all by himself.'

I unbuttoned my breast pocket and took out Bang's small silver lump. Cradling it in the palm of my hand, I regarded its incomprehensible inscriptions. Nearly worn away, the characters seemed to be emerging from a lost time, but the faint lines of the butterfly evoked a disappearance into clouds of wispy scratches. It made the engravings all the more mysterious. I tried to intuit their meaning, but thinking in ancient Asian was a pretty tall order. Just holding the thing though, conjured up a heat wave of feelings for Bang. My head swam in a current of thoughts about her. 'Is she beaming into me from forty klicks away – praying for me like she said? Has she sent something with me, her doppelgänger?'

Bang had been with me all day. I'd welcomed every thought of her, a beautiful wood nymph darting in and out of my consciousness. The tease was one thing, but in another way her intertwining presence bothered me. 'Is she getting in the way of my leading the platoon? Has my decision making been a little off pace? One second I'm trying to outfox a sniper and the next I'm burying my face in her hair. Trip-wires are running through my mind, while her fingers are plucking them to one of her epithalamic songs. After that, I've got a dead guy blowing up, who could easily have been one of my alive ones, while her face and look are vying for control of what's left of my concentration.'

Her distraction was addictively intoxicating. I couldn't stop imagining her and rehearsing our reunion, while another part of me barked instructions about patience. 'It's all I need. I'll be there soon enough. Soon?! There's no such thing when it's about arriving at her door. I've been away from her for twenty-two hours and it seems like a year. I'm headed back to her but at what speed, glacial? Hell, I'm sitting on my ass not even moving *that* fast!'

Then, Ruddick and Wiggins kept making cameo appearances among my thoughts. They were about to be stepped on, but I couldn't help but see them slithering into Bang's restaurant. That MACV colonel could easily wind up telling Braccia that he hasn't anyone to swap into their positions. 'Then what? Think rationally, dude, one foot in front of the other – first one, then the other. Right, it's not that easy, not here in Vietnam. The whole country's a circus of contradictions.'

Logic swirled with ambiguities as I scrutinized the woodline for the sniper. It was as if a sheer screen daubed with green, brown, and black slashes had been pulled down in front of me. 'I can still see what's there, but to what effect? What can I trust? I've got to trust something in this godforsaken war. What? That goddesses might not sully themselves so readily? That's the point. Not her beauty, not her heaven-made look, not even her heart-and-soul pledge to me can account for the magnetism. Even the warmth of her personality can't explain how it's making me feel. Isn't it why I keep thinking that our meeting was the product of some unknowable sorcery? I felt it then. *I feel it now. I love it.*'

I closed my hand around her locket and held it tight, thinking. 'Bang is the solution to everything, my problems with Maureen, her mendacious friends, all the dilemmas of this war, and the imponderables of our love. But aren't *I the master of my fate?* And *the captain of my soul*?'[6.]

I squeezed the locket harder and felt dizzy. The scent of her hair engulfed me as powerfully as it had when I'd buried my face in it. Opening my hand, I felt a strong sense of emanating heat. Both the locket and my palm were wet with sweat. 'Is this thing warmer than it would've been from just clutching it tightly?'

I switched the locket to my right hand and shook it. From the moment Bang had given it to me, I'd known something was inside. I jiggled it next to my ear and sensed a small, soft object. It struck dully as I jerked it back and forth. 'So it isn't an encapsulated snippet of her divine hair... But what?'

I inspected the seam line that ran around the outer edge. Discreet and razor thin, it looked as though it had never been separated. I rolled it around, checking for the slightest finger nail depression. There wasn't one. The two halves seemed fused together. Impulsively, I dug a thumbnail into it while levering the center against my forefinger. It popped open.

There it was, the two open-mouthed halves sitting in my palm, crying out Bang's admonitions. With a start, I tried to put it back together. Not having a hinge, it'd separated into a pair of strange asymmetrical cups, incapable of being fit back into each other. This made no sense. Despite its ancient intaglio, I didn't expect a Chinese puzzle with only two pieces, nor its contents.

Cradled in one of the halves lay an off-white object about the size of a large bean. I dumped it out into my palm, prodded it with my index finger, and still didn't know. Solid, but without much weight, I speculated on it's being an osseous relic of her dead husband. 'What'd she do, remove some fragment of bone from him and entomb it in this little portable crypt? They do have a lot of reverence for their dead ancestors. And she's so definite about souls... and so much a part of the unearthly that anything's possible. She said his soul had sailed off into the vast Mekong sky and without explanation, it had found me. Yet, I found her too.'

I studied the little thing in my hand. It was still unidentifiable. 'Maybe it's his sunbaked Cartesian pineal gland.'

"Therwhackk! A bullet hit the hooch only inches above me, followed by the simultaneous crack of a rifle shot from the woodline and a yelp from inside. I grasped the three items in my hand with total concentration and rolled to the prone.

"You see him Bugabear?!"

"No Sir, I don't see nothing."

From my right Tra scooted over on his belly, then trained his M-16 toward where the shot had come from. "Him shoot, then go in spider hole," he declared, his attention trained on the woodline.

"Yeah," I said, quickly putting the relic back inside while again trying to align the two halves. Its irregular shape was baffling. Guilt and fear that it might be irrevocable kept making me fumble. Suddenly, I chanced on the right symmetry and firmly squeezed the two sides together, perfectly. Nervously, trembling fingers buttoned it back into my left breast pocket.

I moved next to Tra. The sniper was an island away compared to the potential consequences of having opened the locket. Bang had told me never to open it. Yet like an unthinking child, I'd just gone and done it. Cause and effect hadn't occupied a single brain cell. 'Consequences?! But I didn't lose its contents. Nothing's escaped – that I know of. Bang didn't say what's in there. If it had some real importance, wouldn't she have told me what it was, to make sure I wouldn't lose it? No, she just said I must never open it, presuming I was smart enough not to.'

'She also said that I'm the vessel of her dead husband's soul. It's mindboggling, but not ambiguous. She meant it was me though, not the locket. Okay, nothing's been disturbed. It's tightly back together, with its little-whatever-it-is safely sealed inside.

No matter, Bang's remonstration kept echoing. My disobeying of her instruction brought to mind the story of Venus telling Psyche to go somewhere with a box she wasn't supposed to open. Psyche disobeyed her and found nothing but a comatose sleep. 'What'll I get for disobeying my goddess? What had I discovered, a petrified caterpillar Pupa? But in the end, didn't Psyche get united with her love? Maybe, but he wasn't Venus. Great that I crammed my ass off in that course – can't remember shit. Whoa, caterpillar – that tale did have some sort of connection with a butterfly and the soul. Could Bang know something of this? How?'

"Hey Tra," I said, forcing myself to think of something else. "I think that ain't the snipers wife and kid. It's his buddy's wife and kid. That makes him a number ten buddy, right?"

"I think him want more shoot American."

"Yeah. Come on, let's go back inside and quit tempting the son-of-a-bitch."

In the hooch, everyone was safely sitting on the floor with their backs to the bunker. The woman squatted in the corner.

"You done trying to make a target for that sniper, Sir?" Younce teased.

"Yeah, all done." I picked up the handset on Davidson's radio to tell Mounds what I was doing about the sniper. On Nunziato's, I called the TOC to check on our situation.

"Roger, Tiger Claw, expect birds at your location around Echo-Tango-Alpha, One –Eight-One-Five."

"That's going to be a squeeze. It'll almost be dusk by then and I've still got this sniper on my hands. If they don't get here while I've got daylight, he'll move up and pop rounds straight into the choppers."

"Can't the door gunners suppress?"

"The way that dink rode out TAC-Air, he's not going to be all that impressed by pea-shooting M-60s."

"Roger, what are you recommending Tiger Claw?"

"Nothing yet, wait out.

"Okay guys, listen up. If our choppers run even ten minutes late, we'll be risking a nighttime pick-up with that sniper just sitting out there. He knows exactly what we're waiting for. If I was him and it was almost dark, and I heard the choppers coming, I'd just move up as fast as I could. From behind a dike, I could get off a few good shots right when they're scrambling aboard – bunched up – center of big-dark mass. The much closer range will fix his piss-poor marksmanship. Somebody'll take a bullet. Suppose just one dink with an AK joins Mr. Sniper? It'll be better to wait until morning."

"Aw shit," came a clamor of exasperation. I expected this response, but their aversion to spending another night out here was tepid compared to the protest riot going on inside me. 'I have to get back more than they'll ever know. With some good rack time in my bunk and a sure-fire break tomorrow, I can get to Bang. For that, I'll do anything.'

Okay, here's our alternative," I declared. "We've got two good hours until dusk. We can haul-balls north, across open country to the river, then commandeer some boats. On the other side, we hump-it to the road to Can Duc. I'll have trucks pick us up there. It's a guaranteed way of getting back tonight. What do you think?"

"It'll be damn tight on time, Sir," Starcup offered, "but the reliability of our choppers lately is going to shit. You got me convinced. I ain't trusting no sniper with nine lives to keep missing. Popping us right when we're all climbing in, could get one of us in the back, easy."

"Hell, Sir," Crowder added, "I don't much like the idea of staying out here tonight when we weren't suppose to be here *last* night. The way things've been going...."

"It's a case of either putting our asses in somebody else's hands," I told them, "or just taking care of business ourselves. *Us,* I know I can count on."

"You got that right, Sir," Starcup affirmed.

"Nunzie, give me your handset. I need to run this by the TOC." 'We'll move out immediately, get to the river and cross it as fast as we can. Getting to the Can Duc road will be a snap. If we stay out here tonight, we'll definitely fly back in the morning, but I'll lose access to the colonel. Worse, we could get sent out by Major Grizwell on an ambush tomorrow afternoon – and be right back on the merry-go-'round.'

I wanted thirty-six hours with Bang, but was now willing to settle for only tomorrow's daylight. Tra and Tho with the company's three-quarter ton would take care of the rest. There was no question about it, no matter what, I would get in tonight. I took Davidson's handset.

"Tiger Claw Five, this is Six over," I called to Mounds. "Saddle up, we're heading out, right now. Move up and I'll fill you in on our route." I shouldered my gear. Outside, I looked back at the far hooches. Men were putting on their gear. In the other direction, I surveyed the innocuous woodline from where the sniper had harassed us, then the direction in which we'd be heading.

'Bang my sweet, your new husband... and your old, are on their way.'

CHAPTER 3

As second squad took the lead in front of Mound's approaching file, I rechecked my map. To gain the fastest and most secure route, I set our movement along a stair-stepping series of well-traveled dikes. 'If that dink wants to expend some more of his precious ammo, time's short. We're almost out of range.'

"Ka-pow!" The sniper responded, reading my mind with the pull of a trigger. Few even flinched as the shot echoed across distant patties. The file pressed on. 'If he was looking for a lucky hit, I like his timing. Where was he when we were leaving the hooches, when he'd had half a chance? Maybe just intended that Parthian shot as a salute to our retreat.'

Sticking to hard, well-worn paddy dikes, a couple of klicks fell behind us in the first hour. Then the Nhà Bè came into view. This is where we needed to commandeer a couple of decent sized craft. We'd boated across rivers this way before and my aim was to do it again. But none had been anywhere near this wide. From a slight promontory, I studied its pelagic swath of brown water. As far north and south as its course allowed me to see, it loomed with hopelessness. The entire river was empty. 'Why now?!'

"How you reckon we gonna get across, Sir?" Nunziato asked.

"Nunzie, in a moment, thousands of white doves are going to show up and carry us across – as a sign of love and peace. Which is another way of saying, without any fucking boats, we'll still be standing here scratching our nuts."

"I don't see no doves, sir, but every time I seen this river before, there were all kinds of boats going up and down."

"Yeah," I agreed, we always have plenty of everything when it doesn't matter."

From a canal up river, a sampan putted into view. It turned in our direction, hugging the near shoreline.

"Things're improving," Nunziato observed. "First we got nothing, then that...."

"Yeah, from the futile to the unworkable. If this was a ten-meter canal and enough time for ten trips, it'd do. But even if we had all fucking day, a sampan's too shallow for the chop out there in the middle."

Tra nudged my arm and pointed down river. A huge cargo junk was emerging from a distant bend. Lumbering towards us at a speed suggestive of no movement at all, I willed it on. But as it chugged into open view, I could see that it would be too far out for us to flag over. The westering sun edged lower.

"Tra!" I growled in frustration, "what the fuck are we going to do?!"

"That's what we're all thinking, Sir." Mounds' voice came up from behind.

"There," Tra insisted, still pointing at the craft.

"That one," I said addressing Mounds. "It's a real big one. Get your tickets ready."

"Looks like it's gonna be too far from us when it gets up here," he replied.

"When come," Tra said, "make shoot." I turned to the nearest bunch of guys who could hear me.

"Green star!" I yelled to whoever might have one. "When that junk gets to right about *there*, shoot it over in front of them."

My jaw clenched. It took an eternity for the boat to draw closer, but when it was fifty meters of pulling even with us, Olivera popped the green cluster. It arced out and burst just ahead of the boat's bow. A dozen men waved their arms to motion them over. People on-board watched us, dumbfounded. The junk made no changes in its steady progress up river. Tra hollered to them in Vietnamese to no effect. 'Shit! Okay so they might be too far out to hear what he yelled, but they have to know what we want.'

Tra and Tho simultaneously answered the boat's disinterest with eruptions from their M-16s. Bullets tore into the water just ahead of the bow. The far away faces looked to where they'd impacted the water, but that was all. More seconds passed.

"These fuckers are going to drive right by us!" I snarled. "Hagerty! Put a round out there fifty meters in front of them." The stubby barrel of his M-79 lifted to a low angle.

"Pounk – Blam!" The round exploded close enough for shrapnel to lodge in its wooden hull.

"Tra," I shouted, "tell them that I'll sink their goddamn asses if they don't turn in." But if the junk had taken M-16 bullets to be innocuous, they reacted to the concussive blast of a 40-mm round as if bracketed for a naval gun bombardment. The junk's bow jerked hard to starboard and headed straight toward us.

Approaching the muddy bank, it reversed its engine and pulled to a stop. 'All right! It's a fucking ocean-going coaster and might take the whole platoon in one go. But the damn tide's almost all the way out – the riverbank 's nothing but twenty-meters of soldier-swallowing quickmud.'

The steep bank advantaged the first two guys, helping them slither their way down to the water's edge. But waist-deep, they couldn't reach the gunwales.

"We need somebody on board to haul the first man in," I said, to no one in particular. "That skipper sure ain't it. He's so old, he's doing well to still be at the helm."

From inside the wheelhouse, a wizened face regarded us with stony impassivity, fitting since he'd come around only after concluding we were going to send him to the bottom. The rest of the *crew,* three women and several small children, stared at us from the deck.

"Hey, Sir," Nunziato asked, "is this dude trying to fuck with us – bringing the junk in, but not far enough?"

"No, he knows the weight of thirty fully equipped infantrymen'll ground him for sure. And with the tide still going out, we'd be stuck here half the night. "Starcup! Get your stuff off and climb onboard. Start hauling people in."

Starcup calmly slogged down through the muck, into the water and tossed a looped rope over the dragon-eyed prow. Hooking a boot in, he boosted himself up, swung a leg around the stylized beast and saddled it. Then, drawing himself erect on the forward deck, he clenched his hands above his head, his squad cheering as if he'd just single-handedly seized some freebooting brigand.

Starcup pulled a couple of other guys aboard. They then busied themselves pulling in the rest, the junk inching back a little with each one. When I got myself aboard, I found the skipper yammering at Tra. I immediately grasped the source of the old man's agitation.

The boat's cargo, maybe a hundred paper bags of cement, lay in the center of the low inside deck. Dripping water from all our sodden uniforms and boots had run to the lowest point and was soaking into the bags.

"Gonna ruin some of them bottom layer bags, Sir," observed Starcup. "Can't let cement get wet."

"Fuck it," I snapped. "Ain't my fault he didn't use pallets. And what the hell can I do about it now, have everybody jump overboard? They're already wet."

As the last of the platoon clambered over the side, I worried. We were low in the water, real low. From the shore, the junk's high bow and stern gave the false impression that the middle gunwales could bear all our weight without getting too close to the water line. It was dangerously close. It was a huge boat, but I'd just added over three tons of infantry to an already heavy cargo. The sinking sun told me I didn't have time for two trips.

"Everybody, listen up! Stay put. Better yet, do not move." Several of them looked at me as if to say, *'Are you shitting me?'* They stared overboard at my exact margin of error, while holding their breaths. "Shit, we've got a good six inches to spare," I blurted, knowing it was closer to four. 'We might could toss the sodden bags of cement overboard. No, the paper'll break and just make a bigger fucking mess.'

"Tra! Tell Mister Numb Nuts to bring it around and head for the other side." I pointed at the far bank. "Like pronto!"

A few yelps of Vietnamese got us puttering away from the bank in an excruciatingly slow turnabout. We all sat silently, our backs to the hull. A few hands positioning cigarettes were the only movements, that and eyes. They riveted on the small waves lapping at the gunwales. I focused on the shoreline for a sniper. 'Until we get further out, we're a big fat sitting duck. A single bullet tearing into this thing and everybody'll dive for cover. We capsize. Just one slug takes us all down.'

"Whatever happens," I called out, "like another sniper shot or something... *Do not move a muscle! Even if somebody gets hit.*"

The skipper's idea of flank speed was imperceptibly different from idle. I hadn't believed an engine could turn RPMs so slowly without conking out. Decrepit in its oil-slathered well, it chugged with the sound of two cylinders, pistons the size of number-10 cans. I listened to its metronomic labor, doggedly thrumming the hulk beneath me.

Midway, stronger currents and larger waves from a buffeting breeze boosted the sloshing at our sides. I rehearsed our scene of doom. 'A big one'll overbalast one side. Guys will shift their weight to compensate. That'll let in a greater deluge from the other side. This wooden derelict will be as buoyant as a bank vault.'

"Everybody! One by one, starting from the front, carefully slip out of your web gear." Shortly, piles of web gear, grenades and bandoleers lay in the sloshing water at our feet. 'Most can swim and will make it. But I could lose a dozen men. A fate like that and I might as well just go down with the ship. Survivors coming ashore, unarmed and with no means of calling for help might figure out which way to go, but could they get there? A single dink with a weapon could bag every last one of them.'

While contemplating shades of disaster, I willed the boat to transcend the risks I'd taken. I ground Bang's locket into my chest. Holding it against my heart, I could feel her presence. 'We're going to be okay.'

By twos and threes, men jumped from the junk into chest deep water. With curses about my having made Marines out of them, they draggled themselves out of the muck and onto dry ground. With one leg over the gunnel, the soggy cement bags checked my leaving.

"Hey you guys! Let's pass the hat for ol' Papa-san here for taking us across." Several grumbled that they didn't have anything on them. "Well, some of you must – like we kind of owe him. We messed up his cargo – some isn't worth anything now. MPCs, piastres, it doesn't matter."

'We'll all benefit by getting back sooner, but this particular route's my idea, and ultimately it's up to me. *You've got to pay the ferryman.*'

A damp, raggedy wad of assorted currency was handed up to me. It wasn't much, there being little reason to take money to the field. I fished into my breast pocket to pull out that same seventy bucks in MPCs Ngoc and I had fought over in Vung Tau. Retaining a pair of twenties, I passed the rest to the skipper, his face as quizzical as its immobile expression would allow. 'Our modern-day Charon will figure out the transcendent language of cold lucre. He'll have it exchanged by morning."

The sun dipped below the horizon and imminent dusk served up my next dilemma. Of my two possible routes to get to the road, a hardball cart track was by far the easier. We'd make good time on it, but it was three times further. 'It'll take too damn long! The trucks can't wait for us in the dark. It'll be long past that. The other route'll take us straight to the town. Right, and straight through this sketchy-fucking woodline. This was Mounds' choice when Casswell got wounded. No, he didn't have to decide on routes, only whether to stay put or hump-it in. That's the difference; I've got a little more light than he did, and a lot more *need* to get in.'

Mounds and the three squad leaders joined up with me. I shared my decision and its corresponding map information.

"Here to here – less than a klick," I said, indicating where we aimed to go. The dikes and trail in between defined our route without me having to say it. "I've already called in for the trucks to head out. They'll be waiting for us in about twenty minutes on the east edge of the town. Okay, let's get a move on."

Darkness *does* come quickly in the tropics. Because the sun descends below the horizon at an almost perpendicular angle, it drops from sight in no time. The higher the latitude, the more obliquely it sinks, which takes longer. Jungle twilight also has qualities of its own. At sunset, thick wet vegetation becomes insatiably hungry for daylight and leafy shade begins swallowing penumbral light in enormous gulps. The mammalian world evolved a bio-rhythmic instinct for this advance of dusk and darkness, but civilization had decoupled humans from most of nature.

Yet ever since my immersion in *Order of the Arrow*, I'd been working my way back to these instincts, only to become aware that I was hard-wired at forty-plus degrees of latitude. Vietnam's crashing twilight meant a fifteen minute mental adjustment every night. But the psychology of it was perversely uncooperative. The longer I needed daylight preserved, the faster it faded.

Van Wick, on point, gave a hand signal to stop. I moved up to see what it was.

"'To-die' sign, Sir." He pointed to a small rough piece of wood attached to a stick poked into the ground. Its crudely painted lettering, *Tu Dia*, was sun bleached and faded, but still a warning for all who wished to pass. These signs weren't uncommon, but with a friendly district headquarters less than half a klick away, it challenged how assiduous the local Arvins were in securing their own backyard.

"I'd expect to see this shit back across the river," I grumbled, "but not here. What do you think Tra?" Having Tra put his intuition to it was something I never passed up. VC practices did conform to certain patterns, but I'd seen more than my share of lethal idiosyncrasies from those who set them. There were no guarantees of anything.

"Here, me think numbah ten." He pointed to a desiccated patch on the trail, an indication that it hadn't been used in a good while. Probably it was mined. "Here, go, maybe." A gold eyetooth exposed, he pointed toward another trail just off to the left. It branched from the main one and seemed to run in the same general direction. "Maybe VC. VC make booby trap. All time can go."

"Yeah, when you know where they are, it's just a hop skip and a jump." The first path was straightforward trouble. I could understand his hedging for the other, which was regularly traveled but still within the area marked as being booby trapped. It didn't make sense, but I didn't have enough time for a full session with Tra's mental Ouija board. "Let's go Van. Nice and easy. We'll take this trail that bears off to the left."

"Shit, Sir," van Wyck complained. "This here place is booby trapped for sure. Charlie's advertising it. And it's getting' dark. Ain't no way can we go boogalooin' in there. I was resigning from point today anyway." He looked at Corchado either for support or for him to move up and take over.

"Fuck you Dickwick," Corchado grumbled, "it's still your turn for point – and I resigned from the Army yesterday." The two of them plus Nunziato and several of second squad looked at me to see what would happen next. 'Should I order one of them to go stomping into a *known* bad area or turn around and find us another route? That'll take more time than I have. We'll have to stay out here until morning. Not going to happen. There's no leaving, no turning around and going another way. Not now.'

"I've got point," I said. "Come on. Get behind me. And spread out damn it."

I moved up beyond the sign and carefully checked the surface of the trail. Worn smooth and hard, it was getting regular use. The more I thought of it, the less sense the warning sign made. I proceeded hesitantly down the trail, super alert to every leaf and blade of grass. Nothing stuck out not even in the non-way that it might.

Twenty meters in though, something caught my eye. Bits and scraps of plastic wrappers lay scattered on the ground. Moving up a little closer, I could identify a piece of fatigue uniform, and half a length of a shredded trouser leg that had been cut off. The torn wrappers were from first aid bandage packets and the fabric of the cloth from an ARVN uniform. Less than two meters away, the base of a banana tree had been ripped open and its leaves riddled with small holes.

By the depression in the ground, I could see where the device had gone off. 'Strange there's nowhere for a trip wire to be concealed – hard, bare soil extends from the tree all the way to the other side of the trail. The blast wasn't big enough to blow everything away. No ruse –it's just too strange. It bothers me when I can't figure out the logic of it.'

Moving on, I came to a more heavily vegetated area. Branches and wide leaves overhung the trail. Only a snake or a fool would venture into a spot like this. I sent back for Corchado's killer-eye, a cast iron shipping plug from an artillery round with fifty feet of nylon cord tied to it.

After laying the line out carefully so it wouldn't get tangled, I hurled the eye over the vegetation and down the trail. I needed to get into a covered position. There wasn't one so I used every inch of excess line to get as far back as possible. If I got low enough, the typical exploding booby trap wouldn't affect me. Praying that it wasn't set in a tree, I began pulling in the line.

Half way in I felt resistance. Before yanking any more, I waited fifteen seconds then lifted my head up as far as I could to see what was catching it. The line had pulled through the leaves. I still couldn't tell.

"Well, here goes," I said to no one in particular, then shouted, "Fire in the hole!" I looked behind me. Corchado and van Wyck had their heads pressed against the ground.

I tugged the line a little harder. The branches fell away, exposing a length of green monofilament line. As intended, the killer-eye had snagged it. I drew in more line, but it didn't give way. I yanked the line some more. It gave, but with a heavy resistance. I waited for a cook off. Still nothing. 'It should've just pulled the pin from whatever it is, smoothly, and set it off.'

I looked up again to check it out. "Damn! It's got a grenade hung on it." The killer-eye had done its job and snagged the tripwire. But instead of it extracting the pin, it'd dragged the grenade out into the open. I approached in a cautious crouch. It lay on the trail, both sides of its cotter pin spread and safely folded back. "Man! The tripwire would've snapped before that pin'd come out."

"Sir," van Wyck said, "If it'd been that dink's first day on the job, he couldn't have been that stupid."

"I don't think that he was. Mister Charles is a lot of things, but stupid isn't usually one of them. Makes me feel like the dumbass though, when I can't figure out what the hell he's up to."

Further down the trail, we encountered two more grenades, both rigged in the same inexplicable way. Had they been set on this expedient version of safe, for the benefit of unescorted NVA troops? Tra suggested that so close to a district headquarters, they might be part of a trick. A VC could potshot the Arvins, then scram down this trail. With booby traps already set, he'd just have to squeeze the cotter pins as he passed. Because he'd just been seen running down the trail, the Arvins wouldn't be on high alert for booby traps… until they hit the first one.

'That unfortunate Arvin back at the banana tree must've been caught in a ploy like that. They've probably been avoiding the area ever since. Typical. Now, the VC have themselves a refuge right under Arvin's nose. But, it'll let us boogie down this path like Boy Scouts on a nature trail. Worst thing to happen might be somebody getting a grenade tangled around his foot. Yeah, *just like the one that'd snared that now one-legged Arvin.*'

We were soon through the Tu Dia area, unscathed, but our dealing with the booby traps had cost us a lot of daylight. Darkness fell, insinuating itself around me with a malevolent confidence. As the last of the light dimmed, it drew the air away with it. I felt a sense of suffocation. *'Why? I own this damned jungle.'*

I pressed on, forcing myself as I always did to focus on my surroundings. The gloaming washed the vegetation in stippled variants of brown, among pockets of black. Trees and bushes dissolved into amorphous shapes. Yet, it was an environment that I'd long mastered. Besides, there was only fifty meters of this crepuscular chase left. When it turned into a nearby village trail, we wouldn't have to worry about booby traps at all. A hundred meter dog trot on that and we'd hit the road. Then it'd be just a short bolt to the trucks. *'Bang! I'm on my way!'*

It got darker. My words to Keneally yesterday, when I'd questioned Mounds' actions, echoed in my mind. *'Humping over unfamiliar ground in the dark or even at dusk is just asking for it.'*

"Fuck this trail," I whispered to myself. 'I don't need booby traps I can't see. We've gotten all the free ones we're going to get. So once again, we'll just go where they *don't* put them.'

"Tra!' I barked, holding up at a trail junction, "it's getting too dark. Let's bust through that paddy over there. It's wide open and a little lighter – we won't have to worry about any more shit." He consented with a nod in that direction.

We sluiced off the smooth, hard path and into the boot sucking muck of the rice paddy. Unusually sloppy, our boots sank deeply into it. The surface water reached our knees and slogging through it became more laborious than I'd expected. Anticipating that it wouldn't be a popular decision, I considered turning back within the first ten meters. 'Fuck that too. Whatever their thoughts, this muck isn't *that* deep or *that* thick – like it ain't slimy excrement. We're not turning back for anything and if they really don't like it, they can come up here and choreograph this gavotte in the dark themselves.'

After trudging through the slop for more time than I had hoped, the end appeared as a black mass beyond the slight glint on the water. A large high dike lay between us and one small final paddy. We dragged ourselves toward it. I reached it first and lugged myself up its steep bank by grabbing on to some short shrubs. I crossed over its bare path and stepped down to the paddy on the other side. As I did, something around me suddenly felt very weird. The air and water and ground seemed to fuse into one. My mind told me I was falling, as if into a deep canal. My body felt as though it was weightless, yet at the same time rising to the surface. I inhaled for air, but as I did my remaining breath sucked away. In a floating sensation, I lost all sense of what was up or down, of what was real. The dike, the paddy, Tra, the men behind me, all swirled away. I willed exertion, energy, to move some part of me, to make me know that I was. But no movement registered. I couldn't tell if nothing had happened, or if I just couldn't sense it. At last, a wave of feeling began to flow over me, a welcome coolness. My guys were there, but swimming in the air above me, above the surface of something. They were pulling me out, pulling me back up.

Slowly, the whorl of sensations began to center to a single thought. I was hit. Maybe. I hadn't heard any explosion. Everything was still quiet, like muffled or something. I'd been hit before. I knew what it was like. 'Jesus, something's wrong.'

"Bang. Bang!" I called, but only felt my throat working. I couldn't tell if anything had come out. My God, she wouldn't hear me. "Bang! Bang!!" Please come and get me. "Bang!"

"What's he saying man?" Travis's voice came from somewhere.

"He's got to be some kind of delirious," Younce answered, "like from shock."

"Bang, Bang."

"Yeah, it went bang all right." It was Mound's voice. "Dustoff's on the way. Tra's a fuckin' goner."

"That chopper'd better be a fucking rocket ship in a time warp, cuz he's got to be in surgery two seconds ago." Who was Younce talking about? Tra?

"Oh shit! Oh my Lord," Travis wailed. "I can't do anything with this! I, I – I don't even know where to start!"

'What the hell are you crying about? Travis, you're the best medic we've ever had. You've always known exactly what to do. Besides, I can't be that bad. I don't even feel any pain, just cold. That's got to be a good sign. When guys get hit bad, they're always in moocho pain. Unless they're unconscious, and I'm sure as hell not. The locket! I need the locket.'

"Oh Bang – the locket?!" I tried to focus on what I could see. What I thought was nothing, was actually the sky. Stars were just beginning to come out. The whole great empyrean before me seemed to blossom with them. If I could just concentrate, I'd be able to find that constellation, the one that was going to be Bang's. My vow to her came back to me, that I would have her, or die. 'Her, or die! But it had to be **her**!'

"Bang." It came out softly, the way I'd whispered it into her ear, the way I wanted to now. I squinted my eyes trying to see the vault of stars and was truly amazed. One by one, whole constellations had begun to wink out.

Gavin B. Carney

EPILOGUE

CHAPTER 1

OUR FIRE SUPPORT BASE BECAME a swirl of events in the aftermath of Carney's wounding. The order came down for the battalion to relocate west to the Plain of Reeds. While packing up, loading trucks and lifting out with Chinooks, we came under a furious mortar attack. Our artillery ammo dump got hit and exploded. Four men were killed and fifteen wounded. The place was a madhouse. The next day though, we were all back to moving, then setting up at our new location, Fire Support Base Alison. Carney? Before he was medevaced to Japan, I was only able to get to Saigon once.

Mondo was in Intensive Care at 3rd Field Hospital, wounded as severely as one could be and not be dead. In spite of the hoses and tubes, respirator and God knows what else, they told me he was 'stable.' We couldn't talk. He was unconscious, in an induced coma. One of his doctors gave me a horrifying litany of the damage he'd taken, a head injury, perforation of organs, broken bones, and possible paralysis. Numerous fragment wounds to the extremities were the least of it. I had to ask; 'What is his prognosis?' The doctor believed Carney would live but beyond that was extremely guarded. A series of surgeries were planned. The first two would be done immediately on his arrival in Japan.

Two months later, I DROS-ed to Fort Ord, California. I learned by way of Carney's parents that he was still in Japan, though about to be moved to Walter Reed Army Medical Center. My pressing desire was to see him as soon as he arrived there, but things got complicated. I'd been assigned as acting executive officer for the Garrison Commander, a colonel with a passion for golf and the delegation of work. The latter's full support of the former, kept me chained to my desk. My wife, Denise, was pregnant with our second child and experiencing medical problems. Our son Michael had just turned three and suffering with scarifying bouts of asthma.

Finally, after months of trying, I got to talk to Mondo by phone. He was struggling mightily with cognitive issues and his speech was severely affected. When I asked him a question, no matter how simple, there were long pauses while he fought to retrieve an answer, sometimes for so long that I'd try to make it easier by moving on to another subject. That tactic only frustrated him and exacerbated his difficulties. It was painful for both of us. He boasted he was improving so much that another brain operation was contemplated. Others involving skin and bone grafts were also in the works.

Multiple surgeries struck me as encouraging. When the docs quit was when you had to worry. At least there was something to work on, some goals. Mondo insisted he wasn't really paralyzed, just couldn't walk, whatever that meant. To be with him, his sister, Gigi, moved to a nearby apartment. Her view was clearer and sounded hopeful, although circumscribed with Mondo listening from his bed right next to her.

During subsequent phone conversations, I thought Mondo seemed to be making gains although always vague about his overall condition. He'd give me medical information, procedures, evaluations and all sorts of non sequiturs regarding hospital goings-on, but never a definitive status. He was disjointed in a way that made me think he intended to divert me from knowing the bottom line. Gigi's take tended toward a repeating of what noncommittal doctors had told her: 'His progress is encouraging. Will it continue? Hard to say.'

Nine months later, I got an opportunity to catch a hop from Travis to Andrews Air Force Base. Mondo was still at Walter Reed and I spent two days with him. He remained wheelchair bound, but his mental capacities were definitely improved. He said that with this or that therapy, he'd be walking soon. It seemed fanciful to me. Noticeably scarred, he was gaunt and much older looking. But, Mondo's spirits were high and it was a happy reunion for us both, although for me tinged with sadness. This wasn't the hard-charging Mondo I remembered. I felt like the invincible guy I knew was still back in Vietnam.

After I return to California, Mondo was transferred to the Army's hospital at Valley Forge, Pennsylvania. Then, he disappeared. It wasn't that Carney had actually vanished, just that I lost track of him. He'd gotten medically retired from the Army and transferred to a Veterans Administration care facility. I couldn't locate where. It didn't help that my go-to source of information, his sister Gigi, got married, changed her name and relocated with her husband. Only years later did I learn that his parents had retired and moved to Florida. This was long before the internet, so finding people who might be anywhere in the country required the services of a private investigator, and even then was far from a sure thing.

I left the Army during this timeframe. Denise, I and the kids moved to West Milford Township, New Jersey, where I took a job with a financial services firm in nearby Manhattan. Every day I commuted into New York City. Successive jobs and the normal demands of a young family proved significant diversions. It's tough to admit, but my life had little room for the past. Vietnam became relegated to just that. Personal reminders of the war were rare. In my business circles, few had served in our Armed Forces. Fewer still had gone to Vietnam and none had seen actual combat. No one ever asked me anything about my experiences there. I offered none.

Through the early seventies, spontaneous moments of nostalgia did break through, usually in conversations with Denise. During the communist takeover of Vietnam in 1975, media commentary came at me like insults borne on the tips of ice picks. The tragedy of the *Boat People* was perfect for their derisive reportage. 800,000 desperate souls, with half of them drowning, starving, or murdered by pirates during their escapes, were lumped and labeled as the mere hangers-on of a corrupt regime getting out with their ill-gotten loot. We were told that in a now reunified and purified Vietnam, there'd be no room for the likes of such elements.

Then came the horrifying Cambodian genocide. Communist Khmer Rouge psychopaths wantonly murdered two-million of their own people. When TV commentators weren't describing the bloodbath as the revolutionary omelet's broken eggs, they were standing on their heads to blame the United States for it. "Communist excesses," their favorite euphemism, were "regrettable, but ought to be viewed with an understanding of the aspirations of a people's revolution and its rejection of the deep seated injustices of its colonial past." With grave voices, they put their fingers squarely on the catastrophe of *our great American misadventure*, claiming that if the United States hadn't made things worse, then it was the actual cause.

The entire political left opposed our efforts in Vietnam from the start, so our ill-conceived intervention, the failure of our efforts, the collapse of South Vietnam, and the imposition of a communist dictatorship, were all quite predictable. Vietnam they instructed, was finally united and at peace. Wasn't that better than war? Then, they established these opinions as incontrovertible fact and closed the book on Vietnam.

It was excruciatingly hard to take, but that's just what I did, in silence. Then the bad became the bizarre. Surreal fantasies such as "Apocalypse Now" were treated as if they'd been documentaries. The antithesis of what I'd done and fought for began morphing into a collection of falsehoods. Those who controlled the ink, the microphones, and the cameras created new truths about the war, and not surprisingly, they went from bad to worse. The acuteness of this pain made me cut myself off from everything connected to Vietnam, a country for which I'd once had enormous affection.

My broodings over the unfolding events in Southeast Asia and my longings to suppress them had its limits. Abruptly, I became aware of a compelling need to find Mondo. As I thought how I'd let years pass, I became filled with self-recrimination. Where had all the time gone? It was no good to wonder why he hadn't contacted me, because the onus was on me. I hadn't paid the price he had. God only knew how much he'd paid. Now, I needed him.

Where to start? After a dozen futile phone calls, I drove up to his home town in Rhode Island. I went to Mondo's high school first to learn what I already knew that he'd graduated in 1962. Although the eighteen years that had passed didn't seem like much to me, the first two office staff I met were only around twenty years old. They referred me to colleagues twice their age, but neither had any recollection of a Gavin Carney. It was no help that one, a guidance counselor, fondly recalled his sister in the class of '63.

The city police department was my next stop. Mondo's father was a retired cop. I wasn't sure of his rank, but knew he was already retired when we were in Vietnam. Mondo's parents had their children late.

My visit to the Police station gave me more evidence that eighteen years is a long time. Still, I got the names of retired guys who would know Chuck Carney. Back in my motel room though, when I repeatedly called every number, none answered. Finally, a wary-sounding woman picked up. And yes, she knew the Carneys, her husband having served in the department. She also remembered that their son had been badly wounded in Vietnam. His parents had moved to Florida but she didn't know where. Her husband would know, but he was on a fishing trip with his brother in Maine. She gave me the name of another couple who were sure to know. They lived in Cumberland, a nearby town. Armed with their address, but no phone number, I got in my car to try and find them.

It was a small Cape Cod house on a quiet residential street. No one was home. My respect was growing for the frustrating footwork of a detective's existence. Here I was a non-detective trying to find a retired detective. As I was returning to my car, a guy across the street opened his garage door. I learned he hadn't seen anyone home in a couple of days and he didn't know where they'd gone or when they'd be back.

My motel room's phone book did not list their name. Information informed me their number was unlisted. Surrendering to the futility, I decided to hire a private investigator. I drove back home and began calling every PI listed in northern New Jersey. I wanted someone who could convince me that they were a real expert in finding people, but came away suspecting they'd only take me for my money. No one would give me any guarantees they'd come up with anything. My frustration bled into open agitation.

"Paul, I just read this long article about what they're calling Post-traumatic Stress something or other," my wife, Denise, told me. I think you've got it!"

"Put whatever name on it you want," I argued back. "I'm only trying to find an old friend!"

"Sure," she mocked, "everyone is prone to that – out-of-the-blue getting totally preoccupied with a friend they only mentioned three times in ten years."

"I spoke with him on the phone a lot of times when he was in the hospital and flew all the way from California to see him when he was in Walter Reed. That's more than a mention."

"So when was that, back in seventy-one?" she scoffed. "Whoop-dee-doo. Three times since then?"

The truth of Denise's words poured jet fuel on the fire. After networking with guys at work, I finally connected with a PI up in the Bronx by the name of Nazaryan. Based on a credible recommendation, I met with him and paid a retainer. In turn, he promised to get working on it. The most valuable piece of information I had for him was Carney's Social Security Number which I got from an old set of Army orders that pertained to me and other officers in our battalion.

Mr. Nazaryan got back to me two weeks later. Carney, he informed, was receiving disability compensation from the Veterans Administration. He'd also learned from a VA contact that Mondo's funds were being sent to The Woonsocket Savings and Trust.

"That makes sense," I commented. "That's his home town, but when I went up to Woonsocket, I came back empty-handed. Problem is… will the bank give up his address? They'd have to know it."

"Yeah, they'd know," he agreed, "but might or might not give it up. It always depends on the individuals I speak with. They won't give it to me over the phone for sure. Somebody might if I go in person and just happen to meet the right manager. Sometimes you get lucky. This could be trickier than that though."

"Why?" I asked.

"Well, my contact in the VA had sort of a current address for him. It wasn't anywhere in Rhode Island. It was care of a bank in Paris."

"Paris, France?!" I exclaimed.

"That's the one," he affirmed.

I was stunned. Possibilities whirled in my head. Had he gotten so well he'd gone back over there to wallow in his old haunts? In spirit maybe, but definitely not the man I'd seen at Walter Reed. Mondo's permanent damage was just too extensive. Had he gone back to Lisette, his old girlfriend in Paris? The way he'd described their breakup, it seemed more likely he'd gotten back with his old fiancée. I'd asked about Maureen when I'd seen him at Walter Reed. He'd been disinterested in the subject. What I got out of him was their relationship was moribund.

"That's all you've got," I asked. "Some bank in Paris is holding Carney's mail?"

"Evidently," he answered. "Some people do that, you know. Banks, lawyers, or other second-party intermediaries receive their mail. Okay, so what do we know here? His compensation goes to a bank in Rhode Island and he draws on it from one in France.

Maybe only his Veterans Administration correspondence goes to that French bank. Some of his medical bills are being routed through our embassy, back to the VA for reimbursement. I'll bet you my fee the VA has his address and that it's in France. You'll have a tough time getting them to give it to you. I could only get the name of the bank because my contact is sort of peripheral. You'll need the address of the branch he's using. I've never done any work overseas so I can't be much help with that."

"I'll keep you batting a thousand, "I said. "I'll go to Paris myself. But I've got to have more to go on."

"That's the way I feel everyday when I begin a case. You always start out thinking that you don't have a hell of a lot. But, you take what you have and build on it straw by straw. Anybody can find our embassy in Paris. Because of Carney's medical issues, our embassy is bound to know where he is. Whether or not you can get someone to cough up his address is another story. Some will and some won't. Part of it'll depend on how you approach them, the more compelling your story, the more likely."

"Okay, that makes sense," I said, already rehearsing how I would introduce Denise to the European phase of my search for Carney.

Taking my PI's advice, I networked every Wall Street contact I had, who might have a connection with French banking, foreign exchange, Bourse de Paris, or anything in their financial sector like commercial real estate. It was frustrating but I did come up with a couple of names to look up. My last stop was Denise, who I won over with the simple offer of a week's vacation in Paris. At least initially I'd won her. She began backpedaling when she found out the cost. I was making decent money, but our finances were tight because we'd stretched to buy a new house.

After I'd booked our trip, Denise solved part of the cost problem. While horsing around in a game of tag with the children, she'd tripped on the edge of the driveway and broken her ankle. I told her I'd postpone everything until she got off crutches, but she insisted I cancel her flight. She'd come to understand how I felt, and since her mother had rearranged her life to take care of the kids, she'd just hang out with them. I'd go alone. Good-naturedly Denise bantered about what lengths she was willing to go to save us money and teased about enabling my rampant post-traumatic stress obsession. What did I care? It was driving me to find Mondo.

Before my flight, I took another overnight drive back to Woonsocket. Nazaryan had convinced me to try and get more info from Carney's bank. I was apprehensive about traveling all the way to Paris with only vague hopes of getting something out of our embassy. A jaunt to Rhode Island wasn't that much of a haul.

I went back to the little house in Cumberland. If they could connect me to Mondo's parents, I'd have a lock on him. There was still no one at home. That back-tracked me to the woman whose husband had been fishing in Maine. No one answered there either.

Without an appointment, I went to Carney's bank in downtown Woonsocket and dropped the name of my Manhattan brokerage firm. I was shown to the manager's office. After relating my story, the guy's wariness softened, maybe relieved that I wasn't there to sell him financial services. It helped that his older brother had been a Marine Corps officer in Vietnam. I took my PI's advice to circumscribe my request and only asked for the branch office of the French bank where Carney had routed his money.

The VA was sending his mail to this bank. He wouldn't be far. No need to push for something they might not have. Luck was with me. I produced the name of the bank and the manager just provided me with the branch's address.

Armed with two thin leads, I boarded my TWA flight at JFK. Eight hours later, I was walking through the bustling concourse of Charles de Gaulle International. This was the first contact my feet had ever made with the European continent. Before Vietnam, I'd only changed planes at London's Heathrow en route to Nairobi when I was in the Peace Corps.

I checked into La Louisiane, a small hotel recommended by a colleague who'd stayed there on a business trip. At Rue de Seine and Boulevard St. Germaine, it seemed pretty well situated, given I had few ideas beyond using my PI's advice to take what I had and uncover things as I went. Several pointers from a helpful concierge and a detailed map of the city, began the process.

With scant knowledge of French, every aspect struck me as daunting. Paris covers an area three times that of New York. One side of my map showed the entire city. The other displayed a wider view, the city and the surrounding region known as the Île-de-France. This was vast, with many more millions of people. Carney was somewhere out there. Locating him would be, how'd he say it, 'like finding a dink in downtown Saigon?' At least pinpointing my first objective, the U.S. Embassy, wasn't difficult. A phone call to our Consular Services office in Paris got me an appointment.

Mr. Bryndell, a few years younger than me, insisted I call him David. Sitting in his Paris office, I pegged him to be at a semi-managerial level. I laid out my story, from my close relationship with this war hero in Vietnam, through his terrible wounding and my loss of contact with him, to discovering that his present residence was somewhere in Paris.

"I need your help in order to find him," I concluded.

"What would you like me to do?" He asked pleasantly.

"Well, tell, me where he is." Bryndell's question annoyed me. I'd just told him the whole story and what I wanted. I tried not to show it. "I understand he's had some medical attention here and the bills are being routed through the Consulate to the Veterans Administration back in the States. You must have something on where he's living."

"Where did you learn these things?" he asked. His tone becoming confidential, as though I'd just divulged a piece of classified State Department information.

"Before coming all this way," I explained, "I did as much homework as I could... Like I said, I've been looking for him for a long time – only recently learning that he was here."

"I can't tell you where he is," he said.

"Why?" I struggled mightily to keep my composure. "You've got to know."

"Yes I do, but I can't tell you."

"Why, can't you?! Is Carney in some kind of hiding?"

"I can neither confirm nor deny that he is. I don't know."

"Why are you saying that you can't?"

"Mister Keneally," he began, "I've listened to your rather interesting story, but with all due respect I have no confirmation that any of it is as you say, or for that matter if your purposes match your story. With regards to Mr. Carney, people – Americans citizens, choose to live overseas for more reasons than I could count. Presently, there are nearly a hundred thousand living in France alone. I would have no knowledge as to how many of them, for whatever personal reasons, have severed all former ties. But I do know that some have. Within the law, they have every right to do this. Your Mister Carney may well be one of them. Circumstantially, it looks that way to me. You must understand – I cannot take it on myself to meddle in people's private lives. Is it not true that he has had a number of years to contact you, but hasn't...?" The question finishing his discourse, Bryndell sat at his desk, one hand over the other. He had the look of supreme confidence, the knowing satisfaction that he held all the cards and, could choose to dispense a favor or not. My heart sank. Petty bureaucratic power could only exist when exercised in the negative.

"I didn't ask you to meddle in people's lives," I pleaded. "I just want you to give me my friend's address – so I can see him again."

"I told you, I cannot give you his address. I will however, send him a letter informing that you are looking for him and can be found .... You mentioned that you were staying where?"

"You're going to mail him a letter, while I wait in my hotel room, for however long it takes for him to get it and decide to answer?"

"The French postal system is quite efficient," he said. "And yes, he might not answer, but that would be an answer too wouldn't it?"

"No," I snapped. "He might be away, traveling and not be home. It wouldn't mean anything."

"Well, if he *is* away for some indeterminate time, then you wouldn't be able to see him even if I did give you his address."

"Couldn't you call him by phone?" I asked.

"I'm afraid we don't have a phone number for him, just an address." We sat there not saying anything. I couldn't think of any other angle. We were finished.

I returned to my hotel. Anger cooled, congealing into a knot of depression. My dispiriting trip to the consulate earned me a bout of power-drinking, but I had no idea where to go. The hotel had no bar and by the look on the faces of a couple I'd seen emerging from the room across the hall, it had little need for one.

Piss-ant Bryndell's intransigence left me with my only other option, Carney's *Banque Nationale de Paris.* According to my concierge, the address was a branch office in the 13th Arrondissment, at the edge of the Quartier Asiatique. She informed that this was where mostly French Indochinese resided. Since the communist takeover, thousands of Vietnamese refugees were immigrating to France and pouring into that area.

What in the world did Carney have going on? He had to be living somewhere near that bank, otherwise he'd be using some other branch office. I knew he had familiarity with the city. But with Paris being a thousand square miles, it seemed an unlikely coincidence that he'd chosen to live in a Vietnamese section of town. I had no idea what he was doing in France, but *this* just made it all the more intriguing.

In 1980, the Paris Metro did not go to the Quartier Asiatique, so following my concierge's advice I took it part way, then taxied to the bank's address on Rue de Tolbiac. After a few awkward moments with non English speaking staff, I was escorted to the office of a congenial, English-speaking Mr. Jolicoeur. I decided to go for broke. If I failed here the entire trip would be a waste.

I described my connections with the banking world, my life on Wall Street, dropping the French names I'd picked up in my research. I followed that with a passionate story of my friendship with Carney in the midst of Vietnam, our tragic separation over the past decade, and my desperate quest to find him. I sketched in details about how the American Consulate Office completely failed me. I played that up big, America coming up short, with my fate now entirely in the hands of France.

Jolicoeur nodded through my mentally-rehearsed recounting of what had happened with an occasional 'yes' marking his continued understanding. He asked no questions. When I finished, he excused himself and went out. Returning, he handed me a piece of paper with Carney's address.

"I have seen your monsieur Carney a number of times," he told me. "He is not difficult to remember, an American, in a wheelchair. He speaks some French."

"What does he do?" I asked.

"Naturally, he conducts his business here – always out at the counter. You told me yourself that some of his mail is being held here for him."

"Yes," I said, "I'm just overwhelmed with the information – having been so lucky to meet you and receive your help. *Merci beaucoup.* You say he's in a wheelchair. Alone?"

"Oui, most certainly," Jolicoeur answered. "Monsieur Carney is in this wheelchair – from the horrible wounds of war which you have described to me. He is never alone. I have only seen him with a woman. Monsieur Keneally, you must excuse me. My staff wishes me to attend to an important issue. I hope your reunion with monsieur – Capitaine Carney will be a most enjoyable one."

My head swirled. So hard for so long, then suddenly when all seemed lost, it was as easy as *that?* It made no sense, but hey, what made sense anymore? Wasn't this Samuel Becket's adopted city? So Mondo was still in a wheelchair. No surprise there. He was with a woman. No surprise there either. Back in Nam, he'd had countless stories about his days in Paris, one more ribald than the next. Maybe that part of him was unchangeable.

CHAPTER 2

ACCORDING TO THE SCRIBBLED NOTE Mondo's address wasn't that far. I walked. His house, tucked among older houses in a laneway a few blocks from Avenue de Choisy was quiet. On a Tuesday morning, most would be at work. I went to the door and noted the top name slot with "E. Paquin" printed on a plastic card. Below it, a piece of torn cardboard was jammed into the slot, with the handwritten name, "*Gen Carney*." I pressed the bell next to it.

"Hold on!" came a male voice from inside. It was Mondo. The door opened and I caught a glimpse of him as he negotiated his wheelchair to open the door wider. He backed up and I moved into better view.

"Thought you could get away, huh?" I asked. A silent moment followed.

"Holy shit..." He squinted at me, to make sure of what he was looking at. "Fucking gaddang Keneally."

"Yup, that's me. Looks like you still have ninety percent of your old brain working. And you've gone and promoted yourself to general? Why the hell not, huh?"

He leaned forward and stood up with his arms outstretched. We embraced. Carney had always been a couple inches shorter than me but he seemed more than that now and was a lot thinner. In Nam, he'd had the body of a decathlon star.

"Captain was all it ever was," he said, "I got promoted while still in an induced coma… guess I missed the party. Gen is my wife, *Genevièv.* Keneally, how the *fuck* are you?!"

"Forget me. You can walk?!" I asked.

"Yeah, if you call three steps here, five steps there walking – places where I don't have any choice. The bathroom and kitchen are too small to get my wheelchair in. We widened the doorways of all the other rooms but no-go on those little ones. There's some big-ass Nineteenth Century supporting beams in there that keep Madame P. upstairs where she belongs."

"E. Paquin," I said. "I saw the name on the other slot.

"Esmeraude!" P's good enough for me. She's my landlady – a real piece of work. Nutty as a fruit cake – and gives me all kinds of shit. I give it back – it's not hard I can tell you. In my heart of hearts, I know she was a whore for the Nazis. Ha! You should hear the hysterics when I remind her of it. 'Ah, the good old days, huh Madame P? *Mehr Schnapps meine Schätzchen.'*

"Same old Mondo," I said shaking my head.

"I'll take *ein bischen* back because P did let me get a carpenter to do the doorways. Then again, the Hun's harlot got all new doors out of the deal." He eased himself into his chair and was rolling it backwards down the hall. I followed him into the living room and sat on a couch. It sure sounded like the same old Mondo, talkative and profane as ever. The strong Rhode Island accent was still there but slower and burdened with a residual slur due to his brain trauma. He was ten years older since I'd last seen him, but looked as though twenty had passed.

"Why in the world are you living here?"

"What's wrong with this place? Nice quiet neighborhood, best apartment I could afford – hell, batshit P's thrown in for the same price."

"No, the place is nice enough," I said, "definitely quaint – I mean here in Paris cut off from everyone back in the States."

"I'm not cut off," he demanded. "Two years ago, my mom and dad both passed away within a month of each other. I talk to Gigi on the phone regularly. Shit, I had no idea where *you'd* gone, although I did try to find you in the Philadelphia directory once. But you weren't there."

"That's because I never went back. When I got out of the Army at Fort Ord, Denise and I moved to New Jersey."

"After striking out with Philly," he continued, "I had no idea of what city or state to go for next. I can't remember what I did. Nothing – I guess I gave up. Hey, did you come all the way here just to see me or what?"

"Mondo, I've been looking for you for a long time – recently it's been flat out. I drove up to Woonsocket twice and learned your parents had moved to Florida. There's a slew of Carney's in Florida. I didn't know their first names. I tried Gigi too, but couldn't find her either."

"She got married," he said. "Her name's Schimowitz – lives in Newton, outside Boston – they've got two kids. She took care of me for a long time – almost up to when I came here."

Mondo rolled his wheelchair across the room, standing up when he reached a large wooden built-in. In the sideboard there were several bottles with unfamiliar labels. He reached into the rear to pull one out. From behind, I could see a long elliptical scar creasing the back and side of his skull. His civilian-length hair wasn't enough to obscure it.

"I ain't supposed to drink this stuff – not with the pills I take. So, I confine it to special occasions, this being one for sure. Jameson Fifteen it is. If you want ice or water, it's in there." He gestured toward the narrow kitchen while handing me a glass and the bottle. I poured in a couple of shots.

"Like old times," I said holding mine up.

"Clichéd as that is…." We held up our glasses and smiled. "I meant like when you and I used to sit around in your hooch or mine talking – about all sorts of things – drinking it neat like this – whenever we could get the hard stuff. Mondo, to me, Vietnam will never be any kind of cliché."

"Won't ever be for me either, "Carney said, taking a sip from his glass. "Not then, not now. Never!"

"When I came in, Mondo, you mentioned your wife, Genevièv is it? *She's…?*"

"Yeah, I'm married," he said, in a tone that implied I should've known. "She's gone shopping at Tang Frères down on Avenue d'Ivry – there or Paristore –probably both. They love to go, like every friggin' day. She'll be back any time now. Hey, enough of my *down and out* Parisian interlude, what the fuck have you been doing for the past – what is it, eight years since we spoke on the phone?"

"Compared to Orwell's 'down and out' experience in Paris," I responded, "I've been living a life of luxury …. I work in Manhattan in the financial district. I've been with several firms. We have a house out in Passaic County – West Milford. Tommy's in the eighth grade now. Catherine was born in seventy-one. She's in the fourth. I commute into the city all week, work in the yard on weekends and do stuff with Denise and the kids. Her parents and a married sister don't live far so we see a lot of them. And here *you* are… in this apartment – on Rue What-the-Fuck, at the ass-end of Paris – France! You used to disparage the crap out of them – the Frogs, remember?"

"Yeah," he said, "I still do, when it's called for. But a lot of what I told you in Nam was residual ire from Lisette – she was the one I lived with back in sixty-seven. Man, that girl was so good and so *ba-a-a-ad*"

"Ha," I laughed, "I can still remember some of the stories you told me about her."

"I don't know where she or any of my old pals are now.... Scattered to the four winds I guess. I still enjoy taking the piss out of the Frogs though. *They* love talking about Vietnam – experts that they are on the subject, from the fucking day they're born. You know Keneally, they've got a big-ass communist party over here. It draws down a sizeable chunk of the vote – Marchais and his gang – fucking Russian puppets. Then, they have the Socialists, who're really big – that's Mitterrand – dudes been drooling for the Presidency for years and probably'll get it in next year's election. Hand it to them though, at least in France they call themselves what they are; not like in the States where commies and socialists hide out in the Democrat party. A lot of the French are straight-ahead good guys too. Many have gone way out of their way to help me."

"I met one of them myself," I said, thinking of Mondo's bank manager.

"As for Vietnam," he continued, "they do know something of the history – having fought and lost there too. They followed our war even closer than Americans did, but never comprehended why *we* were there. It didn't help that way too many of them saw it through the lenses of *Le Monde* and *Le Nouvel Observateur* – to say nothing of all the commie ash-and-trash rags out there. Go to war to oppose communism? Why? They can't fathom why after they'd smartened up and left, we replaced them as if we were fighting the *same* war. They think we should've vicariously learned what not to do from them. And our apparent ignoring of their experience, can only be proof of our bewildering stupidity. So-o-o-o, from their vantage point our loss was not only predictable, but preordained."

"Don't they get that our military in Vietnam was infinitely more powerful and capable than theirs was?" I asked. "A French defeat was inevitable. Our defeat wasn't."

"Irrelevant. Because of their loss, they've concluded that no force of *any* size could've beaten the communists – as logical as *that ain't.* It makes for beaucoup interesting dinner conversations with them..."

"Not sure I'd take to that sort of social life. That *you* have is a real mind blower."

"Food and wine's always good. And although a minority, there're plenty of Anti -communist French around. We read *Le Figaro* and *Le Point* as best we can." He motioned his glass toward several newspapers lying on a coffee table. "Translating for me what I don't get, helps my French and her English."

"In my hotel, I got a copy of the International Herald Tribune. It's in English."

"Yup, and as they say– only good for lining the bottoms of budgie cages. Anyway, my wife's anti-communism is usually the final word on a lot of these arguments. She should be home any time now."

"Believe me, Mondo, I can't wait to meet her. Let me say again, I'm amazed at how you've made a go of living here. – stunned at the progress you've achieved since I last saw you."

"Give a gung-ho soldier sufficient time – like years and years, and he's bound to surprise you. And you know I'm a gung-ho soldier."

"The most gung-ho I ever met. Which leads me to… what exactly do you do all day? You can't just be sitting in this apartment."

"No Keneally, not if I'm *gung ho.* I have a structured routine. It's super important, but some involves sitting here – writing – putting down things about Nam and our time there. I guess you could call it a manuscript, with you starring in it as my confidant – just like you were. My working title's *'Mekong Meridian.'* It's my brain exercise. Any kind of sustained concentration's helpful, and the kind required for writing has opened new doorways, to chunks of the past in this case."

"Mental pushups is what it is – gives me windows to stuff that'd gotten cutoff. For a long time, my final days in Nam was just one big black space in my head. Some still is – the time after I got shot in the thigh by that dink pistol. But I've been able to isolate the rest, like putting events on glass slides under a microscope: Chopper insertions, contacts, things we said, even my thinking at the time." Mondo had brightened while explaining this. He was brimming with enthusiasm. "Thanks be to God, Keneally. When we last talked, I couldn't capture a whole thought. I'd start one and would lose its ending, then I'd forget the beginning. It was like you were saying things at triple speed, and I'd hear one word, get stuck on it, while you were gone in a cloud of dust. I was so fucked up I wanted to escape from myself. Depressing, and dangerous."

"I'm sorry, Mondo. I apologize. Believe me I got on myself, knowing I hadn't had enough patience."

"Keneally, you don't need to. It was me! It was like that with everybody, even Gigi. Besides, if our roles were reversed I'd have been worse toward you, self-centered and impulsive as I am – was. I'm much slower now." He tapped the armrest of his wheelchair.

"Hmmm, so I play the role of confidant in your memoir? My providing you with sound advice could take up a whole book by itself."

"Ha!" he laughed, "that's why I shrunk the time frame down to just days before I got blown away. You were a huge part of my existence in that battalion, the only guy I could talk to. We had some good officers, but they didn't live next door, and not always around when I came in. Who knows if any could've understood or cared about me like you did?"

"You were easy to understand," I said, "except for your fearlessness. I never understood why your otherwise considerable knowledge didn't temper it."

"It's the opposite. What I knew was how I overcame fear – how I calculated the risks."

"Maybe, Mondo. I still see it as a contradiction."

"I guess what happened proves you were closer to the truth than I was." He slipped his hand into a pouch under his chair's armrest and pulled out a small black automatic pistol. "But, *happiness is still a warm gun*, then and now. *'Little Walther'* here helps protect me and my wife.... It's not a lot of firepower, but I sleep better *knowing* I'm not completely defenseless. Ha! Naked is okay, but the two together?! Fuck that shit. – or *nique ça merde* as the case may be."

"Mondo, now I *know* you haven't changed."

"Oh yes I have. Now, I realize that I was so fearless, I didn't even listen to my own advice! One of the last things I said to you before I got blown away was that, left to their own devices, my men were prone to slack judgements – not the disciplined ones you have to make – doing it the hard way. I always did, except that one last time. Yeah, I told myself I was doing it the hard way, while allowing my emotions to push sound judgment aside.

It cost me… me and her both. But then, Colonel Braccia once said to me; 'Don't let your successes go to your head, and never let your failures go to your heart.' I did though – preoccupied with that fatal error. It filled my heart with self-pity. And when Vietnam was finally lost, it made a home in there – until I saw it all for what it was. It wasn't me. It was the enemy of me. So, I attacked and killed it. It's what I do." He smiled, took a sip from his glass, and slid the gun back into its pocket.

"You're not still fighting the war are you?"

"Au contraire, Keneally. It's the same jug fuck, history that can't be changed. So, I've just chosen to look at it from a different angle – as an academic exercise, instead of harboring it as an emotional experience. It's my choice, why not?"

"So keeping it academic as you say, do you think the U.S. could've won in Vietnam?"

"Yes," he answered adamantly, "and we should have. We had sufficient forces and the public gave us enough time. But we wasted both. There were military strategies we could've employed, but didn't. Our fucking *'best and brightest'* chose not to win."

"You really think LBJ and the rest made such a choice?" I asked.

"Not directly, but their bungling decisions made our loss inevitable. Nixon's Vietnamization might've worked if it had happened earlier than sixty-nine, if the communists hadn't begun violating the Paris Accords before the ink was dry, and if our Congress hadn't cut off all support to South Vietnam."

"I agree Mondo. Remember Walter Cronkite proclaiming to the nation 'that's the way it is'? We'd lived up to our pledge to defend democracy and did the best we could. By the time the treaty got signed, the media'd had over *five* years to pound his summation into America's collective head."

"Fuckin'-ay, Keneally! That pompous stuffed shirt's idea of 'Living up to our pledge…' was a demonstration that we'd stand up to communist expansion. Defeated? Hmmm, no one need worry about that! They just forgot to tell all the dudes out there who were dying in the cause of sending the commies a message. I think Cronkite's mentality was epitomized in Gerald Ford's comment that 'our long national nightmare is over…Yeah, a*in't no biggie – time to just write off our losses.*"

"Do you see yourself as one of those losses, Mondo?" I asked.

"Back a ways I did, in the beginning. One time, I saw this TV movie, *Sticks and Bones.* It was adapted from a play. *It depressed the fucking shit out of me. But Gigi would have none of it:* 'You're disturbed because *that* isn't you – disturbed even more because you know it's what they want you to be, broken – a fitting fulfillment of the Vietnam War they're now constructing!' That smacked me right upside the head."

"Do you remember that Navy LT, anti-war protester, John Kerry? I asked.

"Was he the dude who threw a bunch of medals somewhere down in Washington?"

"He's the one," I said. "He testified to some Congressional committee that we were all just a bunch of Genghis Khans, pillaging and raping the length of Vietnam. He didn't invent the bullshit, but may have given birth to it on a national scale. The lie's been growing ever since."

"That's why I told myself back then… maybe it was Gigi who said it; 'Why do *you* need to see a movie about Vietnam, especially one calculated to propagandize the ignorant?' I don't. I'll never watch another."

"That was around the time I began making serious gains, mental and physical. 'Losses?' Try guys like Prine, Dean, Spot,

Tra.... I'm happily married, sitting here in Paris drinking good Irish whiskey with an old Army pal. Where are they? I'd say they lost a lot more than I did. Try and recover from that willya."

"I take your point," I said, contemplating the fates of those he'd mentioned. Pouring myself another belt of his Jamison, I realized I hadn't heard or even thought of those names since leaving Vietnam. Yet, I was struck with him sitting there in his wheelchair, disabled as he was, but seeing himself as *recovered* – ovbviously from where he'd been. "This perspective of yours Mondo, this change of heart – this– how'd it start?"

There wasn't a single point," he answered, "but I remember one coming from a book I read, *'Man's Search for Meaning'* by Viktor Frankl. He was a Jewish psychiatrist who was sent to Auschwitz and Dachau. In surviving, he describes how he made sense of the hellish ordeal he was in. If there's anything that'd traumatize somebody into total mental non-functioning, it'd be a Nazi death camp. But Frankl explains how even in the most absurd, painful, and dehumanized situation, meaning can be found. Once it is, things become different, even suffering. His ideas helped point the way for me – helped me make sense of what'd happened to me – both good and bad."

"Suffering? Tell me more about your physical condition."

"The ol' ledger's got gains and losses – plenty of shit still giving me trouble. Even though I didn't get hit in the front of my head, the cerebral area, other things got affected – yeah, plenty fucked up." He tipped his head and pointed to the scar that I'd seen before. "But let's see... I told you about my morning schedule. Afternoons, we go places – my physical exercise. We go to a center that's helps Viet refugees – plus more that we do through church. It's mental too – finding meaning in the incredible tragedies some have gone through. Building my comprehension of Vietnamese – Herculean as that is. French too. We go to mass in both languages. Most evenings, we read, often to each other – finding my *meaning*. And where I don't, I impose it. Hah! – what's true and good, is true and good." A creak at the front door caught our attention. A woman's voice called out in French. 'Gave' was all I could comprehend.

"I'm in here, baby," Carney answered. In a moment, she was at the living room door looking in. It was *her*.

"O-o-o-o, je to ne salvias pas que vous aviez un invité," she said, entering and going over to Mondo's wheelchair. Bending over, she kissed him on the side of his head. Her hair was so long it spilled over the wheel and touched the floor.

"This is Paul Keneally," he said. You remember me telling you about him – my best friend in Vietnam." She held out her hand, her face having the expression of someone speed reading a huge card catalogue for an obscure footnote of memory. It was the same indescribably beautiful face that'd been branded in my memory when she'd come searching for Carney in Vietnam. She still had her own unique look, the startlingly perceptive eyes and a warmhearted way of looking out of them.

"We've met," I said. "Remember, at the front gate of our fire-base, a few days after Gavin had been wounded. We only spoke for a few minutes... you came to find out why he hadn't come back to you. You cried when I tried to explain."

"Oui – yes. I remember this. You tell me what happened to him." She looked at Carney. "You want me stay?"

"Of course I do."

"Oui. I must put up these foods. Then, I will come back." She hesitated, looking concerned after noticing Carney's glass. *"Petit, no?"*

"Yeah, yeah, it's only my first – still half full." He held it up to show the proof of it. She nodded pleasantly and went out to the kitchen.

"As my Denise would say, *'Holy Mother of God!'* Mondo, how in creation did you pull this off?"

"I worked on it." he said. "We both did, from different ends."

"*How?!* When?!"

"From the time I really could – only a little at first, and that was a couple of years after getting hit. A lot of that time is still pretty fuzzy. My brain was fucked. Half the time I thought I was dreaming. Sometimes I'd dream I was dead. When I was awake, I could mistake it for just another part of a dream. It's hard to describe a dream and being awake as the same, but they are if you can't tell the difference. Anti-convulsive meds did good and bad – I still have to take them. The sheer act of trying to think in some linear way helped. Every second I could, I did – like I said, my cerebral cortex wasn't damaged, just *des choses plus importantes...* but that's another story. Eventually, I got to doing something at least part of everyday – like an exercise regime. The part of my brain that was okay, had to get the part that'd gotten disconnected hooked up, and like plugged back in. That mightn't be how it is, but it's the way I perceive it. Science isn't sure about self-repairing pathways, but put me in the camp that believes you can help the process. I'm still at it."

"So, trying to find her... for maybe seven years. It started with a longing, like what'd happened to her after I got wounded. As I got into trying to find out, to look for her, it turned into a relentless, craving hunger. I agonized over every dead end and dry hole, driving Gigi nuts. She was already the best sister a guy could ever have. But I couldn't expect her to go it one better by being part of my obsession, by getting inside of it with me. That was actually a good thing though. Frustrations goaded me into doing more things for myself, until I was finally able to move on with my own life, and she with hers. I only hit pay dirt nine months ago. Protective as she is, Gigi came to Paris with me – to make sure I was going to be okay, that and needing to meet Bang, to see for herself what the whole thing was about."

"I can totally relate to how Gigi must have felt," I said. "I'll bet it seemed crazy, especially when years had gone by – years with ... nothing."

"It's crazier than you know. Gigi and I definitely argued about the impossibility of it all. She'd indulged me for a long time in my working on it. Suddenly though, it was all different when things *happened*."

"Don't get me wrong, I had my moments – thoughts about her reaching some abject loss of *all* options... and marrying someone else, or that she was dead. Then I'd shake that off and decide that I'd have to find the truth of it, whatever it was. At the base of the whole thing though, both Bang and I had constructed a reality about each other. We'd poured into it all of our own personal needs, our desperation, my mental and physical isolation, Bang's need to get out... escape. People often indulge in this, mistakenly seeing the other in a way they want them to be. Eventually reality sets in and everything falls apart when the truth is revealed. But in our case, the fantasy and the reality were exactly the same. I don't know, maybe inescapable desperation and self-created fantasies were the only things capable of sustaining us all that time. But at the airport when we first saw each other, it was all the proof we needed – that it was true – that it'd always been real – *preposterously real*."

"Hey back up a minute," I interrupted. "When I came in, you told me Gen was your wife. The name out on the mailbox – *Geneviėv* was it? She's..." I pointed to the kitchen. "She's Bang."

"They're the same. She adopted *Geneviėv* before I found her. To compound matters, she'd also taken to using her paternal grandfather's French surname. Ha, to throw me off her trail I told her. See, her father took his mother's family name when the French left Nam – to kind of help re-Vietnamize himself. Good thing Bang kept switching back and forth, because of living here with so many Viets. She'll always be Bang to me. As my wife, she's legally *Geneviėv* Carney. When we go back to the States, I hope it won't slip to Jen out of convenience – and definitely not Gen-na-veeve... *'Bang'* is so friggin' cool, I'll have to make sure it wins out."

"You're going back – to live? When?"

"Yeah, soon," he answered. "I gotta have more gaddang brain surgery and Boston's my best bet for what I need – not that the French docs haven't been good. In fact, they've been extraordinary."

"Brain surgery? What's *this* about?"

"I don't know," he said as though frustrated that he'd opened the door to my question. "I've been having a little setback. Ha! *Détérioration, déclin, dégénérescence....*" Mondo parodied the French with over-enunciation. "The Frog docs throw all that crap at me – freaks the shit out of Bang. There's some weird-ass EEG activity going on – some kind of blood-flow thing – gears need a little oil. My mobility used to be better, but hey, we're only talking like a marginal percentage or something. Everybody's got their ups and downs. I just need to step up my work-outs – get my Ranger blood pumping like I used to."

"Mondo, I sure hope it all works out. You know, I can't get over how fantastic Bang looks. How old is she?"

"Thirty-four."

"And her hair. You always liked girl's hair the longer the better – seems even longer now than it was last I saw her back in Nam."

"It was much shorter for a while… When the shit was going down, she cut it all off." He swallowed the rest of his drink and stared for a moment at the wall. "She's got it back to being pretty good. The day I first met her it was perfect, but since we're together again she's been improving on that – being magic hair, the more the merrier. Just the brushing can be a two-person job – the chignon knots platted in back or the braided wheel on the side of her head definitely are."

"You brush her… ah, 'magic hair,' Mondo?"

"It's not like that Keneally," he objected. "It's because of my getting fucked up and the nerve damage and all."

"And the connection between that and her hair is…?"

"Okay, so to put it in terms you can understand; it's like this…. My cock wouldn't report for duty. He'd kind of roll out for action, but then start malingering. Maybe from a combination of damage, the pills I have to take and habit, he'd just turned into a lazy-good-for-nothing, goldbricking REMF… until I got Bang back anyway. Mentally, I set up a bivouac in her hair and got lost for a week. Hmmm, what d'ya know, *'she summon big dragon into marital bed for special help…'* And before you know it, I'd destroyed her twenty-inch waistline, temporarily anyway. Magic my man, fucking pure-T magic."

"Your fairy tale life aside, she's pregnant?" I was wondering about that when she came in."

"Yeah, four months. It wasn't as easy as I implied though." Mondo's voice turned somber. "I had my injury, she had hers. It took months. But we stayed focused, all day every day, on the nexus of *us.* The baby's another reason I want to go back to the States – at least for a while. She does like it here in '*Petite Asie.*' First, it's France, then there're lots of Viets. Since last year, quite a few have arrived. Because she speaks excellent French, she can help a lot, explaining the strange Frog ways and bureaucratic things like filling out forms. Man, there's Viet jibber-jabber going on in here all the time. I'm working hard at learning it, but they talk too fast for me. Hell, more often than not, I'm half lost in French. Anyway, our helping Viets who've escaped the communists, is most of our afternoon regime. She was one of them, you know..."

"One of what? I asked. "She *is* Vietnamese and obviously one who managed to get out."

"Yeah," he answered, "of course that. I meant she's one of the '*boat people.*' She's one of the lucky... One of the unlucky. The flotsam of hell."

"I've read a lot about them since the fall of Saigon," I added. "Too much of the reportage is sympathetic to the communists for my liking. There're a few stand-up Americans who're helping though. Huge numbers of Viets are getting to The States – many more than France. Hundreds, maybe thousands are being picked up at sea and taken to refugee camps."

"Make that *hundreds of thousands* escaping," he corrected. "Yeah escaping communism... like who'd want to do that, right? A third, maybe half of them are being lost by boats sinking in the middle of the South China or Thai Gulf. It's horrendous. Just think of setting out with a dozen people packed into a rickety, seventeen-foot boat, for a *five-hundred mile* trip across the friggin' ocean! It's suicide. But they don't care – anything to get away from the communists. It's so completely out of control that last year the UN High Commission on Refugees had to come up with an agreement, the 'Orderly Departure Program,' a super-duper deal with all the Southeast Asian countries. It works for some but not others, because now Hanoi has to *'approve'* of those they want to let out. For anyone who gets disapproved, the boats remain their only resort."

"How did Bang get *here?*" I asked. "You've told me about working on it, but not how you actually succeeded in finding each other."

"The story of her getting here, Paul is a long horribly painful saga. Up front, it was one of those invisible, eight-hundred-pound gorillas in the room, until she walked me through every tortuous detail. How she got through it alive is a gaddang miracle one. But how she's still even slightly sane after it all, is even more miraculous. How both of us worked through it together – the marital-bed issues I mentioned... Her psychological trauma had to be worse than my neurologic ones. But then, mental pain can be overcome. Desiccated nerves? That's harder. She's an angel with a steel wire running through her. Her pulling it together, made my recovery possible. If it isn't all miraculous, then miracles don't exist.

"How much can you tell me?"

"I'll give you my condensed version. After I was wounded and still at Third Field, Bang attempted to see me but the fuckers at the gate wouldn't let her onto the hospital compound. So, several times a day she showed up trying different guards. Finally one dude gave her a nod on the qt. Locating me in the ICU, she told the nurses she was my wife. They let her sit at my side, for hours. But it was the day I was being medevaced to Japan. After that, she had no idea of where I'd gone, just Japan. Hospital staff might've helped her locate me, but the place seemed so foreign and intimidating, she felt lost. And with me gone, she didn't believe anything could be done there, even if she could get back in. Seeing me in such shape though, swollen-to-shit, bandaged, tubes-sprouting-from-everywhere, oxygen, fucking coma and all, filled her with resolve, to get to me."

"Problem one, she didn't know a single American, and didn't have *ein*-fucking piaster to her name. Networking with friends in Saigon, she eventually met some sympathetic American officer. He suggested she return to our firebase, to find friends of mine who might have current info – someone like you who she'd already met. She did, only to learn that our battalion was *gone* – I suppose to the plain of Reeds like we'd planned."

"Yes," I said, "we started moving out there only a week after you got hit. We had a bad mortar attack from 'the Snake' right then and that only accelerated the move."

"Eventually, she learned where y'all were," Mondo continued, "and could've taken Viet busses as far as Tan An. But you guys were way west of there. No Lambros and hitching a ride on the back of somebody's motorbike would've been iffy. None of that area was secure, especially at night. And such a trip could've easily run past dark, with nowhere to stay. Just the idea of her as some wandering waif out there was unthinkable. With no money anyway, she continued working things in Saigon. Naturally, Americans just took her for some officer's pretty mistress, looking for her dude who'd gone home and left her behind – a dude who wounded or not, might not want to be found."

"As the months pass, things got worse. The U.S. was steadily pulling out, until except for our embassy there wasn't any American presence at all. But pursuing that angle, she found a helpful Viet employee who learned I'd been medevaced from Japan to Walter Reed. Problem was, by then that info was two years old. All she could do was pine over her isolation and lack of options. She improvized an address for Walter Reed and wrote to me, but I'd been shipped to Valley Forge so never got anything. That didn't break her faith though. I couldn't write, because my memory of her address was hopelessly scrambled."

"Three more years went by. She persisted in trying to immigrate to the States but with no previous connection with us and so many competitors, it was a no go. Then Saigon fell. When the Communists moved in, things turned chaotic. The restaurant where she lived was forced to shut down. She and the family who owned it became destitute. She moved around Cholon for two years, half starving. The communists instituted some kind of 'wolf ticket' deal and because of her family's anti-communist past, she was barred from most employment. When one of her close friends got sent to a re-education camp, her fretful worrying turned into outright fear. Things became steadily bleaker."

"All sorts of rumors and bogus stories swirled about, generating nothing but false hope, until people realized the only possible escape route was by sea. Increasing numbers of South Vietnamese were attempting it. Bang finally made the decision to leave by boat, hazard her way as a refugee, to America and me. She was desperate to leave and determined to trace me down."

"She and a couple friends planned extensively through all their trusted contacts. Finally, they went to Na Be and boarded a boat after dark. It was crammed with 70 people of all ages. Scared and hopeful, they just chugged down river, out into the South China, and headed west. They wanted to get to Singapore, but gauging the cross-gulf trip too perilous, they struck for Thailand."

"Two days out pirates hit." Mondo's expression and voice turned grim. "Bang's boat was completely defenseless, boarded by a pack of armed dudes, Thai animals. They straight-off shot and killed two Viet men who resisted. All the people were robbed of everything they had and every girl between twelve and thirty was raped. A day later, their engine failed. Adrift in an equatorial ocean, food and water ran out."

More pirates came and off-loaded all the terrified girls. Bang was one. The pirates linked up with other vessels. They got sold several times – more rapes. Eventually, they forced the girls onto a small uninhabited island called Kohl Kra, fifty miles off the southern coast of Thailand. Those who've been dragged there call it 'Hell on Earth.' Pirates take girls from boats all over the Gulf and strand them on it."

"Fishermen turned pirates come from all over, rape the girls and take off. The few unarmed Vietnamese men who make it to the island, can't help. Resistance means on-the-spot murder. Girls try to hide in the island's interior vegetation, but it's too small. They're hunted down and raped. When sighted on the horizon, Bang would go to one of the barren rocky islets nearby and hide in a tiny cave, more a hole full of water, where she'd bury herself. Other girls caught trying that pissed off the pirates, so they just killed them – to teach the others a lesson – plenty more where they came from."

"Finally," Mondo concluded, "Bang got saved when a Thai Navy patrol craft came along and took everyone to a mainland refugee camp called Songkhla – one of the many all over Southeast Asia. But from what I hear, Kohl Kra is still under pirate control. They just keep restocking it with newly captured Viet girls. It tears my heart out. I want to go there and protect them from these horrors – just kill the fucking pirates. I've run the whole operation in my head a hundred times – with a squad of dudes – shit I could do it myself – ambush and gun them down, scuttle their boats off shore... But I can't." He struck his empty hand onto the arm of his chair.

"You're right about this being a saga, Mondo," I consoled, imagining the old physically fit Mondo, standing over a pile of bullet-ventilated ex-pirates. "It's absolutely horrifying. How'd she get from Thailand to Paris?"

"Well, at Songkhla, aid workers and French doctors from their *Association d'Aides des Réfugiés d'Asie and Médecins Sans Frontières* enlisted Bang as a translator. She begged the authorities to get her on the USA immigration list, but failed. Then some doctor used his influence to get her onto a French one. She took it, figuring she'd have a better chance getting to the States from France than waiting it out in that squalid camp, then maybe winding up in Australia."

"Man oh man. So she comes to France. How did you find her here?"

"Actually, *I* didn't, although like I said before, I'd been trying for years – made a zillion contacts with Vietnamese in the States. They have a tight community, but so many were coming to America that the tracking couldn't keep pace. Most of their organizations were ad hoc arrangements. Lots of them only knew their own experience, their particular camp at that time, maybe Indonesia, Malaysia, the Philippines... I ran down every lead, and spent thousands on overseas phone calls. That was my obsession. Many I called couldn't speak English well enough to help me. As for the American bureaucrats involved, I just went in circles. There were people coordinating the resettlement and knew what was up, but those I got hold of didn't have what I wanted. Hell, they didn't have Bang... Half the time, I couldn't get the right phone numbers and when I did, they just rang and rang. Frustrating? I got cross-eyed loco with it."

"But you said you didn't find her..."

"Yeah, I flat-ass failed. But *she* didn't. Once here in Paris, she got the French Embassy in Washington to help. Some saint of a person there found out where I was. So fucking simple! I had a listed phone number so they called Information, got it, and just gave it to her. Then, she called me. My God, I thought I was going to have a four-barreled heart attack. Almost ten fucking years! Neither of us could talk. All we could do was cry. I booked a flight here that same day."

"You tied the knot then and there? You said back in Nam you weren't going to waste any time. What a round-about way of getting there." Mondo and I both laughed.

"I remember that!" he said, as if a revelation. "It was in your hooch, the last time we were together in Nam."

"Well, actually it was in your hooch and not the last time we were together. I came up to Saigon before they medevaced you out, but they had you in an induced coma."

"Hmmm, yeah. That shit can make you a little sleepy. Ha! I lost a few weeks there, probably more. How'll I remember an experience I never had? When they woke me up, I was leaving Japan and I didn't even know I'd gotten there."

"So, tell me more about your getting married – a regular wedding?"

"Of course," he declared, "as soon as we could. Hey Bang! C'mon in – leave that crap for later, Baby." She came back in and sat on an end table next to Mondo's wheelchair. In a frilly, loose fitting blouse and soon-to-be untenable jeans, her hair flowed over her shoulders like a waterfall of glistening ink.

"I think you and Paul want something to eat?"

"Sure, but first fill Keneally in on our wedding."

"We marry in *Chapels Saint Louis de la Salpêtrière,*" she began.

"Excuse me, but that's…?"

"Saint Louie's over at the hospital," Mondo offered, "big ol' church. Both were built three-hundred years ago and have incredible histories. I've been getting my care there – it's not far."

"All my friend come to our wedding, Vietnam people," Bang explained. "On this day Gaa-vin walk long way with me."

"Yeah," the whole aisle," he added. "All the way out of the church. Pure Ranger willpower. Nowadays we get out and I work out at the park – after a fashion. I get a little better and then I don't… Bang says I'll improve if she gets us a dog – a little poodle to go along with a nice fur coat, so she can look more French."

"No, I do not!" Bang cried out over Mondo's laughing. "Paul, please you must not listen to him. I am Vietnam girl!"

"Private joke there, Keneally. Can you just see her… *her,* walking down the street with one of those tweensy-ass poodles – both their noses sticking up in the air?!"

"No-o-o-o, I guess not," I replied, with a smile to Bang.

"Paris ceremony…" she continued, "Ga-vin maybe already say to you, we believe we are married in Vietnam, from two day before Gavin hurt. We have each a heart, but beat together same time always. Monsieur Hugo say this also; 'to love another person is to see face of God.' I think this true, no? Love make us together, even when we far away and suffer much pain."

"We've worked a lot Paul, together on our mutual… I want to say *trauma*, but to call it that, defeats what we've been doing. Like I said before, not necessarily burying it – or putting it behind us, but making sense of it."

"That reminds me," I said. "By coincidence, not so long ago I read a Holocaust book myself, Jean Améry's *"Beyond Guilt and Atonement."* He mentioned something similar, in claiming to not have 'clarity' on what he went through in surviving, and hoped he never would. He defines clarity as something concluded, a settled case, which would necessarily be relegated to history. Améry wants nothing to be resolved or settled – remembering becoming *mere* memory."

"Yeah, you don't bury it, you use the living experience of it to make yourself new – better than before. What happened to me – Bang too, didn't diminish us. It added. It's our choice, bemoan or embrace. But it's not *all* that."

"Go back to Frankl and the part where he got all transcendental with his natural surroundings. In a concentration camp? Like how's that even possible? Well, he credited his survival to it. This is important. Mental survival comes first. The physical follows. So here's the kicker. Bang, who never heard of Frankl, was doing the very same thing during '*the bad times*' – consciously imposing part of her reality with another just as valid reality."

"And this alternate '*reality*' was?" I prodded.

"Her natural world, as it was at the time. She laid it out for me while recounting those events – how she survived by turning the island into something mystical, consumed with the shapes of clouds, sunrise, changes in the ocean's moods… yeah, to the point of befriending the weather and tides, and allying herself with a real-life world of crustaceans and sea-anemones – for entertainment! Force *out everything* else and you leave no space for anything except what you *allow*." Mondo looked to Bang for her take.

"I catch small fish when sea go out, Bang offered – *Petites piscine's les rockers – basin…*" she formed her hands like a small pool of water. "I make this my world. All time I do this, so not be broken. Our mind is for us to decide. What we think cannot be under control of others and other thing. When you let, it control you – then you are lost."

"You just pretended that horror was something else?"

"No, it's not pretending in the least," Mondo vigorously shook his head. "Both are real, so it's about which one you let occupy you. Distilled, it's a choice of either what will destroy you, or what'll allow you to survive, *mentally*. The key is, you're what you *will* yourself to be. Do that and you have a fighting chance to survive physically – with a mind that's not so traumatized that it's worthless."

"My own struggles were physical first and mental second and even that was more brain than mind. I found out that you can will resilience or you can will devastation. That's your choice. My body had huge limitations, but then I wasn't a hopeless captive of bestial psychos. Living with Gigi was paradise in comparison. But there was this inexplicable gap. Bang's triumph became its keystone. I mightn't be able to take it to some orphic place like turning Thai mothafuckers into mother-of-pearl mollusk shells.... but I can dig the principle. Then, just having her is an entire world unto itself; but it's still up to me *to allow it.* That's more indispensable than my having her. So I did, and *let* her fill up every last cubic millimeter. It made me whole again."

"Arriving at this hasn't ben easy, but the effort and need to get there has dammed near fused us into a single person. Like Bang said, when we told each other back in Nam that we were married, we just decided it was so. Why not? It's within our power to decide such things or not. From there, we just acted on it, as best we could – believing as we do."

"I think when we not find each other," Bang added, "we never marry another person."

"*If* we hadn't," Mondo corrected. "We wouldn't have out of pure stubbornness to prove ourselves right. Crazy as shit, huh?"

"Yeah," I laughed, "unbelievably crazy. But is it stubbornness for love, or the *idea of love?*"

"Both, one must have," Bang insisted. "Love cannot be alone, but first need faith for love to be." She looped her arm over Mondo's shoulder and looked at him. "This we have."

"The way you made it endure through these past years, by way of all that you've described, acting on it like you did, is as undeniable as it is incredible. But let me ask you something else, Mondo." I looked at Bang and hesitated. "It may be a delicate subject at this point – and perhaps only serving to satisfy my morbid curiosity...."

"Go on Keneally, our non secret is our not having any secrets."

"Well, it's because it occupied much of the last conversation we ever had. So whatever happened to Maureen? What'd she do when you got wounded?"

"Ha! Miss D," he laughed. "She came to see me a few times – early on when I was laid up. That period is still pretty fuzzy. Gigi filled me in on most of it years later when I could make better sense of it. Maureen was definitely fucked-up distraught over me when I was at my worst. Gradually though, as I got my faculties back – we're talking well over a year here – the gulf between us kept growing. We never broke up. She kept fading further into the far distance until she just wasn't there any more."

"It'd all begun with me though. Before I got hit, I'd already emotionally cut the connection between us. Hell, I'd already mentally married Bang – even though through my early hospitalization, her existence had turned into some kind of apparition. Maureen was physically there, but Bang haunted my consciousness, however jumbled and barely functioning it was. There but not there – not even ectoplasm." He looked to Bang and chuckled. "And no way did I have enough working gray matter to bring Bang up to Maureen – like to tell her how I was *already married, yeah, to a Vietnamese* apparition*?!* But I sure would've if I'd been capable."

"Maureen had signed on for *me*, but not my… situation – not if it was as bad as it was. The war'd tested our relationship and it'd already failed. Then there I am, reduced to mincemeat, stuck in Walter Reed and Valley Forge hospitals. She had her ceaseless gerbil wheel of academic pursuits, way up in Waltham."

"I was useless on the phone and knew it. She'd call and I'd make Gigi talk. Maureen's commie friends were cluing her in that a breakup with a guy in my condition and who held the beliefs that I do, was, *'all for the best.'* The irony is, they were right! If she'd thrown herself at me when I was at my lowest, taking over what Gigi was doing at the time of my greatest need, and when Bang was a vast universe away, even dead for all I knew, I might've just given in, succumbed. According to Gigi, Maureen got her Ph.D. and is teaching somewhere in the Boston area. That's her world and'll never be anything else – don't know if she's married or not. Hey, I wish her well. And *that,* Paul is the end of it."

"What did you mean by *succumbed*? You might give in to what?" I asked.

"Her, Maureen. I might have used her love for my own care needs – easily rationalized with the state I was in. *That* would've kept me from looking for Bang, as soul-stompingly tragic as that would've been. But sticking with Maureen would've created a neurotic symbiosis and fed my worst traits. I'd have become diminished for sure. Not to worry! There were greater forces at work."

"My isolation helped me reorder my mind and reconnect loose gray matter. It was a case of bad actually being good. My mental rehabilitation drove my preoccupation with finding Bang, and vice versa. In her desperation, she was calling out for me – and in some way I heard her. It wasn't a fantasm at all. It was flesh-and-blood real. I regularly prayed that I'd find her. God obviously knew our pain. But He didn't just put us back together. He gave us a sign, and the strength to persevere. We did the rest – *she...*" Simultaneously Mondo and I both looked at Bang.

"When things are very bad for me," she said, "All times I asked for help – from God, from all angels, the Martyrs of Vietnam, and Vi. Gaav-in, I know he was bad hurt and far away. He could not help. But the others are with me. Every day they help. All time, I remember monsieur Hugo say; 'Sorrow is fruit. God does not make on branch not strong to hold up.' When I hide in cave, I pray 'Mary... pray for me, now and at hour of death.' But it is not this hour. I am alive. *Militaire* come and save."

"Bang's something of a devotee of Victor Hugo," Mondo offered, "a kind of inspiration since way back, years before we met in Nam. But during what we call "the bad time,' he came to take on greater meaning."

"Paul, you have read *Les Misérables*, no?"

"I'm afraid not," I said, "but maybe my stay in Paris will stimulate me to."

"You must for many reason. Hugo tell us, the best happiness in life is when we know we are loved. I believe Ga-vin, wherever he was, had love for me. In this bad time, I have peace because I know that night in my soul make stars. I look up at same stars Gavin can see. I know this when hide in hole and make stones over." She got up and retrieved a tattered paperback from a book case behind her.

"I want read you how Hugo explain this. Pardon please, I must translate French. 'Lovers who far away, cheat absence by thousand ways. They make their own reality. They cannot see each other – cannot write. But they find so many way – mysterious way to send message to each other... sound of wind, the light from stars.' Gavin think this Hugo number 10 but for me very number one..."

"Whoa Bang, my criticism only has to do with my... I just don't have a door to his thinking like you do that's all. Door?

More like some metaphysical time portal. But, it's all part of what we've been talking about."

"Ga-vin, I forget say one thing," she said with an impish smile. "'Far away lovers cheat absence.' Remember day we meet, you say me cheat with flower cards *not* good. When I am on island, I cheat absence – it very good."

"Bang, you're too funny." They laughed heartily together. Her words, though broken English breathed pure sincerity. She'd hung everything on something so thin, yet believed so profoundly. People risk heartbreak all the time, but not total annihilation of the self. But even that risk ultimately didn't matter, given her circumstances. Whatever her beliefs, they'd strengthened her mental fortitude not just enough to get her through physically, but with enough sanity to claw her way here, and retrieve Mondo to boot. Their marriage was a wonder, but the road to it was beyond wonderment.

"Who's Vee?" I asked. "Did I hear that right– among the angels and saints?"

"Yeah, you did," Mondo answered. "He was an Arvin hero, who got killed in combat in nineteen-sixty-eight. Calling on his intercession is what she means. Vi was Bang's first husband. He occupies a place of honor in our house – as well he should, a genuine hero, who got Bang and I together back in Nam."

"He got you together?! From what you just said, he was KIA before you ever even got to Vietnam, right?"

"Dead as you can get," he agreed. "That part is way too complicated for me to explain…"

"I bet it is," I said, my skepticism tempered by the centillion-to-one odds against their implausible reunion. Complicated was the wrong word for what it would be.

"Paul, I need tell you," Bang said, "before in Vietnam – it is twelve years, Vi was taken from me. Then, Ga-vin come – to protect me. The communists try take him too. But he is now with me always– to keep away all that is bad and evil. Inside him is same like Vi, perfect for me. Ga-vin saved me from breaking of my mind and my heart. When first we meet in Vietnam, I tell him, 'I know you Ga-vin. I understand all that you are.' I make no mistake." Mondo smiled and squeezed Bang's hand.

"I've described to you before, about how every time I went outside at night and the stars were out, shining on me, it reminded me to pray for you – not *just* then."

"Bang," I said, "I agree with you about Mondo here. He's exactly as you say, but I already knew that. Thank you for taking care of my friend."

"I'll drink to that," Carney toasted with his glass. "So let me finish up on a thought here, before I take you to one of my favorite French eateries. It came to me when I was telling you about Maureen. You see, love is all around us in this world. But that doesn't mean it isn't elusive – and if you can get hold of it, it doesn't mean it can't get away from you. I don't think you actually have to grab and trap it, but because it's invisible, you can lose track of it. Bear with me here."

"Some loves are also bigger and more powerful, so they're harder to lose. What we put into it though, made it much harder. Sure it *was* fantastically idealistic, but we ignored that and lived up to it anyway. So in doing that, it became too big to lose, even through all of what I told you and more. That's Bang and me. We are the cure for each other's pain, the pain we suffered. Together, we have none. Few know the predations of war more than we do. But in the end, *it* put us together. In our lives, our love is its product"

"This is so," Bang interjected. Vietnam is now in the past. It is also true of our pain. We are here." She motioned to mean their living room as its replacement.

"Ha, yeah, "Mondo joked, *"prisoners of the infamous Madam P–* o-o-o-oh the pain! But seriously, in some unknowable metaphysical way, the separate hells we went through weren't the random, accidental events of war, but tests to forge the steel of our love. Another part of love is trust – the bigger the love, the greater the trust. That's how I've come to measure it – ours." He glanced over to Bang, for agreement. If trust could be put into a facial expression, hers read nothing but. "It's big enough to both endure and support everything that's happened. I'd willingly die for her if I had to. I *know* she would for me – without a second thought. It's all in the way you think about these things: If only I'd made it back to those trucks –less than a hundred yards and none of this would've happened, neither my injuries nor any of what happened to her. Has there ever been a more colossal error?"

"Ga-vin!" Bang exclaimed with a sudden burst of emotion. "I tell you, do not speak of this. Many times we talk of this. It is not so!"

"Okay baby, just a small lapse there," he said contritely. "So I'll stick to trust. Back in the War, it was critical that others had your back, others you trusted – to know they'd be there. It came to that."

"You know, Paul, my Recon dudes were as good as any in Nam. But as an officer, you're mentally apart from them. I was connected to the battalion's officers, but outside of you, not so much. Now as for those orchestrating the war, they were as remote as the Man in the Moon. I felt like I was fighting the war alone. Finally though, I found Bang. She joined me – a female personification of an ally I could totally trust. It's what Bang has, that no other girl I ever met had. I don't know how I knew it, I just did. It decided everything for me. Sure her looks came first. Of course they snagged me. They'd snag anybody, but all the love and woman stuff went on top like icing."

"Then there's the Vietnam part, her being Viet and her brutal experiences with communism. But trust is in the heart, the commitment to be there to the death. We both think in these terms, unconditionally. With Maureen, it was *all* conditional. Everything was dependent on something else. Nothing was absolute. But with Bang and I, our world is full of absolutes. They're all over the place. Our rendering commitment down to absolute trust came from our having been betrayed."

"By whom?" I asked.

"In my case, by our political and military leaders. They sent me to Vietnam to defeat the communists. Good idea. I tried to do it with all my might. But really they had no intention of defeating them. They just said they did. In reality they wanted to hurt the communists just enough to get them to back off, but never to defeat them. That made it perfect for the communists. So to get us to fight this loser, our politicians lied to us. Their prosecution of the war, their strategy and their results prove it. They screwed the thing up from start to finish, got fifty-eight-thousand of us killed, and came away with *nothing*. Need I mention the Arvins? Talk about getting screwed. Hundreds of thousands of those poor bastards were killed and they lost their whole country! The Paris '*Peace Accords*' were a farce, but our Congress's subsequent actions couldn't have been more reprehensible if they'd been in the direct pay of the Soviet Union and Hanoi."

"Paul, they lied to me, to get me to fight. They probably preferred that I not die, but if I did, oh well. Of course my travails are a picnic compared to Bang's. Betrayal is the story of her life, a never-ending river of it, culminating in an ocean of depraved wickedness. Until me that is.... That's where all the bad shit stopped. As long as I have a breath in me, she will never worry again. I don't have to worry either. Dude, Bang's got my back!"

CHAPTER 3

On November 13, 1982, America's national Vietnam Memorial was dedicated. The media covered it in full, it being a perfect occasion to remind Americans of its standard narrative on The Vietnam war, our country's "ill-considered misadventure." Their recently created version of the "Vietnam Vet," provided provocative sidebars. He was in conspicuous attendance at "the march to the wall." Costumed in ratty jungle fatigues, festooned with full dress medals, and multiple unit patches, they spouted teary, clichéd maunderings on their guilt-stained participation in the war. Addled tales of enduring trauma were told and shown again and again. The cameras couldn't get enough of them.

Where were the real heroes of the war, those who'd won the Medal of Honor, the Distinguished Service Cross, the hundreds of thousands who'd served honorably, come home and rebuilt decent lives? Few of them ever got the microphone. They didn't advance the pre-ordained storyline that a war as bad as Vietnam could only spawn more bad. Whatever is beyond revulsion, I felt it.

New York City organized a major event for Vietnam veterans in the spring of 1985. Only a week after the media had wallowed in the 10th anniversary of Saigon's fall, this ticker-tape parade was ballyhooed as a belated "Welcome Home." The city turned out big. Emotions ran high. Despite honorable intentions and genuine tributes paid, I wasn't sure how much of it was a mass expiation of guilt or a mass engendering of it. I stood at the periphery of the crowd during the dedication of Vietnam Veterans Plaza on Water Street and the fireworks display over the Battery. I watched the parade as thousands of vets came across the Brooklyn Bridge into Manhattan. I felt it was important that I be there, but at the same time, felt no connection with anything I'd ever experienced in Vietnam. When I allowed Mondo into my thinking, I felt even less of a connection. At the ceremony, many names were mentioned, most had been killed. Exploits were described, all decidedly brave and courageous. But I didn't know any of them.

Along the parade's route of march, I went into a crowded bar just off lower Broadway. The first person I ran into, a business acquaintance, struck up a conversation. He had some vague recollection that I'd been an infantry officer in Vietnam and after a couple of drinks, decided he needed to share with me his having been an anti-war activist.

"I have to say Paul, Vietnam was a huge waste," he commented. "And quite frankly, I feel a sense of pride for having worked to stop it." I took the bait.

"You've got that right," I agreed. "The war certainly was a waste. The problem is your actions contributed more to making it one than they did to stopping it. Those who died though won't ever have an opportunity to address that with you, not since you're going to Hell for it." I'm normally a pretty reticent guy and that was the first time I'd had an uncorked exchange in the fifteen years since I'd returned. Years passed without my having another.

In late '94, I was in Washington on business and stayed at the Willard. One evening after dinner, I walked over to the Vietnam Memorial. It was my first in-the-flesh visit to "The Wall." At eight o'clock, it was dark. A light breeze brought a chill to the air. Random cars on Constitution Avenue seemed aimless compared to the river of traffic I'd seen earlier. The memorial was well lit. Two couples strolled about reading names on distant panels.

I knew what the place looked like from pictures, but first hand it was very different from what I'd expected. Too sparse for my liking, I couldn't find the power that was said to be inherent in its simplicity. Neither could I see, "The Gash of Shame," to which detractors referred. I riffled through the index book, immediately overwhelmed by the sheer number of names, while their 170 corresponding black panels pulled at me. I moved on down the sidewalk. In the declivity between the angled walls, I was struck with an unexpected feeling. The ever-present sounds of ambient traffic overhead, faded away. A kind of quietude settled on the place like a soft blanket. The lower I got, the more muffled it became.

I had a panel on the W side in mind. Several dozens of names had been added to The Wall since its original completion date. In order to keep the chronology right, they'd been etched in margin spaces originally separating groups of names, but it didn't seem like they'd been able to stick to that. I needed to go back and check the book, but decided to go over and take a look at the statue first. Idly, I walked around the three elevated figures.

Frozen forever in bronze, their struggle to represent all the men of the war, seemed more fatiguing to them than their eternal combat mission somewhere off in the vague distance. They were facing the names of the dead, surely better than moving on and leaving them behind.

Cast with faces aimed at capturing all the physical exhaustion and psychic fatigue of combat, their dull-eyed expressions struck me as closer to simple stupefaction. Maybe that'd been the sculptor's subtler intent. The tuned-in, those who understood, the self-ordained cognoscente of the war just hadn't gone. Hadn't it been proof of brainless stupidity to have allowed Uncle Sam to send you to such a place as Vietnam, while simultaneously affording you half a dozen ways to avoid going? Their definition of smart was having figured *that* out. Something else caught my attention.

Further up the sidewalk, two guys in camouflage were manning some kind of display. One of them had just gotten out of a makeshift bamboo cage. They were packing up for the night. I went on over to check them out. While flipping through pamphlets they hadn't put away yet, one of the guys stirred to engage me.

"You been in 'The Nam'?" I nodded and a pair of rigid forearms eagerly thrust at me. They'd appropriated a rudimentary 'soul shake.' "Welcome home brother," they both intoned, with a practiced seriousness. They asked if I was up on the ravages of Agent Orange and PTSD, and was I aware of all the MIAs who were still rotting in tiger cages in secret POW camps, with the full complicity of the US Government! I told them that I'd read of the possibility, but had no way of confirming or denying it. That was the wrong thing to say. They both spoke at once to straighten me out.

In just a few moments, they ratcheted up my skepticism as to whether they'd ever even set foot in Vietnam. Given that our experiences there had been so divergent, I felt guilty for doubting them, but one of the two forced me to speculate if he'd spent a year of his life at Firebase Haight-Ashbury and on patrol in Golden Gate Park. It seemed like he was looking for a way to reclaim time wasted by garnering a little nobility from those who actually had some. How could *we* be 'brothers?' Listening to their litany of residual ill effects from the war, I couldn't help but think of Mondo, once taking a dink bullet like it'd been a joke. By stridently pushing their points, they kept trying to spur me into their fraternity of concern. Instead, they cornered me between weariness and a desire to turn over the cage with them in it. I walked back down between the Memorial's walls. I was ready now, to see and stare, and cry in front of Mondo's name.

Back in my hotel room, I was still annoyed by the incident at the cage, but at the same time felt totally reconnected with Mondo, the war, the truth and the reality of what it had actually meant to me. I was unwilling to let two jackanapes with a cage commandeer my war, my memories, and my friend. Carney sure as hell wouldn't have walked away from those two. He'd have had them for lunch. The war wasn't about us, I could hear him saying.

No. The war was about why we fought. We fought to stop the relentless advance of communism, totalitarianism in whatever form it took. We tried agonizingly hard, some of us did anyway. Too many thousands of souls gave it their last measure of devotion.

I read a lot about the war since that day, sticking mostly to authors who knew of what they told, preferring actual participants to the keen-eyed "impartial" observers. Vicariously slogging through rice paddies of black print on white paper, I relived my days in Vietnam. Book by book, it eventually goaded me into returning.

The Vietnam of 2002 swallowed me in a fabulous whorl of sights, sounds and smells. With Denise and my godson, Vi, at my side, I immersed myself in the land, trekking back to all the places I'd once been, including my old fire support base. Not a hair's trace of our old bunkers remained, although the entrance road was still being used. Now flanked by hedgerows and new ramshackle buildings, I could only roughly estimate where the entrance gate and guard bunker had been. With some closer study, I decided that a mound of packed earth had been formed by the ancient contents of broken sandbags. This was it.

"Back in '69, Vi," I said through a burst of bitter-sweet feelings, "our front gate was right there. I drove in and out countless times, but only stood on this ground once before – the very spot where I first saw your mother. After your dad had been wounded, I was sitting in the orderly room. A call came down through battalion that a Vietnamese girl was at the front gate looking for Lieutenant Carney. The NCO who'd handled it hadn't been aware that he'd been wounded. Knowing immediately who she'd be, I tore up there in my jeep. She was dressed in a lilac-colored Ao Dai and was standing outside the guard bunker, alone – right about here."

"'Bon jour. I am Mã̲ Thị Cây Bàng,' she said. Her expression was clearly pained. 'I have come for Trung úy Carney. He did not come. He has told me for sure, but he do not.' Her composure began to falter. 'There is problem I think.' She handed me her ID card, as if this unnecessary act of formality might somehow move me. I was paralyzed with the sight of her. She was everything your dad had claimed. More." Vi looked at me with full comprehension. Recalling the scene, I thought of Mondo's description of her, and how he'd failed to capture the unearthly beauty that had stood before me. I'd decided that an accurate description was beyond the English language, but it was the situation that had me. I'd wanted to say the right thing in just the right way."

"'Ma'am, he's been wounded,' I told her. 'He was very seriously injured, hurt.' She stood there staring at me with an expression she might've had if she'd just been struck in the back by a bullet."

"'No,' she protested, 'it not can be possible! We make married – us together make. You understand?'"

"Yes, he told me," I answered, not knowing what the hell else to say. '...Ma'am, he is – was – it happened four days ago. He is in Saigon, at Third Field Hospital – near the airport.'"

"'No, she demanded, 'I think you not know. I give him *bùa hô-mang* – he put in here.' She pointed to my breast pocket."

"'What?!' I'd thought. Your dad had shown me the weird little thing, and told about it being some sort of talismanic thingamabob, but just that morning I'd separated it from his personal effects that were to be sent home. I'd put it in my shirt pocket intending to ask the scouts what they thought it was. How did she know I had it?"

"'My God, I have it,' I said. I unbuttoned my pocket, took it out, and placed it in her hand. In an instant, tears sprang from her eyes."

"'He not do what I tell him!' Her body seemed to tremble from the realization. She grasped the thing tightly in her hands. Squeezing it and looking skyward, she began to shake violently. I made a move to comfort her, but she bent down to pick up her bag. Her hair was so long that some of it flopped into a patch of wet mud, but as she straightened not even a single molecule of dirt had clung to it. The memory brought back the recollection of Mondo telling me of her being so beautiful that nothing could defile her. Somehow, he'd known from the start."

"From that spot, Vi, your mother just turned around and began walking away, her lacquered shoes finding the hard dry ridges between the tire ruts. She was a dozen feet away when I heard it, the keening. I could only see the back of her parasol as her mournful cry wailed off across the old rice paddy. I watched her just shrinking into the distance, until she turned onto the main road out there and finally disappeared, forever so I'd thought."

Standing on that exact spot, thirty-three years later, I continued reminiscing with Denise and Vi over what had then come to pass. They both knew the story, but this was my take, now infused with my being on the same ground, and breathing the same air that we'd once mutually shared. Bang's scrabble-life existence in a communist dictatorship, her ocean survival in an unseaworthy boat, unspeakable horrors in the Thai Gulf, an island hell, and the privations of the refugee camp was the definition of harrowing. Mondo's pain and debilitation through all those years was another kind of saga. To then rediscover them both in their Paris living room seemed so fantastic as to be more a dream than a reality. It was as if they'd both risen from the dead.

Sometimes I wonder if Bang had existed at all, or like sylphs and dragons inhabiting the air and sky, only in that time and place, as if in another dimension, a heavenly complement to Mondo. Strange, because for me, even he too had an existence indivisible from 1969's Vietnam and our subsequent reunion. There was a genuine, larger-than-life sense of fantasy about them both, despite knowing they were as real as me.

Vi, Denise, and I lingered on that road where I'd seen Bang walking away. In the distance where I'd lost sight of her, beyond the hedgerows, fruit trees, and roofs of dwellings, I could see the old District headquarters. In what struck me as a painful insult to so many lives, the blood red flag with its communist yellow star flapped in the breeze. Maybe it had been unavoidable that Mondo and Bang would be no more. They'd found it so hard to coexist with that flag and all the innocent dead on which it stood. I suddenly felt very sad about having lived so long and so well with all of it.

Paul M. Keneally

FOOTNOTES

1. From "Story of Isaac" by Leonard Cohen, Sony/ATV Music Publishing

2. From "A Day In The Life" by John Lennon and Paul McCartney, Sony/ATV Music Publishing

3. From "She's Not There" by Rod Argent, Marquis Music Co. Ltd.

4. Ibid

5. Ibid

6. From "Invictus" by William Ernest Henley

Made in the USA
San Bernardino, CA
12 June 2017